I0634017

# Deep in the Place
# of the Dead

# DEEP PLACE IN THE OF THE DEAD

by

## MATT ERLACHER

Southern Pines, NC, USA

Deep in the Place of the Dead

Copyright © 2024 by Matt Erlacher
Published by Vigil Press, Southern Pines, NC
All rights reserved.
Printed in the United States of America.
Book design and cover design by FREE PINELAND! Productions. Cover
photographs courtesy of www.alamy.com. Author photo courtesy of the author.

Paperback ISBN 978-1-963436-03-7

For information about and permission to reproduce selections from this work,
please write:
Vigil Press
RE: Reproductions
PO Box 2312
Southern Pines, NC 28388

No parts of this publication may be reproduced, stored in a retrieval system, or
transmitted in any form or by any means, electronic, mechanical, photocopying,
recording, or otherwise, without the prior written permission of the copyright
owner. This book is sold subject to the condition that it shall not, by way of
trade or otherwise, be lent, resold, hired out, or otherwise circulated without the
publisher's prior consent in any form of binding or cover other than that in
which it is published and without a similar condition including this condition
being imposed on the subsequent purchaser. Under no circumstances may any
part of this book be photocopied for resale.

This is a work of fiction. Most of the characters herein are completely made up,
but some are based on real people, but their words, thoughts, and deeds are
fictionalized. Same for the places and place names.

*For my wife,*
*perhaps the*
*most patient woman*
*in the world.*

A note on Bosanski (Bosnian) pronunciation:

| Letter | Pronunciation |
|--------|---------------|
| Č/č | *Ch* as in *ch*alk |
| Ć/ć | *Ts* as in i*ts* |
| C/c | *Ss* as in *s*ee |
| Š/š | *Sh* as in *sh*oe |
| Ž/ž | *Zh* as in mea*s*ure |
| I/i | *Ee* sound as in *s*ee |
| J/j | *Y* as in *y*ou |
| -sz | *Zh* as in mea*s*ure |

# PART 1: LIBERANDO DOWN

*The fall of man did not introduce evil; it placed us on the wrong side of it, under its rule, needing rescue.*
—N. D. Wilson

PART I: LIBERANDO DOWN

# 1

AUGUST 1, 1943
ABOARD THE B-24D "JESSICA JOY" AT 4,000 FEET
AGL OVER NORTHEASTERN BOSNIA, YUGOSLAVIA

*SO THIS IS HOW I DIE.*

Captain Michael Goodman tried to adjust his goggles with his one good hand, but it just made things worse. Two-hundred-knot winds howled through the Jessica Joy's shattered nose compartment and flight deck. Shredded wires from the instrument panel whipped at his bloodied face. He fought the control wheel to keep the broken bomber flying level, but it was like she *wanted* to go into a spiral. None of the instruments worked properly, so fixing crooked goggles did nothing for him. Goodman scanned the sky above, but he knew the German *Luftwaffe* was done with him. He refocused on keeping the plane airborne as long as possible. But to go where? Returning to base at Benghazi was impossible. Same for the British aerodromes around Cairo. The Jessica Joy dipped her nose and gently rolled again. *C'mon, JJ! Keep your nose up!* He manipulated the throttles and pumped his pedals to counter the drift. *C'mon, please!*

His thoughts returned to his crew. *Did anyone make it out?*

The only thing Goodman could do for them was to keep her aloft long enough and with enough altitude to give everyone a chance to bail out. And then to notify anyone listening of their location. But there would be no rescue. Not this far into enemy-controlled territory. He had failed to keep his crew safe, to keep *her* safe, so he had to try something to atone for his sins. *I owe them that much.* He shook off the tinge of guilt and scanned the terrain below. *Where the hell am I?* With no instruments and no maps, good enough was all he had. Goodman toggled the radio from the intercom to the external channel and squeezed the push-to-talk on his throat microphone.

"Mayday, mayday!" he yelled over the noise. "This is romeo four-niner juliet! Mayday, mayday! This is the Jessica Joy. I am on a heading of two-six-zero…distance…" He played with the math of wind versus airspeed versus ground speed in his head and continued. "…three-zero-zero miles west of Checkpoint Delaware. I say again, three-zero-zero miles west of Checkpoint—"

An air pocket hit the plane like a giant baseball bat, and she dropped a hundred feet in half a second. Goodman's chin hit his chest when the wings suddenly caught lift again. His throat microphone pulled tight and choked him. He yanked it free, and the cord came loose, melted at the end that was supposed to be plugged into the jack. He pulled the entire assembly from his neck and threw it to the floor.

"Dammit!" he screamed at the wind.

The instrument panel snapped free from the frame and wedged itself against Goodman's left leg. He roared at the pain. A blast of heat on his neck. He turned his head but could see nothing behind him except a glowing, smoke-filled crew compartment. *There's nobody left*, he thought. *There's no way I'm getting out of this.*

That day's mission over Romania's Ploesti oil complex went wrong before they even got off the ground. The control tower at Benghazi cleared the *Jessica Joy* to taxi across the path of another aircraft accelerating for take-off, and the two nearly collided. Then the squadron leader's damn fool of a navigator missed a checkpoint and delayed their arrival over the target area by a critical seventeen minutes. Goodman's navigator caught the error, but mandatory radio silence precluded taking or advising any corrective measures. They *had* to stick with the plan. He *had* to follow the leader. He *had* to stay in formation. The iron-clad and irrevocable law of strategic bombing: stay in your place in formation. Pilots get relieved of their commands for failing to do so sufficiently. He saw it happen time and time again. So, he obeyed. And his crew died for it.

According to the plan, the enemy gun crews who were supposed to be asleep at time T-0 when the 376th Heavy Bomb Group arrived over the target area were wide awake at T+17 *after* the planned second wave dumped their explosives all over the Astra Romana oil refinery. The Jessica Joy was the second aircraft to pass over the flak train parked *exactly* in her flight path at less than two hundred feet above the deck. Goodman saw the gunners' faces an instant before they unloaded an 88mm high explosive shell into his nose cone.

The blast shattered the nose compartment and threw Goodman's navigator and bombardier into the void. Goodman and his co-pilot, First Lieutenant Danny Dockery, strained with every muscle to keep the Jessica Joy from plowing into the ground at the sudden loss of aerodynamics. Dockery jettisoned their ordnance load and several tons of high explosives littered the farmer's fields below. That single act allowed them to pull the *Jessica Joy* to four thousand feet and escape the gunfire over the target zone. However, without a nose cone to cut the air cleanly, they plowed through the warm, heavy air. Fuel consumption jumped two hundred percent. When Goodman saw that instrument needle jump, he knew they would never make it back to Libya or anywhere else in Allied territory. He set his mind to getting as far away from the target as possible.

*The Mediterranean is too far. Maybe Turkey?* he thought. *Turkey's no friend, but it's not the enemy, either. I can make that. Heading one-three-five.* He banked the plane accordingly—right into a black swarm of German Messerschmitt Me-109 fighter-interceptor planes.

The interceptors tore into the Jessica Joy's thin aluminum skin with thumping 20-millimeter cannon fire. He could smell the attackers' exhaust in their first pass. He listened to his tail gunner and both waist gunners die in that attack. Engine number two blew up shortly after and required fire suppression. Goodman put the nose down and banked hard to avert the next attack, and the 109s never materialized again. *They must have diverted.*

To avoid the German fighter bases and air defense batteries to the south, Goodman changed heading to two-seven-zero. *Yugoslavia's got to be easier*, he thought. *Fewer German fighter bases in Yugoslavia. Maybe I can get back to the original return route to Africa over the Adriatic Sea and then the Med. Maybe.* A friendly combat air patrol would pick him up and escort him until he had to ditch into the drink. The chance of recovery by allied ships is better in the Adriatic than the Aegean. That was it. His command decision. *I'll ditch in the Adriatic via central Yugoslavia.* Goodman pressed on his throat mic.

"Hey, Danny." Goodman kept his eyes forward, scanning the terrain and the sky. Yelled again, louder. "Danny, can you look up the…" The sudden emptiness felt like his co-pilot had just walked out of the room. Goodman turned his head.

Lt. Dockery's head rolled toward him and gaped with lifeless eyes. Goodman looked away. "Dammit, Danny!" he screamed into the wind. He felt his chest tighten. He blew a long breath. *I still have this plane to land. Someone might be stuck back there.* He set his mind to the task.

"C'mon, *JJ*," he said to his plane. "Just keep your nose up."

Navigating across the eastern Yugoslav lowlands was a matter of counting rivers. Three hundred miles of green farm fields cut by large, sparkling rivers. The Tisa, the Sava, and the Danube all passed below without incident, though successively at lower altitudes despite his best efforts. Western Yugoslavia, however, was all mountains to the coast. He needed to maintain altitude to get over the mountains.

Another dark blue river swept under the aircraft. *That's the Drina*, he thought.

The green foothills began immediately. Goodman tore his eyes away from the ground and habitually checked his altimeter, but it was still just a hole in his instrument panel. He peered out the window and estimated eight hundred feet above ground level. From what he could recall of the route brief, eight-hundred feet above the ground at this point was thirty-two-hundred feet above sea level. The highest peaks were over six thousand feet above sea level. *No way I can gain that altitude.* He looked up to see the green wall of mountains and higher, snow-capped peaks far beyond. Goodman shook his head. *There's no way I'm going to make it to the coast.*

He searched the jagged horizon for a place to set down. A string of contiguous farm fields, a straight piece of road, anything—even a riverbed that ran straight for a thousand feet would do. There was nothing but forested mountains all the way to the horizon in every direction. *There's nowhere to go.* Goodman despaired for the first time. The 376th Heavy Bomb Group would have to go without tail number 42-9559 for the remainder of the war.  Then *JJ* started to drift again.

Goodman worked the control wheel to flatten the wings, but the controls were sluggish. *What now?* He had already increased hydraulic pressure. He pulled back harder. Nothing. *Maybe a cable got stretched*, he thought. He eased the wheel forward and pulled back again when he felt a sudden pop. *What the hell is this?* Now, the wheel moved freely in his hands. *No, no, no!* The Jessica Joy began to roll to starboard, slowly at first, and he tried to correct it with the rudder pedals. Her nose edged slightly as he pumped, but the roll continued. He slid sideways into his harness as the blue sky scrolled away from his view and the green mountains rotated over his head. *No, not yet!* He torqued the wheel hard to the right and stomped on the right pedal all the way to the floor to no effect. Now, he was furious.

"I'm not done yet!" he screamed again.

He pulled back on the throttles and alternated shoving his left and right pedals all the way in and out. He timed that with feathering the weaker props and jamming the more responsive throttles forward as the plane continued its roll unabated. The instrument panel lifted—or fell—off him, and he pulled his leg out. He screamed in rage at his powerlessness.

A violent tremor shook its way from behind him, punctuated by ear-splitting screeches of wrenching sheet metal. *She's falling apart! Time to bail.* He pulled back on the throttles. *I'm out.*

His fingers searched his seat harness to unbuckle it when the instrument panel fell against him again, but this time, it pinned both his legs above the knees. *No!* he cried out. He frantically squirmed and pushed against the instrument panel, but it would not budge. *I'm trapped!*

Dark blue sky filled his view again with the last roll the *Jessica Joy* had in her. Then a brilliant flash caught his eye. Engine two sprayed oranges and yellows into a boiling swirl outside the flight deck. *Combusting aviation fuel*, he reasoned. *Beautiful*. He closed his eyes, and the warmth surrounded him. The strangeness of the feeling never really sank in. But he did indeed feel the pain in his legs fade into numbness. He let go of the control wheel and drew his arms into his chest. *This is it*, he thought. Tears streamed from his eyes. But panic gave way to calm, and he opened his eyes again. Peace. Detached peace of an observer who knows everything will be alright. He watched the horizon of distant mountains disappear behind a tree-lined ridge. The forest rushed up at him. Severed treetops disintegrated on all sides. Engine number four burst into flames, but Goodman ignored it. *I never had that talk with you, Dad. I'm sorry.*

On the slope below, trees groaned and bent under the Jessica Joy's wake. The port-side wingtip clipped a tall and solid conifer, and she nosed downward into the forest. She cut a swath of severed trees for half a mile before touching rock. The impact knocked Goodman unconscious, and the aircraft tumbled down the mountainside. In this final act, at her fiery end, the Jessica Joy saved his life.

# 2

AUGUST 2, 1943
HIGH SETTLEMENT, INNER MAJEVITSA RANGE,
NORTHEASTERN BOSNIA, YUGOSLAVIA

THE OLD MAN IN THE LONG WHITE TUNIC was bent with age. He teetered precariously on the twisted wooden cane wedged under his ribs. His breathing was strained, almost wheezing. Pungent pipe smoke filtered through his gray mustache and beard before it swirled out of the stone-and-mortar pavilion. A bead of sweat dripped over his deeply furrowed brow, traced his eyebrow, then descended across his temple, only to be lost in his beard. He shifted his weight to watch an eagle make wide arcs in the air. When it passed out of view, he cleared his throat to speak.

"Zoran Mehmetović Dudovic…"

At nearly seven feet tall, the other man in the pavilion dwarfed the elder. His great shoulders were made broader by a thick leather vest over heavy woolen shirts. The leather shoulder strap of a Russian-made submachine gun crossed his front. A great, curved sword hung on his hip opposite the revolver in its holster. A bandolier of bullets cinched up his firm, muscular middle. Sunlight had found the sword hilt and reflected a spray of speckles upon the stone walls.

"Yes, Nusret Mufti?"

"Zoran Mehmetović, I am no mufti," scolded Nusret the elder. "We must remember to not elevate ourselves, or each other, beyond where God has placed us. You are a great warrior, from a long line of warriors. Let that be your contentment."

Zoran narrowed his eyes and exhaled through his nose. "Yes, Effendi." His eyes shifted to the ranges of mountains, valleys, and sky.

"Are you ready for the council meal?"

"May I ask for one more moment, Effendi, to contemplate the matters before us?"

"Yes," the Elder acquiesced. Then, he, too, turned his eyes toward the thousand-foot chasm to their front.

The pavilion itself was carved into the crest of a steep, stony slope, with a plunging view of dark green valleys far below and a brilliant blue sky above. A jagged black-and-green horizon separated the earth from the heavens. All these men could see, and some distance beyond, was the Majevitsa, their ancient territory and sanctuary. Steep-banked rivers and heavily guarded canyons in between densely forested mountains protected them from the hostile tribes of Bosnia, Serbia, and Croatia. Here, however, only a low stone wall separated the men from the great void. The exhilaration

Zoran felt never diminished, no matter how many times he came to this place.

*Here, I will rule one day.*

The warrior turned his gaze upward from the green valley below to the blue sky above. He saw the eagle, but he imagined the manmade dangers. In the air, not unlike that eagle, the courageous and terrible German *Luftwaffe* pilots were the masters with their scout reconnaissance planes, fighters, and dive bombers. He had not heard the warbling drone of a reconnaissance plane for several weeks. Like that eagle searching for its next prey, the German scouts prowled the skies. *We're due for an attack*, he thought. *Long overdue.* He closed his eyes and listened to the wind. *When will it come? When will you come, you heathen dogs? When will you again attack my House of Peace?*

A third man approached from a stone pathway. He paused just outside the pavilion.

"Yes?" said the elder. "Do you wish to see your master?"

"A thousand pardons, Effendi,"—the visitor bowed his head—"but something of importance requires Zoran Pash—" He caught himself. "Something requires Zoran's attention, Effendi." He bowed slightly deeper.

The elder man took his pipe out of his mouth and scowled. "You may come." Smoke wafted lazily from his mouth and nostrils.

"Thank you, Effendi," said the visitor. "Zoran," he whispered. "News from the northern hills."

"What news, Milosz?"

"There is a story of a plane crash in the northern range, somewhere west of Hozjak."

"A story is of no interest to me." Zoran turned back to the low stone wall.

"It is more than a story," said Milosz. "A large plane, a bomber perhaps, British or American, landed in the forest."

"West of Hozjak?" Zoran kept his eyes on the rugged horizon. "Then the Germans surely have it by now."

"Yes, Pasha. But they left it."

"Then there is nothing for us there."

"Zoran Pasha, there is a pilot. Reportedly, he is alive."

"Alive?" Zoran turned around.

The elder cleared his throat. "Zoran Mehmetović," he said. "Time draws near for the council meeting. Is this something you would share with the council?"

"Yes, Effendi." The interruption irked Zoran. "I will share as soon as I can collect the relevant information."

He turned and pulled Milosz by the arm out of the small room.

"Now, how do we know this news of an American or British bomber and pilot in the woods west of Hozjak?"

"A messenger carried the news," said Milosz. "He described the crash and the pilot. A reconnaissance patrol discovered the pilot still alive, but barely. They took the pilot to a village in the northern range."

"They did? On whose order?"

"I do not know," said Milosz. "Perhaps they thought it was urgent—"

"Perhaps it is a trap," Zoran grumbled. "And the village will be burned to the ground by nightfall." He pulled on his salt-and-pepper beard. "Who got there first? Surely the Germans or the Ustaše did not leave a living pilot behind. Were there others alive? How badly injured is this pilot?"

"These answers I also do not know."

Zoran scowled. *My people are acting without thought to consequence. The Germans will come with their filthy Ustaše dogs, who will rape and torment my people again. I do not know when or how. But they will come, and we must be prepared. I must know for certain about this pilot. We cannot be taking risks like this but, if this story is a true story, and the pilot is real and he is alive, then this is indeed valuable. He is worth a thousand fighting men, if I ever had that many. But I cannot send just anyone on this task. It must be done correctly and with the utmost haste.* He thought for a moment. *She will know how to handle this.* "Where is Amira Effendim?"

"She is conducting safe passage for the widows and orphans from the Lipovica valley. Tonight, she intends to attack the German checkpoint on the Zvornik highway."

"Send a messenger at once," said Zoran. "Your fastest rider. Bring Amira here, immediately. She will handle this matter with the pilot. Also, send for the doctor from Potraš to join her. If this pilot is injured, as he is likely to be, then the doctor will be more important than you or I."

"Yes, Pasha."

"And Milosz…"

"Yes, Pasha?"

"Keep this quiet. Tell the doctor he gets *one* nurse to assist him, and only one. And he tells no one where he is going nor whence he came. Tell him only that I sent for him. If too many people become aware of this, then it will only be a matter of time before our enemies descend upon us and deprive us of this…opportunity."

"Yes, Pasha." Milosz bowed slightly before retracing his steps up the path.

A long, solemn cry echoed across the valley. Zoran lifted his eyes in time to see the eagle pivot on its head into a tight, spiraling turn. It beat its mighty wings once, then drew them in. It reached an incredible speed and struck at a mountain goat high on the rock face. The unfortunate beast shrieked until it hit the rock face several hundred feet below. Its body tumbled and came to a stop at the uppermost edge of the scree field. The eagle alighted on its kill as the echo spread the story of its victim's end. Zoran Pasha thought on this as he turned and followed the elder out of the pavilion.

# 3

## IN AN UNKNOWN PLACE

GOODMAN'S FEET DRAGGED like he was wearing cement loafers. He ran, but he moved in slow motion. He always ran. And then he fell sometimes. But not this time. A small hand on his head brought a small voice. The voice soothed him but faded away quickly. A warm, sticky, foul breath of air smothered him and he could not move. Something large, heavy with presence – malice – moved over him. Gray-black smoke swirled and thinned to reveal wrinkled, scabby skin. Claws emerged and held him. Lips, stretched and cracked, penetrated by fangs that sank slowly into flesh. His own? He did not know. He watched it all happen, a detached observer. But it was indeed his own flesh. He lurched upward at the pain that seized him. Someone cried out.

"Shhhhh…shhhhh…" The small hand again on his forehead. He thrashed under his blanket.

Something heavy scraped on something hard. He heard muffled voices beyond the pain. People talking. Two? No, three. A woman's voice, firm and authoritative. Then a man's voice, deep and flat. His sister's voice, small and anxious. *Wait, Maria? Here?* He fought to remember. *Little sister, why are you talking like that? What language is that?*

His identification tags clinked on his chest. *They know my name.* Essential elements of information, known only to him and the United States Army Air Corps raced back to him. Goodman. Michael Amancio Goodman. *That's my name. Michael from my father, Amancio from my mother.* Service number 60244623 from the Army. Blood group A-positive. Roman Catholic, by familial default. "Who are you?" he tried to ask, but nothing came out.

Goodman felt his arm lift, like someone detached it from him, with just a nub at his shoulder. A pinprick. *What is…why…who, who is doing that?* He wanted to react, but there was a thick feeling that made his head swim. He pushed through the fog and willed a response. A single, nondescript groan came from deep within. Someone again shushed him.

*There! Someone! I'm here! Please see me!* Suddenly exhausted again, he let himself sink. He thought he heard singing. So strange. *Where are you?* The blackness enveloped him again. *Help me.*


Goodman's mind crawled through the blanket of fog. His family was arguing. No, *he* was arguing. Arguing with his father over something… His decision to drop out of college? No—dropping out of law school? *No, I can't remember. Or maybe it was all of it.* The memories faded. Then a light came back to him. This time, he was aware of the darkness that surrounded the light. *This is an improvement*, he thought. Strange words came to his ears. He took his first deliberate breath. A hundred knives stabbed his chest. And then the pins and needles of pain across his face. Hot, like fire. He wanted the burning to stop. Someone placed a cool, wet cloth on his chest, and the burning lessened. But only slightly. *Who's there?*

"Mom…" He whispered to his mother. "Please tell Dad…tell Dad that I…I'm sorry I didn't…" She turned away from him. "Mom! Wait! Please, go…tell, wait, Mom?"

He heard his mom whisper. Something about Dios. God.

Someone whispered to him, but not in English. It was not Spanish, either. And there was something else. *My mother doesn't smell like that. Who are you?*

More whispers in that strange language again. *Is that Russian?* His thoughts climbed the ladder of alarm. I'm not home. I'm…somewhere. *How could the Russians be here? The Russian front is nowhere near here.* The cloth went away from his face, and he shivered. His left shoulder throbbed with pain. He had to stop the shivering. He felt a scratchy blanket drape over his wet skin, but the shivering intensified. His teeth chattered. In time, the shivering stopped.

A new presence moved to his side. A hand on his forehead. The cool of a wet cloth. A soothing, motherly voice whispered over him.

"Shhhhh…shhhhh…"

He looked with his one good eye as far as he could. Twin reflections of orange lamplight looked down on him. He saw the eyes blink, and the lamplights returned. The cloth lifted from his forehead. A delicate whisper.

It was not Maria's voice this time, but another female voice. *Who is this?* Goodman opened his mouth to speak, but the air caught in his throat, and he coughed. His abdominal wall flexed for the cough, and spasms of pain reverberated across his body. He coughed again and bent in half with the contractions, and then again with the pain. He tried to spit and let out a choking gasp. Heavy footsteps came near.

Someone said something urgently. Heavy hands forced him down. He felt the pinprick again. *A needle.* He pushed back feebly. *Don't do that!*

"No!" he finally cried out.

He writhed and twisted.

A woman's voice yelled out and more hands restrained him. The needle sank into his arm and a warm, smothering sensation moved up his arm and washed over his brain. His will to fight evaporated, along with his will to move, to think, to remain awake. Shapes, smells, voices, and everything else melted into a numb fog. The gray-black blanket covered him once again. *I...I don't...I don't...don't want...*

A brown darkness surrounded him, broken only by a solitary orange glow. He blinked several times until the orange cloud sharpened to a flickering pinpoint. *A candle.* Again, someone was close by. He remembered the pain, and he kept his breath shallow. A pungent, earthy stench wrinkled his nose. The air moved over him.

"Who are you?" he whispered.

That someone shifted close to him. A girl's voice spouted a flurry of incomprehensible excitement, and then she was gone. A slant of blinding daylight illuminated the far wall, flickered, and then shone brightly again.

"Where am I?" he whispered.

No response.

He scanned the room as far as he could, but the pain in his neck pushed back. From what he could see, the space was as small as it felt in the dark. Not more than ten-by-ten. The ceiling looked maybe five or six feet above the floor and was filled with hanging bunches of onions, roots, dried fruit, and herbs of various kinds. A pathway through the herbal forest connected his bed with the bottom of a set of stairs on the opposite side of the room, where light had reflected on the wall. Shelves of jars and boxes lined the other walls. The smell subsided as if knowing what caused it lessened its offensiveness. He let his aching eyes rest again.

Heavy footsteps clomped on the floor above and then down the stairs. A bearded man and a woman stood over him, both in olive-colored wool tunics and wearing peaked military caps. Two more people were partly visible behind them. The woman turned up the burner on the lamp, and her face glowed as she hovered over him. She picked up his wrist and looked at her watch, then turned and said something to the others in severe but melodic tongue. A man by the stairs uttered some deep, monosyllabic response. The lamplight moved to hover over Goodman. He blinked. *Who are these people?*

"You are safe here," said the woman. "Please do not move."

Hers was the voice he had heard earlier but, in *English with a British accent!* Goodman felt his excitement grow. *Did the Allies recover me? Is this the escape network?* He turned his head to see her better, but the pain was excruciating.

"You must not struggle," she said. It was indeed British English, but there was another, more brutal timbre intertwined within. "You are weak from infections." He distinctly heard the "s" on the word infection. More than one.

"Where am I?" He managed the words before he coughed again.

"You are in a safe place," she repeated. "Stop talking so you may rest."

"Where am I?" His breathing was labored. "Am I back? When did I get evacuated? How long… how long was I—"

"There is no evacuation for you," she said. "Not now, and not soon. You have a fever. You must rest."

"Please tell me something," said Goodman. "Who are you? Am I going to die?"

"I am a nurse. You are safe. You do not get to know my name or the name of this place and, no, if you follow my instructions, you will likely not die."

"How far are we from the coast?"

She snorted. "We are *very* far from the coast. We are in the mountains."

*I remember now*, he thought. The river. The mountain ridgeline. The crash. Danny's dead eyes.

Someone else came down the stairs and handed something to the nurse. The Nurse promptly dismissed her.

"Da, madam." It was the girl's voice from earlier. Small and childish, but with that same, indelicate tone. Light footsteps scuffed back up the stairs.

The man standing over the nurse grunted some inquiry at her. Something about her answer triggered his departure. Dust filtered down on Goodman as the man walked across the floor overhead. A door slammed shut. Goodman squinted against the dust in his eye. The nurse wrung out a rag and wiped his face, and then scrubbed up and down his left arm, then his right. She rinsed the rag in the bowl and wrung it out again. *I need more information.* Goodman cleared his throat.

"Are you with the resistance?" he asked.

"The resistance?" she repeated. "If by resistance you mean we are fighting the Germans? Then, yes."

"So you are with the Partisans."

"No."

"I thought the Partisans were the resistance in this part of Yugoslavia."

"We are not Communists," said the nurse. "But they are here, too. Unfortunately."

"Are you Chetniks?"

"No! The Serbian militias are like a herd of swine roaming the countryside. They are helping the Germans sometimes. And sometimes they are helping themselves."

"Sorry," said Goodman. "I didn't know." That wasn't part of any intelligence briefing he had heard.

"Yes, perhaps you should stop talking." She resumed washing him. Goodman jumped at the pain.

"No, really. I'm sorry," said Goodman. "I'm just trying to understand this situation I'm in."

He winced again as she rolled him over onto his side to wash him, and again when she rolled him back. *I need information,* he thought. *I still don't know who this is. Where's the rest of my crew? Someone else could have made it out…*

"Ow," he groaned. "That hurts."

She smirked. "I imagine it is very painful. But you are fortunate. You should have died on the mountain. It seems you have only some minor bone fractures in your shoulder and ribs, and some trauma to your head." She wiped her brow with her sleeve. "A surgeon was here and saved your life from your internal bleeding. My sutures seem to be doing well, so long as you do not move too much. As I said, you have an infection, but you appear to be winning that fight. Many of us thought you would die."

"Did any of my crew make it?"

She gave him a blank stare.

"Anyone else from my plane?" he asked. "Are any of my men alive?"

"There was no one else when we found you."

He thought about Danny, his co-pilot, and the others of his crew. His brothers. His family. That's what they were since he walked away from his birth family. *If I had internal bleeding, then I want someone to monitor for sepsis and hemothorax.* "Can I see a doctor?"

"You do not need a doctor." The Nurse rolled him to his other side, causing him to wince again. "If you see another doctor, it means you are going to die soon. Do not pray for a doctor."

The Nurse laid him back down when she finished washing him. Dropping the rag, she reached into a canvas shoulder pack. She inserted a needle into a glass container and pulled back on the plunger before leaning over him. He felt the needle poke into his skin.

"You use morphine?" asked Goodman.

"Yes," she replied. "When we have it."

He felt the fluid warm his vein as it flowed. "The pain isn't so bad…"

"It will be when this wears off. You move too much when you are in this much pain. Your body must rest in order to heal." She placed the syringe back into a container. She withdrew a pill box.

"You have good medical supplies?"

"No," she said. "This is all I have."

"Am I your only patient?"

"No. I have many. But I am supposed to use the medicines on you first."

Goodman thought he detected a trace of bitterness in her voice. *Or is it just the strangeness of her accent?* "Why?"

She said nothing as she dumped and counted flat, white pills into her hand. "What is that?" he asked.

"It is sulfa," she said. "It is for—"

"Infection," he interrupted. "I know." He swallowed the pills with the water she poured into his mouth.

"You know medicine, yes?" Her voice peaked as she packed away her things.

"Some," he replied. "I was in medical school when the war started. Where are you going?"

"So you were supposed to be a doctor?"

"Sort of."

She pulled the blanket over him and stood up. She pushed her hair behind her ears. "Now, I will tend to my other patients and make my report. Jasminka will be down to feed you. Do not fight her. You need to save your strength."

"Who's Jasminka? When did I fight her?"

"You have done that a few times," she replied. "But I suspect you were confused due to the fever."

"I apologize," he said. "Who is she?"

"You will see her again shortly."

The Nurse dimmed the lamp and carried her pack upstairs. The door closed, and he was alone in the darkness. He slept.

# 4

## AUGUST 2, 1943
## HIGH SETTLEMENT, INNER MAJEVITSA RANGE,
## NORTHEASTERN BOSNIA, YUGOSLAVIA

ZORAN PASHA HANDED HIS SUBMACHINE GUN, PISTOL, AND SWORD to his man, Milosz. A faithful and most-trusted deputy, Milosz was the only man in the Majevitsa who had come close to death more times than Zoran. He withdrew to the door and exited quietly, leaving his commander with the council of their fathers. Zoran sat on the bench and waited for the council.

He tweaked his wife's worry beads between his thumb and forefinger as the council members settled into their seats in the smoke-filled chamber. The council was an enduring constant, as it was meant to be, even in these troublesome times. Times when survival was the driver of all decisions. They had all seen days like these before. *But not exactly like these days*, thought Zoran. *For in this time lay opportunity, opportunity to rise above mere survival. To prosper, even. To Prosper!* He felt his heart soar at the possibility. He almost stepped forward involuntarily out of excitement, keeping to his natural inclination for action. His people lacked only someone to lead from a place of courage and determination, not of fear or survival. Or merely *to lead*, as he thought of it. The ideas are synonymous: to lead is to be courageous. As Pasha, Zoran would not, could not, repeat the sins of omission of his father, or his fathers before him. For his generation led with fear and trepidation. And thus, they lost ground, literally, and moral authority. He would not because to lose ground now meant extermination. But to lead now, and do it with the correct authority, he needed this council's endorsement. But these men were small-minded, petty, impotent, and fearful. His heart contracted slightly at the thought. Maybe one or two possessed something manly between their legs, perhaps. *Why do I try with them? Why do I need this endorsement?* He watched the ancient elders of his people shift in their seats, exchanging platitudes. *They're wasting time*, he thought. *I will be Pasha.* He exhaled loudly to break the stalemate without speaking before his elders. *I am Pasha. I will lead them.* He stood to be acknowledged.

Nusret Effendi, the Elder Councilman, lowered his pipe to speak. "Salam-u Alaykum, Allahov vojnik," he uttered. *Peace be upon you, soldier of God.* The other council members dipped their heads as they echoed.

"And peace be upon you, Nusret Effendi, men of my father's council." Zoran bowed at the waist.

The Elder Councilman gestured for Zoran to sit. Zoran pulled his seat closer to the council's semi-circular table and sat down. The single open window cast orange, late-afternoon sunlight across Zoran like a spotlight. It swirled thick with dust and tobacco smoke. He felt the warmth.

"By the name of the Prophet, peace be upon him," the Elder Councilman began. The others around the table murmured in reply. "We require news of the coming harvest." All eyes lifted and shifted from Nusret the Elder to Zoran.

"Effendi," said Zoran. His eyes moved across the other elders. "Men of this Council, the harvest from all regions will be sufficient for the peoples of the Majevitsa."

"Sufficient, but not plentiful…" the Elder Councilman added. All eyes went to Zoran again.

"No, Effendi, it will not be plentiful. There will be minimal grain for trading. The loss of the farms in the Lipovica valley last spring means our surplus will be smaller than in years past."

Another councilman removed his pipe. "Last year was a meager winter for some…"

"Yes…and last spring was catastrophic for us," said one councilman.

"Not just for us," another councilman muttered. "But for all northern Bosnia. For the Serbs as well as us."

"Men of the council," said Zoran. "Are we now concerned about the Serbian butchers from across the Drina? Do we also share concern for the black hordes of the Ustaši who betray and murder us village by village? Perhaps then we consider welcoming the heathen Communists who will—"

The Elder Councilman slapped the table with a gnarled hand. "Zoran!" he shouted with an old man's strain in his voice. "Do not presume to sermonize the council on these matters."

"Elders of the council, I mean no disrespect." Zoran dipped his head to which the Elder nodded. "Effendi, I am trying to understand the point of this meeting. The harvest is not for several weeks, and I am already making arrangements for our advancement. I have many things pressing on my attention of which I should provide notice." Zoran paused. "Out of respect for the authority before me," he quickly added.

"Yes, a great many things," said the Elder Councilman. The others nodded and puffed on their pipes. "Which is why we seek information to guide our thoughts and prayers as we draw our priorities." An awkward silence followed, and Zoran watched their eyes and hands, the primary tools of council politics. *They aren't*

21

*sure of how to ask me, to challenge the one thing they want to know the most, now that they know they cannot control this meeting.*

"Effendi, what are the priorities of the council?" Zoran sat back to watch how this unfolded.

Every single one of the councilmen kept their eyes fixed on Zoran. Not a single glance flashed across the table, not a look exchanged, not a downward bounce of the eyes. *This meeting has been scripted out*, thought Zoran. *The council has been told to shut up. And, of course, they do.* He glared at the man in the faded red fez. Red Fez wanted power. But he was a little man. A weak man. *A perfect fit for the Council.*

"What news of the stories of many German divisions crossing the Sava?" The Elder Councilman returned to the script.

"There is nothing to them, Effendi," said Zoran. *Is this your method of softening me? Or avoiding me? Say what you really mean to say, you cowards.*

"Nothing at all?" The Elder Councilman pressed.

"There are no new divisions of Germans crossing into our country," said Zoran. "No more than already existed here. The news you hear is movements for logistics, nothing more." He kept his composure. Or at least he thought he did.

"What of this inquiry bothers you, Zoran Mehmetović?"

"Honorable men of this council," he began, carefully. "You may listen to the fantastical rumors of travelers who seek free meals and our protection for a night's rest. And you may listen to the stories of the old women, who busy themselves with gossip and their petty intrigues against one another. Or you can heed the information I bring to you day and night. I am a river of news to this council and, may I say, secret disclosures of great value, am I not?"

To the right of the Elder Councilman, another elder with a faded and stained burgundy fez cleared his throat. "You dispute all other sources of information?"

All eyes switched between Zoran, the councilman with the fez, and back again.

"Yes, Effendi," said Zoran. "If I do not know it, how can I trust it?"

"You do not hold a monopoly of information of relevance to this council."

"What information of relevance to this council have I not brought to your attention?"

"There are other sources," said the Fez.

"Indeed," said another councilman.

"But Zoran has always been faithful and true," said the Elder.

Zoran watched the councilmen exchange glances. *They're fishing. They want me to attack them, to insult their obligations, attack the traditions. This trigger I will not set off. They're divided,* he thought. *Why would I unite them again by speaking?* Most of the councilmen put their pipes back into their mouths, which Zoran knew to be both a muzzle and a signal of acquiescence. *There's dissent, but they won't say it in front of me.* Their eyes flicked between Zoran, the Elder Councilman, and the Fez, and then quickly dropped to the table in front of them, where they stayed for an impossibly long moment. The Fez cleared his throat again and turned to the Elder.

"Yes," said the Fez. "Then there is that." *The cue.*

"What is what, Effendi?" Zoran looked at the Elder. *The time is now. Now we peel back the skin.*

"Zoran Mehmetović, you are a great warrior and a respected patriarch within the Majevitsa," the Elder placated. "You are known well beyond the foothills in all directions, even to the northern banks of the Sava and across the Drina. No one challenges your position—and your authority as such."

"Except the Germans, the communist dogs of the Russians, the Serbian Chetnik regiments, the Ustaša demons in black," Zoran countered. "And *this* council."

"We do not challenge your resourcefulness and your usefulness in your proper place—"

"My proper place?" Zoran stood from his chair and pipes fell from pursed lips around the table. "You mean a lower status than is the birthright of my grandfathers! Your grandfathers even! You challenge the notion of the *pashalik* and my obligations and duty as *Pasha*. A mantle I have not taken—would not take—lightly. On what grounds do you challenge my status within the Bosna Sanjak?"

The Fez leaned in. "Zoran, those times are past…"

*Not today, Fez.* Zoran approached the table, and the councilmen reeled. "Fear has blinded you!" said Zoran. "Your minds are hobbled by the calamities of the past. You see nothing of the future!" He calmed his tone and quickly added, "I mean no disrespect, Effendi, but I must speak freely if I am to be understood. If the council is to understand how *I* understand these days, I mean…" He dropped his head for a moment. His eyes came up to see if it was safe. "May I speak, Effendi?"

The Elder tugged on his beard for a moment. "Yes, you may speak, Zoran Mehmetović, but watch your steps."

"A thousand apologies to you, Effendi, and to the council." He dipped his head again and was met with a nod from the Elder. Zoran put his shoulders back. "The wars of the past are not the war of today. The past wars burned around us without the slightest intervention from us. Was it not the policy of our ancestors to conceal ourselves in our mountains and bend with the winds?" He paused for effect. "And where did this get us? The Kingdom of the Serbs is gone, vanished forever from the earth, praise be to Allah—"

"Praise be to Allah!" the councilmen murmured.

*Good,* thought Zoran. *They're with me.* He continued. "The Serbs are gone, and we are free, but for how long? There are others who would rule us." He looked and saw his chance. "What is the role of the Pasha over the pashalik?" He did not wait for an answer. "It is to guard and defend the honor and lands—the prosperity—of the Sultanate, is it not?"

"Are you proposing to one day be elevated to the title of Sultan?" asked the Fez. "You aspire to be the Khan of Khans?"

"The historical pashalik had its capital in Tuzla," said one of the lesser, but younger and, in Zoran's estimation, one of the more intelligent councilmen. "Is that not the jewel of the region? To restore the pashalik would require the taking—"

*I dare not speak of my strategy*, thought Zoran. *That would be too much.* For now.

"No, Effendi, I'm not seeking the title of Khan, or of a Beg, for I do not wish to usurp the duties and politics of this council." *Nor do I want to be a part of this charade*, he thought.

"Of course not," said a councilman. "This is no land worthy of a Beg, and certainly not a pashalik, either. And a pasha without a pashalik is a shepherd without a flock. He is a man of empty title, not of honor, but a pretender." His pipe stem left curls of smoke in its wake as he gestured with it before he stabbed it back into his mouth.

"But, Effendi, there *can* be a pashalik!" Zoran leaned in and planted his knuckles on the council table, showing the faded tattoos that covered his forearms and hands. "I am a realist, Effendi. We cannot restore the *sanjak*, much less the Sultan's empire. But we cannot hide from this war as we did in previous times. The forces at work today will crush us or consume us. In the mysteries of the future, there is opportunity! Allah knows what Allah knows, and nothing is carved in stone. Allah has blessed us with the Majevitsa, miles and miles of stone, to protect us. We can still expand our lands and protect what we have. It is there for the taking. We simply *have to try*. Too much has already been sacrificed..." He found he had not taken a breath and inhaled. "I am willing to fulfill the requirements of a pasha. I will be pasha,"—a pause as his spirit soared— "I *am* pasha."

The Elder Councilman placed his worry beads on the table and looked at the faces around him.

"What say you, men of the council?"

"Is this not the voice of a proud and greedy servant who seeks to enlarge his personal wealth and power by taking the whole house?" said the Fez. He thumbed his own worry beads feverishly.

"He talks of Allah's knowledge, but who is he to utter such things?" said the youngest councilman. The Radical. "Allah has said no such thing to any of us. Does Zoran Mehmetović have dreams or visions he has not shared with us?"

*Of course, I do.* Zoran started to respond, but the Elder Councilman spoke first. "The visions Allah bestows upon us are for us alone and not for others, unless interpretation is required."

"Who is to say?" said a third, hinting to the Radical. "Who would interpret these things? There is not a mullah or mufti among us. All the judges and scholars are dead. Is it not true that many years have passed since a muezzin has called the prayers from the tower?"

"Or spoken the words over the newly dead?" said another. Others nodded in solemn agreement.

"Zoran speaks with energy," said still another. "And he has the wisdom of his experience."

"Yes," said the Elder Councilman. "Tragedy is a great teacher. And the Dudovic clan has indeed known tragedy." Several councilmen nodded in sympathetic agreement.

"But that kind of learning is a two-edged sword," said the Fez. "It can result in wisdom that benefits all, but it can also harden a heart against the truths of one's own self."

Several men slowly relit their pipes and nodded in agreement.

"Perhaps the title of Pasha is too encumbered for this time," mused one of the older councilmen. "Perhaps Zoran Mehmetović is more of the quality of an agha."

"What difference does it make?" said the Fez. "If one is a pasha or agha or even a Protector of the Gardens when there is no empire, no greater institution or system of laws in which to seat the ruler above the ruled?" He stabbed his pipe into his mouth and puffed again.

"Men who carried the two-tailed whip of an agha were leaders of slaves," said Zoran. "The future requires broader authority. I seek to administer, to lead. Not to enslave." Then he quickly added, "With the blessings and guidance of the council." He saw his response had no effect, even with the added appeasement. "I have no ancestral agha in my line. The job ahead is greater than this."

"None of your fathers were pashas, either," said the Fez.

Zoran glared at him. *You stupid donkey.*

"There is no shame in that," conciliated Nusret, both hands raised as if separating bitter waters. "The formal lines have all been severed. This is not the first time such things have happened in our lands. Even in prior times of foreign conquest, there were mechanisms for re-allocating and restoring title and honor."

The Fez rose slightly in his seat. "None of those mechanisms exist any—"

"Effendi," Zoran stood to his fullest height to look down on the council. "I *am* Pasha. There is no other way to move us forward in these uncertain times. At least none that this council is willing to consider." He paused long enough to see the council waiting for the Elder's lead. "Are there other items on the council's agenda for today?"

The Elder Councilman cleared his throat to preempt anyone else from speaking. "What of the news your deputy brought you prior to this meeting?"

Zoran hoped that he had forgotten. But he dare not lie. "There is a report of a foreign pilot in the mountains of the northern range. If this is true, then I will sell him and use the proceeds to fund my campaigns to the east—"

"And provide for the shortfall in the harvest?" said the Fez.

"Yes, that as well," said Zoran. *I'm done here.* He bowed very deeply.

"Zoran Mehmetović," said the Elder Councilman. "This *other* issue is *not* resolved."

"It is for me," said Zoran. "The sooner the people of the Majevitsa reform behind Pasha, the better for the people of the Majevitsa. I will deliver to you the restored pashalik."

The Fez and the Radical protested to the Elder Councilman, as the other councilmen argued with each other. Again, Zoran bowed deeply enough to imply the right level of submission and left his wake in the smoke. He opened the door to a wide-eyed Milosz, who returned his weapons to him and followed him through the anteroom and down the long stairway to the street.

# 5

YELLOW FIRE LIGHT CAST DANCING SHADOWS all around the high stone wall. A young boy and his brothers stoked the logs and retreated to their mother and sisters at the family table when the heat grew too intense. Around the square, old women gossiped, mothers nursed, and young children danced and twirled in time with the *sevdalinka* that grew in tempo as the musicians fell deeper into their collective trance. Zoran observed all this seated with his back against a wall.

But his thoughts were elsewhere. Or, rather, else *when*. In his mind, he was not surrounded by the women and children of other families, but of his own. He could hear the banter of his children, all eleven of them, boys and girls aged four months to eighteen years. He smiled and closed his eyes. Though it was mixed with the present wood smoke, he could smell his wife's hair. The memory was inextricable from the scent of the cleansing concoction her mother used to make for her and his daughters. *What was it? Berries of the mountain lilies? Yes, that was it.* Poisonously beautiful and disabling if consumed. Like her temper. *Meriam,* his lips moved silently. *My Meriam.* His desire for her still grew in him. But now, his obsolete fantasy conflicted with the detestable reality of this night and every night for the rest of his life. *I could not protect you, my tree of roses…*

"Amidža Zoran…?"

Zoran wiped his face and turned to the girl.

"I have food for you, Amidža." She blinked, and her smile turned downward. "Are you alright, Amidža?"

Amidža. *Uncle.* To the adults, he was Zoran Pasha. To the children, he was Amidža Zoran—Uncle Zoran—for he was literally or spiritually an uncle to hundreds of children in the region. He loved them dearly, perhaps more so now than ever. He shook his head to himself and looked into the girl's eyes.

"Hvala, my little flower." He thanked her and took the plate of food. He turned back to her when she did not withdraw. Her eyes overflowed with worry. He put a hand on her arm. "Do not worry, little flower. I am well."

The girl hovered for a moment. "Do you miss your children, Amidža?"

A God-forsaken Chetnik could not have struck deeper into his soul. He found no air for his voice and smiled falsely.

"Daughter! Come back here at once!" Little Flower's mother called to her. "Leave Zoran Pasha alone." The girl retreated, but kept her eyes on him as she sat down.

Zoran clenched back the tears. She reminded him far too much of his own Little Flowers when they were her age. All of whom were now gone. All except one. One last Little Flower who was not so little anymore.

A commotion of horses and voices broke him out of his emotional spiral. Milosz, who had been sitting some distance away, rose and strode to the gate. He conferred with someone briefly and gestured toward Zoran. Zoran straightened his tunic and arranged his hat. The familiar figure rounded the gatepost and strode toward him. A long, dark ponytail flicked like a horse's tail.

"Zoran Pasha!" she exclaimed. "What is—"

Zoran raised his hand. "Amira, please…" He gestured for her to follow him. They recommenced when they reached a place out of sight, away from the light of the fire.

"Papa—"

"What is the trouble, Amira?"

"You remove me from my mission to destroy the Germans and make me travel all this way? Why?" she demanded. "So what of this pilot?" She clenched her jaw and breathed loudly through her nostrils.

*Just like her mother*, he thought. *A beautiful, strong woman.* Perhaps too strong. "Amira," Zoran began. "Amira, my daughter, please understand the importance of this man to me. To us."

"He is no concern of ours," she replied. "If the information about him is even close to the truth, he's probably already dead."

"He may indeed be dead," said Zoran. "But if he is not, and we can save him, then he is very valuable to us."

"You mean for the bounty." She crossed her arms. "To whom would you sell this man?" She waved her arm in the air. "Who among our enemies would rather give us their money than kill us?"

"Amira, is that a real question? You know how—"

"Papa," she interrupted. "This man, whoever he is, his mother will miss him. That is her sadness. Not ours. The Germans also have mothers, and they will miss their sons, too, when I kill them. One is our responsibility, the other is not. We owe nothing to the British or to the Americans. They feed the communist Partisans who seek to starve us. We owe the Germans our bullets. We owe our family *many* dead Germans. Our duty—"

"Yes, you are right," Zoran assured her. *I must end this debate now.* "But right now, this pilot is more important to me than a hundred dead Germans. There will be Germans for us to kill tomorrow. And the next day, and so on. This pilot is ours for a fleeting time. We must make of him what we can."

Amira's arms tightened in their fold across her chest. Zoran's chest tightened. *I can't lose my last—my only—daughter.* In similar situations with his wife, Zoran could wait her out and there would be peace and unity once again. But he had no idea what would drive Amira away. Forever.

"So, please, Amira, escort the doctor to the village and make the pilot safe in a place where he cannot be found." Zoran looked down at Amira's glare. "Do this for me, Amira."

"And then what?"

"Then it is up to Allah and the doctor to make him well. Or not. Either way, you will return to your mission after you do this thing for me. You have my word."

"Very well, Father." She unclenched her jaw.

"Now, please, my daughter," said Zoran. "Eat something."

"No, Pasha," she said. "If I am to do this thing tomorrow, I will do it now."

*Again*, Zoran thought, *just like her mother.*

Amira spun around and strode across the plaza to her second-in-command, who bolted upright as she approached. He was visibly dismayed at what he heard, but he rallied dutifully.

"Gather the fighters," she said. "We depart immediately." One by one, her men received the news with long faces and sent their eldest children to retrieve their horses from the well. Under protest from their wives, Amira's men quickly shoveled food into their mouths and downed their last gulps of slivovitz. The men of her company bid farewell to bitter women and confused children and mounted up to re-form their march columns according to habit. Without further words, the company followed Amira out of the stone plaza and into the darkness.

*Allah be with you*, thought Zoran. *Please bring her back to me.*

The clip-clopping gave way to the sounds of the wind in the trees, the chattering of children, and the scolding of mothers. Mothers whose eyes Zoran manifestly avoided. He poured the entire mug of slivovitz down his throat to deaden the pain in his chest. It made no difference. He pictured Amira. His daughter. His last.

*My Little Flower.*

*⸙⸙⸙*

# 6

## AUGUST 22, 1943
## A ROOT CELLAR IN AN UNKNOWN VILLAGE

DUSTY SUNLIGHT FLASHED DOWN THE STAIRS and cast long shadows across the far wall. Goodman's eyes moved to the creaking door, and the girl called Jasminka bounded down the stairs. She put down a bowl down next to him and turned up the lamp.

"Dobar dan, Effendi!" *Good day, sir!*

Her crooked, toothy smile gleamed in the lamplight as she gently propped up his head with the pillow. She straightened his hair, as well as his blanket, before she commenced to talking to him, or *at* him, rather. He just opened his mouth to take the spoonfuls of broth when she hovered it over him. It tasted like chicken vegetable soup. There was no substance, however. Just broth. He felt the warm liquid travel every inch of his esophagus down to his stomach. The saltiness burned his cracked lips and throat. He wanted to slow down and take a breath, as his nose was still swollen. But every time he opened his mouth to breathe, she dumped another spoonful of soup. She talked and talked. And he understood nothing of what she said.

She was young. *Twelve? Thirteen, maybe?* It was clear she was genuine, and whatever it was she was telling him was meaningful, at least to her. This went on until the broth was gone. She carefully wiped his mouth several times and smiled at him. He ventured their first two-way conversation.

"Jasminka?" he asked.

"Da!" Her face lit up like Christmas morning. Wiping her hands on her apron, she leaned in and started talking again, even more excitedly this time. She stopped suddenly and sat upright. With an air of satisfaction, she stood up and flattened her dress and apron with her hands. She took the bowl and towel upstairs and bounced back down to sit next to him. Suddenly at a loss for words, or maybe just enjoying the moment, she smiled at him with her hands in her lap. He tried to force a smile, but it hurt too much. Jasminka tucked the blanket around his shoulders and turned down the lamp.

Exhausted, Goodman let his eyes close. His mind clouded over, and he dreamed peaceful dreams.

# 7

IN HIS CELLAR, DAY AND NIGHT WERE NEARLY INDISTINGUISHABLE. His waking periods were foggy and tired. His sleeping periods were still turbulent with pain but improving. Occasionally, he had nightmares, but mostly not.

When leg cramps or back spasms seized him, Jasminka would hear him grunting and race down the stairs to mop his brow with a rag and whisper or sing to him. She would wait patiently until he was calm again and, eventually, her feet would pitter-patter back up the stairs. The empty hours between sleeping and eating left time to think. The kind of time when Goodman deconstructed his entire life and tried to rearrange decisions and pick alternative endings to select conversations. *Too* much time.

*Maybe I should have stayed in medical school*, he would think to himself. *Or maybe I should have just done what my father wanted and helped my brother close business deals. No*, he would argue, *I burned that bridge a long time ago.* None of that was going to be a reality for him. Not that the possibility of getting out of here, wherever *here* was, was real. He could likely die here in this God-forsaken cellar. And then someone, perhaps the people upstairs, would bury him in a hole in the ground. And then there would be nothing. The thought made him feel small. Insignificant. Pointless.

# DEEP IN THE PLACE OF THE DEAD

He could hear those other people upstairs, but he only ever saw the Nurse and Jasminka.

In moments of empty optimism, Goodman came to think of them as his instruments, like in a cockpit. Like the short hand on a clock, the nameless Nurse would visit him every third day to check his pulse, his temperature, and his bandages. She worked his arms and legs to check for mobility, then gave him unmerciful shots of antibiotics in the buttocks weekly or something like that. Her only words were medical directives concerning hydration or cleanliness.

He wished she would be more forthcoming with her medical assessments. He knew a thing or two about human physiology, after all. His self-diagnoses seemed to confirm that the nurse was well trained, but he wanted to know what decisions were being made about him based on his condition. This she would never acknowledge. Occasionally, she would accommodate his requests for translation. He tried to commit the terms and phrases to memory, but it proved very difficult.

Jasminka's visits also marked the passage of time, but more like the long hand. She was his very reliable and friendly chronometer. Three times a day, she would feed him, and she would stay longer and longer each time to talk to him now that he could remain awake. She always wore the same long striped skirt and apron. Sometimes she wore a kerchief over her hair, sometimes not, and she was almost always barefoot.

She would happily engage him in conversation in Bosanski, as he understood her language was called. Caught up in her talking, and she would absent-mindedly wave the spoon around his mouth without feeding him for several minutes. Or she would forget that her patient was in pain until she brushed against his wounds. He would lurch, and she would exclaim and apologize repeatedly. Goodman learned the words *'pardon me'* very early. *Izvinite.*

She tried to teach him Bosanski, and he gave it an earnest effort. But they often tried too much too quickly, and he would exhaust himself. One day, she held up an apple for him and said something unintelligible. He attempted to repeat what she said, but it caught in his throat, and he coughed. Jasminka smiled patiently.

"Apple," said Goodman. "That's an apple."

"Ah-pul," she repeated. Then she repeated the previous word, "Yabuka."

"Ya-*booka*," said Goodman.

"Neh, neh!" she giggled. "*Yah*-buka."

"*Yah*-buka."

Her eyes sparkled at the victory.

At first, they worked on only tangible objects like food, tools, clothing, and things easily found in his ten-by-ten-by-six-foot space. Then counting. *Jedan, dva, tree* was one, two, three. The first abstractions were things like: yes, no, good, bad, up, down, in, out, and such. Their ability to learn bigger concepts improved substantially when Goodman got his mobility back in his arms. Now he could gesture, which meant they could do verbs. What a difference that made! His vocabulary expanded rapidly after that. It became a game he called "pointy-talky" and it made the hours fly. Even if it left Goodman exhausted.

Events upstairs would trigger new rounds of the pointy-talky. A rather violent rainstorm gave rise to weather terms. Village life above ground brought words describing social activities, pleasantries, and news of the mountain villages, which he understood sparsely at best. A small village school convened four times each week, and Jasminka would bring her small chalkboard down, and new vocabulary followed. The arrival of a patrol of the *vojniki*, or friendly soldiers as he came to understand them to be, introduced weapons and other military-related terms and concepts— at least as well as a thirteen-year-old might understand them. Occasionally, Jasminka would teach him *nevalje rijeci*—the bad words—but only when Baba, her grandmother, was not around. Often, their attempts to impart specific words with wildly animated gestures and verbal noises would leave them laughing until a cramp would send Goodman into a fit.

One day, Jasminka was especially coy in her approach. Goodman could tell she was hiding something under the towel in which she carried the soup. She set it down on her lap and lifted the bowl, but Goodman did not take it. She looked at him quizzically.

"Što?" *What?*

"Nište." *Nothing.* He searched her eyes for a hint of what she was keeping back.

"What?" she asked with a slight peak of concern in her voice. "Why you do this? You are not well?"

"Dobro sam…" *I'm fine*. He smirked at her.

"Then…what?"

"You say me."

"Me say you…what?"

"What's under your towel?"

She smirked. "Nište." Her eyes glinted with excitement as she slowly withdrew a badly scuffed and rusted revolver with a short barrel. She gripped it and aimed it at him.

"No!" he yelled and swatted the weapon out of her hand. It clattered against the floor next to the bed. He picked up the pistol and tried to open the cylinder. It was rusted shut. The hammer was also so badly corroded it barely moved.

"Jasminka—" Her face was frozen in shock. Her eyes watered to the brim. *Oh, man. I just scared her.* "Jasminka…" He softened his voice. "Jasminka…much danger…" He saw a tear drip down her cheek.

Her voice cracked as she spoke. "I…I want show you…to…pištolj ne funkcionira…"

"I get that it doesn't work, but…but no put the pistol to me…" He gestured with the pistol toward his pillow. "Žao mi je, Jasminka." *I'm sorry.*

She wiped her eyes and sniffled loudly. "Nište."

"You have more pistol?"

"Neh."

"Other weapons?"

"Neh."

"Ok." He lowered his head to see her eyes. "Jasminka, I no want you hurt. Da li razumiješ?" *Do you understand?*

She nodded and sniffled again. "Da."

They sat in silence for a moment.

Sometime around lunchtime on day twenty-seven—according to the nurse's medical notes—Jasminka crept down the stairs with unusual stealth.

"Imam tajnu," she whispered. *I have a secret.*

"Jasminka…" He was about to scold her after pistol incident the other day. *She'd better not have another weapon.*

"Neh, Mikel," she called him by name. "No pistol."

*Good*, he thought to himself. *Maybe we're back to our old game.* "Another secret?" Goodman forced a smile. "What secret?"

Her grin widened, and she took a leather-covered flask out of her chest pocket. Jasminka removed the cork and took a whiff. She scrunched her face and gave it to Goodman. It smelled of burnt sugar, but fruity. Jasminka snatched it back and took a quick swig of it. Her face crumpled, and she let out a squeal. She gave it back to him and giggled a little too much. He smelled it again, scowled, and took a small sip. Despite the hint of fruit in its aroma, it tasted like a mouthful of scorched pennies. She laughed at the look on his face. He coughed, which did nothing for his healing ribs.

"Make fire, yes?" She pointed to her throat.

"Da," said Goodman. "Make fire!" He cleared his throat and wiped his mouth with his sleeve. "Where did you get that?" he asked in English before trying again in pidgin Bosanski. "Who bottle?"

She giggled again as she took the flask from him.

"Slivovitz," she said and sniffed the spout one more time before replacing the cork. "Baba slivovitz." It disappeared into her apron pocket.

It surprised Goodman that the apparently devoutly conservative Baba would partake of alcohol. *But*, he reasoned, *everyone has their vices. And everyone has their secrets. So why not Baba, too?*

"You put up," he said, pointing at the flask and then upstairs.

"Da, I go," she said. Then she lowered her voice. "I have secret!" Her eyes darted to the stairs, then back to his.

"More secret?"

"Da," she said, as she sat on the side of his bed. She continued when she had his singular attention. "In village… *špijun*." She waited for his response.

"A what?"

"Špijun." She sat back with an air of triumph.

"Špijun? I not know word."

"A man look thing, people, secret." She contorted her face at trying to explain the concept. "He look…for secret!"

"A man who looks for secrets?" He put it together. "A spy?" He pointed with his fingers from his eyes, scanning around the cellar, then he put his index finger to his lips. "Shhh…" He scanned the room again.

"Da!" She beamed. "Špijun…in village."

"In village? You village?" He pointed up at ground level. "How you know this?"

"My friend talk me." *Her friend told her.*

"Oh, really?" He smirked slightly. "How friend know?"

"Other friend talk friend."

"Friend talk friend talk you?"

She saw his patronizing look. "She talk me." Her tone was very matter of fact.

"Da," he replied to be conciliatory. "You say truth."

"Spy look *you*." Her index finger went from her eye to his chest.

An icy wave washed over Goodman. "Who talk that?"

"Friend."

"How friend know me?"

Jasminka shrugged and averted her eyes to refold his blanket.

"Jasminka," he said. "You talk friends me?" He pointed at her, then opened and closed his thumb and fingers like a duck's beak, and then pointed at himself.

Instead of responding, she dropped his blanket and quickly disappeared up the stairs.

Goodman laid his head back down. *I guess it was inevitable that she would talk—if her friends didn't already know about me. Hell, the entire village probably knows about me. But then, why would the nurse keep me in such strict secrecy?* He concluded Jasminka couldn't possibly know what she was talking about. At least not about a spy. *Kids and their imaginations.*

# 8

## AUGUST 31, 1943

MOST DAYS, JASMINKA BOUNDED DOWN THE STAIRS with an innocent joy that was matched only by her moodiness on her off days. In this, and numerous other ways, her mannerisms were not completely unlike Goodman's little sister's. He recalled how Maria had had her up and down days in her adolescent years. The more he thought about them, the more similarities emerged. Was it the constant time together that made it appear so, or had she actually come to look like Maria? Same black hair, childish features, dark eyes. Jasminka had definitely carved out a place in his heart. Almost like Maria. Goodman wondered if he would ever see his little sister again. His heart sank at the thought. The sound of Jasminka bounding down the stairs once again cut his brief malaise short. His face brightened instantly.

With his next meal, Jasminka also brought down something flat wrapped in cloth. *Oh, man, what now?* he thought. She held it on her lap with both hands the entire time she watched him eat, a Cheshire cat grin across her face, and said not a single word. Even when he asked about it, she merely smiled and swung her feet back and forth. He felt his blood pressure increase. She took care to protect her secret item even as she retrieved his bowl and spoon when he finished eating. She sat back down and could barely conceal her excitement. He waited in vain.

"Šta?" he finally asked. *What?*

Cheshire cat grin.

"Šta ima?" *What you having?* He smiled back at her, unsure of what to say next.

"Šta imaš," she corrected. *What do you have?*

"Šta imaš," he repeated and thanked her for the correction. He reached for the edge of the cloth. She withdrew it. "Neh!" she said playfully and pulled the concealed object away.

"Molim?" *Please?*

"Neh!"

She was baiting him. *It's too flat to be a weapon. It's not a container of any kind. I think I can relax.* He exhaled loudly. *I can play this game.* "Okay," he said. "Neh intersovan." *Not interested.*

He swung his feet back onto the bed and interlaced his fingers behind his head as he laid back. One last flick of his eyes toward her before he closed them. He kept one open.

"Neh!" she laughed. "I show you." She unwrapped the object, and he watched her hold it up for him to see.

He opened his eyes to see a wood-framed, sepia-toned photograph of a family. A *large* family with at least sixty people depicted. Some, mostly men, were standing, and most of the women sat with young children on their laps. The men of military age were all holding rifles, wearing conical fez hats with black tassels on one side, and one was in an army uniform wearing a pistol in a holster and a sword on his hip. A long line of children of increasing height stood across the front of the photograph. Flanked by all those children, seated in the center, was a familiar-looking woman with an older, bearded man next to her. A toddler sat on the lap of the girl next to the old woman, frozen in time as she reached for the woman in the middle. Goodman looked at Jasminka and then back at the photograph. He pointed at the woman in the middle.

"Baba?" he asked.

Jasminka's Cheshire Cat smile bobbed up and down. Then she pointed at the toddler. "Ovo ja."

"That you?" said Goodman. *She looks more like a doll in the photo than a child.* He looked at the woman who held her in the picture. "Ko?"

"Moja maijka," she said. *My mother.*

Goodman pointed to the man with a large mustache standing behind her mother. "Tvoj…"

"Otac," she said. "Moj maijka i moj otac." She put her two index fingers together. *This is her mother and father*, thought Goodman. Jasminka sniffled. He saw her discretely wipe a tear. *Poor kid, everybody is gone except for her and Baba.* He felt pressure well up behind his own eyes. Her finger circled the entire group of people. "Moja porodica."

"Porod—?"

"Po-ro-dica." She rolled her r's and put an extra emphasis on the "tsah" at the end.

"Porodica," he repeated, and she nodded.

"Family. This is your family."

She nodded again.

He pointed to the rows of children. "Ko?"

She pointed to each in succession and said, "Brat, brat, sestra, brat, sestra, brat, brat…" This went on for some time. Brothers and sisters. *Holy cow*, he thought. *Thirteen brothers and sisters*. She ended with a brother who towered over everyone else in the photograph. He pointed to the other children of various ages. "Rodzak," she said. "Rodzak, rodzak, rodzak, rodica, rodica, rodzak…" Male and female cousins, twenty-two of them. *Sounds like my relatives from south of the border. Endless cousins.* He thought about his mother and her enormous family, most of whom still lived in Mexico. Jasminka had stopped talking, and he looked up.

"What?" he asked. Her eyes were red and moist.

"Ti." She pointed at one of her brothers. "Moj brat." *Her brother.* "You"—she said something he did not understand—"my brother." She put her finger to her eyes.

"Ja?" *Me?* Goodman scrutinized her face. *What is she saying? Something about me and her brother.* "You want me look for him?"

"Neh." She shook her head. "*You look him*," she finally said in their mutual pidgin Bosanski.

Goodman looked at her, then at the boy in the photograph again. *He looks just like me.* Jasminka smiled through her tears.

"You look him," she said again. Goodman nodded. He knew it was probably the most vulnerable she had ever been with him. He did not know exactly how to respond to this moment.

"Tvoj brat?" he said. *Your brother?*

"Moj brat." She nodded as she wiped her tears.

"What him called?"

"Emad."

Goodman repeated the name. "Emad."

He was about to ask how old he was when Jasminka suddenly threw her arms around his shoulders and squeezed. She pressed her head into his shoulder. It was only a moment, but a small wetness soaked into his shirt from her tears. *This poor kid has been through a lot. I can't imagine what it's like to live in her shoes.* He let her stay there, with her arms locked around his shoulders. *Hard to believe the war that I file with my flight report each night is the same as the one that does this to kids, to families. I only bomb the military targets. Who declared these people to be a military target?* His eyes moved back to the photograph. There appeared to be older sisters or cousins standing together in the second row. They all had long, dark hair, dark eyes, and elegant, stalwart faces. *Definitely a family trait.*

"Ko ona?" *Who is she?* He pointed to the tallest female seated next to Baba, the one holding little Jasminka.

"Ona maja tetka." *She's my aunt.* Another flurry of tears ran down her cheeks.

"I on?" *And him?* Goodman asked of the young man to her aunt's left. He was tall, broad-shouldered, and held two smaller kids in his arms and one on his shoulder. "He called Musa." She wiped her eyes again and managed a smile.

"Musa," repeated Goodman. To him, Musa looked like he had a friendly face. But there was something else, more of an intuition than what Goodman saw in the photo. *He looks like a survivor. Wonder where he is now.*

# 9

JASMINKA SAID NOTHING when she brought his dinner to him. Goodman questioned if he had handled things right when Jasminka opened up to him earlier. Twenty minutes later, she retrieved the bowl, again in silence. Horses clip-clopped on the ground outside and voices greeted one another. *There's the nurse*, he thought. *But two horses. And she's not due for another couple of days.* Moments later, the nurse descended with a companion behind her. The man's mustache and beard flowed over his chest. He wore a mismatched uniform of sorts, grimy with sweat and dirt. He had a military rifle slung over his shoulder. A long bayonet in a scabbard, hand grenades, and leather ammunition pouches ornamented his belt. A faded splatter of blood speckled his legs. And, finally, a new stench entered Goodman's abode with the visitor.

"Who is this?" he asked the Nurse.

The Nurse ignored him and spoke to the soldier in Bosanski. He understood enough now to know that they wanted to move him soon, or something to that effect. Jasminka came back down about a minute into the conversation. Now, standing next to the adults, she looked very young indeed.

"Where is your pain?" asked the nurse. Same question every time. But this time, he had an answer prepared.

"My left knee hurts." Goodman tapped on the splints. "But mobility is improved." He raised his hands high, then lowered them. "My lower back is stiff, though." The Nurse translated what Goodman said for the soldier. He replied, and she tuned back to Goodman.

"I'm going to help you sit up," said the Nurse. Then she turned to Jasminka. "Ti!" She pointed to Goodman. "Pomozi."

Jasminka moved to his side where she and the Nurse helped him sit up and rotate his feet to the floor. His knees were very stiff. His head swam a bit.

"How does that feel?" asked the nurse.

"Nije loš," said Goodman. *Not bad.* An optimistic exaggeration.

The Nurse backed away and let the soldier take hold of him. His breath was putrid. He lifted Goodman by the shoulder, exceeding Jasminka's helpful reach. He backed away once Goodman stood on his own.

"Now," said the Nurse. "How do you feel?"

Goodman recognized what this was. This man is not the doctor the Nurse warned him about. This man had to do with security. Tactical operations. *Maybe he is the guy who decides when I get to go home. You don't get to know about the headaches. You'd never move me if you knew I had a concussion as bad as this one.*

"Good," he replied. "Sore, but this is alright." His lower back was killing him. He put a hand out to steady himself on the post next to his bed.

"Where is the pain now?"

"Everywhere." Goodman hoped to see a crack in the Nurse's armor. She blinked and put her hands on her hips. He tried again. "My back is stiff. Knees, mostly. Feet feel okay," he said, wiggling his toes. "Does this mean I'll be leaving soon?"

He felt a slow dullness eclipse his brain. His vision blurred and went black. He teetered slightly and lost his grip on the post. The Nurse caught him under the arm and sat him down again. She watched the color return to his face. One by one, she lifted his legs onto the bed and pulled his pillow under his head. *Dammit.*

"You require time to build up your stamina," said the Nurse. "You may move about, but only for short periods of time. Drink water, much water. Clean water. Make her boil it for you." She nodded at Jasminka. "You must build up your strength. You may walk around outside for exercise. But not during the day. And only in the fenced area behind the house. No lights, only at night. Do you understand?"

"Yes, ma'am," Goodman said as agreeably as possible. "Razumijem." *I understand.*

The nurse repeated her instructions in Bosanski for Jasminka.

"Da, madam," said Jasminka. "Razumijem." She looked at Goodman, and a slight smile made her freckled cheeks grow.

"You must obey my instructions," said the nurse in Bosanski, wagging her finger at him. "Only at night. And no lights." She turned to Jasminka and spoke slowly enough so even Goodman could understand. "If the sun is up, he is down here! Do you understand?"

"Da, madam," Goodman and Jasminka replied in unison.

"Bring him more water," ordered the nurse. "And boil it!" Jasminka's smile disappeared.

"Da, madam." Jasminka lifted her skirt slightly and pattered up the stairs.

"And for you," the nurse continued in English. "It is most important that you remain secret. The Germans and the Ustaši are very active this season. There are spies everywhere." *Like Jasminka's friend said. That's confirmation. The kids know. But do the adults? Do I tell her about that? Does it make a difference if I'm leaving soon, anyway?*

"Then the sooner you get me out of here, the better, right?"

The nurse simply glared at him as Jasminka returned with a clay pitcher and a cup.

"And who will carry you? Jasminka? Me?"

"He could." Goodman gestured to the soldier. She ignored him.

"I understand," he said solemnly.

Jasminka poured water into Goodman's mug beside his bed.

"So?" said the Nurse.

"What?" said Goodman.

"Drink!"

Goodman drank the mug empty, and Jasminka dutifully filled it again. The nurse continued to stare, so Goodman emptied the mug again. He belched. The nurse gestured to Jasminka to fill the mug once again. She complied.

"Do not ask me about leaving here again until you can walk without falling down." She and the soldier trod heavily on the steps, and the door slid shut.

Goodman laid his head back. *I'll give myself a week, maybe two, and then I'm outta here.*

The nurse and the soldier talked briefly with Baba before they departed. Goodman and Jasminka looked at each other as they listened to the horse hooves clip-clop away until the village sounds were all that remained. *I'm doing this*, he thought. *I need to get out of here.*

"Pomoch?" said Goodman. *Help me?*

"Ja pomožem!" she replied.

Jasminka went to his side as he swung his legs over the edge of the bed. He propped himself up with his arms and dragged himself toward the post. It was tough, but he tried to stand up. He felt his knees buckle, and he reached for Jasminka. She put his arm over her shoulder and reached as far as she could around his waist. She braced herself as he put just a little weight on her.

"Hvala." He thanked her.

"Nište." She smiled.

Once he was up, he shifted weight onto one foot and took a step. His head bumped on a ceiling rafter and dust filtered down on them. Jasminka laughed as she brushed the dirt out of her hair. Goodman ignored the sore spot on his head and smiled back. He took another shaky step.

# 10

## SEPTEMBER 4, 1943
## WESTERN MAJEVITSA FOOTHILLS

DARK GRAY CLOUDS ROSE IN THE WEST. The insects swarmed around Zoran in the warm, humid air. In self-defense, he swished his whip of horse tails from shoulder to shoulder. He nodded to Milosz's comment about the coming storm. Their heads turned abruptly when a whistle echoed from the forest. *The messenger,* thought Zoran. *One of ours.* He checked his watch as the boy entered the field.

"Three trucks," said the boy, out of breath. "From the south. Non-military. Approximately twelve men, armed, but also not military. Tuzla registration plates."

Zoran dismissed him, and the boy ran back to his father on the cliffs overlooking the southern approaches. Zoran stroked his beard.

*They come from Tuzla. Probably not the Ustaša. Most likely not Germans. This patrol is too small and too far from the main lines of communication, even for the Waffen-SS. We will wait,* he decided.

Another ten minutes passed before the sound of diesel engines reached Zoran's ears. Soon, road dust filtered through the trees, and the trucks downshifted to make the turn into the field. A farmer leaned on his rake next to his towering haystack to observe the strangers entering his land. Zoran's machine gunners kept their sights on the vehicles as they bounced across the field. A pale blue flag waved from the driver's side window of the lead truck. Zoran folded his arms and postured. *Right time, more or less. Right place. Right signal. Mikhail is here.* The trucks lurched to a stop in the soft earth.

# MATT ERLACHER

"Zoran!" A voice rang out across the field before the door slammed shut. Sunlight reflected on the bald head and clean-shaven face. High cheekbones cast black shadows on sunken cheeks.

Zoran cleared his throat. "Mikhail! You are late!"

"Of course, of course, Zoran," said Mikhail. Two younger men approached with him, draped with bandoleers and carrying rifles. "But here I am! And where are the Germans? Not for miles and miles!"

"There are dangers other than the Germans, my cousin."

Mikhail waved his hand in the air dismissively. He drew a shiny flask of slivovitz, which Zoran accepted without gratitude when offered. The younger men were Mikhail's eldest sons and his bodyguards, and they all partook of the flask. The sons who would one day inherit the largest industrial mining corporations in northeastern Bosnia. They would also likely inherit their father's disdain for the council and anything associated with its traditions. *Why do the city folk always look down on their country relations?* This simultaneously incensed Zoran and gave him reason to think maybe he should change his own perspective. To shake off the shackles of tradition might be very liberating. But that would also erase Zoran's claim to leadership of the domain.

"Now leave us," said Mikhail. His sons withdrew to the truck's front bumper and his bodyguards stepped out of earshot but remained watchful of their master.

Mikhail Petrovič Sevanović, known to others in the resistance as Colonel Zbrogan, was the commander of the Tuzla branch of the very metropolitan Esnafi Resistance Brigade, and Zoran's urban counterpart. They had fought effectively against the Ustaša militia, but had to broker a truce when the German Army sent the Fifth Waffen-SS Mountain Division to the Tuzla valley. This dynamic gave Zoran badly needed reinforcements over the summer but cost him dearly in cash. But war was not the only channel of relations between the men.

Once commercial competitors, decades of buying, brokering, bartering, and selling had made them indispensable to each other. Zoran chafed at his dependence on this man but took heart at the fact that it was mutual. As their scope of business expanded over the years, so had the level of contact between the families. Marriages cemented a relationship once built on cash flow, which gave each man new access and, frankly, new vulnerabilities. Sustaining business profits while engaged in sporadic combat with outsiders came at high personal costs to them both. Despite the reliance upon one another that made them cousins by the ancient tradition, Zoran did not trust Mikhail, and he suspected this was also mutual.

Today, Zoran needed access to some proprietary knowledge. Mikhail had a finger on every kind of financial conduit in the Tuzla valley—the public as well as the illicit. Like buying and selling human beings. In the underground economy, the best price to be had for a captured Allied airman was with the Germans, but to get to the Germans, Zoran had to go through the psychopathically murderous and fascistic Ustaša. The second-best price was with the Allies directly, but where could one find an Englishman hundreds of miles into an occupied zone? The third-ranked option was with the Titoist Partisans. It was known that the communist Partisans paid very little and charged the Allies exorbitantly for a rescued airman, German or Allied. Zoran would rather burn his own skin than see the fascists or communists turn a profit by his own hand. So, the Allies would get their man back for a price, plus expenses. Mikhail had once subcontracted for transporting something—or someone—he was never willing to disclose. A sudden influx of cash, weapons, and ammunition within a week of the transaction indicated this particular customer had unnaturally deep pockets. National treasury kind of deep. Zoran wanted to know about these pockets and their owner. And if they were in the market for an American pilot.

Mikhail slid his flask back into his vest and looked around the field. His nose twitched at the earthy smell. "What brings me to his wretched farm, cousin?"

"Milosz, would you assure me that the men of Tuzla are provided for?"

"Yes, Pasha," said Milosz. He directed the farmer to retrieve some slivovitz from a wagon. Mikhail's bodyguards followed. His sons, however, remained by their father's truck.

"Are you still playing that game?" said Mikhail as he turned to his sons.

*You are an ass, Mikhail.* Zoran glared at him.

47

"Mirzad," said Mikhail to his eldest son. "Take your brother and enjoy some mountain hospitality."

"Yes, Papa." The sons of Mikhail walked off together.

"Reminds me of your own Mirzad, no?" said Mikhail. He crossed his chest with his hand and kissed his thumb. "God rest his soul. And the souls of your other sons."

Zoran stomped down the emotions inside him. *My sons, my daughters. One day, I will be with you again. But not yet.* "Mikhail, I am here to propose a sale."

Mikhail's eyebrows popped. "This is quite the reversal," he replied. "What do you possibly have that I could want? The harvest is not for another month at least, and I can get what I need through the city markets. Unless..." Mikhail rubbed his chin. "Unless you are offering a brokerage for some other commodity. But that is hardly profitable for me. Is that what you want?"

*You are the ass of an ass,* thought Zoran before he spoke. "You judge too quickly." *Give him nothing,* thought Zoran. *Keep him answering questions.* "Tell me now, do you still have friends from the west?"

Mikhail withdrew a long, dark stick of tobacco from his coat pocket and folded it into his mouth. He chewed it for a moment.

"The Esnafis of Banja Luka? No, my cousin, they are defunct." He spit. "The Germans are thoroughly having their way with the city." He spit again and wiped his chin. "The clans of Banja Luka can no longer offer resistance of any kind."

"No," said Zoran. "I mean further west."

"The Dalmatians? The oil smugglers?"

*Are you going to make me say it? Or do you not know?* "Further."

"Surely you do not mean the Italians!" Mikhail raised his eyebrows. "Perhaps you have read the newspapers? The Italians are no longer solvent. Sure, they would be willing to buy food or livestock. But that is a long way to—" He paused. "But you are not talking about food, are you?"

"I mean the English—"

"Ha!" Mikhail interrupted. "So, the rumors are true. You *do* have him. I thought as much. Rare indeed is the rumor of this magnitude that finds an anchor in truth. Is he British or American? Is it just the one man? Or are there more? Tell me, cousin."

"Not so fast," said Zoran. "We are family, but not that much. First, tell me what I want to know."

"Yes, cousin," Mikhail began. "I still have a friend in Lukavac. Well, I might if he is still alive. I doubt much of his enterprise is still… enterprising."

"Can you find out?" said Zoran. *Don't you hold out on me.* "Can you determine if there is a deal to be made?"

"There will be expenses…"

"Yes, of course, there will be expenses!" said Zoran. "If you come through with your contact, then there will be profits as well."

"So, what if I provide you with the information you need?" said Mikhail. "What is the guarantee of payment? Do not trifle with me. I am not going away anytime soon."

"By our fathers and the Prophet—peace be upon him—why would you think I would not pay my cousin fairly and justly? What cause have I given you for blame? You think me a gypsy vagrant?"

"Calm yourself, Zoran," Mikhail pushed back. "The Turk in you is too gullible. You may be a pasha in your mountains, but I know you better than that." He called to his sons.

Zoran watched Mikhail's men converge on the trucks, including Mirzad, Mikhail's eldest boy. *He even walks like my Mirzad did when he was that age,* Zoran observed. *Every man's son is becoming my son. I see you everywhere, Mirzad.* Zoran breathed in and let out a long exhale. *I miss you, my son.* A mosquito bit his temple, and he cared not one bit.

The engines turned over, and the trucks slowly seesawed over the furrows in the field. The lead truck made a wide turn, and Mikhail's face appeared in the window.

"I will find the information you seek," Mikhail called over the sound of the engine. "And I, Mikhail Petrovič, will broker the deal, and I will name the price!" Blue smoke belched into the air, and the trucks departed the way they arrived.

*Yes, Mikhail, you will broker the deal, you goat turd. I would put your head on a pike if I did not need you now. Maybe once I have power. Once your contacts come to me, rather than to you. Once I have taken Tuzla.* Milosz approached with Zoran's bodyguards.

"All is well, Pasha?"

49

Zoran raised an eyebrow and shrugged slightly. "Yes, Milosz, for now," he said. "Recall the watchers. We're going home."

# 11

## SEPTEMBER 14, 1943
## BABA'S BASEMENT

THE AROMA OF ROASTING MEAT INSPIRED GOODMAN TO BREAK THE RULES. He emerged from the cellar to see Baba busy over the fire. A twenty-gallon cauldron nearly overflowed, with potatoes and vegetables churning slowly in a gentle boil. Baba pushed several skewers of goat meat into the mix. She sang quietly to herself as she did this. *Man, that smells good.*

It was far more than the three of them could eat in a week, but Goodman had seen Baba cook this way many times before. These meals were the household's contribution to the daily feeding of the village's forty or so households of women, children, and elderly. When it was not her turn to cook, Baba spent her afternoons supervising the preparations in other kitchens for that evening's meal. Grandmothers, mothers, and granddaughters across a dozen kitchens prepared the various elements of the meal. The aroma was heavenly.

Everyone had their roles to play, whether they cooked or not. The granddaughters hunted, fished, and harvested. Their mothers inventoried the food stores, baked the breads, taught their children, and watched the hills for signs of their men. The grandmothers salted, cooked, and prayed. This arrangement was universal, except in Baba's house, where there were only Baba and Jasminka to split the workload. Except now, Goodman was allowed to assist, as much as he was physically able to do so. And, of course, only in secret.

Goodman stood a few feet behind Baba, ready to be assigned a task, but she remained focused on sprinkling herbs and watching the stew boil. Bowls with various bits of rabbit and squirrel entrails still sat on the table. Jasminka sat on the far side, slowly scraping fascia from a hide. She shot him a smile and then jokingly scrunched her nose and waved her hand in front of her face at the foul smell of the detritus. He smiled back, and she refocused on her task.

"Pomoch?" Goodman offered to help.

Jasminka nodded with a smile and pointed with her knife at the other hide. He sat down and drew a wood-handled blade from the shelf on the wall. He flipped the rabbit skin over, fur side down, and set to drawing the knife edge as smoothly and evenly as possible across the wet side of the pelt. The bits of fat and smaller chunks of meat that came loose went into the 'soft' pile, to be mashed and cooked into a brick of pâté for later consumption. When she finished, Jasminka scooped the 'soft' pile into a clay bowl and set to mashing the kidneys, livers, brains, and smaller scraps of meat with mushrooms, rosemary, and mint into a rust-colored paste. Baba reminded her to set aside two of the brains for tanning the hides.

"Da, Baba," she replied, and set the rabbit heads on a shelf. She then grounded up a salt rock with a mortar and pestle and sprinkled it over the top of the pâté brick. The lid clanked, and she carefully placed it directly onto the coals under the cauldron. Baba gave her a nod of approval. Jasminka dutifully scraped and cleaned the detritus into a pot and dumped them into the goats' feeding trough. Several minutes later, Baba declared the food ready. She removed the bar from the door and deployed Jasminka to notify the others. This was Goodman's cue to disappear into the cellar.

From below, Goodman listened to the village granddaughters arrive to take the stew to the massive tables in the village center. He had learned there was to be no waste, equal suffering, and nothing to make unnecessary trouble. The trouble was to be equally distributed, but only as far as any household could bear the stress, and no more. Everything had to balance out in the long run, according to Baba. That is how the village had survived the disasters, the empires, she said, and how they would survive this current epside. In this context, Baba had an eye to the future viability of the village, and always apportioned just a little more meat and potatoes to the families with young boys. We need men, she would say. Goodman had never had to think like that before.

After Jasminka finally closed the door, Goodman re-emerged from below to get the bowl of stew she had left for him. He descended quickly to his bed and ate his food by lamplight, listening to the sounds of the women and girls eating at the long tables under the fading evening twilight. The children broke out into song, and shortly, the women brought out an old accordion, several flutes, a stringed guitar-like instrument, and a drum. The melodic droning of the accordion and the steady drumbeats carried the tempo for the numerous vocalists warbling an incantation that reverberated into the cellar. Goodman imagined the older girls twirling and stomping, eyes closed in their trance state, as he had once seen through the kitchen door. That was right before Baba scolded him for being above ground when the door was unlocked.

"Don't tempt the devil," she had warned him. "He'll send the *dirty little men* to find you and use you against your family, your friends." She referred to the "dirty little men" every time something was missing or some mishap disrupted village life. He understood this to mean that if anybody found him, it meant major problems or even death for the villagers. That made sense, he thought. Until the day a small fire broke out directly over Goodman's head and scorched the kitchen floor where there was absolutely no reason for any fire to be. The kitchen fire was nothing but embers at the time. *How did the fire start?* Goodman examined and re-examined the scene. Dirty little men, Baba had mumbled as she supervised Goodman repairing the floorboards. She dismissed it easily, but it bothered Goodman for several days.

His bowl now empty, Goodman laid down on his bed, still hungry. His appetite had been increasing, which was good, if not inconvenient. But he dared not go upstairs again. Not until nightfall. He closed his eyes and listened to the chorus in the village square.

His relaxed state was suddenly disrupted by Jasminka and several of her friends bringing armfuls of bowls and spoons to the wash basin upstairs. They finished quickly and ran happily back outside. Shortly, though, Jasminka re-entered the house and descended the stairs with another bowl with a large hunk of bread soaked with the broth on top of more greens.

"Hvala, Jasminka," he thanked her.

"Molim," she replied. "Baba says we need strong men." She paused on the steps with a grin. "Skroviti." It was her codename for him. It meant *my secret one*. Or something like that.

Goodman laughed to himself as Jasminka slid the door closed again and rejoined her friends. He appreciated her care and helpfulness. He also reflected on all the emotional weight she carried, especially for a thirteen-year-old. Goodman smiled again when he discovered a large piece of meat at the bottom of the bowl, hidden under the soupy greens. He savored it despite its toughness. Baba and Jasminka returned long after dark and restored order to the kitchen by lamplight before going to bed.

Now that the village was quiet, Goodman made his nightly recuperative walk in the goat pens in the rear of the house. Most of the caprines were no longer suspicious of him, except for his nemesis: the large goat with the black face and broken left horn. This one still eyed him as suspiciously now as the first time he invaded their corral almost four weeks ago. It still took opportunities to butt Goodman in the thigh with its one good horn when he stopped paying attention. Jasminka came out and perched herself on the stone wall of the well. She gazed at the stars until Baba called for her. She jumped down and ran inside without saying a word. Goodman remained outside, stretching and performing his calisthenics as per the nurse's instructions. Then Baba called to him with the distinctly sharp voice she used when issuing orders—orders that were not to be questioned. Even Goodman respected these announcements, as they were not without cause. But even this one is different, he thought.

Inside, Baba sat at the table with a cup of tea in her hands and a single lamp that cast a warm glow to the table and her face, but not much else. Another tea sat on the table opposite her. She silently watched him sit down and studied him for a moment. She rarely addressed him directly except for these nighttime conversations. During these talks, Baba was never about the vocabulary building. She always went for the jugular and made him struggle to understand and communicate ideas far outside his ability to formulate linguistically. Goodman often came away with a headache. It was hard to dumb things down enough to communicate across the language barrier, even with pointy-talky. Sometimes, the Nurse or Jasminka helped by translating, but he thought he always missed something in the back-and-forth. He wished his Bosanski was better, but he never shied away from these exchanges, and his 'caveman' Bosanski developed and grew. Trouble now, though, was that Baba never used it in these settings. Fortunately, her slow, clear words were easy for him to follow and he now understood Bosanski far better than he could speak it. Presently, though, her thumb counted worry beads: *click, click, click.* Her lips moved in some silent prayer. Goodman did not understand much of her manners, which seemed close to the Mohammedan ways of the Libyan tribes near his current home airfield. But he knew her well enough now to know that she had something heavy on her mind.

"You are well?" she asked. "You are well here?" This was the first time Baba had asked anything like that. *What's going on, Baba?*

"Da, Baba, better."

"How is your pain?"

"My knees little pain," he said. "My head more good."

"But still there's pain?"

"Da, Baba."

She nodded. "You leave soon?"

*That's a strange question,* thought Goodman. "I know not, Baba," he shrugged his shoulders. "Nurse no say me. You hear more, me hear little." He squeezed his fingers together. He hoped it was enough to hint to her that she could share more. "Nurse say you I go away from here?"

She ignored the question. "You go to see your family?" she asked.

"I..." His words trailed off. *I'll be going back to my unit, hopefully.*

"You do not want?"

*How does she know this?* thought Goodman. Jasminka must have told her about their conversations. "My father, he—"

"Your mother?"

"What about my mother—"

"It is your father's house."

"Da," Goodman answered. *Again, a dead-on shot,* he thought. *How does the old woman know so much?*

"You have brothers and a sister, yes? You do not wish to see them?"

"They married, they family."

Baba tilted her head. He tried to compose a sentence that made sense. "Brother family, brother family, sister family." He paused. "Me no family."

"You do not go home," she said. "You stay in sky army?"

He knew he disappointed her even before she clucked her tongue. A small knot grew in his throat.

"You go to make more war in the sky?" Her eyes zeroed in on the aviator wings still pinned to his collar, and then they bounced upward to the ceiling, to the sky.

"Da."

"You and your father, no love?"

"No, I mean—" *I love my father, but I don't know how to live with his expectations. How do I say this?*

She clucked her tongue again and shook her head. Her gnarled fingers folded around each other.

"Bozhe!" she exclaimed. "Život za život!" She rattled off a long litany of verbiage that he did not understand. *Život means life,* he thought. *Život za život means something like a life for life. But I don't get it.*

"Baba, Baba," he cut in. "I no understand." She stopped clicking her beads.

She exhaled loudly and then enunciated clearly for him in pidgin Bosanski. "Men and fathers… no good. *Život za život* is kill and kill, and not life for life. Men fight, men kill. Men kill to kill. Men fight fathers, men follow fathers. They not know peace. They not know—" She interlocked her fingers, then pulled her arms apart, but left her fingers locked together against the force of her arms. "Family must be strong," she said. "Family make everyone safe. Perhaps you go home. Perhaps you find father love. Go home. Find father. *Život za život*. No kill. No fight. *Život za život*." She clasped her hands together with fingers firmly intertwined.

Goodman knew what she was saying. A life for a life means to forgive. But he had no intention of going home. *There's too much to be undone. Besides*, he reasoned, *home might as well be on the Moon.*

Baba looked at her teacup and stirred the flakes of tea. *Clink, clink, clink* went the spoon. *Click, click, click* went the beads in her other hand. Goodman waited for her to say what she meant to say. Her worry beads stopped clicking.

"You will be leaving soon."

"Nurse say you?" *Interesting that she would tell this to Baba, but not to me.*

"No. Village no safe for you. A man has come."

*Baba, you have my full and concentrated attention.* "Vojnik?" *A soldier?*

She shook her head and sipped at her tea.

"You know man, Baba?"

"Bad man. No good for you." *Was Jasminka right? That stupid story.*

"Špijun?" he asked.

"Vuko," was all she said. *A wolf.* He remembered the night when the wolves came by to steal another baby goat. He and Jasminka defended the goat pens with rocks and sticks late into the night.

"Where man come?"

"Od rijeke," she said. *Up from the river.*

Baba sipped her tea. Goodman knew about the river. The Drina. No one ever came from or departed that way except the children who caught fish in it. Across the Drina was Serbian land. Chetnik land. And up the river a ways was Ustaša land. Very bad lands, allegedly. Or so Jasminka had told him.

"He came to talk to someone," said Baba. *So Jasminka wasn't just telling a story.*

"Someone in village?"

Baba nodded.

"Man know me here?"

She nodded again.

"How do you know?" *Of course, you know, Baba. Somehow, you always know things.*

She quietly sipped her tea.

"What me do?"

"Nothing." Baba fidgeted with her spoon.

"Nothing?" *That's not good enough. If there is a threat, I need to do something. Maybe I can take care of this myself. Protect the village. Protect these people. Myself, even.*

"What you do?"

Baba exhaled and tapped the edge of her teacup with her fingernail. She spoke slowly for him. "We have lived on this mountain for a long time. Men come here and take our men and boys. They come here again."

"When?" he asked.

"Soon," she said.

He struggled to put his sense of urgency into words. "What we do?" he asked. "I must go far. My army." He pointed to the faraway hills. *The Nurse can help. She's the connection to the outside forces.* "Will the Nurse help me?"

"The Nurse," baba replied. "Yes, she will try." *Click, click, click* went the beads.

Baba finished her tea and set it down without saying another word. The conversation was over. She never had to say it, he just knew.

"Hvala, Baba." Goodman thanked her.

She nodded slightly and moved to get up. Goodman came around the table and steadied her by the arm, to which she again nodded. She limped without her cane into her room and went to bed, leaving Goodman to bar the door and turn out the lantern.

Now Goodman wished he had not been so cavalier about roaming the house with the windows open or walking outside a few minutes early to see the occasional sunset. *Someone knows I'm here,* he thought. *I need to lock myself down. Secure my space.* But that did not feel right. *No, I need to get out of here for my own sake, and for Baba and Jasminka. Where would I go? I don't have any idea where I am. But what happens if I stay?*

The spy. A cold blanket of fear spread across his skin.

*Who could it be? A friend of Jasminka's? But would a child do this? How?*

*No way.*

*What about the grandmothers?*

*No, it couldn't be them. They've lost so much already, so much grief in their lives. They're just trying to feed their grandchildren.*

It had to be one of the mothers, that middle generation who had something to lose, but also the most to gain by collaboration. *But which one?* He concluded that there were too many unknowns for him to figure it out. *I know I'm in danger if I go or if I stay. And I don't know the mathematical formula to say which is worse.*

But if Baba knew, then she'd known all along. *Why doesn't she report it to the militia?* Surely, they could resolve it. *If others know I'm here, how much warning would I get if they come for me?* But it was not a question of *if*. Baba had said they *will* come to the village. *They will come for me. And soon.*

Goodman rechecked the bars across the front and back doors before he closed the door over the steps into his cellar. He took the knife he used earlier to clean the skins and put it on the edge of his bed, next to the lantern. He looked at the rusty pistol he took from Jasminka. It might have been twenty years since it was fired or even oiled. Too bad he didn't have his Colt 1911 anymore.

He kept his boots on when he laid down. Sleep evaded him. Long before dawn, Goodman entered the goat pens to walk off the nervous energy, only to joust yet again with the goat with the broken horn. As usual, the stupid beast dutifully defended the honor of his nannies by fighting off the foreign invader. Tonight, however, Goodman found it especially irritating and sat on the far side of the well.

He returned to his bed in the cellar and stared at the clusters of herbs hanging over his head. When Goodman finally drifted off to sleep, German soldiers invaded his dreams by swarming through the village, killing the women and children, tearing houses apart, setting fires, closing in on him. He saw Jasminka lying on the ground. His legs were slow and heavy as he tried to run. He clawed at the cracked skin and fangs sinking into him and finally climbed himself awake when he was about to be discovered. Finally conscious, Goodman clenched his chest and squeezed out angry tears without knowing why. He fought back the fear-memory from the hallucinatory dreams from his first several nights in Baba's basement. *I don't want those things to come back*, he muttered to himself. He did not even know how to describe those *things* he feared. *Dreams are just random thoughts when you're asleep, right?* They don't actually *mean* anything. *Or do they?* He remembered his psychology professors talked about Sigmund Freud and Carl Jung and their theories about dreams. He remembered that they both thought dreams were meaningful, but they disagreed about *how* they were meaningful. That's too much for right now, he concluded. This is no academic exercise. *Am I the danger that Baba talked about? If I go, will they be safe? Will I be safe? Of course not. Am I going crazy? Maybe...* His mind ran in endless circles. When the roosters crowed, he finally sat up, exhausted.

He rubbed his eyes and put his head in his hands. *I can't stay here.*

⚘⚘⚘

# 12

## 0500 HOURS, SEPTEMBER 20, 1943
## BABA'S BASEMENT

THE HOUSE WAS QUIET. *Time to go,* he thought. There was no other way to stop whatever was going to happen because of him. Map folded in his pocket, he checked the knots in his boots. He inspected his small bag of belongings: meat scraps wrapped in cloth, some more cloth for bandages, a wooden spoon, and a small pewter trinket Jasminka had given him. She'd called it her *ginni*—her angel, or something. Lastly, his chief asset was the kitchen knife. He yawned out loud before he put out the lantern. Then Goodman climbed the stairs to lift the door to his basement home for the last time.

He stepped silently onto the floor and lowered the door down gently. He tiptoed past the glowing coals in the fireplace. The floor creaked, and he took a long last step to the rear door. A glance around the kitchen revealed Baba's door was closed. He imagined Baba and Jasminka sleeping in that room. Goodman silently lifted the bar and entered the goat pen. *Hvala, Baba.* He smiled at the idea of thinking in Bosanski. Goosebumps sprouted across his shoulders and back, and he shivered.

The goats stirred as he closed the door, but thankfully, none made a sound. He stepped quietly over the low fence and went down the cluttered alleyway he had studied for weeks. Pausing where it intersected the main road through the village, he realized he had never seen anything of the remainder of the village until tonight. He looked back toward Baba's house. His breath formed a glittery cloud in front of him. The clear, cold sky was just beginning to show a lighter shade of blue in the east. He scanned the stars for the constellations of his childhood and the astral navigational beacons of his adult life as a pilot. *North Star, where are you?* A spread-hand's width between Cassiopeia and the Big Dipper sat Ursa Minor, with Polaris sitting steady as a lighthouse. *The axis of the world runs through that star.* He looked up and down the road one more time and took a step.

Something caught his eye—movement between two buildings several houses away. Were the wolves back? Most nights, he heard them yapping and howling through the hills. But there had been no such sound tonight. His eyes strained to discern the shapes from the shadows amid the clusters of homes. Goodman saw nothing, so he stepped out from the corner of the building. But then he saw them.

Two human shapes, hunched over, moving slowly, deliberately. He saw the distinct outline of a German helmet perched on each of their heads. The long, slender silhouette of a rifle jutted out from the first man's waistline. The second figure raised a hand and pointed into the village. Then he nodded to someone behind them. Several more silhouettes, also armed and helmeted, rounded the bend and walked toward the village center. Goodman shrank back. *That didn't take long. They're already here for me. There's no way these guys are here by accident. That damn girl.*

Goodman eased his way back toward Baba's house. He paused when another silhouette of a German soldier emerged less than twenty yards away, but this one was between him and the house. Goodman watched the soldier's head rotate slowly as he scanned his surroundings. Goodman knew if he moved, the German would see him, but he was stuck next to a long, blank wall. He watched the German's head turn and stop, oriented directly at him. He could not see the man's eyes in the blackness under that helmet, but he knew he was looking directly at him. The German raised his rifle to his shoulder. *Oh, damn.*

Goodman did the only thing that came to mind. He raised his arm and gave a slight wave.

The German's shoulders eased back, and one hand released its grip on the rifle. Goodman saw a small flick of a wave in return. A second soldier appeared behind the first, and they both turned away from Goodman and made their way toward Baba's goat pens. Several more Germans followed. Goodman's mind raced with what to do next.

He quietly advanced several paces and stepped into a narrow space between two stone walls, then waited. The file of soldiers behind him passed by the opening without seeing him. He inched his way to the far end of the gap between the houses and peered around the corners. More Germans approached the center of the village from the north. He stepped back. *I'm trapped.*

A loud whistle shattered the night. From several points around the village, Goodman heard men shout orders, and doors crashed open in every direction. Goats and chickens let out a collective burst of noise, quickly followed by the screams of women. Children's cries punctuated all the others and set a fire inside Goodman, but he stifled it.

*What do I do?* Goodman thought to himself.

*Nothing. I'm certainly not going to take on the German army with a stupid kitchen knife. That damn girl. I should have done something earlier!* Goodman crouched in the dark and shook his head. *Everyone here will die because of me.*

Across the village, German soldiers shouted, and mothers cried out. The argument across the street was especially vicious. Goodman turned and saw soldiers pull a woman and her children out of the house. She put her arms around all four of her little ones, who were huddled in the middle of the street, surrounded by Germans with their weapons leveled at them. Goodman burned with anger. Several Germans exited her house, throwing articles of clothing or utensils onto the road.

A man in a long black coat stood over the weeping mother and spoke to her sternly. She shook her head vigorously as she crushed her youngest child to her chest. The man in the coat turned to the nearest soldier and spoke in a hushed tone before walking away. Goodman's stomach heaved at the sickening thump that sounded as the soldier smashed the butt of his rifle into the mother's head before moving to another part of the village. Goodman watched as the mother quickly herded her children back to their house, but another soldier pushed them out and toward the village center. The eldest daughter attempted to retrieve the family's belongings from the street, but her mother pulled her along, and she dropped everything. They moved out of sight. Goodman quietly side-stepped down the wall until he could see the rear of Baba's house.

Newly emancipated goats and chickens filled the alley. The German soldiers had flashlights out, searching, breaking, prying things open. He could see slivers of light flashing from inside Baba's house. A man was yelling in Bosanski, and Goodman could hear Baba's replies. She sounded meek, almost on the verge of crying. Jasminka screamed something, and then a German yelled back at her. She screamed again and cried. *They're hitting her,* he thought. *Or worse.* Goodman grew hotter with rage. *Stay here. Don't fix this. They'll take me and kill the whole village.* He closed his eyes and clenched his fist around the kitchen knife. *Breathe. Just wait.* Jasminka cried out again.

He turned to stand up, knife in hand, but something obstructed him at the mouth of the narrow space between the houses. The goat with the black face and broken horn stared at him from the road, grinding its teeth. It cocked its head to one side and bleated loudly.

"Shut up!" Goodman whispered at the goat as he shrank from the opening of the alley.

It bleated again and followed him into the space between the walls.

Goodman threw a stone at it. The goat barely noticed the impact on its forehead and bleated loudly yet again. It took another step toward him.

"Get away!" He threw a larger rock but missed. The goat continued to bleat at him. *Stupid animal.*

Suddenly, a dog barked several times before a harsh Germanic command silenced it. *Oh, God! They have dogs. Dammit!* Goodman felt his stomach tighten into a knot. He scrambled to the far end of the wall until he heard Germans on the road behind him, too. *I'm screwed. I am so screwed.* He tried to make himself small in the darkness between the houses, but the goat continued its racket. He gave the goat a shove, but it merely blinked and bleated again. *That's it.* Determined to cut the goat's throat, he gripped the kitchen knife and reached for the goat's head, but the animal dodged and backed up, out of reach.

Several pairs of boots crunched down the alleyway. Goodman heard the anxious whining of a large dog and the repetitive commands of its handler approaching. He glanced in both directions. *There's nowhere to go,* he thought. The dog came closer. Goodman could hear it sniffing. He raised his arm to take the first bite and gripped the knife, intending to plunge it into the dog's neck. He braced himself, visions of wild eyes and snarling white fangs surrounded by black fur plaguing his mind.

Flashlights cast shadows along the wall over Goodman's head. The inevitably enormous German shepherd appeared at the end of the wall and reared up on its hind legs. The beast's snarling terrified the goat, and it panicked and ran into Goodman. He shoved it backward, and it wedged its horns between its own body and the wall. It jumped and bleated, scraping its horns on the wall, trapped by its own girth. Flashlights silhouetted the goat as it squirmed hysterically. The German shepherd barked viciously until its handler pulled back on its leash. The dog relented and returned to its master. And then they were gone. Goodman felt the sweat burst from his pores.

Three long whistle blasts sounded from across the village, and more German soldiers filed past the space Goodman shared with the goat. He waited until he could hear no more German voices before he gave the goat a hard, spiteful kick to dislodge it. It ran down the alley, away from Baba's house. Goodman cautiously looked up and down the road from his hiding place. The Germans were all gone, but he could still hear them. He felt dizzy and put his hand on the wall to steady himself. Dawn had turned the sky gray.

He cautiously made his way back to Baba's house. Baba's fence had been trampled flat, and the goats were nowhere to be seen. Her rear door hung open at an odd angle. He stepped inside to see the kitchen table on its side, as well as the chairs, with Baba's cooking utensils scattered around them. Her front door laid flat on the ground outside. The cellar door was wide open. Goodman went to the opening in the floor and saw the smashed bed and herbs scattered all over the floor. Then he crept to the kitchen window and peered over the ledge.

German voices barked commands nearby. A soldier stood just a few paces away from the front door, watching the villagers gather around the large oak tree in the village center. A cordon of camouflage-clad soldiers surrounded them, weapons ready. In the center, an officer shouted over the women, and an interpreter spoke in turn, dictating warnings not to hide enemy soldiers, or something to that effect. Once finished with the announcements, the officer and the man in the long coat turned their attention to a woman on her knees. It was Baba. Jasminka stood behind her with her arms wrapped tightly around Baba's shoulders, her head buried in her grandmother's neck. One of the dog handlers held his snarling animal just inches from Baba's head. The man in the coat leaned in and spoke to her. Baba shook her head in reply. "Neh! Neh!" Goodman could hear her say. Then the man in the coat stood upright and calmly backhanded her across the face. Several women cried out and ran to surround her. Soldiers raised their rifles, but the man in the coat yelled at them. They lowered their weapons.

The man in the coat seemed to pause, to take stock of the situation. Abruptly, he pulled a girl from the midst of the crowd surrounding Baba. The women tried to pull her back, but the soldiers struck at them with their rifle butts. Most of the women retreated, but one woman refused to let go. Goodman could barely contain himself as he heard the impacts of the batons on her body. *I could stop this now if I gave myself up,* he thought. *The Germans know that I'm here. They would stop if I gave myself over to them.*

*Or would they?* He sank down below the ledge.

A loud, sharp crack shattered the early morning air, and all the women screamed. Goodman peeked over the sill and saw the girl lying on the ground. Her mother charged at the man in the coat and—the pistol cracked again—her body crumpled next to her daughter's. The man rotated his outstretched arm and fired twice more. Two more women fell. One lay on the ground, writhing and crying out. He took two steps toward her and fired once more.

He holstered his pistol, and the entire village erupted into a symphony of wailing. *That son of a bitch!* Goodman clutched at the stone and mortar wall that concealed him. He eyed the soldier standing only paces from him. *I can take this bastard,* he thought. He searched for something to throw, something sharp and heavy. *He has an MP40 submachine gun, not a rifle. That's good. I kill him, take his weapon, and shoot as many of the other bastards as I can before they get me.* The German officer barked out commands again.

"I'm ending this!" he muttered. He rose, but something—or someone—yanked him back down to the floor. He scrambled onto his back to throw a punch.

The Nurse put all her weight on him. "What are you going to do?" she growled at him in a muffled voice. "You are going to fight the whole German Army? You? By yourself? You stupid American fool!"

"They want me!" Goodman snarled back at the nurse. "I'm no good to anyone like this. If the Germans want me, they can put me in a prison camp. Then they'll leave here, leave the village alone."

"No! Wrong!" She thrust a dirty finger in his face. "First, they beat you, then they tie you up and force you to watch them execute everyone in the entire village. And then they burn them. Except for one of them." She pointed a finger toward the villagers. "One of those children, who they rape, and they beat, and they spit upon, and at the end they leave her alive to tell of what happened here. *That* is what they do!" He felt a drip of sweat fall from her face onto his. Goodman knew she was right.

*Oh, God! This is all because of me, and there's nothing I can do about it.*

Back in the village square, the officer blew his whistle long and sharp. The nurse let Goodman raise himself up, and, together, they watched the soldiers flick their cigarettes at the women and children before slowly forming into three columns and exiting the village on the main road, heading north. All except the man in the long black coat and one of the dog handlers. Goodman ducked away from the door when the man in the long coat scanned the village one last time. Finally, he, too, dropped his cigarette and walked out with the infantry, with the dog handler eyeing the villagers as he withdrew.

The villagers wailed aloud again as they rushed to the bodies. Goodman watched with deep sorrow as Jasminka picked up Baba's cane and gingerly helped her return to her feet. He took one last look at the departing Germans before he descended the steps to the cellar with the Nurse.

⚜⚜⚜

# 13

## SEPTEMBER 21, 1943
## HIGH SETTLEMENT, INNER MAJEVITSA

ALMOST TWENTY YOUNG COURIERS WAITED for an audience with Zoran. But Zoran would see none of them, so Milosz agreed to hear them out. For Zoran already knew what they would say. It was what their underage network of confederates had already reported over the previous afternoon and throughout the night. It was the same across the entire central range: the Germans and their Ustaša flunkeys had reformed their combined motorized forces along the five main roads deep within the Majevitsa and dismounted infantry patrolled the slopes around three mountains. The villages in these areas were not random locations. *Someone* had talked. Someone collected the information and put the pieces together. Now there was fear in the Majevitsa again.

No German had ever set foot this far inside the Majevitsa. Even in past wars, before the age of mechanized warfare, foreigners rarely ventured into the Majevitsa. The slopes were too rugged in most places. Roads were scarce and too easily defended. Rivers were too fast and rapids too harsh for oar-powered skiffs. The nearest ferry across the Drina was twenty miles away. The nearest bridge of military value was twenty more miles beyond it. Ustaša commanders knew the Majevitsa was a natural fortress, a sanctuary. But no one told the Germans this, so now they are here. Even for them, to venture a military foray here was a high-risk endeavor. It was too much risk simply to spill militia blood. There was only a single commodity worth the effort. The *American*. Zoran hated being forced into action. He stepped outside. *I am compelled to act within my own domain. Allah damn the dogs who force this upon me!*

"Milosz!"

"Yes, Pasha."

"Where is Amira Effendim?" Zoran stood to observe the valley as if he would catch a glimpse of the dust rising from her movement through the forest. "Is my daughter still moving against the Brčko highway?"

"Yes, Pasha. She attacks another Ustaša garrison outside the city," said Milosz. "That attack will be today."

*That's too far away*, thought Zoran. Couriers can travel quickly, but not fast enough. *She'll never make it in time to be of use.*

"It will be a full day's hard ride to the villages for her," Milosz continued. "The town of Lopare is much closer. It is only a half-day's march over the mountain. But the home guard there is very small."

"What about the others?" asked Zoran. *My forces are scattered and I need to fight my enemies in my own house tomorrow.* "The families are resting, yes?"

"Yes, Pasha, as you directed," said Milosz. "The first of the families reassembles tomorrow evening. The remainder will reassemble over the next several days." He paused. "Again, Pasha, as you directed."

Zoran loved the miscalculations of others but resented his own. He nodded that he understood what Milosz was saying and dismissed him to return to the messengers.

Zoran turned inward. *Should I move the foreigner? Or should I leave him alone?* Too much movement, perhaps any movement, could bring unwanted additional attention. *Should I move my people into position for the opportunity? For the necessity? Do I leave the dust where it lies?* A cloud obscured the sun. Zoran closed his eyes and felt a wind on his face. An unwanted chill spread goosebumps across his shoulders. He had no confidence in his decision.

"Zoran Pasha!"

"What is it, Milosz?"

"This child is from the western slope…"

The chill was no longer merely unpleasant. The western slope. The *American*.

"She says the Germans searched the village early this morning. They killed some of the women, and they beat one of the elders. She says they were searching for the foreigner, the pilot. They found the place where he sleeps."

"How does she know of the pilot?"

"It is a small village, Pasha."

"And she is sure it was Germans? Not the Ustaši?"

"She is certain, Pasha."

"But they did not find him?"

"No, Pasha. Not yet."

Zoran clenched his jaw. He went back and forth over which aspect of the situation irritated him more: the Germans in his mountains at all, his inability to strike at them immediately, or their proximity to the hidden American. Or all three at once.

"There is more, Pasha," said Milosz. "She says the Germans did not happen upon the village. There is an informant. She says the Germans did not take the informant when they departed."

"And the child knows this how?"

"It is a small—"

"A small village, yes, yes," Zoran finished the words. This confirmed his fears. The Germans know about the American. Now it was up to him to act. To act was Pasha's prerogative. His right hand found his revolver and his left rested on the hilt of this sword. *Yes*, he thought. *I am compelled to clean my house of the wolves.* The damned wolves.

"Milosz."

"Yes, Pasha."

"Assemble the sons of the council, but only those who can make the ride." Zoran straightened his tunic. "And send the messengers back to their families. Instruct them to tell their fathers that they are to reassemble their forces and meet us at the crossing *tonight*. We leave within the hour."

# 14

## BABA'S VILLAGE

"GOVNO!"

The Nurse stood over Goodman and Jasminka like a mother lording over errant children, her hands on her hips. "How did this happen? Who told you this nonsense? What were you thinking?"

"I wanted to *prevent* this from happening," he said.

Regardless, the information about the spy was not wrong. Baba had confirmed it. The Germans themselves had confirmed it when they went straight to Baba's cellar. The days of investigation into the matter had revealed nothing, however, except Baba's and the Nurse's combined wrath. The Nurse was apoplectic.

"When were you told about this...this person, this...this so-called spy?"

"We learned about it about a week ago."

"Who is this 'we' you speak of?"

"Well, first it was Jasminka—"

"You are telling me the imaginings of a peasant girl? This...this *gedzhovitsa*?"

"Well, yes," Goodman answered, not knowing the meaning of the word he agreed to. "But Baba also knew—"

The Nurse crumpled her cap in her fist. "Govno!" she yelled and threw it on the floor.

Goodman watched Jasminka's eyes well up as she glared at the Nurse. *That word. Something about that word.* Jasminka turned and ran up the stairs. She burst out the back door and created a noisy panic with the goats. At a loss for words, the Nurse jabbed a finger at Goodman and cursed again. She stomped up the stairs and confronted Baba in the kitchen, and a heated exchange broke out. Goodman limped his way up the stairs.

"You must tell me the name of the spy immediately!" demanded the Nurse.

"I do not know who it is," Baba replied quietly. "You should leave it alone. Život za život!"

"You *must* tell me!" The Nurse fumed. "Život za život also says we must kill those who kill us."

"Neh!" Baba stamped her cane on the floor. "Život za život. The village must do what is best for the village."

"I have no authority over you," the Nurse declared. "But I have to maintain the security of my patients. For him!" She pointed at Goodman. "For all we know, the Germans might be watching the village right now. I have other patients in other places on this mountain—if they are still alive. Now, I must move them all. I cannot trust this place." *Or you.* The implication was clear.

"You can trust this place," Baba replied quietly.

"How can I?"

"I don't expect a girl from the city to understand," Baba replied. "The village will do what the village has to do. It always has, and we are still here."

"Baba, you must—"

Baba cut her off. "You were not yet born when this village was last burned. Your grandmother was just a girl when the Turks cut the heads off the elders in the square." She paused. "Where were you when the invaders took our men away?"

"I was fighting those who took them!" replied the nurse.

"Yes, I'm sure," said Baba. "You have made great sacrifices, but more will be taken from you, I'm afraid."

"Of course, this is war!" the nurse exclaimed. "I am prepared to sacrifice everything. And everything was in order. Except now, because of you and this village, everything must change." She turned to Goodman. "I cannot move you right now. I will make arrangements for you and return as quickly as possible. Try not to get captured before then. And do not be seen by anyone. Anyone!"

"What do I—"

The Nurse spun around and slammed the newly repaired door shut. Outside, she swung herself into her saddle and kicked her horse into motion. "Yah!" she growled as she galloped away.

Goodman turned to speak to Baba, but she had disappeared into her room. Jasminka opened the door at the rear of the house, but slammed it shut again when she saw Goodman looking at her.

Outside, the goats bleated excitedly again. Still staring at the door, Goodman tried to unpack what had just happened. *What is going on with these people? How did I become the bad guy here?*

Baba opened her door. She spoke slowly, like she did every time she wanted Goodman to really understand her.

"All things are not the same to all people. We must watch and listen and pray. Razumješ?"

"No, Baba, I no understand," Goodman confessed. "What me do wrong?"

Baba pointed a finger at him. "You are wrong. You broke the balance on the mountain, and now the wolves come to my house."

"I no want to be here," said Goodman. "Me want go home." He pointed to the sky.

Baba's face was expressionless.

"Ne razumijem, Baba."

"Perhaps you will one day."

# 15

BABA'S WELL HAD AN ALCOVE built into it about fifteen feet below the stone ledge and just above the waterline. She said that, until today, no one had had to hide there since before she was married. Goodman had spent the last seven hours crouched in the cramped four-by-four-by-four-foot space. Now, the cold thoroughly chilled him. Jasminka served his dinner to him in the bucket when she lowered it to get water.

"You want more blanket?" she called down.

"Neh," he replied. She disappeared. He climbed out for the first time when he saw the stars reflected in the glassy water. Disappointment overwhelmed him at the idea of having to go back down into the well before dawn. He dearly hoped the Nurse would bring help by then.

As before, the goats bleated and herded against each other into the far corner of the corral. Even black-face-one-horn displayed an unusual amount of cowardice. Ignoring the familiar stench, Goodman inhaled deeply and relieved himself through the fence. The futility of his situation consumed his thoughts. He did not know if he should be angrier at himself for getting complacent, at the Nurse for not taking him seriously, or at Baba for not taking action when she apparently knew everything all along. Or at Jasminka, for that matter. *But she's just a kid. There are plenty of adults in this mess who should know better than to let things get this bad. Dammit, I'm not the one who created this situation.* He exhaled loudly. He rubbed his eyes to push away his headache. It worked for a moment.

He looked at the goats and thought about how simple life was for the people back home. They had so little to worry about. He remembered the worries of his parents and the rest of the household staff, the family business concerns, the social calendars, the competition his father instigated between him and his brothers. How petty the disagreements. How silly it all was. All of it. *But here I am. And now I don't know what the hell I'm doing.* He pressed his fingers into his temples and leaned against the fence. It creaked loudly under his weight. He stepped through the shifting goats to the wall of the house.

Goodman had no energy to do his exercises tonight. He arched his back and felt the vertebrae pop. He had no idea what would happen when the Nurse returned. *What they need to do is clean house,* he thought. *Get rid of this spy, whoever it is. Or will the Nurse just move me to a new location? Would it be any better than this place? How much longer before they get me out of Yugoslavia?* He rubbed his eyes again and looked at the sky. How perfectly clear it was.

Goodman marveled at the thousands of bright, twinkling stars. The Milky Way was as clear here as it had ever been in the Libyan desert. Polaris stood out like a beacon, just where it should be. He shivered and raised his jacket collar and tucked his hands into his armpits. *I should exercise,* he thought. Turning to begin his habitual walk, Goodman saw it.

A shadow.

More a shadow *inside* a shadow. Someone was there, standing against the neighbor's wall just outside the corral. The figure seemed to have a feminine shape, maybe a long dress and something over the head. Goodman's skin crawled with dread. *How long have you been standing there?* He caught a flash of striped skirt in the low light before she disappeared. Light footsteps accelerated to a sprint.

Goodman limped across the enclosure and stiffly pushed himself over the fence, leaving the goats in a noisy fracas. He made his way silently down the narrow alley. The ground gave no hint as to where the woman had gone. He paused to listen. A stone clinked on stone, and Goodman ran toward the sound. He reached the end of the alley, where it opened onto the main road. He looked in both directions. Nothing but rows of houses on both sides of the dirt street. *Where did you go?*

Women's voices echoed from his left, and Goodman stepped cautiously. He followed the voices until a door clicked shut some distance away. One small window glowed orange briefly, then went dark again. He stepped behind a low wall and listened. The women continued to speak. It grew to an argument. One voice was distinctly older sounding than the other. An interior door slammed shut, and the front door opened just wide enough to allow a woman's covered head to scan up and down the road before quietly closing again. He heard the woman bar the door, and silence again filled the street.

While studying the house, he envisioned gripping the woman by the arms and hauling her in front of the Nurse to render judgment. Of course, it would be secret, since Baba was obviously not prepared or willing to deal with this situation in the way that was required. He turned back to the house to cement its appearance in his mind. The front door had a uniquely high-angled roof over it, with a rickety, white-painted balustrade extending to the left. Once satisfied, he took his time to return to Baba's house.

Goodman reentered the corral and tried the rear door, but it was still barred on the inside. He went to the side lean-to and rearranged the grain sacks and settled in. *No need to hide, since you know I'm still here. But now I know where you live*, he thought. *The Nurse will fix this*. Or he would do it himself, whatever was needed. He tucked the sacks in around him and fluffed the sack he intended to use as a pillow. It took a while, but eventually, he slept.

# 16

## SEPTEMBER 22, 1943
## BABA'S VILLAGE

GOODMAN AWOKE TO THE SOUNDS OF MEN'S VOICES. Bosanski, not German. *Good*, he thought. *Not Germans. Thank God.* The sky was turning gray. He knocked on the rear door and Jasminka opened it. She barely looked at him and let the door swing halfway open.

Baba, the Nurse, and three enormous, heavily armed, bearded men filled the kitchen space. Sweat and dirt streaked the men's faces, and mud and foliage coated their torn green uniforms. Their rifles banged against the door frame and scraped the walls as they shuffled to make room for Jasminka to move about. She quickly retreated into her little alcove in Baba's room as her grandmother stood expectantly behind a chair. The Nurse whispered something to one of the men and turned to Goodman.

"You are prepared to go, yes?"

"Yes," said Goodman. "But first, there is something you should know."

"What is it?"

"The spy," said Goodman. "I know where she lives." He switched languages. "Špijun." Goodman instantly regretted using the Bosanski.

The Nurse's eyes opened wide, as did the militiamen's eyes. She looked at Baba, and then back at Goodman.

Baba's eyes bulged in anger. "Neh!" she yelled and knocked her chair over as she moved to strike Goodman with her cane. The Nurse caught her arm mid-swing.

"Stojte!" yelled the Nurse. "Baba, čekaj!" *Stop! Baba, wait!*

Baba moved again to strike when a militiaman caught her other arm. Her eyes flamed as she relented, and her whole body vibrated with tense anger. The militiamen looked amused. Goodman did not. *Why didn't just stick with English?*

"Come with me," said the Nurse. She directed the militiamen outside before leading Goodman to the front of the house. More than a dozen other militiamen stood in a semicircle in front of Baba's house, and villagers had also begun to gather in the street. The Nurse raised a hand to keep the men away from her and Goodman. She pulled him close.

"What do you mean?" she demanded. "How do you know who the spy is?"

"I don't know who she is," Goodman confessed. "But I know where she lives. I followed her to her house."

The Nurse clenched her teeth. "I told you to remain out of sight!"

"I couldn't help it! You try sitting in that—"

"You disobeyed my specific directions," she said. "I will deal with this. Where is this house you speak of?"

"It's got a tall roof and a white fence or railing in the front."

The Nurse rolled her eyes. "You just described half the houses in Bosnia."

"I can take you there," he said.

"No," she said. "Wait here."

The Nurse pushed her way through the growing crowd and spoke to one of the militiamen. He pulled his cigarette out of his mouth and blew a column of smoke over his head before glancing at Goodman and saying something back to her, nodding his head as he spoke. He gave directions to his men as the Nurse returned to Goodman. Her face was ironclad.

"Take us there!" she ordered.

She pulled Goodman by the sleeve and pushed her way through the militiamen, who willingly deferred to her. The man she spoke to motioned for his men to follow.

"Who is that guy?" asked Goodman.

"He is our lieutenant," she said. "Now take us to this house!"

Goodman led the Nurse around to the goat pens and carefully retraced his path from last night until he saw the high-peaked roof with the chipped stucco and rotting, white-painted balustrade. He pointed at the door.

"That's the house," he told the nurse.

She pointed. "Are you certain?"

"Yes," he confirmed. "The one I saw looking for me is young."

"How young?"

"Older than Jasminka," he replied. "But not a mother."

"How do you know?"

"She had an argument with her mother when she went inside."

The nurse turned to the lieutenant and pointed to the house. The Lieutenant then barked commands to his men.

His men ran to the front and rear of the house. With a knock, the woman of the house appeared at the door, and her face immediately showed dread. There was a commotion inside, and the men in the front forced the door open wide and pulled the woman into the road. A moment later, the lieutenant came around from the rear of the house with his arms around a teenaged girl. She wore a blue-and-white striped skirt. Her hair was in disarray. She thrashed and screamed at the men around her. The mother tried to run to her daughter, but another man held her back. She was half his size, yet he struggled to keep her under control. Both mother and daughter let out a cry, and a chorus of women joined them as they emerged from the surrounding houses. The nurse clamped her hand over the mother's mouth and told her to shut up. Immediately, she quieted but her eyes remained wide and desperate. The lieutenant had his hand over the girl's mouth and nodded to two other men to grab her arms and legs. She tired quickly, and the other women and girls moaned and wailed, gesticulating wildly with their hands. The nurse yelled in vain to quiet the crowd. Goodman involuntarily stepped forward, but a large a hand pushed on his chest, halting him. The militiaman's face said *do not interfere.*

The lieutenant and the Nurse took the girl a few paces away from the crowd and questioned her. *This is an interrogation,* he thought. The girl shook her head at every question, sobbing and speaking in broken sentences between raspy breaths. Goodman couldn't hear the quiet words of the nurse as she knelt next to the girl and asked her something. The girl stopped crying and looked at Goodman. She slowly nodded her head. The nurse took her firmly by the chin and spoke to her again. This time, the girl clenched her eyes shut and wept. The Nurse rolled her eyes and spoke to the lieutenant. He puffed on his cigarette before responding. She rose and spoke to Goodman.

"She says a man caught her in the fields several weeks ago and threatened to rape her and her mother if she did not help him. She was supposed to look for foreigners. For you." The nurse wiped her brow. "She says she did it to protect her family."

"Who was this man?" said Goodman.

"She says she doesn't know."

The lieutenant scoffed. "*Naravno!* Of course, she knows. How could she not know?" He wiped his nose on his sleeve and put his cigarette back into his mouth. "Did she tell him of our special guest?"

"She won't say," the nurse replied.

"Make her."

The Nurse pinched the girl's jaw and growled into her ear. The girl twisted her face away. Then the Nurse looked briefly round the scene, reared back, and smacked the girl across the face. When the girl hit the ground, her eyes were wide with shock. The girl's mother screamed and struggled, but the militiamen held her fast. The surrounding crowd of women let loose with a collective wail. Goodman's heart sank. *I can't believe this,* he thought. *I didn't want all of this. I just thought they would arrest her.*

The Nurse pulled the girl up by her collar and slapped her again. Her head jerked backward, and the surrounding women wailed again. Frightened brown eyes met Goodman's as the Nurse forcibly turned the girl's head toward him and growled again into her ear. The girl shut her eyes and shook her head. When the Nurse asked again, the girl shook her head more vigorously. Goodman's gut clenched with regret as the Nurse stood and let the girl slump to the ground again, where she sobbed into the dirt.

The lieutenant stepped in and knelt in front of the girl. He calmly took her head in his hands. He said something and pointed at her, then at her mother, and waved. Goodman caught the word *kill* and then something about fire. The girl nodded. The lieutenant spoke to her again. She nodded again and spoke much too quickly for Goodman to understand. Her voice trailed as she collapsed onto the ground and sobbed. Her mother knelt beside her and held her head off the ground. Goodman tried to fight the urge to intervene and make it all stop, but he couldn't.

"Molim," he said to the Nurse. "Please. Let her go. She's not a threat if I am gone, right?"

"You have no idea," the Nurse replied. "You have no idea what your presence has created here."

"What do you mean?"

"There is a bounty on your head," she said. "A very large reward awaits anyone who assists in your capture."

"There is a what?" It took Goodman a second to process this new information. "Large? How large?"

"Large enough to make people do evil to each other."

"Well, why don't we—"

The Nurse ignored him and turned to the lieutenant. They stood conversing for a moment amid the growing cacophony of wailing and crying. The lieutenant pointed around the crowd, then around at the hills surrounding, and the nurse nodded in agreement at whatever he said. He directed his men to approach. One man bound the girl's arms behind her, while another held her fast. The Nurse caught the mother's arms and pulled her away while other men moved in to assist with tying up the girl and pushing back the villagers. Goodman looked around at the crowd that had gathered and caught sight of little old Baba standing some distance away, leaning on her twisted cane. She looked right at him. Suddenly, shame and embarrassment assaulted Goodman.

"Gather your things," the Nurse barked at him.

He had to shake himself free of Baba's iron stare. "What are you going to do to her?" he replied.

"What do you think we do with traitors and spies?"

"But she—"

"Do not interfere!" commanded the Nurse. "You have done enough already."

The lieutenant directed the remainder of his men to part the sea of women and girls now in anguish as he moved the bound, gagged, and blindfolded girl back toward the tree at the village center. The nurse and some men shoved the women and children out of the lieutenant's way. One militiaman was already there. He casually tied a noose to a length of rope and threw it over a limb to a comrade on horseback. He lit a cigarette and leaned against the tree, disinterested in the hurricane of emotion that swirled around him. Goodman could not believe what he was seeing. *They're going to do it right here? Right now?*

Baba stepped forward and called out, her cane in the air. A burly militiaman stepped toward her threateningly, but the Nurse stopped him. Baba spoke at length while the lieutenant's men pushed the girl toward the tree. Baba spoke passionately and gestured at Goodman, the girl, and then back at Goodman. He saw tears streaking down Baba's face and looked away as regret once again overtook him.

Above the wailing, the Nurse called to the lieutenant. He paused his men, and the two of them spoke to Baba. Baba pounded the end of her cane into the dirt several times as she spoke. The girl's mother wailed where she stood, still restrained by a militiaman. Goodman could hear the Nurse say something to the lieutenant about protecting the family. The lieutenant nodded in agreement and motioned for his men to remove the rope from the tree. They would be taking the girl with them for "bezbjednost." *As a precaution. Good,* thought Goodman. *They aren't going to kill her after all.*

By now, there were several wounded men—some on makeshift stretchers and some walking with bandages—gathered in front of Baba's house. The rest of the men stood casually nearby. They smoked or talked between themselves, seemingly oblivious to the drama taking place not twenty yards away. The lieutenant motioned to Goodman to join the group of wounded. He hesitated, but the Nurse walked to him briskly.

"Now you follow orders," she said, pushing him toward the wounded men. She took a long farmer's coat and hat from one of the other men and shoved them into Goodman's arms. "Wear these so you do not look so much like a foreigner."

They were stained and reeked of old sweat, but he put the coat around him anyway and placed the black, broad-brimmed hat on his head. That was when he saw Jasminka.

She gazed at him with wide, bloodshot eyes. Her cheeks were wet, and her arms hung limply at her sides. Goodman approached her apprehensively, testing for a reaction. There was none as he knelt in front of her.

"Jasminka... I—" He tried to speak clearly, but it came out broken. "Izvinjenja." *I'm sorry.*

She gave him a forlorn look. He unpinned one of his Air Corps insignia pins from his collar and put it in her hand. She looked at it blankly and put in her apron pocket. Her eyes drifted to some faraway place. Goodman stood and backed away. *This is not what I wanted this day to be like.*

Jasminka sat down on the step behind her and pulled the pin from her pocket to look at it more closely. She did not look up until the Nurse swooped in and snatched it out of her hands. Her little face burst into bewildered tears.

"You fool!" the Nurse shoved the pin into Goodman's hand. "Keep this to yourself. Do you want to kill her, you idiot? If the Germans find this, they will know enough to justify executing her and everyone else in this place! Stupid, stupid fool!"

Goodman's anger spiked in response to the Nurse's rebuke, but he knew she was right. He made no protest as she checked on her various patients. The war had now changed forms for him—again. The rules he knew no longer applied to his situation, to his life in this place. He was no longer a patient, secreted away in a root cellar. And he certainly wasn't a damn pilot anymore. He was now an unarmed, handicapped, foot-propelled alien in foreign territory without a clue as to his location. *I can't stay. But now what?*

The Nurse returned to him, towing the girl with the rope still around her neck and bound at the wrists. She stumbled to a halt in front of Goodman. He looked at the rope in the Nurse's hands, and then at the girl. Her knees shook visibly. The rope was wet and gritty in his hands when the Nurse shoved it at him. Goodman's head swam as he raised his eyes to meet the Nurse's. *No way. No way am I going to be the one to take her out of the village like this.*

"Do not let go of this." The Nurse had to yell over the sounds of women wailing. "No matter what happens, do not let go of this rope. Do you understand?"

"I'm not going to be—"

"Yes! Yes, you are!" The Nurse looked him straight-on. "You will do this."

She stormed off before he could reply. Goodman stood there, speechless, with the rope in his hands in front of the entire village. He saw hatred everywhere around him. *Yup*, he thought. *I did this*.

# 17

WITH A SHOUT FROM THE LIEUTENANT, the column of militiamen got underway. The nurse charged Goodman with carrying a bloody, unconscious man on a stretcher. He wrapped the end of the rope around one of the poles, lifted his end of the stretcher, and followed the man in front. His shoulder immediately ached under the strain. The girl's mother begged and pleaded with Goodman to release her daughter, despite the other men's attempts to obstruct or push her aside. Baba was a statue. Goodman fumed with his own emotions. Angered at the situation, angered at Baba for not preventing this from happening. Angered at himself for…for what? *What should I have done differently?*

At first, the lieutenant moved out quickly, and a gap opened between his lead group and the stretcher bearers. He barked at them to catch up. As the walking wounded and stretcher bearers got their legs warmed up and adjusted to the loads they bore, their speed increased but only somewhat. The girl's mother pulled on Goodman's arm and pleaded for him to stop. His shoulder burned with pain. *Won't someone get this woman off of me?*

"Pomozi mi!" Goodman called out. The man in front of the stretcher ignored him.

The lieutenant directed two men to shut her up. They grabbed the woman by the arms and shoved her down the hillside. She cried out, then stumbled, caught herself, and climbed hand-over-hand to close the distance. A militiaman stood over her and prevented her from getting back to her feet. Finally, she slipped and fell on dry leaves and slid down the slope. She wailed aloud, and the forest echoed behind them. The girl wept as her mother's voice faded into the distance. The Nurse threatened the girl, and she stifled her crying, but it did nothing the alleviate Goodman's feelings of anguish at having to pull her along. Goodman began to sweat profusely. He was already winded and felt his strength ebbing away quickly. *Damn this!*

After a fast mile, the patrol took a hard turn uphill. Maneuvering the steep and densely wooded path was difficult for the stretcher bearers and the walking wounded, but the lieutenant and the nurse showed no mercy with the pace until they reached the first ridgeline. The column hurried down the far side, and stretcher bearers strained and failed to maintain their grip. Some men struggled to keep up and they faltered and fell against trees or simply went to the ground. One stretcher required the nurse to stabilize the wounded man before moving, and everyone passed them up. Goodman's left shoulder throbbed under the load. He felt his lungs burn with the need for air. His left leg cramped painfully. The downhill side was short, and another long slope welcomed them. Several more of the injured fell behind, and Goodman lost sight of them.

"We need to stop soon," he muttered to himself. "This is a mess."

"So, I see American pilots are not too fragile," said the Nurse, who suddenly appeared in front of Goodman. "Do not let go of her." He scowled at her.

"How long until we let her go?" said Goodman.

The Nurse's eyes widened. "What?" she exclaimed, wiping a lock of sweaty hair from her face. "She is not going to be released! What did I tell you before? Do not interfere. We only agreed with the old woman to not kill her in the village. Besides, cutting her throat in the forest is easier than hanging her by the neck in the village. Even the old woman knows this. You are a fool."

The nurse shook her head as she rushed back down the hill. The constant tug on his arm reminded him that the girl was only ten feet away. *They are going to kill her anyway,* he thought. *If I'm not in the village anymore, then she's not a threat to anyone, right? What the hell? We should just let her go once we're a safe distance away.*

They rested with the others at the top of the hill. The girl was no longer resisting the rope, which was fine with Goodman. The Nurse arrived behind them, carrying the next stretcher. She placed it down on the ground and looked downhill to see how far behind the last of the stragglers were. Apparently satisfied that they would catch up soon, she knelt down to inspect another of the stretcher-bound patients. She cursed out loud and began to unwrap a bloody limb. A bead of sweat dripped from her nose. She pointed to Goodman and then to the man on the stretcher in front of him.

"Check those bandages," commanded the nurse. "Fix them if any are loose. You know how to do that, don't you?"

Goodman glared at her but complied. She directed him to another patient. And another. One of the leg wounds Goodman tended was deeply gangrenous. It reeked horribly, and he reared back, covering his nose. He placed the filthy sheet back over the body and moved to check the soldier's pulse, then looked at the face of his prisoner. *Why didn't she give this guy any of the sulfa?* He spit to try to get the sensation of rotten flesh out of him, and his mind put two and two together. *Because she gave it all to me.*

He shook the thought away and examined another blood-soaked bandage. More red, swollen tissue surrounding graying, dead tissue. Massive infection. Unless they were headed to a regular hospital, this young man's days were numbered. Probably in single digits by now. Goodman rewrapped the wound. *No, definitely in the single digits.* He sat against a tree and looked at the girl at the end of the rope.

The girl looked too young to be a spy. She should be in school, or feeding goats, or doing the laundry. *This is my fault,* he thought as he looked around. No one was paying any attention to either of them. *I could let her go.*

The lieutenant quietly ordered two men to search ahead on the trail, and they were quickly out of sight. Those who carried weapons observed the surrounding slopes and the trail ahead. All others, including Goodman, sat by their stretchers or lay on the ground. Below their position on the hill lay a single-lane road, partially hidden by a handful of thick, leafy trees. The sun was well into the morning sky, and its location told Goodman that the trail, and the ridge it followed, went in a northwesterly direction. Birds chirped, and a black squirrel jumped between trees. The wind whispered high in the treetops. Except for the condition and attire of his current company, there was no indication of the war that surrounded them, nothing that Goodman had imagined of life outside the village.

The scouts returned after a few minutes, the older of the two waving his hand back and forth. From the reactions of those around him, Goodman deduced this was the "all-clear" signal. By then, the nurse had inspected and secured all the bandages and straps for their wounded.

The lieutenant directed everyone to rise. The walking wounded helped each other up, and Goodman took the rear set of stretcher handles again, still holding the rope. Labored breathing filled the air as the patrol quickly picked up speed again.

The lead man suddenly veered off the trail and into a small ravine. Goodman heard water running, then felt the cold dampness of nearby water. *Here? On a mountain?* The group halted in the flatness surrounding a spring-fed pond. The water poured out of the rocks above in a small waterfall. Everyone set their stretchers down and made straight for the water's edge. Goodman remained with his stretcher. And the prisoner.

A boy collected water containers and set to filling them two at a time directly from the spring. Several men pushed the floating dust and insects from the edge and commenced sipping the water. Each took a long drink and splashed his face. Once they were satisfied, the healthy members of the party poured water into the mouths of their wounded comrades. Goodman's medical training had taught him that men with severe wounds should not be drinking this much water, but he kept it to himself. Then he realized he had not drunk any water since leaving the village. He tugged at the rope and guided the girl to the water's edge where they drank. The lieutenant suddenly barked at him.

"What?" Goodman responded.

The nurse stomped over to the girl and yanked her back by the rope, causing her to choke and spew water into the air as she fell backward. Goodman instinctively rose to oppose her.

"I was giving her wa—"

"No!" The nurse cut him off. "This is not for her."

The girl cowered behind Goodman's legs, gasping for air through the rope that was now tight around her neck. The lieutenant appeared next to the nurse.

"She needs water," Goodman retorted. "How am I supposed to drag her along if she passes out?" Both the nurse and the lieutenant looked at him with their faces set in stone. Goodman fumed. "I'm not going to—"

"Shhh!" The nurse, the lieutenant, and everyone else dived to the ground. Goodman failed to react quickly enough, and the lieutenant pulled him down by the coat. The echoes of a truck grinding its gears rose to them from the road below. The engine roared. Then a second engine roared. A third truck followed a few seconds later. The lieutenant and another man scurried to the top of the ravine and signaled to everyone to prepare to move.

One of the stretcher-bound wounded writhed in pain, making a low moaning noise that quickly grew louder. Two of the militiamen pounced to silence him. The nurse scrambled through the cluster of men to stab a small sedative applique into the man's thigh. The muffled screams subsided and Goodman watched the man's eyes roll back into his head. Everyone sat listening for any sign that the commotion gave away their position. The trucks continued to lumber along the road. After a minute, the sounds faded.

The lieutenant jumped down from his perch and hurriedly directed militiamen to protect the rear and then motioned for the remainder of the patrol to follow him. A look of concern between men told Goodman that this was out of control. He reached for the poles to lift the stretcher when he noticed the rope was gone. He spun around to see flattened wire grass where the prisoner had been not thirty seconds earlier.

# 18

SEPTEMBER 22, 1943
A WOODED RIDGELINE IN NORTHEASTERN BOSNIA, YUGOSLAVIA

GOODMAN LET OUT AN AUDIBLE GASP. He scanned the mouth of the ravine and surrounding woods. "Where'd she go?" He spun around. "No!"

The man on the front stretcher handles turned around. His eyes opened wide with recognition of the disaster that had just occurred. The lieutenant was already several yards up the trail.

"Stojte!" the man called out quietly to the stretcher team ahead of them. "Stojte!"

They turned and halted, irritated at the disruption of the already arduous task. "Stojte!" They passed the word up to the front. The Nurse came running.

"What is the meaning—" She started to scold the men ahead of Goodman when she saw him standing there with no rope and no prisoner. "Govno!" She flew at Goodman. "What did you do?"

"She was here, and then she wasn't," he stammered.

"You let her go!"

"No, I—"

"Shut up!" She immediately looked up the ravine and scanned the hillside before taking off at a sprint toward the mouth of the ravine. She waved to the lieutenant, who then came running with three of his men. A man at the head of the patrol pointed over the crest.

"Ona je tamo!" he yelled out. "Na putu!" *There she is! On the road!*

Everyone scrambled up the short slope and peered through the underbrush. Goodman saw her, too. Hands bound and blindfold around her neck, she ran downhill, trailing the rope behind her. She tripped and fell, but returned to her desperate, clumsy sprint. When she reached the road, she turned toward the trucks and ran. Goodman's eyes met the Nurse's. She was enraged. The lieutenant arrived to see the girl running along the road, more than a hundred yards away.

"Do we chase her?" the Nurse asked. She huffed through her nose.

"Neh," replied the lieutenant. "We are too close to Zvornik Polje. We must move quickly." He glared at Goodman. "She is already dead." He hurried to the front of the column of men and stretchers that lined the path.

"Do you know what this means?" she said. "We are very far from safety. What do you think will happen when she is found?" She clenched her jaw. "They will come for us now, and we will all pay the price! The villagers, too!" She scrambled through the brush after the lieutenant, cursing out loud.

"Idemo! Idi!" the lieutenant barked to his men. Two of the militiamen remained on the crest above the pond to observe the ravine, while everyone else lifted stretchers or helped a wounded man to his feet. Now they moved *fast*. Nearly everyone stumbled at first, trying to transition from kneeling or standing on crutches to nearly a full sprint. The cramps swelled up in Goodman's legs again. He stumbled and caught himself. *Can't slow down,* he thought. *Can't stop for anything. Dammit! How could I let her go?* He cursed himself under his breath, wishing the girl dead. He tightened his grip, lowered his head, and put one foot in front of the other.

Everyone struggled to keep from falling down the descending slope. The lieutenant, the Nurse, and the scouts soon came back to help the struggling stretcher bearers and walking wounded get through the knee-deep muck at the bottom and up the far bank. Once they stumbled up the bank, everyone collapsed in exhaustion, panting heavily. Goodman's mouth was dry, and sweat plastered his shirt to his skin under the heavy coat. He wanted to lay his head down, but one of the militia fighters prodded him when he closed his eyes. *Oh, God, when will this end?* He sat up and felt the sweat roll down his forehead and burn his eyes.

Shortly, the two scouts returned and gave their report. The conversation was jumbled, as they could only speak in short phrases with their heavy breathing. Something about a road. The lieutenant turned and gave directions. The fighters would cross first, then stretchers would cross one at a time after he and his men investigated the area across the road. *Okay*, thought Goodman. *Progress. Or something. Here we go again.* Everyone got up.

When it was his turn, Goodman and the other stretcher bearer scrambled across the road. They almost ran into the stretcher team in front of them on the far side. The woods were not very dense here, but the steep incline was a big problem. Goodman put his head down and they charged ahead. They passed the stretcher in front of them and almost closed on the one further ahead. Sweat stung his eyes. *Almost there*, he thought. Just g*et to the top...then we can rest for a minute...*

Suddenly, there was a yell from the road behind them, and a rifle shot shattered the serenity of the surrounding woods. The echo seemed to swim around them through the forest. *What was that!* Goodman spun around to look. He caught a glimpse of men in black uniforms swarming like a wave through the woods. A second shot chased the first. Everyone ducked his head and went to the ground. Another shot pierced the air, and Goodman heard a high-pitched buzz. He looked over his shoulder. Suddenly, the air filled with gunfire. The lead man on the front stretcher handles yelled at him to hurry and get up. *Shouldn't someone be returning fire? Why isn't anyone returning fire?*

Finally, someone fired back. Goodman heard the lieutenant and the Nurse barking orders, and the rifleman fired, re-cocked, and fired again. *Okay*, thought Goodman, *let's move!* With renewed energy, he pushed on the stretcher from behind.

The deafening sound of machine-gun fire thundered at them through the forest, and any remaining discipline on the militia's part evaporated like water on a hot stove. The lieutenant yelled something furiously and let loose with his submachine gun, a pitifully small sound compared to the machine gun that chewed through the trees around them. A second machine gun opened up and cut down the stretcher team behind Goodman. The many screams of pain shocked him into a panicked sprint. *Run, dammit, run!* Then the lieutenant's gun went silent. Men were running away from the road and getting mowed down by black-clad men behind rifles and machine guns. Goodman watched them fall—one, then two more, then another and another. The patient on the stretcher was now fully conscious and moaning loudly. Goodman looked up at the man at the front of the stretcher.

"*Idemo!*" Goodman shouted.

Together, they ran as fast as they could. Goodman's hands, arms, and legs screamed with fatigue as they hustled to get over the low crest ahead of them, out of the line of fire. But it was too late. The stretcher in front of them fell sideways and took all the stretcher bearers down with it. The man at the front of Goodman's stretcher stumbled over them as they struggled to get up. Bullets buzzed and snapped all around them. Goodman felt a sickening twist in his stomach just like the hundredth of a second before the first anti-aircraft shell exploded in front of the *Jessica Joy* on their approach to their target at Ploesti. Now he felt far more helpless.

The lead man suddenly jerked sideways and smacked into a tree. Goodman and his stretcher went down with him. The whole stretcher spilled sideways, and the wounded man fell onto the rocky ground. He gave a muffled yell and kicked his legs frantically.

"Get up! Goodman yelled to the man up front. No response. Goodman gave the man a shake. But the man did not move.

A bullet smacked into a tree a couple of yards in front of Goodman. Another bullet smacked into a tree right behind him. Goodman flattened himself onto the rocky, leaf-covered ground. Several more rounds snapped through the branches over his head. Suddenly, the bullets ceased. There was some far-off yelling, and then silence. The only thing he could think of was to hide. *Don't move!* he thought to himself. *Don't fucking move!*

The Nurse suddenly appeared at the side of a tree about ten yards ahead of him, near the crest of the hill. She had a pistol in her hand, and her eyes darted everywhere. She saw him and silently motioned for him to move to her. He crawled slowly and quietly toward her. She pointed to him and then to his left, into a small patch of low ground. He slid into it and continued crawling toward her. Blood ran down her cheek and neck from unseen wounds. Two more rifle shots rang out, and the nurse crouched down behind the tree. He crawled around a gray, jagged rock that was about two feet high and saw the nurse and two stretcher bearers with their wounded comrade in a slight depression in the ground. Her pistol was the only weapon among them. *OK*, he thought. *There's only a few of us left. Does she know where to go?*

The Nurse whispered angrily to the other men, who nodded their heads and turned to crawl toward the dense greenery behind them. Then she turned to Goodman. "Follow them! Go!"

"What about you?" whispered Goodman.

Ignoring him, she moved to the largest tree between them and the road and peered around it before shrinking from what she saw. "Idi!" she growled at them. The two men sprinted in a low crouch away from her location, leaving their unconscious man on his stretcher. Goodman looked at the man on the stretcher and then back at the nurse. *Do we leave him?* The thought went firmly against his instinct. *Could we even think of carrying him?* The Nurse slowly took aim with her pistol around the base of the tree. He could only watch as she fired.

The spent casing pinged off the tree trunk and clinked into the rocks. She fired again, paused, then fired three more shots. She cursed as the reply came flying back at her. Chunks of wood and sheets of bark peeled off the tree. She flattened against the ground and covered her head. Dark-colored bark and yellow wood flew in all directions. Leaves and sticks showered down around her. The trees behind Goodman showered him and the wounded man with splinters and chunks of wood. The nurse frantically turned and saw Goodman still lying on the rocks, gaping at her.

"Dammit, you fool!" she yelled. "Run!"

# 19

"RUN!"

The nurse nearly stepped on Goodman as she sprinted for the dense brush behind him. He got up to follow her, but yet another burst of gunfire sent him diving for the ground, this one close enough to deafen him. The bullets smacked her around like a heavyweight boxer had set to kidney punching her. She caught herself and dived headlong into the underbrush, but her medic bag snagged on a branch and held her back. Another burst of gunfire knocked her to the rocks. Hard. Goodman twisted around and saw a smoking muzzle poking out from behind a tree just a few feet away. *He doesn't see me!*

Goodman was furious about the Nurse. And about the wounded man he dumped on the ground. And about the wounded man next to him whom he was about to abandon. He picked up a fist-sized rock and went to the near side of the tree. The gunman stepped around the tree and Goodman drove the rock right into his face. The man grunted loudly and fell against the trunk. Goodman hit him again, and he tumbled backward, taking his weapon with him. Goodman reached around the tree and grabbed for the weapon. Blazing heat from the barrel seared his forearm, but he pulled on it anyway. The attacker blindly clutched at his weapon, and Goodman hit him twice more with the rock before the man let go, spewing a fountain of blood from his mouth. Goodman choked on a lump of bile in his throat. He spit and looked at the weapon in his hands—a German-made MP–40 submachine gun. *Okay, now what?*

In that instant, Goodman caught a glimpse of what was beyond the tree. The hillside swarmed with black-clad men with rifles. Gunshots popped and echoed as they worked their way through the bodies lying on the ground between the road and the hillside. *They're killing the wounded!* A rifle cracked, and the bullet thumped into the tree next to him. *Oh my God! I need to get out of here!* Goodman pushed away from the tree and fled.

He stumbled over the rocky ground, toward the Nurse, who now lay gasping and choking, soaked in her own blood. A root snagged his foot and brought him to the ground, face-to-face with her. Desperate blue eyes locked on his for the briefest of moments. She gasped repeatedly for air that escaped through the holes in her lungs in a bright reddish froth across her back. Her lips moved, but he heard nothing. Goodman scrambled back to his feet and plowed headlong into the thicket.

Branches snapped him in the face. He tripped and fell, but caught himself on a small tree and ran again, stumbling and falling forward.

Behind him, voices called to each other, and gunfire erupted again. Bullets ripped through the thicket. The heavy farmer's coat suddenly jerked him sideways. The snag held fast as he pulled, so he fired the weapon one-handed into the woods behind him, not bothering to aim while he pulled free of the heavy coat and pushed through more thick brush. He emerged onto a downhill slope of enormous, moss-covered trees.

Goodman climbed over a fallen tree trunk and collapsed. It was eerily quiet except for the blood pounding in his ears. He peered over the top and saw no one chasing him. *Do I run? Do I stay here?* He wiped sweat from his eyes before he caught a flicker of movement in the thicket he had just run through. He aimed and pulled the trigger.

*Click.* Smoke wafted lazily from the muzzle. He squeezed again and looked at the chamber. *Out of ammo. No!* He scanned the trees downhill, away from the enemy. Nothing. Good. *Run!*

Suddenly euphoric, like he was flying down the hill, he dove into the brush. He stumbled, caught himself, and started up the next slope. Hand over hand, he made for the top. His left leg throbbed with a massive cramp, and it slowed him down.

*Run!*

His lungs screamed for air, and a new pain burned his head. He felt a warm trickle on the side of his face and wiped at it. His whole sleeve came away covered in red. The steep slope brought him to a near standstill as rocks and roots forced him to climb slowly. He reached the crest and slid down the other side in a cascade of dirt and rocks. As distant gunfire echoed from behind, he looked over his shoulder before pushing himself to stand up.

He stumbled repeatedly, willing his wobbly legs to move, one after the other—left, right, left, right—until the ground flattened and the forest thinned out across a floodplain with a stream that snaked across it. *Not good for hiding*, he thought. *But better for running.*

*Wait.* He slowed down. *What was that?*

Someone yelled, but it was muffled, like a loud whisper. Goodman scanned the tall grass around him. Two men waved at him from the dense brush along the stream. They called out to him again.

"Druže!" *Friend!*

They waved him over, but he hesitated, unsure of who they were. Instead, they ran toward him and motioned for him to follow them. When they got close, he recognized them from the Nurse's patrol, and a wave of relief washed over him. The distant shooting faded to nothing as they splashed across the stream.

They collapsed next to each other behind a fallen tree at the base of the next slope, coughing and choking on the dust in their throats, their chests heaving for breath. Goodman slumped on the cool earth and tried to estimate how far they had run. *A mile? Maybe more?* He had no idea. It was difficult to tell in the hilly terrain. He also had no idea how far their attackers would go to pursue them. Goodman peered over the log but saw no one behind them. He settled back to the ground and looked at the two men who lay next to him.

They were stretcher bearers who were with the nurse, so they, too, had dumped their wounded comrade and ran. Being with these two made him feel less inhumane for leaving a wounded man to his guaranteed death. Or did it? *They did it, too*, he reasoned, before pushing the thought away.

"Hvala," he said. They nodded in return.

*But still*, he thought, *who are these guys?* One looked to be seventeen or eighteen years old, but the younger was maybe fifteen. Regardless, they were survivors. *Did anyone else get away?* He looked back again and saw no one crossing the flood plain. The two boys merely sat and stared at him with hollow exhaustion in their eyes. *Can I trust these guys?*

One said something to him, but it was as if he was underwater. Still mostly deafened from the gunfire, Goodman gestured that he did not hear him. The two boys talked hurriedly to each other, then they said something to him again, but it was unintelligible.

"Ne razumijem," said Goodman. He gestured again to his ears.

The older one repeated what he said, but slower and louder. He said they had no water, no food, and that Goodman had their only weapon. But, he said, they had an idea where to go. Goodman hoped it was true, for he had absolutely no idea where they were. Regardless, anywhere farther from here was better than here.

"Gdje?" he asked. *Where?*

They motioned for him to follow. The younger one helped Goodman to his feet and strode ahead, leaving Goodman to limp his way after them. He peered over his shoulder, alert to any sign they were being pursued. *Good, nothing.* But there was a stone of sadness in him that no one else had escaped. They zigzagged up the grassy slope to the tree-covered crest, down the other side, then up the next. The sun blazed on their backs. The trio paused and hid every time they thought they heard a noise behind them. *Maybe they're imagining things?* thought Goodman. *Maybe they can hear better than I can right now.* He wiggled his fingers in his ears to stop the ringing.

They were exhausted and thoroughly drenched with sweat when they got to the crest of an especially steep ridgeline, the highest one nearby. They pushed through a patch of mountain holly with needle-pointed leaves. Here, they collapsed next to a large rock that was cracked down the middle. The older boy peered around the rock to observe the route they had just taken. A cool wind blew over them. It felt good. He laid his head back against the rock.

His hands ached from clutching the submachine gun, so he wrung them out and cracked his knuckles. His tongue stuck to the roof of his mouth. He massaged his left shoulder and stretched his legs. His knees were killing him. He could hear the blood throbbing through his ears. And the headache. The headache was its own special kind of pain. He pressed his fingers into his temples.

One boy tapped on Goodman's shoulder. He motioned for him to rest. *Rest? Now?* Goodman squinted at the sun. It sat behind the trees on the next ridge. He had completely lost track of time—they had run all day. Goodman sat down next to the rock and watched a v-formation of geese sweep across the sky. He let his head fall back against the mossy rock and fell asleep without realizing it.

Some indeterminable time later, Goodman awoke to a cramp in his left calf. He grasped his leg and rolled with pain as other cramps seized him in both legs. He massaged them repeatedly. The pains subsided after a while, but the stiffness remained. *Man, I need water.*

There was no moon, but the night sky looked blue, and the exposed rock look gray under the stars. He shivered and refolded his arms tightly across his chest, feeling the empty space on his wrist where his watch used to be. *How long did I sleep?* He propped himself up against the rock behind him. It no longer radiated any warmth, and he wished for the farmer's coat the nurse had given him. He sat upright, looking around for his companions.

Goodman peered into the bluish darkness and saw nothing to indicate they were still there. He crawled the few feet over to where they sat earlier and felt around for any object or artifact of their presence. The small depressions in the ground where they had been sitting were cold. *Where are they? They didn't leave me, did they? No way.*

He whispered into the darkness. "Hey!" He heard no response. "Hey!"

Only the night sounds came back to him. He stood and called out quietly. Silence. *What the hell? Where did they go?* He stepped into a shadow and stumbled on a root. He steadied himself and called out again, louder this time. No response. Again, he called out, practically yelling.

Nothing but echoes from the tree line below him.

*No. They would not leave me.* He called out again. More silence. *Maybe they did leave me.* He looked up at the stars. *Oh, God, please help me.*

# PART 2: TUZLA

*Through me you pass into the city of woe:*
*Through me you pass into eternal pain…*
*All hope abandon, ye who enter here.*
— Dante's Inferno, Canto III

# 20

SEPTEMBER 22, 1943
A MOUNTAINTOP IN THE MAJEVITSA, IN NORTHEASTERN
BOSNIA, YUGOSLAVIA

GOODMAN LOOKED FRANTICALLY FOR HIS YOUNG COMPANIONS. He stood fully upright and saw only black shadows broken by greenish-gray rocks surrounding him. *Where could they be? There's no way they would have left me here. Would they?* He scanned the woods nearby. *Sure, they would. Why not? They left their wounded on the road.* He looked around again. *And they left me, too.* He shook his head and made his way through the large boulders that constituted the peak of the hilltop.

*Wait.* He paused. *Is that snoring?*

To his great relief, Goodman found the younger of the boys sound asleep, propped up against a boulder. The boy reeked of slivovitz when Goodman drew near. He reached carefully and shook the boy's shoulder.

"Govno!" The boy cursed out loud and nearly jumped into the air before rubbing his eyes and stretching. He pulled out a small flask from his pocket, unscrewed the lid, took a swig, made a half-hearted offer to Goodman, then withdrew the offer and took a long drink.

"Gedje drug?" Goodman whispered. *Where's your friend?*

The boy shrugged and gestured down the hill.

"You know this place?" Goodman asked. "Where are we?"

Another shrug as he stifled a cough.

"You live here?"

Again, the boy said nothing.

Annoyed at the boy's reticence, Goodman sat down next to him and drew his knees up to his chest. Distant black hills pushed up against the starry night sky. Not a single light shone from anywhere below the horizon. An owl hooted from somewhere below them. Another hoot echoed from across the valley. Goodman accepted the boy's second offer of the flask and returned it. As they listened to the owls, Goodman felt his head swim with the effects of dehydration and alcohol. *I shouldn't drink any more.* He wanted to remain lucid, prepared for any contingency.

Quiet, crunching footfalls announced the return of the older boy. The two boys conferred in a whisper and, having agreed, motioned for Goodman to come with them. Something about a farm, they said. He followed them down the mountainside and across a ravine toward another ridgeline.

The holly grew thick on the next slope. It snagged and pulled on Goodman's clothing, and he held up his forearms to fend off the hundreds of invisible knifepoints that thrusted for eyes, necks, and anywhere soft. There was a steady flow of hushed profanity in Bosanski and English as the trio descended the ridge into thick tree cover.

Before they were obscured, Goodman read the stars. He had entered the forest, headed southbound, and descended the slope by numerous switchbacks. There was no chance he could find his way back to the village anymore. *Southwest is generally the right direction to the Adriatic.* Then he shook his head at the idea of walking the hundred-fifty-odd miles through at least two more mountain ranges to the Dalmatian Coast. *Not gonna do that today. It might come to that, though.* He pushed through the thicket.

The next high ground was mostly devoid of trees except those that ran along a vine-choked stone wall. A black, triangle-shaped peak of a house rose above the vines behind a gate. The boys leaned into one another.

"Mustafa," said the younger. "Go see the man."

The one called Mustafa stepped cautiously toward the gate and tried to push it open. The metallic clink was absurdly loud in the still night air and drew a bark from a dog inside the compound. Mustafa leapt backward as the enormous beast hit the gate at full speed. A second dog joined with a snarl that sounded more like that of a lion. A third canine appeared and reared up on its hind legs, standing taller than Mustafa. All three were kept at bay by the large gate, but claws and teeth that shone in the night reached between the bars. A sudden, sharp whistle drew the dogs into submission. The beasts withdrew to the house as their master stepped out, holding a lantern over his head. The long barrel of a gun reflected the yellow light.

"Ko je tamo?" said the man. *Who is there?*

"We are friends of the Majevitsa, effendi!" Mustafa called out. "It is Mustafa Mehmetović, Effendi!"

"You are Mustafa Mehmetović?" The man raised his lantern slightly higher and stepped toward the gate.

"Yes, Effendi," said Mustafa. "And you are Raza Effendi Milovač."

"Yes, I see," said Raza Milovač. "Boys, put down your weapons."

Two other figures stepped from either side of the house. Starlight reflected on the long barrels of their weapons, which were pointed at the gate.

"Stjepan! Ivan! My sons, lower your weapons!" said Raza Effendi.

Raza's sons complied as he closed the distance to the gate. His dogs paced back and forth at the house, unable to sit still.

"There are three of them, father!" said one of the sons of Raza.

"Who is with you?" Raza demanded.

"My cousin Radoslav is with me, Effendi…and…a friend, Effendi," said Mustafa.

"A friend? Show yourself, stranger!" demanded Raza. "Tell me, who are you?"

Goodman hesitated.

"Govori!" Radoslav hit Goodman on the shoulder. *Say something!*

Goodman tried to compose a sentence, but the man called Raza cut him off.

"Stranac!" *Stranger!* Raza abruptly stepped back from the gate. "You cannot bring a foreigner here! You must leave. We have nothing to do with foreigners." His sons raised their weapons again.

Raza raised his lantern and aimed his shotgun with one arm. Mustafa backed away from the gate with hands raised high.

"We do not want trouble, Effendi!" he said. "We are looking for my uncle, Zoran Pasha!"

"Zoran Mehmetović? He is no pasha!" Raza scoffed. "And he is nowhere near here. What business does Zoran have with foreigners?"

"He is my uncle, Effendi," said Mustafa. "And he desires that we return to him with the foreigner."

"How do I know where your crazy uncle is, boy?" Mercifully, Raza spoke slow enough for Goodman to understand. "Last I heard, he was on his mountain, but who knows?"

"He is not there, Effendi."

"Then I have no idea what to tell you but that he has likely gone back across the river to make war in the valley again," said Raza. He finally lowered his shotgun. "But God would curse me if I told you to cross the river. The good people have all fled from there if they can. All who remain are the dead and the cursed."

"If my uncle is there," said Mustafa. "Then we must go there. I must deliver the foreigner to him."

Raza's reply came slowly. "Then go with God, Mustafa Mehmetović. You will follow the road to Josef Djordjevic. Do you know him?"

"Da, effendi," said Mustafa.

"Good. He is a Christian, but he will help. What your uncle wants with a foreigner I cannot know, but good cannot come of it. He is *loša sreća*."

Goodman recognized that phrase. *He's calling me bad luck, a curse.* Baba's discussions with the village women were filled with such talk. Raza turned and called to his sons.

"Stjepan! You and your brother take them to the river so they can be in the valley before the sun rises. Hurry!"

His sons climbed quickly over the wall rather than exit through the gate.

"And Mustafa!" Raza called. "Tell your uncle that Raza prays for him."

"Hvala, Effendi," Mustafa thanked him. "Bog s'tobom." *God be with you.* Goodman had heard the women in Baba's village use that term as well.

"Bog s'tobom." Raza called out from behind them.

The woods quickly engulfed them on the narrow trail.

"Where go we?" Goodman asked. *Hopefully toward the coast.*

"We're going to the Tuzla valley," said Mustafa.

"What in Tuzla valley?" asked Goodman.

"Tuzla City."

"Man say Tuzla people dead," said Goodman. "What wrong in Tuzla?"

"It means the war is there, like everywhere," said Mustafa. "Raza Milovač is a stupid old man."

The sons of Raza led Goodman, Mustafa, and Radoslav out of the woods and along an overgrown downhill trail for quite some time. Goodman felt a wet cold bite at his nose and ears as they descended. Presently, they departed from the main trail to a large, rocky outcropping. An old stone dam lay perpendicular to the water's flow, creating a stairstep from placid smoothness on the upstream side to glistening white foam frothing twenty feet below.

"Cross here." Stjepan pointed along the dam's crest to the black trees on the far side.

"Is there no bridge?" asked Mustafa.

"Not for you," said Stjepan. "Follow the trail over the mountain. Do not follow the river—the villages there are not your friends. And,

Mustafa Mehmetović, my father is old, but he is not stupid. Do not bring foreigners onto our lands again."

Mustafa dipped his head politely, then turned and led Goodman and Radoslav down the trail to the dam. He did not know why, but Goodman was glad to be away from Raza and his sons.

"Stay away from the river!" Stjepan called before he and his brother withdrew into the forest.

Mustafa stepped cautiously onto the first stones of the abutment. The narrow ledge was cracked, and chunks were missing. Radoslav followed his cousin down onto the narrow ledge.

Goodman looked back up the trail leading to Raza's house, then to the cousins leading him over the dam. *Do I even follow these guys? They don't seem to know where to go any more than I do.* He looked at the stars. Polaris was still clearly visible.

The river, the trail, and the dam presented Goodman with a binary choice: cross the dam and go northwest with Mustafa and Radoslav or go back past Raza's house and angle south. He looked over his shoulder. *Southwest is the correct azimuth for the Dalmatian coast. I need to be going that way. Along the river. All rivers lead to the sea, right? But Raza's son said to stay away from the river. Away from the villages. I have no food or supplies, and no functioning weapon. And the people around here obviously don't like foreigners. Again, do I trust these guys enough to follow them?* Goodman watched the boys step cautiously along one of the broken portions of the dam, and water rushed over their feet. But they kept moving. *At least they know who to look for,* he thought. *Which is a load more than what I know.* Goodman lowered himself down the bank and onto the dam. To his right, the stars reflected brightly in the black mirror, and cold spray sprinkled him from roaring foam twenty feet below on his left. He cautiously stepped heel-toe-heel-toe across the top. The ancient masonry stayed true, and he crossed without incident. Mustafa and Radoslav each lowered a hand and heaved him up the far bank.

"Hvala," Goodman thanked them. *Maybe this will be okay*, he thought.

"Mali problemi," said Mustafa. *Small problems.*

The trio passed over the next mountain without seeing another house or farm until the valley on the far side. It was then that they found what Mustafa called the "Christian's house" on a hillside above a series of cultivated clearings. A dirt lane snaked through the fields from somewhere unseen. Radoslav and Goodman hid behind a woodpile while Mustafa approached the front door and knocked.

A man opened the door with a hunting rifle in his hand. There was a brief exchange of hushed words, and Mustafa waved them forward.

"Ne reci ništa," Radoslav whispered. *Say nothing.*

The man peered over Mustafa's shoulder, right at Goodman and Radoslav as they approached.

"Mir na vas," said the man. *Another way of saying 'peace be with you.' The Christian way.* It, too, was spoken in Baba's village. *It seems these people get along as well as the Christians and Mohammedans did in the village. At least on the surface...*

"Mir na vas," replied Mustafa.

Goodman kept his mouth shut.

The boys exchanged more hushed words with the man as he silently closed the door and led them away from the house. The trees thinned, and they could see the black outlines of other farmhouses. They crossed a dew-covered field to another man who was waiting next to a crumbling, stucco-covered building with a hunting rifle across his knees. He stood slowly, and the men greeted one another with hushed voices and kisses on both cheeks.

"He will help you," said the Christian.

The landowner called out, and a girl's voice replied from somewhere inside the house. The men bid farewell to each other, and the Christian disappeared back up the trail.

"Salam alaykum, Effendi," said Mustafa with a hand over his heart. *Peace be with you. The Mohammedan way.*

"Wa-alaykum as-salam," replied the man. He spoke quickly to Radoslav and pointed across the field. A young girl exited the house carrying a wooden box covered with a cloth. "Go with her."

She led them to a hay shed on the far side of the pasture. There, she pulled opened the door and motioned for them to climb a ladder built into the inner wall. Radoslav went first, then Mustafa. Goodman took the box from the girl and handed it up to Mustafa.

"Hvala," Goodman thanked her, glad to be in a place that seems safe again.

She looked at him curiously and said nothing as she departed. Mustafa and Radoslav had already opened the box and were sifting through the contents when Goodman made it to the loft. Mustafa lit a candle and handed it to Goodman while Radoslav distributed handfuls of radishes, chunks of crusty black bread, and several small cuts of salted meat. And the inevitable clay jug of slivovitz. They ate everything in the box, drank the slivovitz like it was water, then pinched the flame and fell asleep in the hay. Each of the boys had made a small nest for himself in the hay, and Goodman followed suit. *This is a lot warmer*, he thought. *The insulation makes sense.* Goodman wrestled with the alcohol as it soaked into his brain. *Where are we going? I think we generally went west-southwest, but I can't tell if I'm making progress toward the coast. Who is Zoran? Who does he work for?* He yawned loudly, then tucked his arm under his head and slept next to his weapon.

# 21

## SEPTEMBER 23, 1943
## A FARM IN NORTHEASTERN BOSNIA, YUGOSLAVIA

STARTLED, GOODMAN OPENED HIS EYES. He clutched the cold metal of his submachine gun. He gasped hard. *What! What's happened?* The one called Mustafa shook him hard.

"My uncle wants to see you," he said.

Goodman exhaled and put his hand to his racing heart, and then to the corroded pistol in his pocket before rubbing his eyes. He exhaled a long breath and rolled over, slung the strap of his weapon over his shoulder, and climbed down the ladder on stiff and painful legs. He reached the floor and faced several armed and bearded men. One man dwarfed the others, but it was difficult to tell by how much because he had to stoop to avoid the low rafters. He turned and looked at Goodman in the eyes.

"So, you are the American airplane driver who drops the bombs on the Germans." The man had a voice as big as his frame. "Salam alaykum."

"Wa-alaykum as-salam, Effendi," said Goodman in his most respectful voice. He held out his hand, but the large man just stood there. "Ja sam Captain Good—" Mustafa cut him off.

"My uncle is not effendi, he is *pasha*!" Mustafa whispered into Goodman's ear.

"Ne razumjem."

"Pasha! Zoran Pasha!" Mustafa gestured with his whole hand.

Goodman turned back to Zoran and apologized. "Izvinite, Zoran Pasha." *What is a pasha? I don't know what a pasha is. Jasminka didn't teach me this, and the nurse never mentioned it.* For a brief second, he resented her for it.

"Govorite naš jezik, stranac," said Zoran. *You speak our language.*

And there's that word again, thought Goodman. *Stranac. Foreigner.* Zoran's enormous hand reached for him, and Goodman shook it. Zoran's vice grip crushed Goodman's hand while giving it a single, distinct shake. Goodman did his best to offer a friendly, confident expression, but he felt better when he got his hand back.

"I have teacher," he said. "Ja sam Captain Michael Goodman."

"Ja sam Zoran Pasha Dudovič Mehmetović..." Zoran kept talking, but it was way beyond Goodman's comprehension. It must have shown because Zoran Pasha repeated, slower and louder. Goodman still understood very little.

"Ne razumijem, Zoran Pasha," he said. "I understand only little." He pinched his fingers almost together. Zoran turned to his comrades and laughed. Then he turned, and a rock-hard finger poked Goodman in the chest.

"You no talk, foreigner! You pssst!" Zoran Pasha swept a finger across his lips. "Razumiješ?" *Do you understand?*

"Razumijem," said Goodman. *So this guy doesn't want me talking. I get it. I think. Does he know he's supposed to get me out? Does this guy even know about the escape network? I need to ask him.*

Zoran Pasha lifted his pants by the belt before he turned to his compatriots and said something evidently humorous. Something *stranac* something, he said. The group laughed. Goodman heard it one more time, followed by more laughter. Now it made him self-conscious. He wished he had learned more of their language while he was with Jasminka, though he was not sure what good it would do him in the face of ridicule. From what Goodman could understand, the group commenced discussing how to move him and the cousins, Radoslav and Mustafa, out of the area. Down into the valley, they said. The Tuzla valley. *The valley of the dead people.* Whatever that meant.

The weapons these men carried were as varied as their personal appearances—rifles and submachine guns of German, Italian, Russian, and other European manufacture. Pistols, too. And knives. Bandoleers heavy with ammunition crossed their chests. Each man had one or two of the pineapple-style or German potato masher grenades. The boots and threadbare olive-green wool shirts with epaulets came from some unrecognizable European military stocks. Animal skin vests and long capes covered their shoulders. Fur hats topped matted gray or graying hair. One man was bald.

"Prati me," said Zoran Pasha. *Follow me.*

He and his men retrieved the reins of six horses from the young girl from the night before. Jets of warm breath emanated from the horses' nostrils and swirled into the cool, humid morning air.

"*Stranac*," said Zoran Pasha. "Možeš li jahati?"

Goodman did not know what *jahati* meant. He knew he was being asked if he could do something. Then Zoran bounced his hands up and down together to simulate riding a horse. It would have been comical if Zoran himself did not present such a massive and somewhat terrifying figure. *Ride. Jahati means ride.*

"Da, Zoran Pasha," Goodman pointed at himself. "Jahati konju." *I ride horse.*

*Riding should not be too difficult*, he thought. Though Goodman had not ridden in years, he remembered riding with his family for years as a kid. There were hills there, too, but not like these.

Mustafa took the reins and mounted swiftly, and Radoslav climbed on the same horse with an assist from his cousin. Zoran mounted a massive horse with amazing ease, given his large frame and weight. The others mounted their horses and steered them toward the tree line. Goodman felt the clomp-clomp of hooves through the ground. The immense size of Zoran's horse fit him perfectly, and he towered over Goodman.

"That is good," said Zoran. "You ride." He pointed to a smallish pony with a simple leather saddle and braided rope for a bridle.

Zoran kicked his horse into motion and led the group around the barn out of the pasture through a gap in the fence. Though the sky was fully lit, the sun still sat behind the hills, and the woods were dark. Goodman managed to get his horse to trot and coaxed it alongside Zoran.

"Izvinite, Zoran Pasha," said Goodman. "I have question."

"Da."

"You help me out from Yugoslavia?"

"There is no more Yugoslavia, as you say, stranac," Zoran replied. "There is only Hadž."

"Hadž?"

"Da. Hadž."

"I not know this word."

"It is the place of fire," said Zoran. "It is the place of dzhavo."

*Dzhavo.* Goodman recognized that word from Baba's stories. It meant Devil. Jasminka would tell stories of how Baba's circle of old women from the village would engage in spiritual battle against the unruly imps like the dirty little men, and of their dark master, the Devil. The source of all troubles. The father of all lies. *Dzhavo.* They seemed to take it all very seriously. Goodman inwardly scoffed the first time Jasminka described it to him. But things happened that gave him pause.

"You send me out, da?" Goodman asked again.

Zoran Pasha looked askance at Goodman for a moment. Then, slowly, deliberately, he spoke. "Stranac, the road is not flat. We have many enemies. I will take you to your people, as you say, but first"—he kicked his horse to maintain speed—"for now, your way is my way. Now, šuti."

"Da, Zoran Pasha." Goodman understood enough to know that first, he was supposed to shut up, and second, he was along for the ride. He steered his animal into line behind Mustafa and Radoslav. Horse hooves clip-clopped loudly on the stony ground.

Zoran led them into the dark forest. A sharp two-toned whistle echoed from the darkness, and Zoran replied with two whistles. They proceeded into the midst of a large company of men, also on horseback. The volume of small sounds and glowing cigarettes told Goodman there were at least a hundred men. The group circled around Zoran, and he issued orders. He mentioned something about killing pigs: *Jebene svinje*—fucking pigs—was the precise language he used. Jasminka had loved to teach him the bad words, and they stuck with him.

"We will go into the valley after we do this," Zoran told his men. They murmured in agreement.

*What did that mean?* wondered Goodman. *Do what? What are they going to do first?*

Zoran prodded his horse back onto the track. Two long columns formed behind him. Hundreds of horse hooves clunked heavily on the path. Two horsemen trotted ahead, their horses stumbling slightly as they disappeared into the dark. Goodman caught glimpses of the gray sky as they moved uphill until they reached the crest of a long, narrow ridge. Farms and pastures filled the valleys on both sides. Slight whiffs of fog or white smoke hung low in the cool morning air. They circled a round hilltop, and Zoran raised his hand. The horses came to a halt.

Two other men on horseback passed Zoran and took up position about twenty yards to the front, weapons at the ready. One of them whistled a simple birdcall, which was echoed a second later from a long way down the path. The new arrivals approached.

"Is it as we thought?" said Zoran, not waiting for them to stop.

"Yes, Pasha," said the lead scout in a low voice. "The way is quiet. They number not more than forty, though one man less than an hour ago." He promptly shoved a body off the back of his horse onto the side of the trail. The corpse flopped to the ground like a rag doll. A broken spear protruded from the dead man's chest. His khaki shirt was dark with crimson. Goodman could not help but stare. *They just dumped him right there on the ground.*

It certainly was not the first time Goodman had seen a dead body. His first experience was seeing a cousin who had been caught in a cattle stampede. He was ten years old. Then in Africa, there had been dozens of bodies on stretchers or in body bags carried away to the Mortuary Affairs tent behind the surgery back at Benghazi Field. But there, the bodies were treated with reverence, piety, even. The bodies of dead Italian and German soldiers were treated with equal respect. Certainly not callously dumped on the ground in a heap.

"Very good," said Zoran. "Bog hoće." *God wills it.* Another of Baba's sayings.

Zoran and his scouts reined their horses around, and the columns quickly resumed a steady pace. The scouts led Zoran and his force down a narrow branch trail that descended steeply from the ridge. They halted and spoke quietly to Zoran, gesturing down into the valley. Zoran scanned the forest and nodded in agreement.

The rising sun lit the uppermost treetops on the far side of the valley with a red tint. Through the trees, Goodman could see a small farm in the middle of a pasture that was at the base of the valley. It was surrounded by numerous tents and several dozen horses divided between two large corrals. Wisps of white smoke hovered over the encampment.

"The fucking pigs are dead," Zoran muttered. "Perfect. You did well." He dismissed his scouts and turned his head to speak and waved to others to approach.

"Foreigner," Zoran grumbled.

"Da, Zoran Pasha," said Goodman.

"Can you shoot that thing?" Zoran pointed at the submachine gun on Goodman's back.

"Da." *What does he want me to do?*

"Good." Zoran swung his pointed finger toward several men dismounting their horses. "Get off your horse and go with those men. Now, you will see justice in Bosnia."

# 22

ZORAN'S HUNDRED OR SO FOLLOWERS DISMOUNTED and readied their weapons. In two waves, they quietly worked their way downhill through the boulders and trees. Zoran continued to issue commands with an urgent but hushed voice. He waved a man over to him. Goodman heard him refer to the man repeatedly as *sochnik* or *sosnik* or something like that. The only thing Goodman understood was that the man was to watch the *stranac*. Me. The foreigner.

"I don't need a nanny," Goodman muttered to himself. When Zoran finally dismissed him, the man lifted his hat to straighten his hair as he approached.

*That's odd*, thought Goodman. The man wore a grimy, well-worn business suit with a tie pulled loose and a hat, like a fedora. *But a suit and tie? Out here?* The man said nothing and motioned for Goodman to follow him.

Another wave of militiamen checked their weapons and adjusted bandoleers and other equipment while two boys took their horses' reins. The boys led the animals some distance to the far edge of a clearing where they let the animals graze on the tall weeds, the reins tied together in a loose knot. *My first ground assault*, thought Goodman. The idea was exciting at first, but then the reality of the situation sank in. *Where do I go? Isn't there some sort of signal, like a whistle or flare or something?* Every war movie he had ever seen rushed through his head. He had no training for this. *I need ammo. I*

112

*know that much*. He turned to follow, but a large hand blocked his way.

Goodman looked past the bandoleers, knives, and perspiration-matted animal fur vest to see a bearded, barrel-chested militiaman pointing to the boys with the horses. Goodman pointed a finger at himself as if to say, *me too?* The man nodded. Goodman shook his head at the man and pointed to himself, and then at the group of men headed downhill. The militiaman growled something at him. Goodman clenched his jaw as he backed down and unshouldered his weapon. *How am I supposed to protect myself without any bullets?* He unlocked the magazine from the receiver and held it for the man to see that it was empty.

"Bez mecima," said Goodman. *No bullets*. He had the Nurse to thank for that bit of vocabulary.

The bearded man ordered a compatriot to give Goodman a full magazine. He did so begrudgingly, and the two of them hurried after the others, who had already disappeared into the woods. Goodman fumbled slightly while inserting the magazine into his weapon. He glanced one more time at the backs of the men headed toward the valley. Goodman took the leather straps in hand and followed the man in the suit. Dew immediately soaked his pants. *Guess I'm watching the horses with the kids*, he thought.

Another group of men approached with their horses and handed their reins to Goodman and the man in the suit. Rather than heading toward the valley, this group of men moved along the road across and out of the clearing.

"They are protecting the rear of the assault force," said the man in the suit. His near-perfect British English caught Goodman by surprise. "You are a bit out of place here in the Majevitsa. How is it you find yourself a guest of the great Zoran Pasha Mehmetović Dudovič?" He paused, but Goodman volunteered nothing. "You are the pilot, yes?"

Goodman cautiously shook his head, not wanting to engage in any conversation. *Zoran said to keep quiet. I've already been outed by one spy. Besides, why is he asking me these questions?*

"No… I think you are." The man took a step toward Goodman. "You do not look like one from the Majevitsa. I assume Zoran told you not to speak. It is not a problem." The man took a drag on his cigarette and blew out through the corner of his mouth. "I also am not from the Majevitsa. Nor do I have the mountain accent. Yours is very different, however. To a farmer or other ignorant peasant, your accent sounds very much like Spanish."

"It does?" asked Goodman. *And when did you hear me talk? I've only spoken to Zoran and the guy who gave me ammo.*

"Yes. That will work well for us, I think."

"If you say so," Goodman said. "What do you mean 'for us?' And how did you know who I am?"

"My name is Marić, Tomislav Marić." He extended his hand to Goodman, who shook it. "Please call me Tomislav."

"My name is Goodman," he said. "How did you know who I am?"

Tomislav raised his finger and reached into his inner breast pocket. He offered Goodman a crooked, slender, hand-rolled cigarette. *I haven't had one of those in two months.* The craving came back immediately. He took it as Tomislav clicked his lighter. Goodman took only one puff, and a wave of hot, acrid smoke immediately assaulted his throat and sinuses. Several hot strands of tobacco burned his tongue. The heat seared his throat and made him cough. His eyes watered as he cleared his throat and spit several times.

"Yes, my sentiments exactly." Tomislav patted Goodman on the back as he spit on the ground.

"What the hell *is* that?" Goodman scowled as he wiped his mouth on his sleeve.

"The local tobacco houses learned the *beedi* method from the Bulgarians, and the Bulgarians learned from the Turks, who soak the tobacco in spice as a sealant. It does not last long, and so it is stupid, but it is their way." He drew on his own cigarette and let the smoke puff out of his mouth.

The nicotine hit came in a sudden rush and he felt a swirling sensation that relaxed him. He blinked his mind back to steadiness. *This is about as bad as the stuff the Arabs smoked outside the gates at Benghazi*, he thought. *Tastes terrible.* Goodman picked several more strands from the tip of his tongue and took another puff. "This is all that is available here in the hill country. The cities have better, but"—he waved his hand to the forest—"we are not in the cities."

The last of the militia interrupted them by forming up and picking their way through the woods toward the valley.

"So, we just stay here with the kids and watch the horses?"

"Yes," said Tomislav. "We will bring the horses down when the attack is complete." He paused to take a drag. "Your rank is captain, yes?" Again, the directness of the question was unsettling to Goodman.

"Yes, how did you know?" Tomislav pointed to the dirty, but distinct silver twin bars of the U.S. Army insignia for the officer rank of Captain. Goodman tucked his collar back inside his coat.

"Do not worry," Tomislav said. "I will not broadcast it. This is a difficult place, and there is no need to make it more so."

"Right," said Goodman. *I don't want to answer any questions*, he thought. He pretended to spit out another strand of tobacco. "What was it that Zoran called you? *Soch-nik?*"

Tomislav laughed out loud. "You caught that, did you? Your Bosanski is better than one would think. Yes, he calls me a součeznik. It means actor or pretender."

"Why does he call you that?"

"Because that is what I am. I'm an actor." He touched the brim of his hat and tipped it forward, bowing slightly.

"An actor?"

"Yes, you see, I was once a stage performer at the Zagreb National Theater Company. That is in Croatia, far away from this place. I have performed all over Europe to audiences of hundreds that have included kings, prime ministers, ambassadors, generals, admirals, and other various forms of bourgeois aristocracy." He paused for a second. "I was quite good, nearly famous, mind you."

"*Nearly* famous…?"

"I have played many supporting roles, but I was never the lead in any production," he confessed. "I was the lead understudy for Hamlet in the company's 1938 production in Madrid. Yes, that was the peak of my career before Germany invaded Poland. Everything changed after that." He looked at Goodman. "You know Shakespeare, yes?"

Goodman really knew nothing about Shakespeare or anything else that he was supposed to have read in secondary school. He decided to play it off. "Not personally," he said.

"Not personally?" Tomislav laughed. "Yes, we will do very well together." A yellow-toothed smile spread across his face. He took a long drag on the remaining half-cigarette. "Seriously, do you know of Shakespeare in America?"

"Well, yes," said Goodman. "Americans know about Shakespeare."

"But you are not a patron of the theater?"

Goodman looked at Tomislav. *Do I trust this guy with anything about me?* he thought. Not sure what he was looking for, Goodman searched Tomislav's face for something—anything—that would indicate what was in store if he answered truthfully. *Do I lie? But then, what difference would it make? He already knows the basics: I'm here, I'm an American pilot, and an officer. If someone wanted to kidnap me and deliver me to the Germans, there's all the info they need to verify. And it's not like he was searching for me. After all, he wasn't the guy who was coming to Baba's village at night and talking to that girl, telling her to find me. He didn't find me. I came to these guys with those two kids from miles away. It's pure chance that I'm here.* Goodman shrugged it off.

"My family is," Goodman finally admitted. "Well, my mother is. But I was a student before the war. I didn't have a whole lot of time for theater." His cigarette had burned out, and Tomislav flicked the lighter again for him. "What other languages do you speak besides English and Bosanski?"

"Technically, I speak Croatian, as I am from Istria. But you would not know that," Tomislav mused. "I also speak German, Hungarian, my French is good, and Italian, of course…"

"Of course," Goodman chimed in. "So how does a *nearly famous* actor find his way to…wherever we are right now?"

"We are in the Majevitsa mountains," Tomislav replied. He took a moment to answer. "Not all politics are acceptable to the fascists. In fact, only fascist politics are acceptable to fascists. I'm the wrong kind of socialist." He took another drag and continued. "I had occasion to learn Spanish a few years ago, but my skills are a bit rusty," Tomislav admitted as he attempted to light his next cigarette from the embers of his current one. He failed and drew his lighter again. "And you? Do Americans speak languages other than English?"

"Well, I speak some Spanish, but it's Mexican Spanish. My mother is Mexican. I grew up in Texas."

"Is that in Mexico?"

"No, it's in the United—"

The sound of machine guns tore the morning quiet to pieces.

# 23

HUMANS AND HORSES JUMPED at the sudden cacophony of gunfire from the valley. Birds flew into the air, cawing and screeching as the ripsaw of machine guns shattered the morning air. Goodman, Tomislav, and the two boys fought to maintain their hold on the reins of the panicking horses. The volume of gunfire was tremendous and lasted for almost a full minute, transmitting layer upon layer of echoes throughout the woods and reverberating off the far side of the valley. After a brief pause, they heard several explosions and more gunfire. The machine guns let up, and the smaller cracks of rifles and staccato puttering of submachine guns took over. Then there was the popping of pistol shots. A machine gun opened up again with a final, long burst of fire that echoed in the valley for an absurdly long time. There was one last crack of a rifle, then silence except for Zoran's voice booming out from the valley.

"Well," said Tomislav. He smothered his cigarette with his shoe. "That is that."

Two more pistol shots rang out in the valley. A man yelled out, and another pistol cracked.

"Oh, yes," said Tomislav, blowing a thread of smoke into the air. "And then there's that."

"What was that?" asked Goodman.

"Zoran does not take Ustaša prisoners."

"Whoa," said Goodman. "They're executing prisoners down there?"

"Well, yes." Tomislav shrugged.

The thought made Goodman uneasy. *Is everyone here psychotic? The Germans murdered the women in the village. These guys murder prisoners.* He smothered his cigarette butt and listened intently to the sounds of men shouting. Then he heard another rifle crack. But this one was from the north, across the clearing rather than down in the valley to the south. Goodman and Tomislav looked at each other in alarm.

"That was from over there!" Goodman pointed across the clearing.

Several more shots rang out, and the boys abandoned their horses. They ran toward Goodman, pointing into the woods behind them.

"Run!" they yelled.

Bullets snapped overhead, and the horses jerked at the knot that bound them together in a wild-eyed panic. Goodman froze. *What happened to all the men who went that way? The enemy is in the valley!* Gunfire blasted his ears. Tomislav yelled something, and Goodman dropped to the ground and scurried away from the attack on his hands and knees.

Four of Zoran's militiamen sprinted past him. Goodman turned back to look for the remainder of the militia who had gone that way. *That's it? There should be at least ten of them.* Several black-clad men with rifles and large black caps emerged from the woods. Goodman flinched at the snap of a bullet launched by a tiny, yellow-white muzzle flash. He stumbled backward, caught himself, and ran into the woods after Tomislav.

Tree branches snapped into pieces and bullets smacked into tree trunks, sending Goodman's heart racing as he scrambled to get away. A tree right in front of him threw bark at his face. He sprinted over the rocks and took cover behind a fallen tree not more than twenty-five yards into the woods. Tomislav was already there, hiding in a nook between the large trunks, a pistol drawn.

Goodman looked toward the valley. He saw no one coming to meet the attack and shrank behind the tree. The attackers called out to each other as they probed into the tree line, coming to within a few yards of Goodman and Tomislav. Two of them argued, and the remainder continued into the woods toward the valley. Goodman clutched the weapon to his chest and tried to calm his breathing. He dared not look over the tree trunk. *Keep your head, dammit! Stay down, keep yourself together and you'll get out of here alright.*

Then, a boy's voice cried out. Goodman could hear footfalls of men running toward him. One boy climbed over the fallen tree that concealed Goodman and Tomislav and kept running. A moment later, several of the black-clad attackers leapt over the tree in pursuit. *Maybe they'll keep on going. Maybe Zoran and his men will get them.*

Goodman peered over the top of the tree and saw that they had caught the boy. One man had his foot on the boy's chest, and another was poking the boy's face with his rifle's hot muzzle. The boy screamed and struck at the man's leg futilely. He begged them to stop.

"Are you going to use that?" Tomislav growled and pointed at Goodman's weapon.

Goodman stood up and aimed his submachine gun at the cluster of men. He squeezed the trigger. Nothing happened. Goodman looked at his weapon. *What the hell is wrong with it? It's loaded. I don't get it. Stupid thing's jammed.* The attackers glanced up and saw him. Two of them raised their rifles, and he fell backward against the tree.

From very close range, several pistol shots sent the attackers scrambling for cover. One of the black-clad men fell onto the rocks. Another slumped against a tree. His rifle clattered against the stone and slid away from him. Goodman looked up in amazement at Tomislav, standing fully upright with his arm outstretched. His pistol cracked again. One more attacker went down. Several rifle shots sent Tomislav behind the tree next to Goodman again.

119

"Here!" Tomislav reached over to Goodman's weapon and flipped the bolt lever out of the safe position. "Now, shoot something!"

Goodman rose to his knees and peered cautiously over the tree trunk while Tomislav reloaded his pistol. At first, there was no sign of anyone except for the boy still lying on the ground, whimpering in pain. Suddenly, three attackers emerged, and Goodman squeezed his trigger and sprayed bullets across them. The lot of them went down. One survivor retreated on his hands and knees until Tomislav stood and put him down with several shots. More gunfire ensued, but this time from the opposing direction. The forest suddenly filled with Zoran's militiamen firing as they moved from tree to tree. Tomislav ducked down next to him.

"Stay down!" Tomislav yelled over the gunfire. Goodman sank next to him. They hid until Zoran's militia ran past them toward the clearing.

His ears ringing, Goodman peered over the tree. The black-clad attackers were still down. Goodman approached slowly with his weapon raised, sweeping the muzzle back and forth across the attackers' bodies. Most had just crumpled to the ground in a heap. Two others looked around frantically, gasping for air, their black uniforms shiny with fresh blood. Tomislav stepped over a rock and fired one more angry shot into each of them and watched them expire. Dark red stains expanded across the rocks. Goodman stood up to get a better look, captivated by the sight of the blood and the men's frozen expressions on their faces. He wanted to look away but found he could not. *They were okay just a minute ago. Sure, they would have killed me, but...I got them first. Tomislav actually got them first. Then I did. This isn't war—what is this? Okay, don't overthink this. This isn't me. This isn't my doing. I had to do this.* He felt satisfaction that he had indeed killed these men who would have killed him. Even so, this is not what he was trained for. *I'm not even supposed to be here.*

One of them groaned and moved slightly. Goodman stumbled, surprised that such a horribly wounded man could still be alive. The man clutched at his rifle with clumsy, blood-covered hands. He tried to raise it at Goodman, but it slipped from his fingers and slid away from him. Then Goodman got a good look at his face. *He's just a kid! He can't even be fifteen.* Goodman felt himself withdraw. The boy's eyes were wild with fright. *Do I help him?* Goodman's medical training rushed into his head.

"You need to finish him." Tomislav pointed at the dying boy.

"But he's—"

"Do it!"

Goodman hesitated.

"Do it!"

Goodman barely aimed and fired his last four rounds into the boy's bloody body. He died with a loud rush of air and a groan. Goodman stood transfixed for a moment before he heard the other boy crying. *I just killed a wounded kid.* Goodman was angry with himself. *What's wrong with me? That's wrong where I come from. Immoral. And it's a war crime according to the Geneva Conventions.* He felt a knot in his stomach. The militia boy next to the rock cried out, and Goodman went to him. *Maybe this one I can help...*

The boy's face was full of fear, his chest heaving rapidly. He looked to be alright—except for the two singed and bleeding welts on his cheek. *Kids killing kids.* Goodman felt sick and angry that these boys were made to fight on both sides of this war. His doctor's mind kicked in finally, and he reached to examine the wounds. *This won't be too bad to keep clean.* He turned the boy's head to examine the other side, but the boy swatted Goodman's hands away. He rose on his own and gave Goodman a hard shove that knocked him off balance. The boy let loose with a string of curses and stomped off through the rocky ground, wiping his tears. Goodman stood up to follow, but Tomislav stopped him.

"Let the boy go."

Goodman stepped back to watch him leave. He felt a wave of anger at both the boy and Tomislav. *Who the hell fights like this? These are just kids.* He wanted to strike out at someone, anyone. If he had had it, he would have fired another entire magazine into the air just for the power of it. He wanted to fight. To do something, anything, with his anger. He didn't know what he wanted to do.

Someone shook his shoulder. Goodman's head spun like it was on a hair-trigger.

"You must breathe, American Captain." It was Tomislav. "Breathe."

Goodman blinked and shook the awful feeling away. Tomislav was right. He blew a long breath outward.

He looked down to see Tomislav rummaging through the dead men's clothing and equipment. Tomislav took a pouch of tobacco from one dead man and a pair of glasses from another after peering through the lenses. He yanked a body over and opened the man's shirt and pocketed the cash from his wallet, which he then tossed aside.

"What are you waiting for?" said Tomislav. He gestured at the next body.

Goodman took the hint. He shouldered his submachine gun and knelt to pick up one of the attackers' weapons of similar design. It was identical, in fact. German made. He changed his empty magazine for a fresh one from the leather ammo pouch still looped around the dead man's neck. Goodman then took the entire ammo pouch and put the strap around his own neck. Otherwise, the man had only an identification book. Ivo Manić, born 1912, from some unpronounceable town. Goodman could only read what Jasminka had taught him from Baba's own tattered identity book.

Several militiamen ran past. Goodman was shocked when several of them pulled knives and hatchets from their belts and set to slashing necks and smashing skulls. Blood-splattered and grunting heavily, the men moved off toward the clearing to search for more victims. *I'm going to vomit*, he thought. He looked away and breathed deeply for a moment. But then his eyes went back to the bodies. He flinched at what he saw.

"Why do they do that?"

"The same reason I told you to finish him." Tomislav began to remove boots and pistol belts from the bodies. "Only then do we know that none of them are pretending to be dead." He extracted several rings from the fingers of the man in front of him and pocketed them. "None of them will come back to recognize us and kill us." He fished through a leather pouch before tossing it aside and untied the dead man's boots. "And so that their families will be reminded of what happens to all who fight us, if the bodies are ever returned to their homeland." He dropped the boots in a pile at the feet of one of the deceased.

Goodman held his breath and was opening another dead man's jacket when he heard horses clip-clop over the rocks. Zoran dismounted and stepped over the large rocks with long strides. He looked grim.

"Did you do this?" Zoran dismounted and stepped over the bodies as he strode toward Goodman. He could barely understand the rest of what Zoran was saying.

"Zoran says that you stopped a bad thing," Tomislav translated. "That God has blessed you—and us—today."

Goodman exhaled with relief. Zoran gestured again at the bizarre arrangement of bodies on the ground. He spoke, and Tomislav translated again. "You stopped the pigs…God hates the pigs…he smiles when they get butchered." Then he added, "Ustaša. Nazi swine. Those are the pigs."

Goodman tried to speak but his Bosanski failed him, and Zoran cut him off.

"Yes, I know some of my men are *kukavice*." He grumbled out loud as he glared at the groups of militiamen now making their way back to their horses. Everyone noticeably avoided eye contact with him.

Goodman got Tomislav's attention. "What's a *kukavice*?"

"It means cowards," said Tomislav. "Or traitors. Zoran hates cowards and traitors. He thinks they are just different words for the same thing." He crammed a wad of looted bills into his pocket. "He's going to punish the men who failed to stop the attack against us from the rear."

"Did he say that? How do you know that?"

"He will." Tomislav tilted his head toward Zoran. "Just wait."

Zoran's eyes locked onto the four men as they rummaged through bodies by the large rock, and he strode quickly to them. They alerted to his approach, but too late to avoid getting grabbed. Zoran caught one and punched him in the back of the head, sending him headlong into the dirt. He tried to get away, but Zoran grabbed him again and heaved him into the air. He landed over a log with a loud exhale and did not get up again. His friends sprinted into the trees.

"*Kukavice!*" Zoran's voice echoed throughout the forest. "Milosz!"

"Yes, Zoran Pasha," came the reply from a man about half the size of Zoran.

"Milosz, get them!" He pointed at the retreating men. "Bring them to me!"

"Yes, Zoran Pasha."

The man called Milosz marched off, barking at others to round up the fleeing men.

Zoran knelt to pick up the boy with the welts on his face and held his head in his giant hands to inspect the burns. "Yes, I think you will not forget this day, eh?"

"Neh, Amidža Zoran," said the boy, wiping his tears and wincing at the pain of the raw skin on the side of his face. The boy spoke at length, half crying, half so full of rage he could barely speak. At one point, he pointed at Goodman and then jabbed his finger into the air and at the ground like he was shooting a pistol at the dead bodies. Goodman's heart sank. *I hope he's not telling Zoran about Tomislav yelling at me to shoot the wounded.* Zoran patted the boy's head rather roughly as he looked at the bodies on the ground around him. And then he looked at Goodman before he turned back to the boy. Goodman quietly cursed at himself for not being more aggressive. *These guys obviously don't value human life very much. What is Zoran going to do to me?*

"What do you think of this?" Zoran asked the boy.

The boy spit on the body nearest him, then winced as the skin pulled on his raw burns.

"Good boy," said Zoran. "Now get your friends and gather the horses."

"Da, Amidža!" exclaimed the boy, still fighting back tears. He ran off, blowing his nose on the ground and wiping his eyes as he went.

The man called Milosz returned with the three runaways under armed guard. They looked at their compatriot, who still had not lifted his head after getting thrown over the log. To Goodman, they looked like someone had just shot their dog in front of them. Milosz ordered the armed men to back off, which they did. Most of the others in the surrounding woods tried to avoid looking, but not Goodman. He stood transfixed by the suspense playing out before him.

Zoran towered over the threesome and put his hands on his holster and sword hilt.

"Look at me!" His voice boomed.

The men flinched and looked up at him, their knees quaking. Zoran raised a pumpkin-sized fist and slammed it into the face of the first man. He flew backward and fell to the ground. The others flinched again, including Goodman.

"Do not move!" Zoran's voice boomed again.

By now, everyone had turned to watch. Zoran's second swing hit the next man hard enough to lift him more than a foot off the ground. He collapsed with a great rush of wind out of his lungs and curled up on the rocky soil. The third man's knees shook as he braced. Yet he straightened up and locked eyes with Zoran.

With his fist still hanging eight feet in the air, Zoran demanded something of the man. The man stood stone still.

*What is he saying?* thought Goodman. He prompted Tomislav to translate, which he did in a hushed voice. "Zoran dares the man to fight him. He asked why he stands firm now after running like a coward in the battle."

The man in front of Zoran said nothing, but instead raised his right hand. Two narrow bones protruded from the bloody, raw flesh where the middle, ring, and little fingers used to be. Zoran's expression changed. Then he raised his other hand, which was also covered in blood.

"This is Ustaša blood!" the man cried out, almost sobbing.

Zoran lowered his fist and stood fully upright. "This is a man!" he declared to the forest and the men in it. Tomislav translated again. "Though slightly less of one now that some of his parts are gone." Zoran smiled at his own joke. No one else did. "Now someone stop this man's blood from leaving his body." He turned back to the man in front of him. "Good thing you still have your trigger finger."

"Da, Zoran Pasha," replied the man.

A young militiaman with a medic bag over his shoulder ran up and assisted the man to the ground. The injured man raised his hand to let the medic do his work and proceeded to pass out. The medic caught his head before it hit the rocky ground and laid it down carefully. Goodman instinctively moved to assist, but held back.

Zoran turned to Milosz and pointed to the men he punched. "I don't want to see these men again. From now on, they work with the animals."

Milosz looked at them still lying on the ground. "Yes, Zoran Pasha."

Zoran motioned to Goodman. "You!"

Goodman froze. *Oh, no! Am I next?*

"You do not work with the animals! You may fight with the men. Do you want to stay with the animals?"

"N-Neh, Zoran Pasha…"

"Good! Do you want to see who this was?" He pointed into the valley. "Do you want to see the men who attacked you on the road?"

Goodman's mind raced to put together a sentence in Bosanski. "Men no Germans?" he asked.

"No, these pigs are much more dangerous than the Nazis."

# 24

THREE MEN FROM ZORAN'S GROUP NOW LAY DEAD in the field next to their dead horses. A short distance away, near some tents and a small cluster of farm buildings, most of which were now burned or on fire, lay dozens of dead, black-clad soldiers similar to those who had attacked Goodman and Tomislav in the clearing.

Closer to the farm buildings and tents, the setting assaulted Goodman's senses. First was the vague, uncertain vision of dead bodies covered in blood partly obscured by tall grasses. And then the dark, shiny blood on the ground. Lots of blood on the ground. Carcasses of dead horses were intermingled with the men's bodies. Discarded rifles and hats littered the grass around the bodies. So many bodies. Some severely mutilated, split open, entrails spilled out onto the ground. And there were women's bodies, too. His head spun with the clouds of flies that cast swirling shadows on the morning grass. *These guys are raging lunatics*, thought Goodman. *How does someone fight this way?*

He squinted his eyes and wrinkled his nose as he tried to stifle his gag reflex as his senses reeled from the acrid combination of smells. He followed Zoran to a muddy, manure-littered animal pen.

Zoran said something to him he did not understand. Zoran abruptly gestured for Tomislav to translate.

"Do you recognize any of these men?"

Goodman immediately regretted it when he saw them—hands tied behind their backs, throats slit, and agony etched into their faces. Goodman heaved dry eruptions of stinging bile with his hands on his knees. He spit and forced himself to stand to see what Zoran wanted him to see. He wiped his eyes and, finally, he did recognize the dead men. They were the stretcher bearers from the original group that took him from Jasminka's village only the day before. The lieutenant was there, too, also dead. His arms and legs were bound, and his boots were missing. All their boots were missing. *What is it with the boots? How did everyone end up here?*

"What…why are they here?" Goodman asked Tomislav, who then translated for Zoran.

"They were going to be sold to the Germans," said Tomislav after Zoran's matter-of-fact reply. "This detachment of Ustaši were going to sell these people to the Nazis. They killed them when we attacked so they could not be released."

"But why?" exclaimed Goodman. "Why would they be here, tied up like this?"

"If you do not have a gun, you are like cattle," Tomislav repeated Zoran's words. "You are for sale or for slaughter."

*Okay, I understand that*, thought Goodman. *But these people all live here.* "Ask Zoran why would the Yugoslavs do this to each other," he said.

"That might not be a good idea," said Tomislav.

"Ask him."

Tomislav turned to Zoran. Zoran's eyes shifted from Tomislav to Goodman.

"Listen to me, stranac," Zoran spoke to Goodman, and barely gave Tomislav time to translate. "There are no Yugoslavs, as you say. Not anymore. The Germans have invaded, and the Ustaši"—Tomislav paused in the translation—"the Ustaši sold their souls to the gods of fascism to make Croatia rule over Yugoslavia. Then there are Marshall Tito's communist bastards who want to make our homeland into a worker's paradise or some such nonsense. They will make us slaves to the Russians. From across River Drina, the Chetnik pigs want to restore their kingdom." Tomislav paused when Zoran did. "They all want to control Yugoslavia, and perhaps more. But none of them have room for us in their Greater Serbia, Greater Croatia, or whatever they want to call it.

"Right now, the Ustaši are more…how you say, zealous, yes? Yes, much more zealous than the Nazis in their pursuit of power, but we kill Nazis and Communists, too, when we—" Tomislav cleared his throat. "—run out of Ustaši to kill." He gestured at the bodies and burning houses. He cleared his throat and spit a wad of phlegm onto a nearby body.

"So, who are you?" asked Goodman. "I mean, what do you fight for?"

"I fight for my people," Zoran proclaimed, gesticulating with an outstretched arm. "We are of the Majevitsa, and this is my family, my army. These are my hills. I command ten thousand fighters from the mountains of Bosnia. We fight to restore our home."

Goodman looked around at Zoran's men and boys sorting through the detritus. He did not see ten thousand fighters. He estimated about a hundred at the most. "So, who were these people?" he asked.

"These are the pigs who attacked you on the Tetima road," said Zoran. "These are the Ustaši, one and all." Zoran looked at the surrounding hills as he finished his thought. "These are *our* hills, *our* land. But here, now, they hunt us. So, we kill them. Život za život."

*Život za život.* Goodman remembered Baba's words. This is what she was talking about: a life for a life. Simultaneously the cause for forgiveness for past transgressions and the excuse for perpetrating blood feuds that have spanned generations. *This is the other side of what Baba was talking about,* thought Goodman. The ironic and terrible play on words had made Baba cry. Now, seeing it in action—again—with his own eyes, he saw why. *These are people who live here killing their neighbors. And in the cruelest ways possible.*

"Hey! Hey!"

The sudden exclamation jerked Goodman's head around. A militiaman was in the pen holding the executed prisoners, examining something. Or somebody. Goodman was the second to join him, right after Mustafa leapt the fence. Together, they knelt in the mud next to the body, and Goodman saw the ankle-length, striped skirt covered in mud and blood. His heart pounded. *The girl spy.* Her arms were bound and there was a cloth over her eyes. A large patch of blood covered her back. Goodman searched for the source of the bleeding, and he found two holes in her back, both of which penetrated through to her front. He immediately searched for something to stop the bleeding, but a strong hand grabbed his arm. It was Mustafa who gripped him.

"Pasha! Pasha!" Mustafa yelled excitedly, but the rest of what he said was beyond Goodman's understanding. Goodman felt the firmness of Mustafa's grip, restraining him from touching the girl. *He doesn't want me to stop the bleeding*, he thought. *They want her to die.*

Zoran's shadow fell over Goodman and the girl. "Ko je ona?" *Who is she?*

"She's the spy from the village, Pasha," said Mustafa.

Zoran put his hands on his hips. "So, this is she." He looked at Goodman. And Goodman looked down at the girl.

Mustafa released his grip on Goodman's sleeve and stood next to Zoran.

"What does she know?" Zoran asked.

"Him." Mustafa pointed at Goodman.

"What else?"

Mustafa shrugged and Zoran stroked his beard. "If she breathes, we must know." He waved to the man he called Milosz. He approached with two more men.

*The girl's barely conscious*, thought Goodman. *She's not even close to being able to speak, let alone answer questions. How could they think of interrogating her in this condition?* Goodman shook his head. Knowing the conditions in which they treated the wounded, he figured she would be better off if she died quickly.

Milosz climbed over the broken fence and examined her. He turned her head and pried open an eyelid before letting her head hit the mud again. "Who are you?" barked Milosz. The girl was silent. "Nište," said Milosz.

"Nište," Zoran repeated. "Kill her."

"What?" Goodman blurted out. Tomislav pulled at his arm.

Zoran turned away with Milosz, who gestured to his men. One man drew his pistol from under his belt and shot her. Goodman was the only one who flinched. Then the man replaced his pistol and casually stepped over the fence the way he had come.

Goodman was speechless. *He just did that.*

Tomislav tugged on his sleeve again. "Let us leave here…"

Goodman stood and followed, absent any reasoned purpose, unable to get beyond replaying in his head what he saw. *Her mother knew what was coming*, he thought. *Somehow, she knew.* Tomislav led him back through the camp to where the militia piled newly liberated horse-drawn wagons and several donkeys with newly liberated weapons and supplies. Men laughed about the treasure trove now in their possession. Goodman watched and listened to the grotesque looting spree, still feeling sick. He spit several times but failed to get the spicy taste out of his mouth.

"How can he do that?" Goodman blurted to Tomislav.

"Do what?" said Tomislav flatly. "Kill a person who spies for the enemy?"

"Yeah."

"What do you propose to do with spies?" said Tomislav. "What should we do with her? Take her to a hospital? Build her a house? Spies are more damaging than a thousand armed soldiers. Excellent spies are worth ten thousand or more." He paused. "Or one American pilot."

"Maybe..."

"You are new here," said Tomislav. "Perhaps you should simply do what I tell you and keep yourself to...yourself."

Goodman looked back at the girl. *He's right*. He looked at the men and boys scavenging through the belongings of the newly dead. Then it occurred to him that he, too, should gather more ammunition and whatever else he could use.

Goodman went to his knees and picked through the bodies lying around him outside the pen. He avoided looking at the faces. The first was thoroughly picked over. The next body he came to was barely recognizable as a woman's body. He was instantly repulsed by what he saw and withdrew.

*Oh, my God. I can't believe I'm doing this. But I need to eat.*

He moved to the next body, where he withdrew a box of matches from the inner pocket of the man's coat, but to his horror, his hand came back to him covered in blood. He frantically wiped his hands and the box on the grass before stuffing it into his pocket. He picked up and discarded a lice-infested hat and pocketed a lighter that did not work. *Maybe I can trade this*, he thought. He kicked aside a blood-saturated leather ammunition pouch, and one of Zoran's men snatched it up and slung it over his shoulder. Two other men fought briefly over a lambskin coat, slinging curses and punches at one another. The first one came up with the coat in the end. Goodman returned to his own half-hearted looting spree but came up empty-handed except for a thread-bare blanket, the empty lighter, and the matches.

Another militiaman slapped Goodman on the shoulder. Goodman's eyes followed the pointed finger to a line of loaded pack animals. Tomislav was already there, holding a rope tied to two skinny, mangy horses loaded down with crates of wilted greens. He welcomed Goodman with a somber face and a cigarette in his mouth. He held up a second cigarette, already burning, and offered it to Goodman.

"It will help with the smell."

Goodman took it and drew in a long, scorching drag. It burned. He coughed, then spit out a few tobacco strands and drew in again. The swirling sensation was almost immediate. He forced his mind to other places and other times as the sunlight scrolled across the field of bodies that littered the valley floor.

Holding the horse made him think of home on the wide-open back range, with all of Texas spread out for miles and miles. Camping with his siblings, watching out for his kid sister, Maria. But the world around him forced itself upon him. The dark hair of a dead woman a few yards away reminded him of his last image of the nurse. Her bloodied backside and crazy, wild eyes. Then he thought about Jasminka and her tearful, pallid expression as he backed away from her just moments before he departed her village. He shook away the memories, but the dark, furious look in Baba's eyes stayed with him.

*What am I doing here?* he thought. *How am I going to make it through this? I need to get out of this place.* He remembered the reprimand his commander was about to sign for neglecting his administrative duties, after just having been promoted to flight lead. He remembered how threatening that document was for him then. *God, I wish I had taken that butt chewing right then and there. I can't believe I actually argued with the colonel,* he recalled. *I got my way. I kept my position as flight lead. And now…now, I'm here.* He subconsciously shook his head.

*I should have kept my mouth shut. Then I would have been in a different place in the formation over Ploesti and…and I wouldn't be here.* Goodman became lost in thought, and it was the bright orange flash and acrid smell of kerosene ignition that jerked him back to the here and now. Zoran's people torched the entire farm, bodies included. The sudden heat wave made him blink. Unable to tear his eyes away from the flames, he took another long drag on the bitter cigarette and coughed it out. He wished he had done something, everything, differently that morning back in August. *I should not have argued. I should have taken that reprimand. And the demotion.*

He took another drag and blew it out. *But now…now, anything to get out of here. Anything.* He cleared his throat and spit to get the taste out.

*This place is hell.*

# 25

## A VALLEY IN THE OUTER MAJEVITSA RANGE

SANCTUARY LAY SOMEWHERE AHEAD, at least according to what Tomislav had said. The sky had turned orange, and the valley was cast into darkness. Zoran's lieutenants rousted their men from their rest break. Goodman stood up and stretched and lent a hand to help Tomislav to his feet. In short order, the brigade was moving again. By last twilight, they had trudged up a dirt road that snaked over a heavily forested hillside, giving the wagons and the wounded a tough go of it. They crossed over the ridgeline and proceeded down the other side just as the last gray light faded into another clear, starry night. The moon cast the countryside in shades of blue-gray-black, punctuated with the rare yellow twinkle of a distant fire.

The columns merged into a long, slow, single file as they passed over a rough stone bridge. The men guarding the bridge greeted the brigade loudly, and the men exchanged handshakes and shoulder slaps as they passed. They had passed a frontier, some kind of boundary. *This must be the safe area*, thought Goodman, his thoughts limited to sleep. Or food. Food and then sleep. *Yes*, he thought. *Food and then sleep.*

Finally, the long, tired procession veered off the road and into a broad pasture. Campfires glowed everywhere. A farmer directed the pack animals to a large barn on the far side of a field.

Open at both ends and well-lit inside, the interior of the barn was piled high with weapons, ammunition, and crates and bags of supplies. Goodman mimicked what he saw others doing and unloaded his horse. When he finished, he followed Tomislav out of the barn.

"I will find us a place to sleep," Tomislav said. "And some food."

"Okay, thanks," Goodman replied, but Tomislav was already out of earshot. "I'll… I'll just wait here."

Men meandered off and formed small groups. Each group met up with comrades who sat in circles around the fires. Someone started playing a ukulele or similar stringed instrument, and a voice crooned into the night. The smell of roasting meat and vegetables filled Goodman's nostrils and made his stomach growl.

"Here," said Tomislav, handing Goodman a jug with some liquid sloshing inside. "Have a drink."

Goodman lifted the jug and immediately smelled the burnt metallic sugar smell of slivovitz. He took a drink and winced as the liquid fire passed over his pallet and assaulted his throat and nasal cavity. Goodman closed his eyes as the warmth descended upon his empty stomach with a vengeance, then emanated across his body to his extremities. His head swam. *I'm already drunk*, he thought. Two days of almost no food, a lot of exertion, and only a little water.

"Milosz!" boomed Zoran.

"Da, Zoran Pasha!" The short, bald man stepped to Zoran's side with Tomislav behind him.

"Get our stranac something to eat." Zoran turned to Goodman. "You… eat!" he boomed, pointing and then making a cup with one hand and a scooping motion with the other.

Milosz conferred quietly with Tomislav and another person, who was invisible to Goodman. Tomislav shifted his weight and, in so doing, he revealed the third person, who was partly illuminated by a nearby fire. Goodman saw long, dark hair pulled back into a ponytail under a folded garrison cap. *A woman! What is a woman doing in this group? She must be another nurse.* She looked at Goodman over Tomislav's shoulder.

She held herself differently. She stood with confidence, speaking briskly with the two men. Her peaked military field cap was slightly crooked and formed an apex to her narrow, bony face. The ambient blue moonlight on one side of her face and the orange of the firelight on the other made her face appear to be of two different people. His male instinct struggled to determine if she was pretty or not. Suddenly, he realized she was looking at him.

"Ya!" she barked. The world came racing back to him. She was talking to him.

"Shto?" he managed to say. *What?*

"Jesi li jeo?" *Did you eat?*

"Umm…neh, I no eat," he finally replied.

"I get you food." She turned abruptly. "Prati me." *Follow me.*

She led Goodman and Tomislav to one of the groups of men who were sitting or lying down on the ground, drinking, laughing, and talking loudly around a fire. The men fell silent as they approached, or, rather, as *she* approached.

The woman directed them to give her some of their food. They looked up at her, then they looked at Tomislav and Goodman, and then to their lieutenant, who was still seated. Most of them kept their eyes on their plates. The leader stood and looked her in the eye. She was much shorter than he, but she stood her ground. The man gave her a rebellious salute and stooped to pick up his metal bowl. From the kettle next to the fire, he filled the bowl with some of the meat and several small potatoes and topped it with a ladle full of steamy, droopy greens. He stooped a second time to pour a ladle of broth over it all, making sure it was at her eye level when he did so. She took the bowl and gave it to Tomislav straightaway.

"Još jedan," she commanded. *Another one.*

He took a bowl from the man seated next to him, who protested at first but shrank when his leader threatened to backhand him. He filled the bowl and handed it to the woman.

"Here. Eat," she said to Goodman. He almost dropped the bowl when she shoved it into his hands.

"I will find you in the morning," she said to Tomislav. "Keep him close to you, and let no one speak to him."

Goodman held the bowl of food and watched her walk away. The men around the fire muttered to each other. A couple snickered as she departed. When she was gone, the head man sneered at him and said something Goodman was fairly sure was a pejorative. The whole group laughed out loud. Tomislav tapped on his elbow and led him to a haystack closer to one of the other fires, but still outside the social circle. They sat down with their backs to the hay, just outside of the firelight's reach.

"Hvala," Goodman thanked him.

Tomislav nodded as he slurped at the stew.

"Who *is* that?" Goodman asked.

Tomislav cleared his throat. "For those who speak to her, she is Amira Effendim. And you ought to do what she tells you. Perhaps it is best for you to not speak to her."

"Who is she? Does she have rank or something?"

"Perhaps it is more important for you to eat your food." Tomislav heaved the clay jug and drank the slivovitz. "Here." He handed the jug to Goodman and returned to his plate. "Drink this and ask no more questions. It is time to rest."

Goodman took a gulp from the jug, then shook off the burning in his nostrils and decided he was done with the stuff. He picked out bits of meat and beans with his fingers. *Who is she?*

He used the last of his bread to mop up the greasy broth and tilted the plate over his mouth to suck down the last dribbles. The hot broth ran down his throat. He put down the plate and watched the fires around them. Goodman turned to Tomislav, but he was already buried in the hay, snoring with his hat over his face. Goodman reclined and pulled the ratty blanket around him. It did not cover his feet.

He tossed and turned as his mind played and replayed the events of the last twenty-four hours. This part of the world was more perplexing to him than he had become accustomed in the smallness of Baba's root cellar. Now it felt as if he was paying an additional price for his complacency. He should have tried harder to learn more of the language. He should have asked more questions of Baba. Or the Nurse. So many things seemed contradictory. Like Baba keeping the spy a secret. Or the stern advice Raza gave to Mustafa. *I don't understand these people,* he thought. *This isn't what I thought it would be. Maybe the escape network that command briefed back at Benghazi doesn't really exist. That might be too much to think about.*

*But,* he reasoned, *I'm not dead, or in a POW camp. This—whatever this situation is—is better than that.* He closed his eyes and let the sleep come. The last thing he heard before drifting off were distant wolves howling to one another.

# 26

## SEPTEMBER 24, 1943
## MILITIA ENCAMPMENT IN THE INNER MAJEVITSA RANGE

GOODMAN FLICKED HIS HALF-SMOKED CIGARETTE INTO THE DIRT.

"Okay, Tomislav, what's your deal? You don't look like a freedom fighter. You look like you belong in a bank."

Tomislav laughed out loud. "To fight against our enemies, we come in many costumes. We dress to fit our roles, much like a performance in a theater, no?"

"Sure," Goodman agreed. "But you didn't answer my question."

Tomislav had paused to light a cigarette when one of Zoran's men called out to them from the barn. He waved them toward the commotion of men loading the pack animals. Goodman followed Tomislav to their horses.

"Sometimes, when our part is not yet required on the stage, we must perform other tasks. So, for now, I pull a horse."

"What else do you do?" asked Goodman.

"Whatever is asked of me." Tomislav smiled and looked at the line of horses headed out the door. His horse nudged him repeatedly with her nose. He laughed and rubbed the horse's jawline, then discretely pulled something from his coat pocket and fed it to the horse.

*He's got apples. I didn't see any apples at breakfast.* Tomislav saw that Goodman noticed, and pulled another, smaller apple from his coat pocket and gave it to Goodman.

"Here," Tomislav said quietly. "Horses are like people. It will help if he thinks you like him."

The animal sniffed at it, and two crunches later, the apple was gone. Goodman patted the horse along the jawline, and the horse's nostrils flared again at the residual apple smell on his hand. The loads were heavy, but the horses seemed not to notice. When the packers were done, they led their horses to join the assembled columns now formed across the field adjacent to the tree line. The sun was breaking over the ridge. A rider galloped into the field and steered his horse directly to the group of men that surrounded Zoran.

"Who is that?" asked Goodman.

"That is one of our couriers," said Tomislav. "We depend upon couriers to tell us everything. We do not have the luxuries of telephones or radios or telegraph, so we use the people as our eyes, ears, and mouth as well, when the time comes."

"Interesting," said Goodman. "And who are those men with Zoran?"

"Those men are our commanders," he said. "They are the chain of command for what remains of the families of the Majevitsa."

"What remains...?"

"There used to be many more of them... of us," Tomislav corrected himself, still watching the group that surrounded Zoran. "Last spring was a bad time for the Majevitsa. Especially for Zoran's family and the others in the resistance. Not many of his clan are still alive, nor most of the other major families for that matter. Those who did survive are the foundation upon which Zoran rebuilds his army, his 'Majevitsa Brigade'. Those men"—Tomislav gestured to the group with Zoran—"were the young and inexperienced of the commanders. Now, they are the only ones."

"And Amira is one of them?"

"Yes, sort of."

"Sort of?"

"She is more than a commander," explained Tomislav. "Zoran has elevated her to Pasha Kadin Effendi. Normally, that title was reserved for the chief wife or consort of a great household."

"So, what does that mean?"

Tomislav drew and lit a cigarette. "It means she's the last of her kin."

"You mean—"

"Yes, what I said is true. Zoran's brigade was fighting along the Sava when the SS and a battalion of Ustaši attacked the village where his family was hiding. The entire village and Zoran's whole family were killed there."

Goodman thought of the large family in Jasminka's photograph. "Everyone?"

"Everyone except Amira."

"She wasn't a fighter with him?"

"No, she was with the rest of his family. Only his sons were with him."

"How did she survive?"

"They left her alive, but..." His voice trailed off. The lit end of his cigarette burned brightly.

"But what?"

"Only after they did things…"

He took a long drag on it and held in the smoke before sending it out through his nostrils. Tomislav looked away. Goodman took it as meaning the conversation was over.

But the question lingered in his mind. *But who is she?*

The courier pulled his horse away from Zoran and kicked it into a trot toward the barn. Another mounted rider approached Zoran and his lieutenants. Ponytail. It was Amira. She rode easily, like she had ridden all her life. *I've seen that before,* Goodman observed, somewhat longingly. The way a real woman rides, not side-saddle like in the movies. *My mother rides like that.*

She stood in the stirrups to scan the field of men and horses before fixing on Goodman and Tomislav and steering her horse over to them.

"Sa nama," she commanded. *You come with us.*

Then she turned and spoke more Bosanski to Tomislav, too fast for Goodman to catch. She reined her horse back to Zoran and kicked it to speed. Goodman looked at Tomislav, and Tomislav just shrugged.

"It appears the script has changed for us."

"I don't understand."

"I do not write the script," Tomislav said. "We do what we are told."

Two militiamen strode toward them, each leading a horse already laden with small packs stowed behind the saddles.

"Now, these horses, we ride," Tomislav announced. "Do you know how to command something besides an airplane?"

"Yes, I do," said Goodman, taking the reins to one horse. He smirked. "I used to ride all the time when I was a kid."

"Good," said Tomislav. "You have useful experience, but you'll have to adapt and improvise. One never knows when the... *sudbina*—I don't know the English word—will change our plans." He threw the reins over the horse's head and lifted himself into the saddle.

"Sudbina?" Goodman repeated. "I don't know that word."

"Hmmm... I think it is like a dream, perhaps?" Tomislav cocked his head as he tried to steady his mount. "Sudbina..." He gestured in a circle with one hand outstretched. "Sudbina is the power around us that forces our...cooperation...our obedience."

"I still don't get it."

"It is decided for us. You cannot change your sudbina."

"Destiny," said Goodman. "You're talking about destiny."

"Yes, that is the correct English word, I think," said Tomislav. "Destiny." He nodded as he repeated the word under his breath. "All men are subject to their destiny. You are subject to your destiny, are you not?"

"I don't know about that."

"No? You do not feel that a man is part of a larger..." He flourished with his hand. "A larger machine?"

"No, I think that a man can make his own path."

"Yet you are a soldier in the army of the skies, yes? You wear the uniform of a man in a machine that flies, which is part of another, larger machine made up of many machines that fly."

"But I *chose* to be in my country's army."

"Your prime minister did not order you to become a pilot to bomb your country's enemies?"

"President. We have a president in America," said Goodman. "And, no, actually, I had a deferment."

"I do not know this…deferment," said Tomislav.

"I was supposed to be a doctor." Goodman gripped his saddle and mounted his horse. The animal felt bony under its heavy coat. "I quit medical school to become a pilot."

"Truly?" Tomislav said with surprise. "You refused to become a doctor so you could become a soldier and die in a war?"

"Well, no. When Japan attacked my country, I wanted to become something of my own choice, without answering to anyone."

"So, you joined your army."

Goodman saw the look on his face. The irony was obviously not lost on Tomislav.

"Yeah," said Goodman. "Go figure."

Goodman felt the load behind him slide and tried to reach it, but it was Tomislav who steadied it. He held his reins in his mouth and retied the knots to keep the bags in place.

"Do not worry, my friend," Tomislav said, taking the reins in hand. "By tonight, you will be as natural as the knights of old."

"Hvala," said Goodman as he recentered himself in the saddle. "Hvala na pomoći." *Thank you for your help*.

Tomislav fixed his hat on his head and tipped the brim to the side. "Molim," Tomislav said, smiling. "You speak our language well. You must have had a good teacher." He kicked his horse into motion.

"Thanks, I did." Jasminka's sad face appeared in Goodman's mind. He frowned at the memory as he steered his horse around to follow. *I hope she's okay*.

They moved toward the center of the field and halted near the circle of men and horses surrounding Zoran, listening to discussions of plans or logistics or something. Goodman understood almost none of the conversation, but at two different points, he distinctly heard Amira say "Papa" at the end of a sentence. Goodman mouthed the word to himself. *She's Zoran's daughter? Now I know why those guys obeyed her last night.*

"Hey," he whispered to Tomislav. "Why didn't you tell me she's Zoran's daughter?"

"Is it important to know that Amira is the child of the man who calls himself pasha?"

"Well, yes, it—" Goodman scowled. *Yes, it's important. I still don't know what a pasha is, but, yeah, it's damn important.* "You could have told me last night."

"I told you that you should listen to her. What else do you need to know?"

"Ok, next question." Goodman took the open door. "What is a pasha?"

Tomislav's turn to smirk. "A pasha is an ancient term of status and position."

"Like a king?"

"No," said Tomislav. "It is more of a prince, or governor, if you will, of a province."

*That sounds important.* "So, he has an office."

"Only that which he made."

"He made?"

"Yes, the old administration went away when the Hungarians invaded in the last war," Tomislav explained. "Tradition has failed, so others have filled the void."

The men of the militia stirred as Zoran's discussion broke up and his lieutenants dispersed to the groups around the pasture. Those who had them mounted their horses, others helped the wounded into the wagons or formed into marching columns.

"Where are we going?" Goodman asked.

"We move to a new place to prepare for Zoran's next concern," Tomislav said.

"And what is that concern?" Goodman hoped this would be the first leg of his journey home.

"We move toward Tuzla."

*Tuzla.* Raza the farmer gave a warning about Tuzla.

"Why Tuzla? I heard it's not a great place to go."

"It *is* a great place," said Tomislav. "That is part of the reason for Zoran. Tuzla is the seat of government for this territory. It is also the home to the local German occupation army and their Ustaša forces that control the regions surrounding the city."

"Sounds like Zoran's itching for a fight."

"Yes," Tomislav said. "You might say that."

"Why there?"

"As I said, it is the seat of power," said Tomislav. "Zoran would make it his."

"So that's where we're going now?"

"Not exactly. We need to join with others before we can attack the garrisons around the city. It will take a couple of days to do so."

"Garrisons?" Goodman's pulse quickened. "What kind of forces are we talking about? How big?"

"Their number is somewhere in the thousands, likely four to eight thousand infantry. Perhaps as many as ten. They have artillery and tanks, which they keep in several defensive positions around the city, and they use armored cars to patrol the highways. It will be interesting to see how Zoran and the others decide to attack."

"You're telling me that in two days we're going to attack ten thousand Germans and Ustaša who have tanks and artillery in fortified positions?"

"Yes," said Tomislav. "That is what I just said."

*That is ridiculous*, Goodman thought to himself. "I'm not here for a fight," he said. "I'm only here so I can get *out* of here. That's the deal I have with Zoran."

"You struck a deal with Zoran? Really?" Tomislav steadied his horse. "It would be very uncharacteristic of Zoran to make such a deal."

"He said he would get me out."

"Well, I do not know about that," said Tomislav. "Zoran has his plans…"

"I'm not up for this," said Goodman. He pulled the horse around and kicked it into motion. The men around Zoran paused as Goodman approached.

"Zoran Pasha, I talk you, please?"

Zoran looked amused, but a scowl crossed Amira's face. The senior men around him dipped their heads slightly and backed their horses away.

"Tomislav!" Emira barked.

"Many apologies, Effendim!" Tomislav removed his hat. "I was—"

Zoran Pasha spoke. "What is it the foreigner asks of Pasha?"

"You...give...you put me to my people?"

Amira scoffed. Zoran put a hand up to silence his daughter.

Goodman immediately softened his tone. "I ask you, please, Pasha, I go home, yes?"

Zoran's face showed no sign of understanding.

"I go home, yes? Or I fight—" Goodman suddenly realized that he did not know the Bosanski word for Germans. "Tomislav, help me." Tomislav translated.

Zoran's eyes lit up, and he replied to Tomislav. Emira's face reddened, and the blood drained from Tomislav's.

"Zoran asks if the foreigner wants to have a say in his plans."

Goodman felt his stomach tighten. "Neh, Pasha." He suddenly wished he had kept his mouth shut. "I...I...izvinite, Pasha, I..." *I need to find a way out of this. I don't have the words for this.* "Tomislav, tell Zoran Pasha I was wondering how I could be of use..."

Tomislav translated. Amira scoffed out loud again and rolled her eyes.

"You, my foreign friend," said Zoran. "You will be very useful. Just do not get a bullet in your head." Zoran turned to Tomislav and growled something Goodman did not hear.

"Da, Pasha." Tomislav was chagrined. "Izvinite, Pasha, izvinite." He bowed deeply and waved with his hat to tell Goodman to follow him. Goodman caught up with him as they approached the column of horses.

"Izvinite," said Goodman. "I'm sorry."

Tomislav nodded and said nothing.

"What did Zoran say to you?"

"He said I will get a bullet in my head if I do not do my job."

"What *is* your job?"

"To keep you under control."

# 27

The road to Mala Gornje

HORSE-MOUNTED MILITIA WERE POSTED ALONG THE MAIN ROAD leading to a large stone gate of a small town. Goodman saw Mustafa, but Mustafa only nodded discretely. He had the hardened look of a boy who has seen too much of the world and had a grim task to accomplish. He and his fellow riders held weapons ready and carefully eyed the houses that stair-stepped up the tree-covered hillside. A face occasionally appeared in a window or doorway. Otherwise, the town looked vacant. Goodman pulled his submachine gun around to his front.

"Are we expecting an attack?"

Tomislav pretended not to hear him. His eyes, too, searched the hills and alleyways.

"Molim, moj drug," Goodman appealed to him. *Please, my friend.*

"Friend?" said Tomislav. "Friends do not shove friends off the mountain."

*He's right*, thought Goodman. *He's helped me a ton so far. And he's the only one here who speaks English. I need to fix this between us.* "I apologize, Tomislav. Really. I do. I know now that I should not have approached Zoran like that." Tomislav still ignored him. "I did not know that he would react like that. Especially to you."

145

Tomislav looked at him sideways. "You think you know so much, but you do not. You must look with your eyes and see what is right in front of you."

"No, you're right. And I will not do that again." Goodman looked for a sign of acceptance. "Obećavam." *I promise.* One of Jasminka's sayings.

Tomislav looked hard at Goodman before removing his hat. "Yes, I think you will keep your word." He pulled a handkerchief out of his hat and wiped his face with it. "You are the doctor who joined the army when he did not have to. Anyone who admits to such a thing is either highly honorable or a fool. Fools die quickly here." He replaced the handkerchief and put his hat back on his head.

"So, we're okay—you and me?"

"Yes." He put his handkerchief away. "You had another question?"

"Is this a dangerous town?"

"Not especially," was Tomislav's response. "Though it is not a friendly place. This is a Serbian village."

"How can you tell?"

"There is an orthodox church by the square, not a mosque or a prayer tower." Tomislav abruptly reined his horse to a halt and pointed at a whitewashed stone building uphill from the public square. "There is the church." A black-and-white building stood beneath two large, onion-shaped domes.

Tomislav and Goodman reined their horses around to let a column of mounted militia pass. The troupe halted in the center of the town, but none dismounted. The Majevitsa force remained vigilant, with weapons ready. *What are they looking for?* Goodman looked up at the buildings on the hillside. All was quiet. Unconsciously, he put his hand on his submachine gun.

"If this is not a friendly place, then why are we stopping here?"

"To extract payment," Tomislav finally said. "This is called *jizya*, a kind of tax. Zoran taxes his enemies monthly."

"These people fight for the Germans?"

"No—well, yes, in a way. This is a Serbian village. They are Christians, and they used to support the Chetniks, who are not friends of Zoran's family. The Chetniks invaded after the Germans drove away the old royal army units, but after their defeat, the Chetnik forces abandoned their towns and were driven back across the Drina." Goodman remembered the river downhill from Baba's village. Were these the men who Baba warned about?

Zoran, Amira, Milosz, and others halted their horses directly in front of the large, square-shaped building adjacent to the town center square. A very thin man wearing a white tunic with a dark vest and a round, peaked hat emerged. Zoran dismounted and adjusted his collar and bandoleers as the man halted a few paces away.

"He is the village leader," Tomislav whispered. "He will pay homage to Zoran and then pay the jizya."

After some words and exaggerated genuflection, the man gestured to a table with several chairs set out. Only Zoran sat down. Zoran gestured to the man with the vest and hat to sit, which he did. The man uncorked a bottle and poured Zoran a glass of dark wine.

"Watch," Tomislav instructed. "Zoran will not drink until the village leader does."

"Why?" asked Goodman.

"For fear of poison."

Goodman watched as Zoran gestured for the leader to drink, not lowering his hand until the glass had been emptied. Only then did Zoran drink from his own glass. As the men enjoyed their second, and then third glasses, chanting started up in the crowd, and two other men served steaming bowls of food, which they set down on the table. Another pair of men carried a large wooden box with wooden handles. The chanting continued as the men set the box down on a pedestal next to the table. Zoran inspected the box's contents and nodded his head in approval. Goodman felt the tension in the air drain away as the two leaders commenced eating.

"Zoran accepts," said Tomislav. Goodman detected a hint of relief.

"That's not always the case?" asked Goodman.

"Not always." Tomislav wiped his nose on his sleeve. "Its never pleasant when that happens."

*I can only imagine*, thought Goodman.

Amira concluded her conversation with Milosz and remounted her horse. The hundred or so men who rode in with her also remounted and organized themselves for movement. Tomislav nudged Goodman and they, too, quickly re-mounted their horses and fell in line. She kicked her horse—and the column with her—into forward motion. They passed through the entire village and exited onto another main road, horses clip-clopping on the stone pavement.

Less than a mile down the road, another village came into view as the pavement crumbled into large gravel and the gravel faded into dirt. In front of a once-formidable stone and iron gate, an old man wearing a faded, sweat-stained, burgundy fez on his head met the advance guard with a toothless smile and overly gracious greetings. He heaved an ancient hunting rifle over his shoulder and vigorously shook the hand of every man who passed him, welcoming each with a scratchy voice. When he saw Amira, his hoarse praise grew even more emphatic.

"Dobrodošli nazad, Effendim! Welcome back, Hanim Amira Effendim, daughter of Zoran Pasha!" he said repeatedly. "Welcome to Dolinski Grad!" He kissed the back of Amira's hand more than a half dozen times. Another old man, surrounded by younger men, approached from the town.

"Who's that guy?" Goodman whispered to Tomislav.

"That is the mayor of this town."

The mayor leaned in and kissed the air near her feet, with hands waving outward as if he were blowing the kiss toward her. The young men near the mayor followed his lead and began to kiss Amira's boots. She ignored them and flicked her reins.

Goodman looked askance at the display. "What is that all about?"

"Those are the men who would marry the daughter of Zoran. Amira was the youngest of her sisters, all of whom are now dead. Now, she is Hanim Amira Effendim, the sole heiress to a pasha, and all that he would command, more or less."

Goodman scowled. "But kissing her boots?"

"There is significant prestige and power at stake. Traditionally speaking, at least. The man who gains her favor gains much in this mountain region." He paused. "You might even say that man would win everything there is to win here."

"I don't see that working with her," said Goodman.

"To grovel for status is a common practice here in the hill country," he said. "Ineffective with Amira, to be sure, but common."

"Yeah," Goodman observed. "She doesn't seem the type."

Tomislav smirked and flicked his reins. Amira directed the column of horses to the center square and deployed groups of men to the outskirts of the town. She ordered her man Ahmet to post sentries at the gates and to send another group to a rocky crag overlooking the town. The remainder of the men dismounted and rested in the shade surrounding a large well surrounded by a knee-high stone wall. Tomislav and Goodman dismounted and tied their horses there, but they put a large tree between them and the remainder of the militia.

Scores of townspeople flooded out of their homes. Men shook hands with the militia, and boys ran to fawn over the militia's weapons and horses. The massive work horses carrying the machine guns and crates of ammunition drew the largest crowd of adolescent boys. They approached Goodman, but Tomislav waved them off as he drew his flask again. He offered it to Goodman, but Goodman refused.

"What is this place to Zoran?" Goodman asked. "Another town to tax?"

"No, no, no," said Tomislav. "This is a village that was under the Serbian thumb for a long time. That is, until Zoran liberated them some months ago." He unscrewed the lid, drank from his flask, and then sucked air through his teeth at the sting of the alcohol. "Rumor has it that this is Zoran's birthplace."

"Really?"

"Just a rumor," said Tomislav. "But it could be true."

He offered the flask to Goodman, but he refused. Tomislav screwed the lid back on his flask and tucked it away. In the same motion, he withdrew a pair of cigarettes. His other hand flicked a lighter and lit both cigarettes, then he inhaled through both and handed one to Goodman.

"Hvala." Goodman took it and inhaled. Swirling calm ensued.

"Molim."

They listened to the well water gurgle upward from an unseen spring. The clip-clopping of horses drew everyone's attention to

Zoran approaching with the remainder of the militia. Scores of townspeople surged toward him, yelling his name, raising their hands and waving, smiling with arms around one another. More people poured into the square from all directions. Goodman and Tomislav stood up to watch. A wave of mothers with young children approached.

"Zoran Pasha is here!" they cried. "Children! Go to see our beloved pasha!"

Old women reached out for him. Small children darted precariously in and out of the columns of horses. Elderly men stood, bent on their walking sticks, yet energized sufficiently to raise an arm to their heads in an open-handed salute. To the men, Zoran returned many salutes. To the children, he smiled broadly and reached out to touch an outstretched hand, grasp a fist of solidarity, or wave back. It all seemed to be an over-the-top display of melodrama to Goodman. But for whom?

"This is quite the welcome," Goodman mumbled to Tomislav.

"This?" said Tomislav. "This is normal."

Goodman nodded. *Wow.*

Back home, people clapped politely for local politicians during election season whether they voted for them or not. Senators and other high-powered politicians held fancy dinners and fundraisers, but that was for show. A performance for an audience. Here, no one was witnessing the spectacle but the participants themselves. Maybe that was the point. Maybe all of it was contrived, one party for the other, to such an extent that it became the natural, expected way for all parties involved. Like the Senator's dinners. *But, here, there's more. These people seem to genuinely love their Zoran Pasha.* Maybe he was indeed their *pasha*—whatever that meant to them. Zoran's men all stood up to acknowledge his arrival with shouts and weapons raised high. Goodman caught himself feeling the urge to do so as well. *That must be it,* he thought. *They do it because it is expected of them, and they expect of themselves.*

Zoran stopped his horse in the center of the square, where he dismounted and strode into the building across from the well. Several men unloaded large crates from three horse-drawn wagons and followed Zoran into the building. Some of the townspeople tried to follow but were obstructed by militia and townsfolk armed with worn-out rifles and shotguns. One old man chased the adolescent boys away with a stick. The crowd swelled, choking the square, filling the streets, and eventually surrounding the nearby buildings. Goodman and Tomislav joined other men in standing atop the stone wall surrounding the well. The formalities ended and everyone returned to their homes or settled back down on their blankets.

Soon, smells of roasting meat carried on the wind. The crowds returned and converted the village square into a festival. Hunger assaulted Goodman, as well as memories of Baba's kitchen. Goats, lambs, and chickens perished by the dozen, and the streets ran red with blood. Numerous fires threw smoke into the air, and portions of meat turned on spits and skewers. Cauldrons boiled potatoes and vegetables. Soon, every hand was greasy, as were beards and shirtfronts. The slivovitz flowed like water, and people settled down wherever they could, talking and feasting. Villagers and militiamen started to doze off from food and drink. Dizziness forced Goodman to sit down. *I need to slow down.*

"Where is all this food coming from?" Goodman asked.

Tomislav turned and looked at him. "Where did we just come from?"

The Serbian village. Zoran's tax. *Straight out of one mouth and directly into another. That is harsh.* A second round of food appeared as a young boy brought each of them a leg of lamb. The entire leg, including the hoof. The skin was cracked and toasted, and it dripped with warm juice. A girl followed with a football-shaped loaf of bread, cut open and stuffed with vegetables. Tomislav tapped him on the shoulder with a jug of slivovitz. Goodman put up a hand.

"My friend, this is different," said Tomislav. "Much better than the other you have had."

"Very sweet," said Goodman after taking a sip. "But not bad." Dry leaves blew through the square on a cold breeze, and Goodman shielded his face. The militia turned their backs to it and drew blankets over their heads. Goodman reached for his blanket likewise.

From under their blankets, he and Tomislav passed the jug back and forth for a long time. Goodman slumped against the wall when he felt the slumber of a full belly and alcohol smothering his brain. He deliberated as he assembled a thought and spoke to his friend, but no answer came. Goodman looked and saw Tomislav's bag, but no Tomislav.

*Where did he go?* Goodman stood to look around but had to steady himself. He fumbled with his weapon before finally getting it slung behind his shoulder.

His head swam, and he tasted bile burning in his throat. He made his way through the crowded street as soberly as possible. A dried river of animal blood, someone passed out in the middle of the road, and packs of children chasing one another all impeded his already inebriated progress. A young girl walked by, handing out warm bread rolls from a basket, and he accepted one. He was not hungry, but he munched on it anyway, reasoning it might achieve some calming effect on his stomach. He meandered through the crowd and sat down on the steps of the public building.

Suddenly, people backed away from the front of the main building as several townsmen exited. Goodman stood and watched as Zoran Pasha himself crossed the threshold to the growing cheers of several hundred people. The crowd surged again as many more people re-emerged from their houses. Goodman watched with some amazement that this man inspired such gratitude and... worship? Zoran smiled and waved magnanimously to the people, which brought on additional cheers as more people woke up. Several children ran up the steps past Goodman and embraced Zoran's legs, their short arms barely able to reach around his large, muscular thighs and waist. Goodman saw Zoran Pasha smile the biggest smile he had seen since his arrival in Yugoslavia. The crowd was ecstatic. *They really love him here.* Goodman felt himself smile as well.

Then Zoran's smile suddenly took on the artificiality of a mannequin. His eyes went cold as they darted left and right across the crowd. Zoran took a half-step back, like a boxer gaining his stance. A chill prickled across Goodman's arms and back. *What...what is this? What's going on?* Milosz stepped to his side, and Zoran gave him an order. He stripped the children from Zoran's legs and shooed them away. With the subtlety of a man facing a viper, Milosz stepped back and discreetly gestured for Zoran's bodyguard to approach. Zoran remained waving in his fighter's stance as Milosz recrossed the threshold back into the building. Milosz returned to Zoran's side, but now had his pistol drawn and partly concealed in the palm of his hand. Zoran continued to wave, but his natural smile did not return. *What does he see?* His and Milosz's eyes darted back and forth, searching the crowd, looking for something. Or someone. Goodman's brain sobered up quickly and scanned the crowd. Then he saw Tomislav.

Tomislav waved for Goodman to return to the well. Goodman gave a half-hearted wave in reply as he tried to see what Zoran saw. Goodman took a step up toward Zoran as his eyes searched back and forth across the crowd. He saw nothing but smiling faces and hands waving. Then, as if a spotlight suddenly flicked on, Goodman spotted a man with a large mustache, wearing a dirty gray coat, making his way through the crowd toward the steps of the town hall. The man's face was unmoving. And angry. Like a theatrical mask. His eyes were dark, without light, without reflection. *What is that?* Goodman studied the man's face. *Why does he look like that?* Like a gun with a hair trigger on the verge of snapping into action, his body wanted to react, but his mind was still computing what he saw. Or, rather, what he did not see. Before his mind could register the *sense* of what he saw, or put a label on it, or call it a name, a sharp crack rang out in the town square.

# 28

IN THE FIRST INSTANT OF TIME, the crowd seemed not to notice. His mind raced to process the second sensation, having failed to label the first properly. Then a second shot rang out. His mind processed this sensation much more quickly, but the entire town went silent for a fraction of a second, as if the collective mind was a beat or two behind his. In shocked amazement, Goodman watched the man he had spotted fall to his knees. His face, now vacant of expression, hit the pavement with a smack. His arms flopped outward, and a pistol clattered on stone. Then, screams.

The screams filled the air, and the crowd scattered in all directions. People pushed and shoved, tripping and stepping on each other. Young and old were shoved aside, mothers reached for children, and men yelled and fought each other as if suddenly blinded. Goodman crouched low on the steps and wrestled with the strap of his weapon. Another man leaped over the dead man and ran toward Zoran, but two of Zoran's bodyguards tackled the man. They fell hard onto the street and struggled. A third pistol shot snapped past Goodman's head and impacted the step below Zoran's boots. *They're trying to kill Zoran!*

Goodman raised his weapon, but Zoran's bodyguards pushed past him, knocking him to the street. Four other militiamen appeared, dragging an unconscious man with them. Another shot rang out and one of the bodyguards fell. This attacker, too, went down under a swarm of militia, fists thumping and knives flashing.

Goodman finally aimed his weapon, but the action seemed to have stopped. *Is it done?* He thought. *Is that it?* Someone grabbed his coat from behind and shoved him toward the steps. *Who the hell is that?* Off balance, Goodman turned his head and caught a glimpse of another man with cold, hard, dark eyes behind a long stringy beard. Goodman tried to turn around to fire his weapon, but the man behind him kept shoving him.

Goodman pushed back and kicked, grabbing at anything he could find. A hat came free in his hand. He dropped it and reached again. His fingers found long, greasy hair. A bearded face. He squeezed and twisted. The man yelled, and a gunshot went off under Goodman's left coat sleeve. It felt like a hot knife had sliced him under his arm, and he fell. Zoran reacted to the bullet's impact, but rather than fall or retreat, he turned and raised his enormous, curved sword over his head.

Goodman spun around and squeezed his trigger. The attacker's body fell backward, lifeless. When he wiped his face, his sleeve came back smeared with the attacker's blood. A shadow fell across him, and he turned to face the new threat.

Zoran's sword flashed over Goodman's head, and a revolver clattered down the steps at his feet. The owner's headless body fell over Goodman and knocked him down. Goodman kicked himself free and scrambled to get away from the body and the blood that already flowed down the steps and pooled between the stones. Yet another shadow fell over him.

Zoran stood over Goodman, his bloody sword in one hand and his own revolver in the other, outstretched. Zoran, Milosz, and several bodyguards scanned the now empty square with their weapons raised, ready to shoot. Most of the townspeople had fled. Amira and her men came running and took up positions around the square. Goodman gasped for air.

"Stranac! You good, yes?" Zoran looked down at him. He was smiling.

Goodman was still trying to catch his breath and merely nodded in reply.

"You stopped a devil from killing me," said Zoran.

"You. Arm." Goodman pointed at Zoran's shoulder. Zoran looked at the red stain slowly making its way down his arm.

"Ništa," Zoran's voice boomed back at him. *It is nothing.*

Zoran holstered his revolver and reached down with his bloody arm. Goodman reached upward and Zoran lifted him to his feet.

"Hvala, Pasha," said Goodman.

"No, stranac, many thanks to you," said Zoran.

Goodman nodded, still breathless. He checked his weapon and brushed himself off.

Zoran wiped the blood from his sword on the coat of the dead man on the steps and sheathed it. Milosz and Amira barked orders to bring the attackers forward. A moment later, three dead men laid in front of Zoran, two others appeared to be unconscious, and a sixth man, conscious and held on his knees by militiamen, was trembling in fear. He had just urinated himself, and the wet spot expanded over the cobblestones. Zoran pointed at him. "Up!" his voice boomed across the square. His men raised the survivor to a standing position, though he required a man on either side to hold him up. Zoran descended to the street.

"You come from Mala Gornje, yes?" Zoran's voice echoed across the otherwise silent town square.

The man groaned, and his legs trembled visibly. He averted his eyes, but Zoran clenched the man's head with his huge hand and rotated the man's face toward him. Goodman saw that the man's eyes were wild with terror, but the burning pain under his arm made Goodman too angry to ration any amount of sympathy for him. Zoran spoke in a measured tone and tempo, which made his words even more penetrating.

"You watched me leave your dirty little village, and you hated me, yes?"

The man said nothing.

"You wanted to kill me, yes?"

Again, the man said nothing. Zoran released the man's face, and the man almost passed out.

"But you could not do this on your own," Zoran continued. "You are just a little man. There are others, yes? Who told you to do this? Perhaps one of these men was your leader?" Zoran kicked one of the bodies. "No, others sent you. Who ordered you to kill me? Who are the cowards who sent you to die?"

The man tried to avert his eyes again, and Zoran punched him directly in the face. The men holding him let him fall to the cobblestones, where he sobbed and pleaded at Zoran's feet. Zoran spit on his head and turned away.

Goodman suddenly felt a knot in his gut at what might happen next. But the other side of him, the part that was livid that the attack happened, that almost killed him, pushed back. *That guy deserves to die*, he thought. He imagined Zoran ordering the man up against a wall and then shot. Then he felt himself draw back slightly at the thought of execution. After the attack on the farm in the valley, this should not have affected him so much. *Stay back*, he told himself. *This is not your fight.*

"Pasha!" said Amira, already on her horse. "We know who did this. Let us go there now and deal with them."

"Yes, Amira Effendim, you are right." Zoran stood tall. "We return to Mala Gornje."

Zoran whistled, and the whole town square sprang to life. Several townsmen brought their horses to the square as scores of militiamen ran to find their own mounts. Zoran directed Milosz to bring the attackers, those alive *and* the dead, back to the village they had just left. Tomislav and Goodman ran to their horses and mounted up with the others.

"What is Zoran going to do?" Goodman asked, climbing into his saddle.

"I think Zoran will kill a lot of people for this." Tomislav reined his horse around and kicked it toward the gate.

"Wait, what does that mean?" Goodman followed as quickly as he could. *Massacre? Is he going to kill a whole town? Would he do that?* Again, the farm in the valley came back to him. *Oh, he might.*

Zoran was already gone, and Amira was far ahead. Goodman kicked his horse to a gallop in pursuit.

# 29

## MALA GORNJE PUBLIC SQUARE

GOODMAN CAUGHT UP TO ZORAN AND HIS MILITIA LEADERS just as they dismounted in the center of town. The only living thing present was a stray dog that retreated into an alley. Every window was shuttered. The first several houses Amira and her men searched were empty. The public buildings were dark. *They knew,* Goodman said to himself. *Zoran was right. They knew and now they're hiding because they know what's coming.*

Mustafa and his men came forward with a young boy. The child was incoherent, bawling and shaking with fright. He quivered at the sight of Zoran.

"He says nothing of value," Milosz told him.

"Let him go," said Zoran. "He'll tell us everything we want to know."

They watched as he fled. The boy looked over his shoulder before ducking around a corner. He ran up a wide street toward the black-and-white church. At a gesture from Zoran, Milosz directed the men to surround it.

The church building was large and covered in white stucco with a large, black, onion-shaped minaret over the front. The shutters here, too, were closed and locked. Amira met them there and ordered two of her men to pry open the doors. The heavy oak and iron doors held fast.

Zoran drew his dagger and pried a crack in one of the shutters that sealed the windows. Sounds of crying emanated from within. He sheathed his blade and stepped back.

"Send out your elders!" he boomed. "Send them to me!"

Only the sound of his voice echoing off the hillsides came back to him.

"Give me your elders!" he repeated.

There was still no reply. Zoran calmly backed away from the building, then he waved at the church dismissively. "Shoot the walls," he ordered.

Gunfire erupted and shards of white stucco and slivers of ancient, weathered wood littered the ground in an instant. Dark gray pockmarks dotted the church's exterior. The men changed magazines and held their weapons ready.

"Well?" Zoran called out, plucking shards of white from his beard. "Do I burn the infidel church? Or do I swing the elders by their necks? The choice is yours until it is mine!"

A moment later, one of the large doors creaked open with a heavy scraping. A thin man with a white shirt and dark vest emerged, holding an old military rifle over his head. Goodman recognized this man as the one who sat and ate with Zoran at the earlier meeting.

"Drop your weapon, mayor!" Zoran directed. "The next man I see with a weapon in his hands will lose his head!"

The mayor looked behind him, and the clatter of weapons hitting the slate floor echoed from within. Several more men followed their mayor into the small enclosure in front of the church. They huddled together and kept their eyes averted from Zoran. Zoran put his hands on his holster and hilt.

"This is all of your elders, mayor?"

"Yes," he answered meekly.

"What!" Zoran bellowed.

"Y—Yes, Zoran—"

"Did you order your men to attack me in Dolinski Grad?"

"No—"

"No?" Zoran was incensed. "Bring me one of the dogs who attacked me!"

His men who dragged the only conscious prisoner to the front. Behind them, the two unconscious men were deposited behind the group, along with the three bodies. Milosz ordered his men to continue to hold up the sole conscious man, as he could barely keep himself erect. He sobbed quietly. His twisted, bloodied face said everything there was to say. Goodman imagined this was the very image of despair that knows death is imminent. *Good*, he thought to himself. He massaged his arm where the would-be assassin's bullet cut him. The prisoner let out a long moan.

Zoran marched up to him, then raised and fired his pistol into the man's face. The man collapsed on the stones. The elder's faces dropped, aghast at the sight. Goodman, too, was shocked by the suddenness of what he just witnessed.

Zoran signaled to his daughter, and Amira stood over one of the unconscious men. She lifted the man's head by the hair and held her knife to his throat. She looked to her father.

"Is this not another of your men?" Zoran demanded.

One of the other elders let out a gasp. "No! Please!" He stumbled forward, but one of Zoran's men shoved him back with the butt of his rifle.

"Who ordered this attack on me?" Zoran glared at the mayor. The man said nothing. For want of a response, Zoran scanned the faces of each of the elders, one by one. In turn, each averted his eyes.

"No one? Not one of you will stand as a man to face me? Who will answer?"

The elders remained huddled together, silent. Zoran gave his daughter a slight nod. Amira's knife hand swung, and blood poured from the man's neck. She held it for a second and let it drop with a sickening thud. Goodman's mind stumbled on the idea that she was capable of the act. The very act that she just committed. The elders cried out as they struggled on weak knees. Amira wiped her blade on the man's coat before she moved to the other unconscious man. She lifted his head up and, again, she looked to her father. He turned and looked at the elders, who languished out loud. Goodman looked at Zoran, and then at the church.

*This can't be happening*, thought Goodman. He wanted to look away, but he was frozen.

"What do I do now?" yelled Zoran as he marched across the front of the elders. "It is up to you. And you have no time. Tell me!" Silence. "Very well…"

The mayor's eyes had drained of life. He swayed as he stood there, slumped, ashen, and silent. Then, finally, one of the elders spoke up from the rear of the group.

"Please, Zoran Pasha…"

"Ha! Now I am *Pasha* to you!"

"Please, Zoran Pasha, have mercy! Have mercy! We did not order this attack. We do not know who did, but please, Pasha, please let us find him and punish him." The man sank to his knees and begged. "Please, please, Pasha, please…" He laid his head down with his palms up in total supplication. Tears dotted the stones beneath him.

"Do you think I am stupid?" Zoran yelled. "You say Zoran is a fool! Zoran is just a simple, stupid goat herder! A pasha of goats! Is that what you say about me when I am far away? Or do you say that I am not pasha?"

"No, Pasha, no! We do not say such things." The elders shook their heads vigorously.

"I do not believe you," said Zoran. He stopped pacing. "Burn the church!"

# 30

GOODMAN DID NOT REALIZE he had voiced his opposition out loud until he caught the look from Milosz.

Zoran's men sprang into action to bundle sticks together from the barren bushes and trees nearby. Others approached with armloads of firewood taken from the nearest kitchens. "Stake the doors shut," Zoran told Milosz. "Let none out when the fire lights."

Milosz turned and directed another group to carry out their commander's directive.

"No!" the elders called out. "Pasha! No!"

"Shut up, dogs!" Zoran yelled back at them.

Goodman suddenly felt like he was outside of himself, like watching a moving picture of the entire drama playing out around him. Zoran had his hands on his hips. Milosz nervously wiped sweat from his forehead. Amira still hovered over the remaining unconscious prisoner. Tomislav had turned away from the entire scene and was lighting a cigarette. Everyone else was either lighting torches or nervously watching the others do so. Goodman felt sick. *I can't let this go.*

He suddenly had a flash of what to do.

He approached Zoran. Tomislav reached to pull him back, but was too late. Milosz strode back to intercept him, looking straight into his eyes.

"Please, say Zoran he make bad," Goodman stammered through another sentence in Bosanski.

Milosz's eyes moved from Goodman to Tomislav. "I don't understand what he just said." He looked at Goodman, and then to Tomislav again.

Tomislav put himself next to Goodman. "Please excuse him, Milosz, we will not—"

Milosz stepped close. "Take him back to the town square and keep him quiet!"

"Yes, Milosz—"

"Zoran Pasha does not take orders," said Milosz. "He gives them."

"I know," said Goodman. "I will strong Pasha, not weak…" *I think I said that right.*

"What is this?" asked Zoran. Milosz turned to address Zoran, but Goodman spoke first.

"Zoran Pasha," he began. "*Oprosite*, forgive me, but you make thing bad for bad future."

Zoran gave Tomislav a blank look. Goodman regretted—once again—opening his mouth. *I didn't say it right.* Goodman pleaded to Tomislav. "Help me…"

Tomislav stepped forward very reluctantly.

"I think you are making a mistake." Tomislav said to Goodman, and then he translated what he had said.

Zoran laughed, and Goodman felt the pit in his stomach again.

"What does the foreigner know about these things?" Tomislav translated Zoran's words.

Zoran waved for his men to approach the church. Several crackling torches were set to the bundles around the church.

Tomislav tried again to pull Goodman back. "Do you want to get yourself killed?" Goodman shrugged him off.

"Zoran Pasha," Goodman began. "This is not good…"

Tomislav shook his head.

"You know what I'm trying to say!" Goodman exclaimed at Tomislav. "Tell him!"

Tomislav exhaled and cleared his throat. "Zoran Pasha…" he began. After a moment, he stopped talking and Zoran spoke at length. Goodman could tell the idea was not well received.

"Zoran wants to know why," said Tomislav.

Milosz move to Zoran's side and spoke quietly to him. Zoran nodded, then his eyes moved to Goodman.

"Milosz seems to think you have a point," said Tomislav.

Zoran tugged on his beard and looked at Milosz, then at Goodman. "Very well," he said. "I will leave it to their own choice." He turned back to the elders. "Then tell me what I should do! You!" He jabbed a finger at them and lit into them with a long string of curses followed by a statement.

Zoran's voice was the only sound on the entire mountainside. Goodman could catch only parts, phrases at best, but he could put two and two together. He gave them a chance to decide their fate. Something between killing one or killing them all. As much as he wanted to say something, though what he did not know, both Tomislav and Amira were giving him the same fierce look. It was enough to keep him quiet.

"Which is it?" Zoran finally said.

The elders trembled in silence.

"Spaliti," said Zoran. "Spali ga." He turned and walked away.

"Burn it?" Goodman said to Tomislav. "Did he say burn it?"

Tomislav merely gestured at the men with the torches.

"But, that's not… that's not what—"

Tomislav reached for Goodman to shut him up. Amira glared at him.

"Čekaj! Molim!" someone called out. *Wait! Please!*

Zoran stopped mid-stride. He turned.

"Take me." One of the elders stepped forward.

"Who speaks?" said Zoran.

"Zoran Pasha, take me in place of these men and the women and children." The man who spoke was wiry, with graying hair on his head and face. He wore a long black tunic and had a cylindrical black hat on his head. He paused a few feet from Zoran. Beads of sweat made his face glisten. His collar was soaked. "Zoran Pasha, I am Father Budimir. These are my people." He bowed at the waist.

"Ha! An infidel priest!" said Zoran. "You are brave…"

"Please, P-Pasha, please do not punish everyone for our foolishness." He removed his hat. "Please, Pasha, p-punish m-me, n-n-not th-th-them." His hands quivered so badly he almost dropped his hat.

"You are very brave. Perhaps the bravest man here, apart from those who died trying to kill me. Very brave. But your sacrifice is insufficient."

The elders looked at each other. Father Budimir turned and pleaded with Milosz and Amira, but they ignored him. One by one, the other elders stepped forward to line up with Father Budimir.

"Good," said Zoran. "Hope is not lost for the infidels." He turned to Milosz. "Keep the villagers in the church. Take the elders and the last prisoner to the square."

"Yes, Zoran Pasha."

Milosz immediately made the preparations, and Amira led the elders and surviving unconscious attacker down to the center square. As the townspeople realized what was happening, they began to yell and push on the church doors. Zoran's men pushed back and drove stakes into the ground to brace the doors. The long line of militiamen led the village elders to the square. Amira strode quickly ahead of them.

When the rest of the force had assembled, twelve nooses hung from the trees in front of the government building. Militiamen prodded the elders, Father Budimir, and the last attacker to mount chairs placed under the ropes. Father Budimir asked to speak to Zoran as his men fitted each rope around a neck. Milosz said no.

Goodman's mind raced to come up with something to save them. *This isn't war, this is a massacre.*

Father Budimir called out anyway. "Zoran Pasha, may I tend to the men's souls before we are to be killed?" He cleared his throat as the rope was tightened.

"No." Zoran walked away and remounted his horse. "Milosz!"

Milosz opened his mouth to respond, but Goodman beat him to it.

"Zoran Pasha!" Goodman called out. "Život za život!"

Only the wind made a sound.

"What is that you say?" Zoran reined his horse around. "What are you talking about?"

164

"Zoran Pasha, I stop you death in village, yes?" Goodman called out. Tomislav threw his hands up.

"What is this thing you are doing, stranac?"

"I stop you death in village, yes?"

"Ay. So?"

"I stop you death," said Goodman. "Give me a life."

"What does this mean? Give you a life…"

"Život za život. You, alive. Keep one man alive." *Please understand*, thought Goodman. "Molim, Pasha."

Zoran steered his horse almost on top of Goodman. The horse's giant hooves thumped on the stony ground. "You want one of these lives? These infidel cowards of this shit village? Very well, stranac. Tell me, which of these dogs would you have?"

Goodman looked at the priest. "Him," said Goodman. "Release the priest so he can see to his people." He quickly added, "Molim, Pasha." Tomislav repeated everything, even the *please*.

Zoran shook his head and exhaled out loud. He waved his hand at the priest, who strained against the rope around his neck. The nearest militiaman reached upward and severed the rope with a knife. The priest fell to the ground, the noose still choking him. He reached toward Goodman.

"Thank you," said the priest. "God be with—"

"Shut up!" Zoran cut him off and turned his horse. "Milosz! Where are you?"

"I am here, Pasha!"

"See to this thing, will you?"

"Yes, Zoran Pasha."

"And another thing."

"Yes, Pasha?"

"Assign two men to guard this…foreigner…to keep him out of the way."

"Yes, Pasha." Milosz motioned for two men to stand guard over Goodman.

Goodman started to thank Zoran, but Tomislav pulled on his sleeve. *Right*, thought Goodman. *Too much.*

Zoran scanned the faces around him one last time, then kicked his horse to a trot, not bothering to watch the remaining eleven men drop. Milosz called out a command to the prisoners' attendants, raised his hand, and then dropped it to his side. Each of the attendants kicked the chairs out from under their captive's feet. The priest fell to his knees and cried out as the eleven men fought for their last breaths.

"To your horses!" Milosz barked. Men scrambled and mounted their rides.

"Amira!" Zoran called from the main road. "My daughter, listen to me."

"Yes, Papa." She reined her horse around.

"Assign a guard until the people of Mala can organize a watch to keep the bodies hanging for as long as possible…"

Tomislav translated, but Goodman interrupted angrily. "I know what he's saying."

Zoran continued. "Failure to comply is death. Make sure the people know that."

"Yes, Papa." Amira turned and issued instructions to her man called Ahmet.

"And one more thing," said Zoran.

"Yes, Papa.

"And Milosz, this is for you as well."

"Yes, Pasha."

"I want the infidel priest to remain where he is until the bodies fall." Zoran looked at Goodman. "I want everyone to see how merciful Zoran Pasha can be."

# 31

Mala Gornje Public Square

THE ENTIRE BRIGADE, LESS ONE SQUAD OF GUARDS, returned to Zoran's alleged place of birth. Darkness came quickly under fast-moving clouds. The horses shuffled against one another to get the best protection from the cold bite of the wind. Those members of the militia who had not been invited into a household for dinner huddled together on the leeward side of every tree and wall around the public square. Goodman found his own piece of wall, wrapped himself in his woolen blanket, and picked at his food in silence. He had no appetite, so he wrapped the remaining roasted chicken and beets in a rag and shoved them into his coat pocket. He could not shake the images of those men struggling, swinging from those trees. The wailing of the priest still rang in his ears.

Then, as if the townspeople's agony at the deaths of their elders was not enough, Zoran's men had set fire to each house after it was thoroughly looted. Clouds of black smoke dropped ash where they now sat. Food stuffs, clothing, jewelry, metal boxes full of paper currency, and various tools and implements were now in the hands of the Majevitsa militia. What the militia could not carry away they tossed back into the fires. The families of Dolinski Grad were again eating food taken from their neighbors just up the road. Zoran had exchanged the balance of power between tormentor and tormented on that mountainside in less than an hour.

He raised his head when Tomislav returned from dinner at one of the nearby houses. That Goodman had not received an invitation was not what troubled him. Unlike the other houses that had welcomed the militia, there was no husband at the door to this one. Goodman had also noticed that Tomislav was not the only man to enter the home, only to exit less than a short while later with his shirt untucked. Goodman put his head down on his arms across his knees. *Who are these people I'm with?*

"What you did earlier was very dangerous," said Tomislav as he pulled a blanket from his pack and arranged his place to sleep.

*Another lecture*, thought Goodman. "What?" He said with an irritated tone.

"The demand you made of Zoran with that priest. Anyone else would have been beaten severely and maybe killed with those villagers." He paused. "*Only you* could have done that."

"Why?" said Goodman. "What do you mean *only me*?"

"You are a special case," said Tomislav. "You are protected." He nodded at the two guards, who lingered conspicuously nearby. "But not forever."

"You mean because I'm an Allied officer."

"No." Tomislav kicked his shoes off and spread the blanket over his feet. "That is part of it, but you also were shot for protecting Zoran from the assassin's bullet." Tomislav pointed at Goodman's injured arm. "He recognizes that. You cannot be born into that. That is not associated with rank or status." He tucked the blanket around his feet. "That you must *do*. Maybe you did not intend that, but you did it. So now you have his protection."

"Is that what you call this?"

Tomislav shielded his face as he lit a cigarette. He did not offer one to Goodman. "You don't see it, do you?"

"See what?"

"Zoran is protecting you." Tomislav pulled his blanket to his shoulders. "You are more useful to him now. More than just a warm body. But also more than just another gun."

"Hmm," Goodman considered this as he sat back against the wall. *But I didn't see what was coming. Zoran did. He saw something.* "How did he know?" Goodman asked.

"How did who know what?" Tomislav pinched his cigarette between his lips as he cinched his rucksack closed.

"How did Zoran know that there was going to be an attack?"

Tomislav wrapped the corner of the blanket around his toes. "Ne znam." *Don't know.*

"No, seriously," said Goodman. "How did he go from a king's welcome to stopping an assassination attempt?"

"I think you have to look at the time and the place of it," said Tomislav. "Maybe he already knew. You and I cannot know what others know. We can only do what we are supposed to do when and where we are."

"There has to be more than that," Goodman replied. "If he knew, then he could have stopped it before it ever started." He thought about Baba and the spy.

Tomislav shrugged and took a deep draw on his cigarette as he pulled his blanket around him. "Sudbina…"

"I knew you were going to say that," said Goodman. "It's not fate, or destiny, or whatever you want to call it that allowed Zoran to be a step ahead. It can't be. There are too many things going on here to be part of a… machine. Even a complicated one."

"You have your eyes closed." Tomislav let his blanket drop over his shoulders. "The entire universe is a machine. The machine turns, and the stars move, the planets move, day becomes night. The strong men take power, and the weak go hungry according to the laws of the machine. It is as predictable as the seasons. Even a poor man uses the levers at his disposal, and he eats occasionally, or he is no longer a man. And he will continue to be poor and hungry because those are the levers he has. So it is with Zoran, but with different levers. Zoran is important for a time because of the machine."

"So, this… machine… created Zoran? Created this war?" said Goodman.

"No, the machine *is* the war. The war *is* the machine. It is the world that works by war. When the machine runs out of steam, when enough men have died, there is peace for a time, but the machine rolls along. The people who best adapt to the arrangements will be best accommodated by it. Those who fight against it will be consumed. Like that foolish display you put on by claiming the life of the priest. You do that too often, and Zoran Pasha may find you are too expensive to have around." He put a derisive emphasis on the *pasha*.

Tomislav continued. "Same thing with different armies, different countries, different machines. The lesser machines will be consumed or destroyed by the better machines. This is why Germany will win the war."

"No way," said Goodman. "You don't really think that. Do you?"

"None of us would be here if it were not for them," said Tomislav. He took another drag on his smoke. "They are the dominant machine."

"So why am I here?" Goodman asked. "I took off from North Africa to blow up an oil storage tank. I wouldn't be here if the Allies didn't take North Africa back from the Nazis and the Italians."

"No, that is *how* you got here. You must separate the how from the why. The how is irrelevant in the end."

"Okay, so why?" said Goodman. "Why am I here?"

"It is impossible for me to say," said Tomislav. "I have no foreknowledge of events any more than Zoran. Or you. Perhaps you are here for someone else's purpose."

"Why are you here? What is your purpose?"

"I have my reasons." Tomislav flicked his cigarette into the street and shifted under his blanket.

"Is it because of your family?"

"Something like that." Tomislav pulled the blanket over his head and rolled over.

Goodman pulled his blanket back over his shoulders. He tried to lie down, but now his mind was still clicking along conversation's trajectory. *What terrible experiences for Tomislav and his family—and everyone else here—bring people to this point? Like they have no control over their lives.* He remembered what Raza the farmer told him that first night after leaving Baba's village, before he crossed the river. *The people here have no hope.* Goodman shook his head.

# 32

GOODMAN WATCHED THE LAST OF A LONG LINE OF FAMILIES depart the public building across the street. Each family carried with them armloads of liberated clothing and baskets full of bread and vegetables. Under torchlight, fathers shook hands with Zoran, mothers bowed their heads to Amira. Sons carried armloads of coal and wood for their stoves down the street. Daughters carried bolts of cloth, or shoes, or other odds and ends. Liberated, confiscated, or stolen. *I guess how you describe it depends on who you are.*

Milosz stood outside, smoking a pipe while he watched the last family disappear down the street. He nodded slightly to Goodman when they made eye contact. Goodman rose to his feet and crossed the street. They stood in silence until Milosz pulled his pipe out of his mouth.

"Winter is coming," he mused. He took a long puff on his pipe.

"Cold now," Goodman said, folding his arms.

Milosz nodded in agreement. "Zoran Pasha wants to see you when he is done," Milosz informed him.

"Da," said Goodman. "I ask question you?"

Milosz replied, but he spoke too rapidly.

"Ne razumijem, effendi," said Goodman. "Sorry, I must speak and hear slowly."

Milosz repeated himself. "You make fight with lion."

"Da, razumijem." *I understand.* He quickly added, "I know this now."

"But it was important for Zoran to hear," said Milosz. This surprised Goodman. Milosz continued. "You learn our ways and our language quite well, Američko."

"What mean *Američko*?"

"You." Milosz pointed the stem of his pipe at Goodman's chest. "You. Američko."

"American?"

"Da."

Goodman smiled. *He said American, not stranac. Not foreigner.* "Hvala," Goodman replied.

"It is better," said Milosz. "For you to be *un*-seen. And not heard, either. Other men want your head."

*Tomislav was right—I'm being protected.* "Razumijem, Effendi," said Goodman. "Hvala…"

Milosz nodded. "What is your question?"

"The bad men attack Zoran."

"Da." said Milosz.

"You know attack before attack?"

Milosz pulled the pipe from his lips and looked Goodman in the eyes. "Neh." He shook his head and put his pipe back. The embers glowed brightly in the bowl.

"But Zoran see attack, yes?"

"Ask him."

"I know not how ask." Goodman struggled to get the thought into his simple vocabulary.

"Razumijem, Američko," said Milosz. "You may ask him. Shall I get him?"

"I know not how talk to Pasha…"

"Bah!" Milosz dismissed it with a wave of his hand. "You talk Pasha. Pasha talk to you. Wait here." Milosz turned and entered the public building. Zoran emerged a moment later with Milosz right behind him. His eyes swept the street and turned to Milosz.

"You say him?" said Zoran.

"Neh, Pasha," said Milosz.

*Milosz didn't tell me something. What didn't he tell me?*

Zoran gestured to Goodman and Milosz spoke again, but in perfect, but heavily accented English. "Zoran Pasha speaks English, Captain Goodman."

*Wait. What?* Goodman gaped at Milosz, then at Zoran, and then back at Milosz, who just smiled. "You speak English?"

Zoran cleared his throat and smiled. "Yes, I was once a member of the Royal Home Guards in Beograd, the capital city, back in times of the Kingdom of Yugoslavia."

"But…this…I don't understand." *So many questions.*

"I was a guard for the embassy of the British Envoy to the King. We were taught English so we could listen to their conversations and report what they were saying. I was a guard and then a sergeant of guards until 1938, when we were purged from the capital, and I returned home. Only a few people know this."

"Amira?"

"Yes, she knows. She also speaks some English." He paused. "Milosz was my deputy, so he speaks some as well."

*Oh, wow.* Goodman was stunned. *They faked it all this time. Does Tomislav know?*

"Tell, no one, Captain," said Milosz. "No one at all."

Goodman slowly nodded.

"You want to ask me something, Američko?" said Zoran.

Goodman immediately bowed his head. "I...ummm...Zoran Pasha, a thousand pardons for my words. I talk too much, I—"

"Yes," Zoran interrupted. "Yes, you talk much, talk big. You must be a big man in heart to talk to Pasha. You must be lion in heart." Zoran pointed to his chest. "Perhaps small in head, but big in heart, yes?"

Zoran chuckled, and it set Goodman at ease.

"I have few lions," Zoran said. "Many, many sheep. Too many. And there are too many wolves."

Goodman nodded to show understanding. Zoran nodded as well and looked at the black sky.

"You, Američko, you are different. Perhaps it is because you come from far away and you do not have to fear where you live. Perhaps it is something else." Zoran's eyes lowered to Goodman. "You have questions."

"Zoran Pasha, today, what happened in this village, right here on these steps?"

Zoran looked at Milosz, who nodded and put his pipe back in his mouth.

"Come," said Zoran. "Let us walk."

Goodman followed Zoran down the steps and onto the street. Milosz and the guards trailed several yards behind. They avoided the fires along the road where militiamen and townspeople warmed themselves. Most failed to notice them as they passed by.

At one of the larger houses in the village, Zoran led them up a staircase to the rooftop. The wind cut through Goodman's clothing, and he folded his arms against it. Looking over the village and surrounding slopes, Goodman couldn't help but admire the view of dozens of fires twinkling against the black hillsides, the moon's disk smeared to a diffused glow behind the clouds. Zoran paused at the edge of the roof, hands on hips, seeming not to notice the cold.

"What is your question?" asked Zoran.

"Zoran Pasha, how did you know of the attack today?"

Zoran turned and gave a hard look at Goodman. "Do you know what you lack?" he said.

"Many things, Zoran Pasha."

Zoran chuckled. "You may use our words, but you do not understand the correct language."

"I'm still learning Bosanski—"

"Neh, Američko." Zoran pursed his lips. "There is more."

"I don't understand, Zoran Pasha."

"Words are not enough," Zoran spoke slowly, clearly. "You are a stranger here. Many people talk; not many understand. A man can be false with his mouth, but not with his eyes."

"You mean like lying?" asked Goodman.

"Neh." Zoran shook his head. "The world has two languages. The language of the mouth and the language of the eyes. Words can be nothing. You can speak with your mouth and hear with your ears, but they may be false words. It is the—I don't know the meaning in English—the eye-words you must understand. Mouth-words can be truth or lies. Eye-words are always true, but only if you can see with the correct eyes. If you see the world with ignorant eyes, you will not see the knife when it comes for you. If you see the world through hateful eyes, you will have no one to die for you. You must see with both eyes."

"Is that how you saw what was happening today, just before the attack? You saw a knife?"

"I saw the eyes," said Zoran. "Black like darkness. Black like the evil ones."

"The evil ones?" asked Goodman. "You mean the Nazis?"

"No," said Zoran. "The Nazis and the Ustaši are merely puppets. The evil ones I speak of are the ones who come in the night to set fire to a man's barn. Or set free a farmer's flocks. Or turn a child against his father."

"I don't understand, Zoran Pasha," said Goodman, more confused than a moment prior. "Who are the evil ones?"

"They are evil as well, but no, I describe another. They come in whatever form they desire," Zoran explained. "Young men, old women, small children. A goat, or a rat, or some other troublesome animal. We call them *duhovi* or sometimes *ginnii*. Many people are afraid to call them by their real names, so they call them *dirty little men*."

Goodman recalled the conversation with Baba. *Dirty little men.* "The spirits," Goodman said. "Little devils." Jasminka would never talk about them. But Baba had said: Do not be afraid—but be mindful. "You aren't afraid?" Goodman asked Zoran.

"You know of this, yes?" said Zoran, pleasantly surprised by his tone. "No. No, I am not afraid of them. They work *for* me as much as against me. You can know who their servants are by their eye-words."

"And you can see who they are?"

"Yes, because I speak their language," said Zoran. "You must learn to speak their language. You will not survive Bosnia if you fail to read the eye-words."

"How do I learn eye-words, Pasha?"

"Watch," said Zoran. "Listen to ear-words but watch…*watch* for the eye-words."

"Yes, Pasha." Goodman nodded, but he had so much more to ask. These people are so…suspicious. But *I need them…I need them to help get me out. Is Zoran even thinking about that? I need to know.* Goodman started to ask, but bit his lip instead.

He looked at Zoran. The gray lunar glow from above and the twinkling orange points from the many fires reflected in Zoran's eyes. *I have to ask. I don't know if I'll get another opportunity like this.*

"Pasha," he said. "You'll get me out of Yugoslavia? You'll get me back to my people?"

"Yes," said Zoran. "If you live. We must take Tuzla. We must have the upper hand in the control of the city and the entire valley. Then we can negotiate for your safe return to your army, and to your place in the skies."

"Hvala, Pasha." Goodman waited for Zoran to initiate the next move, but he remained statuesque on the edge of the rooftop. *I need to show that I'm thankful.* "A thousand pardons, Pasha—"

"Ništa." Zoran dismissed the additional apology without looking down from the sky.

*Thank God*, thought Goodman. He exhaled loudly. For the first time since leaving Baba's village, he felt under control. Like things might work out. *For now, though, I'm with Zoran. No, not just with them. I'm for them. This is my fight, and then I'll go home. Their war is my war. Then, and only then, I can...can what? Leave?* His heart, and now his gut, were all mixed up. *But this*, he resolved, *this is not my place.* He imagined himself back in the cockpit of the Jessica Joy, with his best friend in the co-pilot's seat, ticking off tasks on a checklist. *That may never be*, he said to himself. *But maybe something close. None of that will be real if I don't go all-in with Zoran. What choices are there? None.* He looked at Zoran, and again at the sky. *I'm here now.* A sense of peace washed over him. *I'm not in control, but I'm not flapping in the wind anymore. Whatever I do to win here is how I get home.*

"Zoran Pasha, hvala."

"Nište."

Goodman turned to the stairs, but Zoran remained stationary. "Pasha, are you going to go to sleep now?" asked Goodman.

"Neh," Zoran grumbled. "Now I will speak to Allah so the *duhovi* do not gain the upper hand against me."

"What should I do, Zoran Pasha?" asked Goodman. "How do I help you fight?"

"The fight will come," said Zoran. "And you *will* fight. I know this now. But you must learn to speak the eye-words. Then you might live to fly your airplanes again." Zoran turned back to the night sky above them.

"Laku noč, Zoran Pasha."

Zoran turned and watched Goodman descend the stairs. *This man*, thought Zoran. *This foreigner. What to do with him?*

Tomislav caught up to Goodman on his way back to the well, where they joined the militia at rest. "All is well?" he asked Goodman after a long silence.

"Strangely, yes," Goodman replied. "I think so."

# 33

## SEPTEMBER 25, 1943
## THE VILLAGE OF DOLINSKI GRAD

GOODMAN AND TOMISLAV WERE CLOSEST TO THE MESSENGER when he dismounted and rushed to Milosz, who then urgently called for all the militia leaders to come to the house where Zoran slept. Word spread quickly through the militia that a large German supply convoy that had passed through some town before sunset last night had not yet arrived on the Tuzla highway. Forty-two trucks, two armored cars, and a single command car.

The militia lit up at the news. A huge German convoy stuck in the hills! What a gift! The region was remote, Tomislav explained, and the only passage through the southern ranges of the Majevitsa was long, winding, and narrow. And the hills were bad for German FM radio communications.

"This is good for us," said Zoran when he emerged from his meeting. "Very good for us." He tugged anxiously on his beard. "Prepare the men!"

Milosz and Amira rousted their men, organizing the force into three columns and taking lead of one each, with the remainder to be commanded by Zoran. Zoran's column would find and attack the head of the German convoy while Milosz led a simultaneous attack from the rear. This would keep Amira's group free from the threat of German reinforcements or counterattack as they attacked the center of the column. Capturing prisoners—as many as possible—was her mission from Zoran. Officers were better, but any Nazi dogs would do. The three columns went their separate ways when scouts reported they identified the road where the Germans sat, sleepy and bored, less than four miles away.

Only an hour later, after a difficult but swift foot march, the Amira's column reached the ridgeline above their target. Amira and

177

Ahmet dashed ahead on a quick reconnaissance of the forest road below. Upon returning, she led her force through a small gap in the ridgeline and down a ravine on the far side. She paused at a large depression in the ground and let her men consolidate around her.

"The convoy is there." She pointed to the dark green trucks evenly spaced along the crescent-shaped road below them. "When this group is distracted by the attacks from Zoran and Milosz, we will attack." She looked at her men and called for her machine gunner. A giant emerged from the group, heavily laden with belts of ammunition and a German-made MG-42 machinegun. He looked familiar, but Goodman had no idea why.

"Musa," said Amira, pointing toward the road and then to a rocky outcropping. "One hundred-twenty meters from there, yes?"

*Musa?* Goodman remembered the name. *Is that Jasminka's cousin? From the family photo?* He searched his memory to match the faces. *It must be him.*

Musa peered through the brush. "No problem," he said matter-of-factly. He confidently patted the long, fluted barrel of his weapon. "From there, yes?" He pointed along the curve of the road. "To there, yes?"

She nodded, and Musa smiled in reply.

Goodman crept forward next to Amira and scanned the valley below. *That's a lot of Germans*, he thought. Tomislav clucked his tongue and gave Goodman a concerned look. Ahmet quickly scanned the road for himself.

"Too many Germans," whispered Ahmet. "There are too many Germans, Amira Effendim."

"Gluposti," Amira replied. *Nonsense.*

"Why are they stopped?" said Ahmet. "We should leave here at once—"

"No, look!" Goodman pointed down the hill at two trucks doubled parked on near edge of the road. One had its hood raised. "Kamion oštećen!" *Broken truck.*

"Get me the boy! Get me Hamza!" Amira quietly ordered. After a moment, a boy who looked as if he should be in grammar school crept forward. Amira pulled him close.

"Hamza!"

"Yes, Amira Effendim!" He saluted. She ignored it.

"Hamza, listen to me now. Tell Zoran Pasha that we have the convoy in front of us. We will take them when he attacks. Now, do you know where to find him?"

"Yes, Effendim!"

"Good. Now, go quickly!"

"Da, Effendim!" He quickly raised his hand in salute and scampered silently from tree to tree until he disappeared over the top of the ridge. Everyone turned their attention back to the road.

A German soldier in mechanic's coveralls emerged from under one of the trucks and spoke to a cluster of officers standing nearby. One of them yelled something, and the German voices rose in volume. A squad of German soldiers emerged from the rear of another truck. After some time, toolboxes clunked in the back of the flatbed. Amira looked at Ahmet, Goodman, and Tomislav.

"Good," she said. "We move when the engines will cover our noise and the *fritzies* are distracted."

Goodman leaned over to Tomislav. "What's a *fritzie*?"

"Fritz is a common German name," he replied. "We call them Fritzie."

Goodman smirked. "We call 'em krauts."

"Krauts?" Tomislav chuckled after a moment's consideration. "Ahhh!" he finally said. "As in *sauerkraut*. That is funny."

Several long and nervous minutes passed as the group listened to German officers shout out commands up and down the long column. After what felt to Goodman like an absurdly long period of organizing, the Germans climbed back into their trucks, and dozens of diesel engines roared to life. The broken-down truck sat silent as an angry sergeant barked orders to his squad.

Amira signaled for everyone to move. Musa led his machinegun crew to the rocky outcropping. Ahmet rose to a crouch and waved the rest of the militia patrol to follow him to the assault line. Goodman and Tomislav quietly slid into a place where they had a good view through the thicket.

Goodman watched the convoy slowly roll past the broken-down truck. As the trucks rolled by, soldiers waved and taunted their comrades who were assigned to the stay-behind guard force. One by one, the trucks topped the ridge and disappeared. Finally, a gray-and-green-painted armored car with a long cannon and a co-mounted heavy machine gun protruding from the turret swerved and skidded past as the driver took the curve at speed. Only a cloud of blue-white diesel smoke remained over the road. Soon, the valley became quiet again. Goodman wondered how long Amira would wait.

Several more minutes passed, and the Germans on the road began to throw sticks at each other and roll over onto their backs. Some of them lowered their heads and dozed in the warm sunshine that filtered down through the bare trees.

"Musa!" Amira whispered. "Make ready your weapon! There are three Fritzies in the rear of the second truck. Do not kill them. There are several more behind the trucks. Kill them only if you have to! Kill the ones in the first truck, and then the ones in the woods."

Musa nodded and lowered his head to squint down the sights. He aimed at the first truck, then shifted his aim to the second truck and back again. He nodded a second time when he was ready.

Amira pressed against the tree next to her and took aim with her submachinegun. Goodman peered over the tree again and looked down his gunsights. He had two Germans in range: one sat at the edge of the road looking at the ground, and the other leaned against the bumper of the disabled truck immediately behind him. They were talking, not paying attention to the forest around them. The sergeant paced around the trucks. Then it struck Goodman what he was about to do.

*I'm killing Germans*, he thought. *I'm about to open fire and shoot German soldiers.* Why did it feel different from the Ustaša men he killed in the forest? Maybe because last time, the Ustaši gave him no time to think or feel. He exhaled nervously. *Where's Tomislav?* He looked around and saw Tomislav sitting with his back against a rock, detached from what the rest of the group was doing, his pistol on his lap.

"What are you doing?" Goodman whispered.

"I'm no good in a gun battle," was all he had to say.

Goodman shook his head and turned his eyes to the Germans on the road. He took aim at the one with his elbows on the bumper.

Amira stood up to a low crouch and unscrewed the caps that retained the pull-strings to three German *stielhandgranaten* stick grenades. Ahmet did the same with three more grenades. At Amira's command, they each yanked the strings and threw them in quick succession down the hill. They clunked against the trucks or landed with a smack on the road. Several Germans looked around at the noises, but only one got out a scream before the grenades fractured the serenity of the forest. Musa's machine gun erupted with an ear-splitting ripping sound that cut the forest air. The entire assault line opened fire, and the road suddenly exploded into dust. Goodman flinched at the brilliant, hot muzzle flashes to his left and right, but he recovered and emptied his magazine at the place where he last saw the German by the truck. His gun clicked empty, and he changed magazines. This time, he aimed again but saw no one to shoot at. So instead, he emptied his second magazine into the truck. Goodman hunkered down when a bullet sprayed him with dirt. He reloaded his weapon.

Musa's ammunition bearers kept feeding belt after belt of ammunition to his weapon, and he kept spewing fire into the German position below. The cab of the lead truck flew to pieces, and glass and blood splattered onto the road. Goodman spotted a muzzle flash through the ferns on the slope. He aimed at it and squeezed the trigger.

Musa shifted his weight slightly, and a German soldier twisted and fell amidst a shower of sparks from a truck's engine compartment. The canvas cover danced with the force of the bullets, and a soldier rolled out and landed out of sight. Another German soldier fell headlong out of the rear and flopped onto the road. A third slumped against the large truck tires.

Musa shifted his fire again to chase a soldier making a dash for the woods behind the trucks. The soldier fell, and Musa shifted back to the trucks. Bursting tires caused the trucks to lurch sideways, and white sparks showered the road. Metal protective panels fell from the truck sides like playing cards. Musa's machine gun fell silent, and his assistants hastily reloaded another belt of ammunition. He slammed the cover down and took aim.

"Prestani pucati!" Amira yelled out. *Stop shooting!* Goodman and the others repeated her command down the line, and everyone slowly complied. Goodman's ears were ringing.

Musa's machine gun emitted a loud ticking noise as the glowing metal parts cooled and contracted. Goodman turned to Amira for her next command, but she was already halfway to the road.

"Atak!" she cried. She sprayed the ferns and laurel with one long burst of automatic fire as she ran.

Goodman heaved himself over the fallen tree and ran toward the smoking trucks, also firing his submachinegun. The entire assault line was right behind him, screaming like a tribe of savages, firing their weapons wildly. The militia quickly reached the smoldering trucks.

Goodman followed Amira to the rear of the second truck. Three of Amira's men scrambled over the bumper to the tailgate, and a gunshot shattered the air. The first fighter fell backward and hit the ground. Several more gunshots followed, and the other two men fell out of the back. One more was severely wounded and screamed when he hit the ground. Amira, Goodman, Ahmet and several others fired into the rear of the truck, and a point-blank firefight erupted. It lasted until Amira and Goodman physically pulled the men back. Three more Majevitsa men were now wounded. All for one truck.

"Govno!" Amira yelled angrily. "Tomislav! Come here, now!"

Tomislav jogged the final few paces down the hill to the last tree before the road. She gestured toward the truck.

"Tell them to surrender!"

"Du musst dich ergeben!" Tomislav called out.

An angry shout came in reply. Tomislav looked at Amira and shook his head.

"What did he say?" said Amira.

Tomislav pursed his lips. "He says, 'fuck you,' and, 'you should go to hell.'"

She vigorously jabbed her finger at him and then at the truck. "Iznova!" *Again!*

Tomislav exhaled before he called out again. Another angry yell emanated from the bed of the truck. Tomislav shrugged. "Same," he said.

"Tell him this is his last chance. We will take him alive now, or we will kill him now!"

Tomislav protested. "He's not going to—"

"Tell him!" she barked.

Tomislav called out once more. Rifle shots from inside the truck sent everyone behind cover. Amira reached around and withdrew a stick grenade from her belt. She pulled the cord and raised it over her head.

"Granate!" she yelled and promptly threw it into the bed of the truck.

It landed with a loud clank. A German screamed, and the blast blew out the canvas on all sides. Fragments of canvas flopped onto the ground, smoking at the seams and smattered with blood. Two men climbed over the tailgate and confirmed what everyone already knew. Three rifles and a submachine gun flew out over the tailgate, followed by several bandoliers of ammunition. With that completed, the militia began a disorderly rummaging of the contents of the trucks and the personal effects of the dead Germans.

Someone cried out, and everyone stood to see what was happening.

Goodman caught a glance of two German survivors sprinting into the woods. Several shots rang and out, and the men veered off in different directions.

"Stop shooting you idiots!" yelled Amira. "Catch them!" She took off running.

She leapt over a fallen tree, and Goodman followed right behind her. Amira caught the nearest German in a flying tackle, but he, being much bigger than she, flung her to the ground and took off again. But before the German could get much speed, Goodman hit him in the lumbar region with his shoulder, and the German went down with a crunch of sticks and maybe a bone or two. He fought back, and Goodman struggled to hold him down. The German was very muscular and twisted to turn himself over.

"No, you don't!" Goodman exclaimed as he punched the man in the side head.

A look of surprise exploded across the German's face. Goodman raised his fist to hit him again, but Amira gave the soldier a solid whack with the butt of her weapon and the German slumped into the ferns. She directed her men to carry him back to the trucks before looking to where the others were still struggling through the thick underbrush in pursuit of the last escaping survivor.

Goodman stood and searched the woods for the other survivor. All he saw were ferns and trees.

"Govno!" she screamed in frustration. "Where is the other one?"

"I see him!" Musa called out from his perch on the slope above the trucks. "Do I shoot him?"

Amira looked toward the woods where her men were still crashing through the laurel. "Kill him!" she yelled.

The brief but violent ripsaw sound echoed through the forest. Everyone waited for his next words.

"Got him!" yelled Musa with a tone of satisfaction. "He's down."

"Bring him back here!" Amira yelled to her men.

"Good," muttered Goodman. *Can't let any of them get away*, he thought. *I didn't get into this fight for nothing.* He felt an intense satisfaction for what they had just accomplished.

Not wanting to miss out on a chance to resupply himself, Goodman quickly returned to the dead Germans around the trucks. He rifled through a soldier's pockets, tossing aside the man's identification book, but he kept a pack of cigarettes, a small pocketknife, and a box of matches. Most of the food in the man's ration box was already eaten, and Goodman finished the rest. *Not terrific,* he thought. *But better than nothing.* Then it occurred to him: *I killed this guy, and now I'm eating his food.* It did not feel as odd as it should have, but Goodman shrugged it off.

Tomislav came up with two full packs of cigarettes and a box of matches, plus a working lighter. He tossed a bandolier of ammunition to Musa's ammo bearers and pocketed three full clips of ammunition for his own pistol.

"Hey!" he called to Goodman. "Here!" He tossed something to him.

Goodman looked up just in time to catch it. It was a lighter marked with the infamous gothic lightning double-S of the Waffen-SS. The other side was ornamentally engraved as well. He pocketed it, and then Tomislav tossed him a pistol. It was a rather worn looking Walther P38, same as Tomislav's. "You may want this one day." Goodman checked the clip. Only two rounds fired. Tomislav handed another pistol magazine to him. It was heavy with bullets.

"Hvala." Godman rubbed off the grime and checked it. It was full.

"Molim," Tomislav smiled grimly. "What's a few bullets between friends?"

Goodman half-chuckled and pocketed the pistol and magazine.

"Here," Tomislav said. He tossed a flask, also engraved but very worn, with a dent across one side.

Goodman opened the screw-top lid and sniffed. *Fruity.*

"The Fritzies drink schnapps," said Tomislav. Goodman took the flask.

"Schnapps?"

"Ja," said Tomislav with an exaggerated German accent.

Goodman took a quick sip. *Very smooth,* he thought. He took a second, longer drink. *Much better than the homemade slivovitz everybody's got around here.*

As the others completed their looting, Amira's men delivered the newly captured German soldier to her with his hands bound and his mouth tightly gagged.

"Roll him over," she directed. She looked him over, rolled his head to one side, then the other to look at the growing lump she put on the side of his head. He had a boy's face, with freckles, and a look of sheer terror in his eyes. Other men arrived with the body of the German that Musa had shot. His head was a bloody mess, as was the rest of him. Finding nothing of interest, they left the body in the ferns.

"Take the one," she directed. She turned to Ahmet and shook her head. "Only one."

"There was nothing to be done," said Ahmet apologetically.

Gunfire echoed from the north, just over the ridge. A large caliber cannon blasted twice, then several more times in quick succession.

"Idi!" Amira pointed at the prisoner. "Get him moving!"

Goodman and Tomislav lifted the prisoner and shoved him toward the hill. Everyone else had already started up the hillside by the time they got back across the road. The prisoner resisted, and Ahmet punched the young German in the stomach. Fritzie grunted loudly and resisted no more. Everyone struggled up the hillside, slipping on the loose soil and rocks, as the gunfire over the ridge increased in intensity.

"Is that Zoran?" Goodman asked.

"Yes! Keep moving!" Tomislav yelled back.

The cannon pounded away repeatedly, and a large tree fell with a groan and a crash.

"Hurry!" yelled Amira in Bosanski.

Goodman looked over his shoulder in time to see the armored car blow a cloud of smoke into the air as it rounded the bend. Its gun traversed left and right, scanning for targets. The next vehicle to appear was the command car with its long antenna swaying back and forth. The armored car opened fire into the woods on both sides of the road. Cannon fire and explosions made the forest air vibrate.

Musa planted his MG42 in the crook of a tree, aimed at the road, and yelled to his comrades to hurry. He shot a quick glance at Goodman as he passed by with the prisoner. He smiled, which struck Goodman as oddly familiar. *That must be Jasminka's cousin.*

Safely behind the ridgeline, Amira and Ahmet reorganized the group. One of Amira's men retied the ropes that bound Fritzie's arms with a knot around his neck and the free end held fast. *Just like with the girl spy,* thought Goodman. On the road behind them, the armored car continued to blast away at the empty forest.

"Everyone, listen!" yelled Amira. She explained that the rendezvous site was eight miles away, and they had to make it by nightfall.

When Tomislav translated, Goodman exclaimed, "Eight miles? In this terrain? Why so far?"

"If they have the forces, the Germans will surround this area within hours and conduct a search-and-destroy operation for us," explained Tomislav. "We must be outside of this area."

Amira raced down the hill, and everyone ran to keep up, including Goodman.

# 34

## A FARM IN THE WESTERN MAJEVITSA FOOTHILLS, BOSNIA, YUGOSLAVIA

SOMEONE SHOOK GOODMAN from his dozing. He rubbed his eyes and heard the engines racing through the woods. *That's not good*, he thought. He sat up in a sudden panic. Everyone was scrambling to gather his belongings in a mad rush. The glow of headlights cast a dull incandescence over the open fields surrounding the farm where they had paused to rest. Heavy vehicles raced down the single-lane dirt track toward the farm.

"Get up!" Tomislav exclaimed.

Amira was barking commands to her people. "We waited too long!" she said. "We must leave here now!"

Goodman shook the exhaustion from his mind and grabbed up his equipment. A burst of machine-gun fire sent him—and everyone else—to the ground. The armored cars skidded off the road, but a thick stand of trees stopped their advance. A machine gun ripped the air, sending tracers through the trees, severing branches, and snapping against the rocks on the far side of the small pasture. Some men dropped their equipment as they ran into the woods. Musa held his MG42 over one shoulder and dragged Fritzie the prisoner by the rope with the other arm. Goodman heaved Fritzie to his feet and gave him a shove. Amira yelled something as she ran to keep up with her men, trying to keep some semblance of control in their withdrawal, but it was all they could do to run.

Blinded by quick flashes of headlights and militiamen wildly returning fire, Goodman ran haphazardly through the dark woods. He tripped and fell several times before running head-first into a tree. Dazed, he got up and ran again. He felt a warm trickle on the side of his face and wiped it away. Someone went down in front of him, and he offered a hand to get them back to their feet. The arm was heavy, and the man never moved. Goodman dropped the hand and ran.

"Tomislav!" he called out. He thought he heard a reply, but the smack of a bullet into a tree near his head refocused him on his own running. He followed the sounds of someone crashing through the trees in front of him, hoping whoever it was knew where he was going.

The group broke out of the forest into a narrow field with a stacked stone wall across their front. When Goodman reached the wall and peered over it to see another road on the far side. Amira yelled for everyone to stop running. They collapsed against the wall with sweaty, heaving breaths, punctuated by coughing and spitting. Someone groaned loudly.

"Ahmet!" called Amira.

No answer.

"Ahmet!" Others joined her in calling out for him. "Ahmet! Ahmet!"

"Shut up!" Amira barked at them. "Musa, Stjepan, Fedad, are you here?"

"Yes," they replied, almost in unison.

"Check the road." She pointed over the wall, and they disappeared into the dark. "Latif, Goran, Fuad! Carry Marko. Tomislav, where is Ahmet?"

"I...I don't know," Tomislav stuttered between breaths.

"The road is clear!" came the reply from the other side of the wall.

"Idi!" Amira called out, and everyone scrambled over. Suddenly, someone yelled to them from behind.

Goodman spun around to see Ahmet with another man under his arm, each dragging a rifle through the weeds. Goodman and Tomislav ran to help, each taking an arm of the wounded man. They heaved him over the wall, where he landed with a loud groan, and then got themselves over. Amira looked around at the group and then at the moonlit road.

"Pozuri!" said Goodman. *Hurry!*

She looked over her shoulder at him, and then at both ways up the road. "We go now."

She led the group across the road, but a steep embankment on the far side stopped the group in the open. Amira and most of the men climbed hand-over-hand to get up, but several slid back down when the loose dirt gave way. The men carrying the wounded man let him slide back down the embankment and roll into the middle of the road. The heavy roar of a truck engine sent everyone scrambling.

"We can't leave him!" Goodman called out to Tomislav.

Goodman shielded his eyes against the glare of the headlights.

"Yes, we can!" replied Tomislav. "And we must!"

Goodman looked at the truck barreling toward them with headlights blazing, then looked at the man lying in the road. The memory of the wounded man he dropped in that first terrible ambush came to him. *I can't leave him. I can't abandon one of us again. Not again*, he muttered. The men carrying the third wounded man dropped him next Goodman and scrambled up the embankment.

Ahmet slid down next to Goodman. And let out a long string of curses as he dropped to a knee and fired his rifle at the approaching headlights. Goodman raised his weapon, too, and squeezed a long burst at the cab. The truck swerved, skidded, and slammed into the embankment in a cloud of dust.

Ahmet squeezed off several more rounds at the truck. Goodman yanked his empty magazine free as one of the truck's headlights flickered out. Then he saw the bright yellowish-white bursts of return gunfire and a German soldier running directly at him, firing as he ran. Goodman panicked and fumbled the magazine. He reached for it, only for a bullet's impact to knock it away. Ahmet fired again and the German soldier dropped and lay still. Goodman finally loaded the magazine and aimed. But he saw Amira leap from the top of the embankment to the hood of the truck and fire her entire magazine into the cab in one long burst.

"She's attacking!" yelled Goodman.

Dark-clad men poured out of the rear of the truck, and Goodman emptied his magazine into the woods where they ran. His weapon clicked empty again as two Nazi Waffen-SS stormtroopers charged at him. One of them fell and did not return to his feet. Tomislav stepped to Goodman's side and dropped the remaining SS trooper with two shots. He ran to the body and fired once more at close range. Goodman reloaded his weapon, but Tomislav's hand blocked him from aiming it. *Why is he stopping me?* Goodman wondered for a split second until he saw why.

Amira and the handful of men with her poured gunfire into the truck from close range. There was no return fire. Pistol and rifle shots rang out and echoed through the woods as the militia chased down and snuffed out the survivors. Goodman turned to Ahmet and the wounded men on the road.

The light from the truck's remaining headlight provided enough illumination for Goodman to see that Ahmet's shirt was matted with blood. And that he braced his arm against his stomach. Goodman checked Ahmet's wounds and saw there was a long cut under his forearm. Goodman tore Ahmet's sleeve and fashioned a hasty tourniquet. Ahmet slumped against the embankment and motioned to the fallen militiamen on the ground next to him. Neither of them was conscious.

Goodman checked them for a pulse. He felt a very weak, irregular throbbing in the first man's carotid artery. Tomislav gently lifted the other man's arm to check, but the volume of blood on the road under him told everything he needed to know. Ahmet muttered a small prayer as he shuffled toward the truck. Amira barked orders to get off the road.

"Man need doctor!" Goodman told her.

"No time for that," Amira barked at them. "We go now!"

"But we can't—"

The crack of a pistol shot cut him off. Everyone turned and saw Ahmet pocketing his pistol.

"He is gone," Ahmet announced.

Amira waved everyone off the road, and her men moved quickly up the embankment and into the forest. Goodman was shocked. *What kind of treatment is that for a fellow fighter? Is this what they do to each other? What if I get hurt?*

The going was very fast and quiet for several hours. Amira led them across farm fields and through acres of woods and across numerous streams. They avoided all roads and carefully skirted a tiny village. This time, Goodman was not the only one struggling to keep up with her. The night seemed interminable, as did the thorns in his arms and legs, sticks in his eyes, and spider webs across his face. Before long, exhaustion set in again. *How much longer?*

At a brief pause, Goodman collapsed next to Tomislav and drank from a stream. "If that farm was the place we were to meet up with Zoran," asked Goodman. "Where are we going now?"

"We are retreating into the Majevitsa," he replied. "Back to sanctuary."

"What will we do there?"

"Rest, eat, plan …

At the bottom of a long, gradual descent, Goodman smelled the humid funk of a swamp. He felt water seep into his boots. Amira led them along a circuitous route, seemingly avoiding the deeper water at some points, yet deliberately leading them through frigid, chest-deep water at another. It smelled rotten, like ancient decay. The mud sucked at their boots. Goodman felt his leg muscles fatiguing. He imagined himself finally not being able to lift a leg and remaining stuck. His vision terminated with images of Amira leading her men away from him, having given up on pulling him free. *Stop thinking that,* he thought to himself. *That's stupid. Don't stop. Just move your feet.*

Finally, Amira pushed forward and led the group abruptly toward higher ground. When they finally paused to rest, the ground felt solid. Wet, but solid. The sky appeared to show hints of dawn. Or was it a trick on Goodman's eyes? He strained, but he could not determine which it was. *Swamp light? Or Dawn? Or just ambient light? Doesn't matter*, he thought to himself. He intended to lower himself to the ground, but he lost his grip and hit the ground rather hard.

Amira set up the group in the middle of a slightly elevated piece of ground. Ahmet quickly posted two sentries on the trail of broken weeds they left behind. The sky seemed slightly brighter to Goodman. *It is sunlight*, he thought. *We've been running all night.*

"We stay here for a while," Amira announced. "But do not sleep!"

Amira dispatched two men to search ahead, toward the gathering dawn. Goodman checked on the wounded, suddenly invigorated by the opportunity to use his skills to help. He put another tourniquet on Ahmet's biceps. *At least he'll keep his blood, if not his arm*, Goodman thought. On other men, Goodman bandaged two severe wounds that would certainly be gangrenous in twenty-four hours if not properly cleaned immediately. He looked over Fritzie the prisoner. He was probably one of the more well-off individuals in the camp. Obviously young, healthy, well-fed and likely accustomed to sleeping on the ground, Goodman concluded his health was not a concern, despite the bruises and open cuts.

One of the wounded men cried out suddenly, and the others pounced to quiet him. He continued to whimper until he passed out. Goodman checked to see that he was still breathing and then sat down next to Tomislav, who was asleep with his head on his knees. *Maybe one of us should stay awake*. Goodman let him sleep. Tomislav gave no indication of acknowledgement of the downpour that started half an hour later. Goodman pulled his coat over his head. Eventually, the rain stopped. Then he, too, fell asleep.

# 35

## SEPTEMBER 26, 1943

GOODMAN SLAPPED HIS OWN FACE in a slow-motion attempt to swat a mosquito. He was groggy, caked with mud, and smelled of swamp filth. He scratched at the mosquito bites that covered his face and neck. The sky was now the same gray as the dense fog that enveloped them in the swampy forest. Most of the men were sitting up, either alone or quietly talking to each other, swatting mosquitos. A couple of the adolescents were throwing lumps of moss at each other, and occasionally at Fritzie, who could only flinch and curse at them in German through his gag. Goodman sat up to look around. Tomislav was still sleeping with his coat over his head. Ahmet was passed out against a moss-covered tree. Musa was awake, but Amira was nowhere to be seen. In fact, he counted that fully half of the men from the night before were absent. *She's still gone*, he thought. *I hope nothing went wrong. Well, nothing more than what happened last night.* He rubbed his eyes and used a tree to push himself up. *How long was I out?*

Standing tall, Musa was the only one looking at something other than his feet or the inside of his eyelids. He held his MG42 with the ammo belt draped over his shoulder, silently observing the dense fog around them. *I know where I've seen Musa before*, Goodman remembered. *That photograph Jasminka showed me. He's the one with the kids hanging on him. I think he's Jasminka's cousin.*

Goodman stretched and felt joints pop at every motion. At six feet and two inches, he was taller than most men in the militia, and Zoran was a good four inches taller than he. But Musa was at least four inches taller still. That MG42 had to weigh forty of fifty pounds, but he carried it effortlessly. *I'm glad I'm on his side*, thought Goodman. *Wait, is he crying?*

Goodman wasn't sure what to do when he saw the moist redness in Musa's eyes. He *had* been crying. Musa glanced over and saw the questions in Goodman's eyes.

193

He spoke slowly, and his voice cracked. "My cousin died on the road last night. I don't know how I'm going to tell my family. He was everyone's favorite." He swatted at the cloud of gnats and mosquitos surrounding him. "He was *the* favorite." He paused again. "You probably don't understand anything I'm saying."

"Žao mi je," said Goodman. "Razumijem." *I'm sorry* was all he could think of to say. Then he remembered.

"When I live in village," he began to compose his best sentence yet in Bosanski. "I live with old woman and little girl. Little girl name Jasminka…"

Musa's eyes opened wide. "Jasminka?" His face suddenly lost ten years. "Gde?"

"I not know where," Goodman stumbled with his reply. "I not know name of village. But village on… on mountain. Jasminka my…" He wanted to say *friend*. "…my Bosanski teacher."

"Ona je živa?" he asked, almost desperately. *She is alive?*

Goodman pretended the Germans had never found the village. Certainly, they never executed anyone for their inability to locate him in Baba's basement. "She alive, and Baba alive, too."

Musa's grimy, emotionally drained face managed a slight smile. His shoulders relaxed, and he exhaled a great breath and looked up at the sky. His smile covered his face. Then it dawned on Goodman. The photograph. Jasminka's family. Musa. Zoran. Amira. *They're all family!*

Musa nodded, then turned back to looking off into the woods. He became agitated and marched off and prodded the men along the perimeter to pay attention. A groan from a wounded man turned Goodman's head. He squatted down on the soft earth and examined the man's wounds. *This is an infection already.* He scowled. *This is a mess. I'm not really a doctor, but I should be doing more.*

"Gde je tvoi bol?" he asked the next man. *Where is your pain?* It was what the nurse had asked him every time she had shown up at Baba's house. After a cursory exam, Goodman decided that the man was generally fine. Old and exhausted and injured, yes, but fine given the circumstances.

Much to Goodman's dismay, the second man, the eldest of the injured, had succumbed to his wounds sometime in the night. His pallid flesh was scraped and scabbed, but there were no open wounds, certainly no obvious bleeding. He searched the man's body and discovered a single hole in the man's stomach under a fold of fat. It was about the size of the tip of Goodman's little finger. He rolled the man over and there was no exit wound. *Dammit*, thought Goodman. *That must have been really painful.* He shook his head. *The guy made no noises, no complaints. And he paid for his stubbornness.* This angered Goodman again.

*Why didn't he say something? Why did I not see this before? Why did I not check the wounded more often? I should have checked again and done a better job. I should have been more aware. Dammit! I should have checked for this. I should have checked.* He bit the inside of his cheek. Hard. He rose and checked the other injuries in the camp. He even checked the young German prisoner, though his act of service was not well received. Fritzie took a swipe at Goodman that knocked him back. The guard smacked Fritzie hard across the face with a stick. Another German curse and another smack with the stick. Goodman felt a wave of satisfaction at the instant punishment.

*Stupid kraut.*

Goodman decided the German soldier deserved no more help and moved on. All the others were stable and conscious—angry after Goodman woke them to check on their injuries, but more or less healthy, all things considered. Satisfied that he had done what he could, Goodman sat down behind a moss-covered tree. The camp quieted down again.

Several more hours passed before a sentry sloshed into camp and pointed into the fog. Musa snapped his fingers, and everyone quickly postured themselves for attack. A sloshing sound came from a fair distance away. A minute later, everyone relaxed as the sentry signaled it was Amira and the rest of her patrol returning.

They were soaked, muddied, and tired, but appeared upbeat. They carried clay jugs, which they handed out. Amira went straight to Musa and started giving him directions. Several others gathered around to hear what she had to say.

"We must go to the Hukič farm," she said, breathing heavily. "It is much farther, but the return route to the first meeting place is impossible. Too many Germans. We move soon."

"What about him?" Goodman pointed at the dead man next to the tree.

"Leave him," she said flatly. "We must move quickly."

Others quickly relieved the dead man of his possessions and left him in the moss, surrounded by trampled ferns. Goodman watched and felt his instinct to preserve the man's dignity battle the urge to get a pack of cigarettes or food or something for himself. He also knew that they hadn't the time, resources, or energy to bury him decently. He felt his empty stomach growl. *We need to get out of here. Away from the Germans. Where is Zoran?*

Everyone quickly gathered their belongings, shouldered their weapons, and moved off the high ground and back into the swamp. Goodman carried his submachinegun over his shoulder for at least a mile before the ground dried out under his feet. The forest canopy opened to reveal a blue sky behind the thinning cloud cover. Amira waved at someone ahead. Goodman saw a young girl on horseback waved back.

The girl led them along a small stream that traversed rolling farm fields. By midday, the stream led them into a large, wooded valley, and finally, to its rocky source. The churning water was refreshingly clean, and everyone gladly scooped it over their heads and slurped it into their mouths. Tomislav scooped his flask into the water and gulped it down before re-filling and giving it to Goodman. He drank.

"Thank you for what you did back there," said Goodman as he handed the flask back to Tomislav. "On the road. You saved my life."

"Yes, I know," replied Tomislav. He gave Goodman a piece of bread from his food bag. Goodman took it and shoved it into his mouth.

"I told you," Tomislav mused. "This place is difficult."

"That's putting it mildly," Goodman admitted. "Every time I think I have this place figured out, something turns it upside down, but it makes sense afterward."

"Stay close to me," said Tomislav. "I know what to do."

"Yeah, thanks," said Goodman. "No good in a gunfight, huh?"

Tomislav pursed his lips. "I do what I have to."

The girl remounted her horse and departed the way she came. Amira said there was a farm at the bottom of the eastern slope, that someone would meet them with food, water, and a place to sleep. Goodman's spirit lifted at the news, as did everyone's. The sun had set again, and the final rays of light revealed a beautiful, sweeping view of the plains to the south and the forested slopes of the greater Majevitsa hills to the north.

They walked for hours, but it went fast for everyone except their walking wounded and Fritzie the prisoner.

"Get up, Fritzie," one man would say after watching him stumble into a bush.

"Hurry up, Fritzie," said another, who shoved Fritzie into the back of the man holding the rope around his neck. He got shoved back again.

"Get back in line, Fritzie." A kick to the buttocks. Another swipe with a stick. Another push, another shove. Goodman smirked at the darkly comical nature of Fritzie's abuse.

*Stupid kraut.*

Goodman still burned inside over the death of the old man in the swamp this morning, and of Musa's cousin on the road last night. Fritzie's people killed him. And Goodman had helped to kill some of Fritzie's people. Now, it was strangely satisfying to have done so. Fritzie now had a pronounced limp, which was slowing him down and not endearing him to anyone. After he fell a final time—and stayed down—Musa picked him up and carried him over his shoulder. The exhausted group arrived at the Hukić farm just as the sky in front of them was turning from dark blue to gray.

A tall gate opened, and Zoran and the entire Majevitsa militia force greeted Amira, Goodman, Tomislav, Musa, and the other men with a muted cheer. Milosz escorted them to a feast of cooked meat, vegetables, and, of course, plenty of slivovitz. Musa dropped Fritzie like a sack of potatoes and everyone promptly forgot about him. Well, not totally. He was placed under guard in a small goat corral. *Screw him,* Goodman thought as he grabbed a bowl and heaped food into it. He shoveled the first mouthful and looked up briefly and saw

Zoran looking at him. Much to his surprise, Zoran nodded and smiled approvingly. Goodman paused and dipped his head to Zoran, the Pasha. He felt like he knew something of what a pasha was now. Zoran responded in kind.

For Zoran, a new thought occurred to him—no, not just a thought, and certainly not a mere feeling. An awareness? Zoran found himself elated that the American was still alive. But it was not the profit motive that awakened him. This foreigner looked just as filthy and wearied as his own people. As if he had always been travelling and fighting with the Majevitsa people. He felt...pride? *Why this pride*, thought Zoran. He watched the American eat and wrestled with his own emotions. *This man is like my son. Can I think this thought? Neh! He is a foreigner. He is not of my blood. He is outside my family. Yet, he is here. Why is he here?* Of course, Zoran knew the logical—the material—answers to these questions. But they were not the real reasons anymore. *This man is more*, Zoran almost mouthed the words. *Do I continue on this road? Do I make him family?* His eyes moved to where Amira stood, eating among her lieutenants. *This woman, my daughter, among men. What of family for her? Perhaps this is why I think these thoughts.* He thought of the future for his family.

Milosz herded Goodman and the other new arrivals into a large, hay-filled barn and told them to sleep. They were to remain there through the daylight hours while they waited for the German counterguerrilla patrols to return to their bases.

Goodman's body slumped in exhaustion, but his brain was swimming with thoughts. *This is my war now*, he thought. *I need to survive. For Zoran, for Amira. For Jasminka's village. I still need to get out, but to survive, we need to win. Like the whole world right now fighting this war for national survival...the Allies need to win. But the entire war is right here, right in front of me. To beat the Germans, and the Ustaša, or whoever they are, and whoever else we need to kill.* Goodman wrapped his coat around him and pulled the hay over his legs for warmth. *Nothing else matters...*

His head swam. He vaguely recognized it as the alcohol. It obscured the pains in his legs and joints, but it also confused his thoughts. He tried to tease out memories of Baba and Jasminka. And what came before, whatever it was. *Oh, yeah*, he thought. *The crash. Flying. The crash, the village. The girl spy.* He started to cry as he pieced together his recent history, he cried until he ran out of tears. Eventually, the alcohol won out and he slept. He slept very hard.

# 36

## A FARM NORTHEAST OF TUZLA

GOODMAN AWOKE TO THE SOUNDS OF HORSES. And then there was the pain. A dull cloud of pain, like a well-rounded rock, had grown inside his head. *Last night. What was last night?* he thought. *Slivovitz. Yeah. Lots of slivovitz. Now, I have a hangover. A good and proper one at that.* He pressed his fingers into his eyes. *Wow, I haven't had one of these since that night in the Royal Air Force officers' club in Benghazi. What was its name…? Doesn't matter.*

Pressure on his bladder drove him to lift himself up under the weight of his condition. He stooped low and took a moment to breathe. He belched foul air. He stepped toward the barn doors and pushed one open. The blinding light stabbed his eyes like fiery spikes. He squeezed them shut and felt his way outside.

Shielding his eyes, Goodman reopened them and focused, and recognized the first of the horsemen to dismount as Zoran's nephew, Radoslav. The one who fled with Goodman with Mustafa from the attack on the road by the bridge. It felt like so long ago, yet he knew he could count the days on one hand. Radoslav glanced and gave him a nod, but Goodman found himself unable to return in kind. Damn, his head hurt. He made his way around the corner of the barn and relieved himself.

Horses, men, and wagons filled the enormous field outside the barn. *Never seen this many before. Maybe Zoran wasn't really lying when he said he had thousands of men.* Other men emerged from the barn, bleary eyed and gray faced, apparently also suffering massive headaches. Tomislav stepped into the sunlight and squinted a grim smile at Goodman.

Goodman exhaled and pressed his eyes again. "Why are you so damn happy?"

"Here," he said. "Try some of this." He held up a large jug.

"Oh, no," exclaimed Goodman, putting up his hands. "No, no, no."

"This is not slivovitz," Tomislav assured him. "It is for *after* the slivovitz. After." He took a long drink, swallowed, and then grimaced and handed it to Goodman. "Here. Drink."

Goodman took it and drank. He spit it out immediately. "Oh my God, that's foul!"

"You need to drink it, or you will have a very bad day."

"Right." He handed the jug back to Tomislav.

"No, really," said Tomislav, pushing it back. "It tastes bad, but it is good."

Goodman took a small sip and swallowed. "Oh... oh, that's awful." He gagged. He cleared his throat and spit.

"Yes," said Tomislav, tipping the jug upwards. "Drink."

Goodman took a larger drink and choked as he swallowed. Some of the liquid trickled down his chin and chest under his shirt. "One more." Goodman drank again and shoved the jug back into Tomislav's arms. "That tastes like vomit." He belched loudly.

"Well," said Tomislav. "There may be some..." He put the jug back down inside the barn door, where it was immediately picked up by someone else.

Two horsemen trotted across the field on their mounts, one of whom also led a riderless horse. Zoran directed Fritzie to be draped across the third horse on his stomach. Several men led another six or seven horses across the field, each with one or two German soldiers already bound and secured.

"Looks like Zoran had more luck than we did," Goodman noted.

Tomislav nodded in agreement. "Appears so."

Fritzie grunted loudly as he was tied down. The man doing the tying paused in his task to slap him on the side of the head, then finished tying him down. Satisfied, Zoran walked away, leaving Milosz to finish giving instructions.

"What are they going to do with them?" Goodman asked Tomislav.

"They will be imprisoned until the need arises for a prisoner exchange," answered Tomislav. "Or they may be sold to the collaborationists or the Ustaši through an intermediary. Or… someone may need a Nazi soldier for their own purposes."

"What does that mean?"

"Here, prisoners or other out-of-place persons are commodities," said Tomislav. "Such as yourself. The Germans have posted a value—a bounty—on all such persons."

"Do I have a bounty on my head?"

"Certainly. I think the last poster I saw said something on the order of one hundred thousand German Reichsmarks for a living Allied officer. I think half that if you are dead."

"Yeah, I am." Goodman considered that for a moment. *I have a price on my head. Dead or alive.* "What could you buy for that?"

"Quite a bit," said Tomislav. "I can buy a horse in Tuzla or Sarajevo for a thousand Reichsmarks. On the black market, a military rifle in working condition is… about a four hundred. A pistol is about the same."

"What about you?" asked Goodman. "How much are you worth to the Germans?"

Tomislav smiled. "Me? Oh, I am not as valuable. I think we are worth around two thousand Reichsmarks each. Alive."

"Alive?"

"Yes, alive. A living prisoner is useful. A dead man is just a dead man, something for the worms. A live prisoner can be branded a traitor, publicly tried, paraded through the streets, executed with a sign around his neck, and then photographs can be made into posters as warnings to others for years. That is a very useful prisoner."

Goodman gave up trying to figure the math of the currency exchange rates. The hangover made it impossible. *So, I'm worth, what? Fifty of the militia or one hundred horses? Or a couple hundred weapons. One fighter with the resistance gets two thousand Reichsmarks. Two grand gets you a handful of weapons or a couple of horses. One Allied airman gets you a small army. And these people haven't sold me to anyone,* Goodman thought to himself. *At least not yet. They've certainly had the opportunity.*

"Is Zoran going to sell me?"

"No," Tomislav laughed out loud. "Well, not exactly."

"Not exactly?

"No, not outright," said Tomislav. "But there is a payment for your safe return."

"I'm sure that it is the way everyone does business in this sort of thing, but… dammit—" Goodman saw his minders again. "Is that why they're here again?"

Tomislav looked over his shoulder. "Yes, that is Zoran's protection of his future profit."

This irritated Goodman. *Is that what I am?* He had reflected on his conversation with Zoran the other night and took it that Zoran thought more highly of him than that. *Maybe I'm wrong.*

Zoran, Amira, Milosz, and several of Zoran's other commanders emerged from the woods, deep in discussion. Goodman saw Amira at the same moment she turned and saw him. She zeroed in on him and pointed a finger.

"Oh, no," moaned Goodman.

"You better see what she wants," said Tomislav.

Amira motioned for him to follow her to the edge of the woods. Once in the shade, she spun around with a serious look on her face. "Musa says you know of Jasminka?" This was the first time he heard her speak English. It was thickly accented, but understandable.

*So that's what this is about.* "Yes," he answered. "She's the one who taught me most of my Bosanski."

"Tell me the true words." There was a pleading in her voice. "What *after* the traitor and the Germans attacked the village? Is she still alive?"

"She was alright," he answered. "She and her grandmother were okay when I left."

"But the Germans killed some of the villagers."

"Jasminka was unhurt." *By the Germans, anyway.* "She is a very good girl…" It was what he could think of to say to make her happy. There was no way he would tell Amira about the man in the coat

202

striking Baba. Goodman did not really know why he suddenly wanted to make Amira happy, but he did. Maybe it was the sudden intimacy of the distress for her family. Was it trust? Did she suddenly trust him, out of necessity for sure, but trust rather than the disdain she had displayed before now?

A wave of sorrow washed over Amira's face as her body bent with agony. She put a hand to a tree and let out a small wail, which she stifled with her forearm. Her knees buckled and Goodman caught her before she fell. She sobbed quietly in his arms, leaving him to carry her full weight. Goodman was almost overcome by the tremors that wracked her body. He felt his own eyes glisten, too.

"Jasminka cared for me." He said. He tried to think of something comforting, something that would give her strength. "She protected me when the Germans came. She is a very brave girl." *What else do I say here?* "She's a lot like you," he finally said. He held her firmly for some impossible amount of time.

Amira took a breath and let it out. "She was my little one…" she whispered. "…when her mother was taken…"

Amira stayed in Goodman's arms as he tried to interpret what he just learned. *So she must have raised Jasminka, her little cousin, for some amount of time,* he thought to himself. *A surrogate mother…*

Gradually, Amira stood on her own and wiped her eyes repeatedly. She held herself up, seeming to try to compose herself, but finding fault with her hair and just about everything she was wearing. She cursed under her breath and finally tied her hair into a knot and replaced her hat crookedly on her head. As he watched her, he found her inexplicably attractive in this moment of vulnerability. A lump grew in his throat. *How do I help you?*

"Amira…" he said.

"Say nothing of this to anyone!" she growled at him, her old voice and facial appearance flashed back into being. Then, suddenly, her features softened again, and her eyes met his. "Thank you for telling me about my little Jasminka. Thank you…" Her voice cracked. It was the softest, most gentle voice he had ever heard from her. "Say nothing! Not to anyone!" She abruptly turned away from him like she was ashamed.

He took a step toward her, but she quickly went deeper into the woods. He watched her disappear into the forest. Then he returned to the camp. A weak cheer rose from the crowd surrounding the horse train for the prisoners. Someone whacked Fritzie the Prisoner with a stick, and his yelp drew another cheer from the crowd. The leader of the prisoner detail mounted his horse and guided the prisoners—along with a wagon full of wounded men—out of the farmyard and up a track into the woods. Goodman walked to where Tomislav sat by the barn door.

"Yes, Fritzie will not enjoy his journey," observed Tomislav.

"I didn't think there was a danger of that," said Goodman. His eyes watched the last of the horsemen kick their mounts into motion and disappear around the gate, but his mind was on Amira.

"Everything is well, yes?" asked Tomislav. He watched Goodman's eyes closely.

"Yes, I think so," replied Goodman. *Better than before*, he thought to himself.

"Good," said Tomislav.

Goodman touched his temples with his fingers. *No more headache*, he thought. He licked his lips. *Still some cottonmouth, though*. The sunlight felt a good measure less painful to his eyes. Tolerable even. He inhaled the fresh air and felt measurably better still.

"Stuff works." Goodman pointed to the jug containing the mystery hangover concoction.

"Yes, quite well." Tomislav lit up a cigarette and offered to Goodman. He took one and lit off the same match.

A cloud bank moved in overhead and gave merciful protection to the many heads in need of shade. The pair returned to the barn and dozed away what remained of their hangovers.

# 37

ZORAN'S REPLY FROM MIKHAIL–Colonel Zbrogan–was positive. But that was all it was. No details. Lots of room for negotiating. *Curse him for making this political!* thought Zoran. *Curse upon me for allowing it to be!* He clenched his fists. It was enough to be vague in the reply. It was annoying to have to call for yet another meeting. The plan was to be made real now, or likely never, with winter approaching. One hard storm and the world was frozen for *another* season.

Zoran observed Milosz and Amira escorting the commanders to his place around the giant table in the center of the barn. Each family patriarch to his place according to the net balance of seniority, capable manpower, knowledge of tactics and, of course, wealth. None of them were by themselves wealthy enough to purchase a wholesale enemy conversion, nor enough to bribe a German to abandon his position. No, these families—and their combined capital—would be much more helpful when the time came to compete with his cousin Mikhail's Unionists for political sway within the Tuzla district's power structures. Zoran knew that they all spoke a common language: blood, then money. *But first*, he thought, *first, I must win this fight.* He nodded to Djavud Effendi Hukič, the landowner and host for tonight, enjoying the honor Zoran gave him by being there. A deep and reverent bow came in reply.

The fathers gathered there had their sons, nephews, and brothers seated or standing around the walls and lofts of the barn. He looked to his own family: Milosz, Amira, and the handfuls of men, not his sons, eager and loyal though they were. Milosz moved to his place by the door, saw to the guard and, satisfied that all was secure, gave Zoran a nod.

*Everyone is ready.* Zoran raised his eyes to heaven. *Allah, if you will it, keep the duhovi from me and my plans. Protect my family from my sins.* He spread his arms like they were wings.

"Patriarchs of the Majevitsa..." he began. His voice boomed even inside the barn. He looked around at the faces of the elders and their advisors, who stopped whispering into their master's ears. *Good*, he thought. *I have them.*

"I have reliable information that the German Army is now in a general offensive against the Communists across the entire region. According to our sources, the Germans have repositioned entire divisions in this pursuit. This has put Tito's forces on the run—" Men cheered and pounded their rifles or staffs on the floor until Zoran raised his hands to calm them. "But as we all know, they have also empowered the Ustaši to become bolder in their attacks against us. We have killed a good number lately, and they have returned to their hiding places. Marshal Tito's Third Corps of Partisans are freezing to death in the Konju Mountains, and the Germans have given chase, and they, too, are trapped in the mountain snows. The next closest German force of any consequence is fully engaged in operations at least a week's march away from Tuzla, and then only after they consolidate, which will take days itself.

"What does this mean for us? What is the choice before us? I say it is to attack! But where?" He paused for effect. "I shall tell you…Tuzla! The remaining German forces, now minimally manned according to sources, are inside their garrisons at Zenića, Gradačac, Zvornik, Brčko, the bridgehead at Slavonski Brod, and, most importantly to us, in the Planina Fortress in Tuzla with its defensive outposts. There remains only a small force within Tuzla, and they do not know about us."

Zoran watched the expressions on the faces around him. *They don't believe me*, he thought. *They're doubtful. They're still timid from last spring.*

"I have struck a deal with Colonel Zbrogan's Unionist brigades of Tuzla to assist us in taking control of the Tuzla valley over the course of the next three days. Tonight, my family will attack the Ustaša garrison at Simin Han. From there, we will attack the Planina over the next evening while each of you will attack the remaining garrisons that surround Tuzla city. It is in this and the consolidation afterward that Colonel Zbrogan's forces will assist us." Zoran stood fully upright and rested one hand on his holster and the other on his sword hilt. "We will overwhelm them from all directions." Satisfied, he turned to Milosz, who stepped forward and spoke.

"We will discuss the information we have learned about the other garrisons with you individually, as that information is not for the ears of others. We will hold the first—"

One elder stood and spoke. "We attack the Planina?" He sounded incredulous.

"You say this as a statement," Zoran countered. "Or as an inquiry?"

"This Colonel Zbrogan, his Tuzla Brigades, you speak of. Why?" asked another. "These Unionists…they are for this, this agreement? And Colonel Zbrogan? Truly?"

"Yes, what of this agreement?" Yelled out another of the patriarchs. "You did not bring us into this negotiation. How do we trust them?"

Zoran tried not to scowl. *Why does he chastise me*, he thought. This was Djavud's great uncle, the leader of the families at Uporovice. One of the stalwarts. Good farmers, good fighters, but bad at business. Good, solid families, though. *I need him with me. The others will follow.*

Djavud's great uncle stepped forward another step and spoke again. "What guarantees do we have that they will fight with us, and not against us? How do we know they will not abandon us as they did last spring?"

Zoran wished he had pressed Mikhail Zbrogan harder about the guarantees. But there wasn't time. Zoran stepped forward. "I have personally discussed these matters with Colonel Zbrogan. We both believe that we were victims of treachery, which led to them returning to Tuzla rather than coming to assist us by attacking the bridges over the Jala and protecting our escape route."

Another commander, a man fifteen years Zoran's senior, stood and shouted. "That very act prevented us from returning to our homes and villages to defend them from the Ustaše battalions! We had to cross the streams, swollen with snowmelt. Some of us died during those crossings! It was days before we could get to our families!" The low murmurs turned louder. The man spoke again. "Zoran Mehmetović Dudovic, pasha or not, we must know that this will succeed. We cannot afford to lose! Not again."

Zoran raised his hands and exaggerated the expression of agreement on his face to quiet the crowd. "My people! My people…please, please listen." Milosz stepped forward, but Zoran discretely raised his arm to say, *not yet, I've got this.* Milosz played it off and casually strode to the other side of Amira. Zoran choked on the memory he was about to invoke. "My people, you know that we…we all lost something last spring. This will not happen! We remember… *I remember* what that means." He watched the knowledge of his family's loss come to the surface. At the same time, he felt a pain in his throat. *Allah, forgive me for abusing my wife's memory. But if this is what it takes to avenge her, then so be it.* "Now is our time to strike! Now is our time to take what is ours, for the sake of our children, and their children! We must be free. They must be free of all outside corruption! Tonight, we take the first garrison, and then tomorrow night, we take them all! For tonight we number hundreds, but tomorrow we will be thousands!"

*Finish them.*

Zoran stood another three inches taller, or so it felt, and raised his fist higher still. "We will *not* fail!"

The elders of each clan raised a fist in solidarity, and the crowd rose to their feet. The haunting chant of a war mantra from Ottoman times grew out of the back rows and consumed the whole gathering. Zoran beat his chest and drew his sword and pistol. He raised both hands into the air and raised his voice to sing out louder than all the others. He smiled when he saw that the crowd—the people, his army—were indeed his. The people in the barn threw themselves together in a moment of zealous ecstasy and cheered one another on, and the younger men danced. The song reached a crescendo, and he looked to his daughter. She stood as solid and unmoved as a stone edifice. Her eyes were on the floor. Zoran's heart sank. His eyes welled up for his little flower.

Milosz came to his side. "Well done, Pasha." When Zoran said nothing, Milosz traced Zoran's eyes to his daughter's. He stepped back and guided the conversations away from Zoran. Eventually, he pulled Zoran back in for the inevitable farewells and guarantees.

After he shook the last hand, exchanged the last hugs, spoke the last word of confidence for the evening, Zoran's smile completely vaporized. Amira was gone. He had already forgotten half the expedient promises he made in those rushed conversations. *The business of war is done for tonight*, he thought to himself. *Now, the business*—he caught himself—*this is not business. This man, this stranger who came to me, now I must let him go, again. Again? What 'again' am I thinking?* He chastised himself for the thought, the betrayal. *This foreigner is not my son. No matter how I think of him, he does not belong here. But still...* He hesitated, then placed a hand on Milosz's shoulder and walked with him around the corner, out of the light.

"Yes, Pasha."

"My friend," Zoran began. "Please, send a courier to Colonel Zbrogan requesting a meeting with him to discuss two topics of immediate concern for us."

"Yes, Pasha."

"First, we need to discuss the taking of the Planina. I'm sure he and his Unions will want to have some say in the methods of securing Tuzla city proper, along with the surrounding garrisons. And this might as well open the door for a future power sharing arrangement. I don't want to discuss that issue yet." *I hate the idea of sharing power and requiring the approval of another man.*

"You have not yet negotiated control, Pasha?"

"No," said Zoran. "Only in vague terms. I want to secure the garrison at Simin Han first, as it will give me an idea of the strength remaining in these surrounding positions. Also, the supply depot there will yield us additional resources against the Germans. Then I can estimate our chances."

"I see, Pasha," said Milosz. "And the other concern?"

"The other concern is this foreigner, this American. I must free myself of him. My dear cousin may or may not have negotiated a broker for his sale and transfer to—" he clucked his tongue "—other parties." It pained him to say it. He had hated to think of it over these past few days. *My son. The man who reminds me so much of my beloved son. My son. My heart.*

"Which other parties?"

"This, I do not know," Zoran admitted. "I did not specify, though I did suggest to him his Banja Luka connection from last year."

Zoran breathed through his nose. *If he must leave me, then please let it be to the British. Then to his own people.* "Though I have no idea if they exist anymore, nor do I know whom Mikhail has been cozying up to as of late."

Milosz nodded. "Yes, Pasha. I understand. I shall dispatch a rider immediately."

Zoran returned to the head of the table and sat down, for he felt the weight of everything such as he had not felt since last spring.

# 38

A DISTANT RUMBLE OF THUNDER kicked Goodman into consciousness. In a moment of panic, he looked around quickly and reached for his weapon. Then, when he recognized where he was, he exhaled. Milosz, Amira, Ahmet, a young fighter named Suleiman, and the other group leaders were discussing the attack plans when Tomislav nudged Goodman with his flask. Goodman shook his head and sat up. Tomislav looked at the tension on his face.

"You did well the other night, on the road," said Tomislav.

"No, I didn't," Goodman replied. "I screwed up. Bad. Those guys—Musa's cousin and that other guy—might be alive if I hadn't been so quick to get on that road. I forced the—"

"Nonsense. You did no such thing. Did you kill any of those men on the road?"

"Just the Nazis."

"You will do well again tonight," Tomislav assured him. "You'll do well."

Two young boys were making the rounds to distribute ammunition disrupted Goodman with his thoughts. They gave him several fully loaded magazines and two of the German potato masher stick grenades.

"They gave me bullets," said Goodman optimistically. "And grenades. I guess they expect me to fight."

Amused, Tomislav replied, "How do you say it…no free lunch, yes?"

Goodman chuckled. "Yup." They smiled.

Another young boy came by with a can of oil and a rag, which every member of the militia used to oil the bolt and barrel of his weapon. Tomislav instructed Goodman on how to remove the bolt, which he did clumsily, and then how to put the weapon back together. "You should learn to do this," said Tomislav.

"Yeah, no kidding," Goodman replied. "Pomoch?"

Tomislav coached him through several complete iterations of disassembly and reassembly, and then talked him through how to remove a jam, ejecting four or five rounds onto the ground in the process. He also instructed Goodman on how to wedge his elbow under his shoulder when firing. "To keep the bullets from spraying out of control," he said. "And now, your pistol."

"This I can do," said Goodman. He removed the magazine, ejected the round that was chambered, and took it apart to its constituent elements. He wiped the pieces down and re-assembled the weapon. Tomislav stuck his cigarette in his mouth and took the pistol and racked the slide several times. "This is rough," he said.

"Yeah, I know," said Goodman. "I got it second-hand." Tomislav ignored the joke.

"Here." Tomislav reached into his coat pocket and handed Goodman a new-looking pistol and two magazines. "It is from Czechoslovakia. Very good manufacture."

Goodman weighed it in his hand and aimed it. He was impressed. "So it is." He inserted a magazine and chambered a round. *Very smooth*. "Thank you," he said.

Tomislav nodded and blew a cloud of smoke. "The bullet hits very hard, this one."

"I'm surprised," said Goodman.

"About what?"

"That you know these things."

"I know things," said Tomislav. "After all, my country has been at war for two years."

Musa and his machine gunners sat down on the other side of Tomislav. They were all smiles.

"You want to see the machinegun?" asked Musa.

"Da!" replied Goodman. He proceeded to receive a course of instruction on the MG-42. After several repetitions, he was handling it like an old pro. Or that was what he thought to himself.

Musa nodded his head in approval. "You...very good," he said in thickly accented English.

"Hvala, moj drug." *Thank you, my friend.*

Everyone stopped what they were doing when Amira and a large contingent of men strode across the field and conferred with Zoran and his lieutenants. The tension was palpable.

"They are to inspect the factory and the ambush site on the road to Tuzla," said Tomislav, nodding toward Amira.

"Like a reconnaissance," said Goodman.

"Yes, reconnaissance, that is the correct word," replied Tomislav. "Amira then will lead the ambush against the German counterattack."

"Amira is going to the ambush?" asked Goodman. "I thought she'd be in the main attack."

"The factory garrison is but one objective. The greater threat is coming from the SS garrison at the Planina," explained Tomislav. "Zoran wants his best force to fight the greatest danger. So, he sends Amira. If we are lucky, the assault force will be done with the factory before the forces from Tuzla can arrive for a counterattack."

"So, the attack on the factory is a diversion?" Goodman asked.

"Hmmm...more of an invitation to attack," said Tomislav. "It is foolish to attack even a partially armed garrison. But if we can get them out of the fortress, where it is very difficult, then our odds are somewhat better."

"Somewhat?" said Goodman. "That is not a very confident statement."

"Oh, I'm very confident in what I said," said Tomislav. "What I'm not confident about is if we know how many SS and Ustaši soldiers there are in Tuzla tonight."

"Well, crap," said Goodman. His nervousness dug a pit in his stomach.

"Perhaps…" said Tomislav.

Musa sat up and asked Tomislav what Goodman said. He translated and Musa smiled. He patted his machinegun and repeated the words "no problem" several times.

Zoran's deputy, Milosz, approached and began giving instructions to the groups around the barn. He included Goodman and Tomislav when he assigned men to the squad led by Suleiman.

"He looks like he's fifteen," Goodman muttered to Tomislav. "Are we really working for him?"

"We are not participating in the attacks," Tomislav quietly replied.

"What?" Goodman was suddenly irritated. "We're not going to attack?"

Tomislav was interrupted by Musa's machinegun team as they got up and lifted their equipment and crates of ammunition to their shoulders, smiling to each other under the heavy load. The remainder of Suleiman's group all stood and bid farewell to them, exchanging jokes and friendly curses alike. Suleiman unfolded a map on the ground and spoke to the group now gathered around. Goodman saw that Suleiman's hands were shaking. *He's nervous*, Goodman thought to himself. *That's just great.*

"We are responsible for ambushing any Ustaši or Nazis returning to the factory from the east once the attack begins," Tomislav translated for Goodman. "There is a rear gate to the factory on the east side which we will block. There are sure to be at least two guards outside the gates, front and rear, and perhaps ten inside the bunker or on the walls. There are between twenty and twenty-five Ustaši pigs inside the factory tonight…"

"We have fourteen men," Goodman whispered to Tomislav. "Fourteen doesn't equal twenty-five. Aren't we supposed to have more than the enemy?"

Suleiman ignored him. "We must not let anyone into the gate, and by no means is anyone allowed to depart through the gate. They must not escape while the attack is going on. Afterward, we go to a farm north of the main road and wait for the others. If the attack on the factory or the ambush to the west fails, we must withdraw back to this place." The men interrupted Suleiman to grumble a little at this last point. He tried to ignore them, but his hands shook all the harder and his voice stuttered. "We will depart from here and go to the edge of town to await Amira and her reconnaissance report." He looked down to fold his map, which took an inordinately long time, then he avoided eye contact with each of the men around him. "We leave now," he mumbled. "Pack up your things."

Suleiman arranged his map case, ammunition pouches, and rifle sling, but got the straps tangled and had to do it again. He leaned his rifle against a fence post, but it fell and hit the dirt with a clatter. When he knelt to pick it up, a baseball-sized fragmentary hand grenade slipped out of his pouch and rolled away from him. Fortunately, the pin was still firmly in place. One of the men picked it up and warily handed it back to him, and then exchanged woeful looks with the other men in the squad.

"Is he okay?" asked Goodman.

Tomislav turned around and shrugged his shoulders.

"That's great." Goodman shook his head. The older, more seasoned men grumbled to one another. "Why is he in charge?"

"We are supporting the supporting attack." Tomislav flicked his cigarette away before lighting up his next one. "And he is a nephew of Zoran." He offered another cigarette to Musa and one to Goodman. "I strongly advise you to not interfere this time."

Goodman put his hand up to receive it with index and middle fingers apart. "Believe me, I won't." They both nodded as Tomislav sparked his lighter. Goodman puffed and sat back.

They watched Ahmet's group exit the barn after Amira's security element passed through the gate. Zoran's contingent had departed some time ago after the other clans dispersed en route to their respective locations around the Tuzla valley. Suleiman motioned for his group to follow, and everyone slowly rose and helped lift the heavy packs for one another. A frigid wind blew as they passed through the gate. The sky had turned from partly cloudy to a deep, dark gray. A single spit of rain hit Goodman on the neck and sent a shiver throughout his body, prompting him to turn up his collar.

# DEEP IN THE PLACE OF THE DEAD

Goodman and Tomislav followed the file of men as they snaked their way downhill, over numerous stone fences, around goat corrals, and between brick and stone houses, and into the alleyways on the outskirts of town. The light was fading quickly, and rain was now a light and very cold sprinkle of needlepoints that hit them in their faces. Yellow-orange lights in windows felt warm to look at, and the smell of burning wood hung in the air. Somewhere, a dog barked, and Goodman shot an uneasy glance in the direction of the sound, as did everyone else.

Suleiman led the column to the edge of a broad avenue and halted. He looked up and down the road and, seeing no traffic or people, hurried across. The next man waited for them to get to the far side and signal that it was still clear to cross. Two more men crossed, then two more, and two more. Tomislav and Goodman had just started to cross when the sound of a truck engine emerged on the wind, coming from the left. Suleiman signaled them to stop at the same time as Goodman and Tomislav scrambled back around the corner of the nearest house with everyone else. Goodman held his breath as a single flatbed truck rumbled by, its frame creaking and shaking with age. The driver and his passenger apparently paid no mind to what was not in their headlights, and the truck disappeared around a bend to the east until there was only the smell of diesel on the wind. *This is for real again*, he thought. Strangely, he felt a sense of belonging, that he now fully shared what was going on around him.

When Suleiman finally signaled, Goodman, Tomislav, and the remaining men crossed the road quickly. Goodman felt relieved when reached he touched brick on the other side. Then the group continued southward through the narrow alleyways.

At the next road crossing, Suleiman halted and looked down the road as far as he could see in the dark. He then backtracked and led the group to an intersection, where he stopped and looked again. He repositioned himself and the squad behind another house, then repositioned again for a third time. The older militiamen exchanged concerned looks. Suleiman backtracked yet again, leading the group on the same route they passed before, back to the broad road. They halted in yet another narrow alleyway and crouched there in the dark. Suleiman looked down the road in both directions and then looked at his watch by the orange glow of a lantern through a window. He cursed and whispered something to the man next to him before he got up and ran across the road, disappearing into the darkness.

A man next to Goodman cursed out loud as he watched Suleiman disappear. Goodman listened as the man whispered something to others next to him. They, too, cursed and shook their heads before turning to their neighbor to share the bad news. Tomislav quickly told them to shut up. They did. And then they all waited. And waited. *What is going on?* thought Goodman. *I don't think he knows what he's doing.*

"Where did he go?" he asked Tomislav in a hushed tone. "Where is that guy?" Tomislav merely shrugged.

After several minutes, one of the men stood to look onto the road, and the others pulled him back down, cursing at him for being foolish. Several men shifted under the weight of their packs. Tomislav stood to a crouch and moved to the front of the line to talk to the man Suleiman spoke to before he left. He returned to Goodman and said nothing. Goodman poked Tomislav and flipped his palm upward to ask, "what?"

"Suleiman said to wait," said Tomislav. "But we are supposed to be in position already. Ahmet is supposed to attack the front gate any time now."

"Well, shit," said Goodman.

"Yes, it is shit now," said Tomislav.

"Where is the factory?" asked Goodman.

"We think it is west of here," Tomislav replied, pointing down the road to the left.

"We think?" Goodman repeated. "So why did Suleiman go to the right?"

"This I do not know," said Tomislav.

Goodman clenched his jaw in frustration. *The plan is already falling apart, and we are nowhere near our position. Where the hell is Suleiman? How do we do our damn jobs if we can't even find the battle?*

# DEEP IN THE PLACE OF THE DEAD

The light sprinkle of tiny frigid pinpricks turned to a shower of ice cold drops, and everyone groaned. Goodman cursed out loud as the first trickle of frigid water penetrated his coat and ran down his spine. Water trickled off the roof right onto the heads of the men beneath, and everyone shifted to get out of the falling water. Then, the trickles turned into streams. The men around Goodman began shivering uncontrollably as the alleyway became a torrent. Then he began to shiver. First, his shoulders twitched, then his upper back, then his chest, then multiple places simultaneously. He listened to his teeth chatter. Water flowed over his boots and soaked his feet. Frustration peaked within him as there was still no sign of Suleiman. And visibility was down to only a few yards.

The shower turned into a downpour, and the amount of water coming off the roofs into the alley was no longer tolerable. Right at that moment, gunfire rang out. The rain muffled it, but it was definitely gunfire. A lot of gunfire. A heavy machine gun opened up. A second heavy weapon commenced fire, and the two guns continued to fire with only brief pauses. The attack was on! It might be working, or it may be failing, and here they sat, in the rain, lost and without their leader.

*This is stupid,* thought Goodman. *These men need a leader. I might not be a ground soldier, but I am an officer.* He turned to Tomislav and said, "You're sure the factory is that way?"

"What?"

Goodman had to yell to be heard over the rain as he gestured down the road. Tomislav stood and walked to the man in the front, who was no longer trying to look out for Suleiman's return. After a frustrating moment of pointing left, then right, and then left again, Tomislav said yes.

"Follow me," Goodman said, gesturing for the men to follow him back down the alley.

At first, they remained motionless, looking at each other. Then Tomislav and the man in the front moved to follow and pulled the others with them. By the time Goodman reached the end of the alley, the entire group was following. The battle was now in a full rage, and Goodman was determined to assist in any way he could. He wiped his face and head, wishing he had a better hat. The heavy machine guns were relentless. No other gunfire was audible anymore. *What does that mean? Does Zoran have heavy guns like that? Or are those enemy guns?*

At an intersection of two alleys, Goodman looked in every direction and turned toward the gunfire. Through the rain, visibility was about ten feet in every direction. He could barely see lights some unknown distance down the road.

"We go that way!" he yelled over the downpour. Three blocks later, Goodmen led the group around a corner. He motioned for the men to gather closely to hear him. They got as close as a dozen men could gather.

Goodman pulled Tomislav close. "Translate!" he said.

Tomislav nodded.

"The factory is that way," Goodman said as he pointed toward the sounds of battle. Tomislav translated. "But I don't know exactly where the factory is, and I do not want to walk into the middle of the battle."

From the middle of the huddle, a man asked, "Where is Suleiman? Where is the leader?" The men only exchanged looks and shrugged. Several men shrank back from the group and murmured to each other. A rumble sounded from the west. Was that thunder or an explosion? Another crack rolled through the night air. *That's a cannon,* thought Goodman. *They must have tanks or artillery or something. God, I hope they don't have tanks.*

"We gotta move!" exclaimed Goodman. "Or we will miss the attack. We must move, or we fail Zoran!"

Everyone nodded in agreement, but no one stepped up. Goodman reached the end of his patience.

"Who here knows this factory?" he asked. No response. He said it again.

They all stared at him, shaking with cold. One man finally raised his hand.

"I know."

# 39

## SIMIN HAN SALT FACTORY IN THE EAST TUZLA SUBURBS

GOODMAN PULLED THE MAN BY THE COAT to the end of the alley. "Is that it?" he asked in Bosanski.

The man nodded. "Yes, this is the back of the factory. The gate is under those lights."

"Good," said Goodman. "You stay here and tell me how many men are there and if the gate opens." The man nodded and peered around the corner. Goodman went back to the others.

"We're here," said Goodman to Tomislav. "But this is a crappy place to attack from. Come with me, bring another guy."

"Wait! What? Attack?" Tomislav exclaimed.

Goodman ignored him and moved through the group. Tomislav pulled Goodman by the sleeve.

"We are not supposed to attack," Tomislav yelled over the rain. "We are supposed to wait."

"Wait?" Goodman yelled back. "Suleiman was supposed to wait." The heavy machine guns continued to pound away in the rain. "Do you hear that?" Another burst of heavy machinegun fire echoed through the streets. "*That* is the attack! And we're just sitting here! I'm not gonna do that."

Several explosions echoed through the town. The heavy machine guns continued unabated.

"Zoran and Amira have their plans," Tomislav conceded. "We should remain—"

"Get those two," Goodman cut him off.

Tomislav hesitated. Of no mind to argue with him, Goodman turned and tapped two men on their shoulders to follow him. The four men moved through the alley and climbed over a low fence. Several goats silently watched them pass through their domain, seemingly oblivious to the rain and the gunfire alike. The gunfire at the other side of the factory let up slightly, followed by two small

219

explosions. Goodman heard some yelling, and the heavy machine guns opened up again. Red tracers arced into the rainy night sky.

Goodman peered around the corner of the next house. The two lights over the factory gate shined like orbs through the heavy rain. He could barely make out the horizontal gate arm in the light. Water flowed over the brick street toward the gate from his position. Goodman saw no sign of guards near the gate, but there was a lighted window to its right. *A guard house, maybe?* He turned back to Tomislav and the other two men.

"We attack from there." He pointed to a four-foot-high brick wall that separated the house from the main road. There was a small stone shed at the left end of the wall, about twenty feet away. A pile of junk and a cart sat parked on its other side.

"Okay," said Tomislav. "So…what?"

Goodman opened his hands as if to say, *this is what I got, take it or leave it.*

"You are determined to attack?"

"Yep, with or without you," Goodman said curtly. "I'd prefer with you. I need your help."

Tomislav nodded his understanding. Goodman could tell he still disagreed. *So what?*

"I'll be right back," Goodman yelled to Tomislav. Tomislav nodded again, wiping rain from his face.

Goodman ran to back to where the group was waiting. Water squished in his boots at every step. The others seemed glad to move when Goodman motioned for them to come. He brought them to the wall and set them down behind it. Tomislav and the other two men were using a large canvas tarpaulin to deflect the rain. Miraculously, there was plenty of heavy canvas, so everyone pulled it over them as Tomislav fed it to them. Goodman stood behind the corner, watching the gate. Then he thought about what was behind them and the fact that they had no good view of the road to the right, where the responding forces would potentially come from. He crouched and ran to Tomislav.

"Can you go back to the alley and watch for anyone coming down the road?"

"Yes, I'll bring someone with me to run messages for us." Tomislav grabbed one of the men and pulled him through the rain back to the alley. "We should watch behind us as well, in case an Ustaši man had a girlfriend and was on his way back to the factory," Tomislav suggested.

"Right," said Goodman. He tapped one of the men under the tarp and pointed to his own eyes with two fingers and then the alleyway behind them. The man nodded and turned. Goodman turned back to observe the factory gate and shivered at the deepening cold.

The gunfire completely ceased on the far side of the factory, leaving only the sound of the rain. Goodman looked for movement at the gate. He saw nothing but the mist of his breath drifting through the rain across the row of men. Steam from their collective body heat drifted up from under the tarp. Goodman looked at the man behind him, who was guarding their rear. He was still there, diligently keeping watch. Several frigid minutes passed before Tomislav ran up to him.

"There are two trucks coming up the road," he said, out of breath. "I can't see what kind they are but, with the curfew, no one would be driving at this time of night except for military."

Goodman shook the tarp to get the attention of the men nearest him. One peered out from under it. Goodman jerked his thumb upward several times, then pointed to his submachine gun and then at the factory. The man understood and alerted his comrades. Within a few seconds, there were eleven weapon muzzles pointed across the wall. Everyone was shivering, and cold weapons rattled against the stone wall. Goodman patted the man behind him on the shoulder, who acknowledged him with a pronounced nod of his head.

A moment later, the gate and the walls began to glow with the light of headlights. A dark guardhouse stood to the right of the gate, but there were no guards visible. The glow of the headlights on the gate area narrowed as the trucks approached. A man appeared from behind the wall and yelled, "Stojte!" while aiming his rifle at the lead truck. The two trucks stopped exactly in front of the wall, not more than a few yards away from Goodman's position. They were both cargo trucks, with the tarps pulled tight at the rear, and the windows of both cabs were steamed over. The driver's door on the lead truck opened, and a man yelled something back to the guard before the guard lowered his weapon to raise the gate arm.

Goodman saw his moment. He looked at the man next to him, crouched behind the wall, his rifle aiming directly at the driver's door of the truck in front of him. He had two hand grenades dangling from his belt. Goodman put his hand on the man's shoulder and unhooked the grenades. The man looked at Goodman. Goodman pointed to himself and the man, then to the grenades and the rear of the trucks. The man smiled.

He put his arm through his rifle sling and said something to the man next to him. The man looked back at Goodman and nodded excitedly. Goodman gave the man a grenade and put a finger through the pull-ring on his own grenade. Adrenaline filled Goodman's veins, chasing away the cold as they stepped over the wall and walked up to the rear of the trucks. The others watched through the dim light as Goodman and the other man reached the rear corners of their respective trucks. Rain pelted his head as Goodman made a gesture of preparing to pull the pin on his grenade, and the other did so, too.

In a brief but sublime motion, Goodman and his companion pulled the grenade pins and simply dropped them over the tailgate of each truck. Through the rain, Goodman heard the grenade roll toward the front of his truck. Both men scrambled back over the wall, and each truck exploded. Men inside the trucks screamed as the canvass was shredded and wood and metal shards flew in all directions. Hot shrapnel pierced one truck's gas tank and caught fire. The gas tank quickly burst and engulfed the rear of the truck. A man fell out onto the road, dead, and another tripped on the tailgate and fell headfirst onto the road. He did not move again. The militia ducked behind the wall as rain and pieces of smoldering wood pelted them. Emboldened by the chaos of the explosion, Goodman stood up and let loose a long burst of automatic fire into the bed of the truck that had not caught fire. The men behind the wall followed his lead and emptied their magazines into the trucks as well. The lead truck rolled slowly forward and stopped when its bumper gouged the outer factory wall. *That went amazingly well*, thought Goodman. *That was lucky.*

Amidst sporadic gunfire, a soldier limped through the flames of the rear truck, his clothes smoldering. The militiamen fired, and he and the driver of the lead truck fell dead. Several shots impacted the guardhouse, shattering glass and splintering wood as the guard at the gate ran behind the wall. The man in the passenger seat of the lead truck tried to run to the gate but was cut down by rifle fire. Another man disappeared behind the wall before the flaming river of fuel that was trickling out of the ruptured fuel tank and down the hill toward the gate reached him. Flames from the rear truck illuminated Tomislav's face as he and another man ran alongside Goodman.

Goodman was unconcerned as a shot rang out from behind the gate. He pointed at the other truck and yelled to Tomislav. "Someone pull the drain plug on that other truck!" He changed magazines and let loose a spray of bullets at the break in the wall that framed the gated entrance. "Gotta keep them back!"

"I'll do it!" Tomislav yelled. He leapt over the wall and ran to the rear of the lead truck. He ran back, and a moment later another river of fuel caught fire, the combined waves flowing through the rain toward the gate. Soon, the whole gate area and guardhouse were engulfed in flames. The militiamen began laughing and shooting randomly into the flames. A light over the gate area flickered out. Goodman finally breathed as he admired their accomplishment.

*Okay*, he said to himself. *What now?*

# 40

A BURST OF GUNFIRE FROM THE ROOF OF THE FACTORY sent everyone back over the stone wall. Bullets ricocheted off the street and walls of the houses all around them. Roof tiles shattered and crashed to the ground. The men hugged the wall, pinned down by the gunfire. *Woah! That was stupid, standing out there like that.*

When the volley slackened, Goodman aimed into the darkness and cut loose with another burst from his submachine gun. Others returned fire, too, but they were answered with a sustained burst from the factory roof. The fires from the trucks illuminated the entire street and wall. Only the dancing shadows from the burning trucks were concealing them from the gunners on the roof.

"We need to get out of here!" Goodman yelled to Tomislav.

"Yes!" yelled Tomislav. He aimed his pistol and fired three shots at the rooftop. Yet another burst of return fire followed his shots.

Goodman yelled, "Hey!" to the men crouched behind the wall. "Shoot up there!"

They looked, and he pointed at them and then to the rear of the house beside the shed. They shook their heads as rounds impacted the wall and the ground immediately behind them. *We need to get some fire on that rooftop!* He pointed at them again, angrily, and then to the back of the house. They shook their heads again. Goodman grabbed one man and thrust him toward the shed. He crouched and ran, splashing through the rain. A trail of bullets splashing in the mud chased him the whole way. The others made themselves as small as possible behind the wall. The man who got up now disappeared around the corner and into the dark.

"Dammit," muttered Goodman. "Where'd he go?"

Tomislav ran to the nearest man and pulled him away from the wall by the arm. Several rounds zipped by him and splashed in the mud. Both men slipped and scrambled behind the corner where Goodman was standing.

"The men don't want to move!" yelled Tomislav, breathing heavily. "I counted three weapons on the roof."

"I know!" yelled Goodman. Several more shots rang out from the factory roof. Then a shot rang out from somewhere to their left. Goodman looked toward the sound but could not see anything. Another burst of gunfire from the roof brought another shot from the left. For a moment, there was no more gunfire from the factory rooftop. Goodman fired a round at the roof. No gunfire returned. Then, the man who Goodman thought had run off re-appeared from around the corner. In the darkness, Goodman saw him wave and thought he saw the man smiling. Goodman gave him a thumbs up. The man beamed.

"That guy's a great shot," yelled Goodman. "Keep him close. Let's go that way before they get more gunners up on the roof!"

The group ran down the alleyway, slipping and falling as they went. The alley led them to another wide street, which ran parallel to the southern wall of the factory compound. Goodman led them to the wall, where they were out of sight from the roof top.

"Now what?" asked Tomislav.

"Let's get in the factory," said Goodman.

"What?" said Tomislav. "We are not supposed to do that."

"What are we supposed to do out here?" replied Goodman. "We can sit in the rain and get shot at, or we can get inside and take this place. Out here, we're just waiting to get killed in the counterattack."

"I don't know." Tomislav frowned.

Goodman grabbed the young sharpshooter. "Put this guy in a place where he can keep those guys off the roof while we get inside."

"Very well," grumbled Tomislav. He disappeared with the marksman down the alley.

"And come back when you're done, I need you!" Goodman yelled after him.

"Okay!" he heard Tomislav yell back.

A couple of minutes later, Tomislav returned. "He is set. It is too dark to see if there is someone up there."

"Right," said Goodman. "We'll move fast." Goodman crept toward the corner of the compound wall. The fires in the trucks had burned out, and the entire area was dark again, except for the single remaining light over the gate.

Goodman turned to Tomislav and the next two militiamen. "Stay close to the wall and follow me."

Goodman turned the corner, now exposed to the light. The gate was forty yards away. Plastered to the wall, he side-stepped closer to the gate. The rain was not as hard here, but he was getting more and more exposed to the light. Goodman turned to Tomislav, who was only a couple of paces behind him, also plastered up against the wall.

"Hurry!" said Goodman. "Can our marksman see us here?"

"I think so," said Tomislav. Goodman waved his arms and pointed with his left hand toward the light. Nothing. Goodman looked at Tomislav and waved his arms again. Goodman pointed at the light with his hand. A shot rang out, and the light exploded in a shower of sparks. Several shots rang out from the factory roof. Another shot from the marksman and silence followed.

"Do we have any more grenades?" asked Goodman. Tomislav turned to the next several men and came back with two. "Good," said Goodman, pointing into the guard house and gate area. "Throw them in there."

Tomislav pulled the pin on one and threw it. It rattled around the brick gate area and exploded. He threw the second grenade and got it behind, but not exactly inside, the guard shack. *No matter,* thought Goodman as the wooden shack, already so riddled with holes, collapsed when the grenade went off. The whole structure creaked and fell sideways, leaving only silence and rain.

"Follow me!" said Goodman. He raised his submachine gun and ran to through the gate area to the east wall of the factory, immediately tripping over a body and almost falling. There was a large vehicle door with a smaller door next to it. Light seeped through the cracks under both doors and through a half dozen bullet holes. Through the holes, Goodman saw that the factory was dimly lit inside, but he could make out several trucks and an officer's car in the spacious loading area. Several men were running around inside, carrying bags or boxes. There was a dead man, surrounded by a pool of blood, lying on the salt- and dirt-covered floor about ten feet from the door. Three men stood in the middle of the floor, leaning on a truck bumper, watching the far door. They did not appear to be watching the rear door, seemingly unaware that it was unprotected. *What are they thinking? Did they not hear the shooting?*

Goodman excitedly grabbed Tomislav's shoulder and pointed inside. Tomislav looked through the bullet holes and shrugged, as if to say, *okay, might as well.*

Goodman, Tomislav, and the others all stacked in a row along the wall, hunched over, leaning forward on their toes, ready to sprint, trigger fingers quivering. Frigid rain trickled down backs and across foreheads, but no one was cold anymore.

Tomislav quietly pulled on the wooden handle, and the door opened slightly. It was unlocked. He lowered his head as Goodman counted down with his fingers, "Three… two… one… open!"

# 41

TOMISLAV YANKED ON THE DOOR AND SWUNG IT WIDE. Goodman and the whole gang of men burst into the loading bay. The three men on the truck bumper stood, wide-eyed and aghast before falling dead on the floor under a burst of Goodman's submachine gunfire, their rifles clattering to the floor. The militiamen chased and killed the men who dropped their crates or bags and tried to run through a wide doorway on the far side of the bay. A man on an elevated gangway dropped his cigarette and ran into an upstairs office without yelling or firing a shot. Goodman made a beeline for the door, stepping over the fallen Ustaša man. Others followed on his heels. A man came around the door and caught a wall of bullets in the chest, which propelled him backward, out of sight.

One of the militiamen threw a grenade through the doorway. It clanked against something metal on the far side and exploded. Goodman barely had time to protect his face from the blast. *Dammit!* He felt a hot sliver on his cheek. His ears rang loudly. Men screamed and yelled on the other side of the doorway. Goodman motioned for another man with a submachine gun to shoot into the room. The man complied with great zeal, his crazed face lighting up with the muzzle flashes. The other militiamen took turns firing wildly into the next room. *Guess they had too much ammo.* A single shot from the far side was answered by no fewer than six of the militiamen emptying their magazines into the darkened space around the corner.

Once everyone was just about deaf, Goodman put his hand out to force a pause in the free-for-all. Goodman quickly popped his head around the corner and, through the swirling smoke and dust, he saw three bodies on the floor and a staircase immediately around the corner. Goodman pointed to three of the men to skirt around the corner and go up the stairs; they nodded in compliance. He then motioned for Tomislav and the remainder of the men to make for the far side of the room.

Goodman held up three fingers again and counted down silently, *three... two... one... go!* The two groups scurried in their assigned directions. Goodman stepped out to cover the doors on the far wall with his weapon. Everyone reached their destinations without a shot.

"Tomislav!" yelled Goodman.

"What?" Tomislav yelled back.

"You good?"

"Yes," said Tomislav. "There is no one here!"

The men from upstairs called down. "Ništa ovdje!" *Nothing here!*

But a second later someone yelled, "Neh! Neh! Pazi!"

Several pistol shots rang out, and the militia fired back with rifles and submachine guns. Someone was upstairs, holding out with a pistol. Another militiaman rattled off several rounds with his submachine gun. Silence. Two men ran up the stairs and fired several more shots.

"Not a problem, not a problem!" said one of the Majevitsa men as he emerged from an upstairs room, sliding a pistol into his belt. The men upstairs were rifling through desk drawers and throwing papers out the door and over the railing. Papers fluttered down like leaves.

Suddenly, everyone heard a voice coming from one of the rooms. The voice crackled with urgency. It sounded German, but something was off. *Static. It's a radio!* They all looked upward and realized it was coming from a radio room. Goodman raced upstairs, with Tomislav right behind him. They burst into the room just as a young black-clad radio operator was about to swing his rifle butt into the radio.

"No!" yelled Goodman. Goodman raised his weapon and squeezed the trigger. *Click!* Nothing happened. *I'm empty!* The radioman charged at Goodman and fired twice, missing both times. Goodman grabbed the wooden shaft of the rifle, and the man looked at him with fire in his eyes.

"No!" Goodman yelled again. Tomislav sprinted through the doorway and fired his pistol. The radioman's head snapped backward and he fell. Goodman, too, fell backward and landed hard on the cement floor with the radioman's body at his feet. Tomislav helped him up.

"Thanks," said Goodman, breathing heavily. "Again."

"Of course," replied Tomislav.

"What is he saying?" Goodman asked, looking at the radio. Tomislav stepped forward and lifted the headset to his ear.

"He is asking for a report," Tomislav said. "I think it is their headquarters in the Planina."

"You can understand it?" asked Goodman.

"Yes, a fair amount," Tomislav replied.

"Well, get on there," Goodman said.

"What do I say?" asked Tomislav. He sat down on the operator's stool as he placed the headset over his ears and lifted the microphone.

"Tell him…" Goodman searched his mind. The radio crackled again. "Tell him we need reinforcements."

"What!" yelled Tomislav, incredulous.

"Tell him!" said Goodman. "That's the mission, remember? We're supposed to draw the Nazis into an ambush, right? Who knows what they'll do if we don't respond? Tell them we fought off an attack, but we need help reinforcing the factory."

Tomislav gave him a strange look.

"Do it!" said Goodman.

Tomislav put his pistol on the desk and held the mouthpiece close. He pressed the transmit button and spoke. "Hallo, hallo! Die partisan sind weg, aber wir brauchen hilf! Jetzt, jetzt!" He released the button, then pressed it down again. "Ende!" he said, then released it again. They waited for the response.

The radio crackled, and Tomislav translated. "Yes, yes, we understand. How many militia… how many wounded… how many dead? Where is Lieutenant Smecker?"

Goodman spoke up, "Tell them... ten militiamen escaped, two men wounded, no dead."

Tomislav just looked at him.

Goodman explained, "It'll tell them there is enough of a threat that they need to respond, but we don't want them to send everything."

"What about their lieutenant?" Tomislav pointed to the man in a German officer lying on the ground with several red stains on his torso.

"Tell them he... he's pissing," said Goodman. Tomislav just shook his head. "Tell them!"

Tomislav pressed the microphone button again. "Hallo, hallo!" He talked at some length, and Goodman understood exactly none of it. They waited. The radio crackled again.

Tomislav spoke up. "They understand. They have already dispatched reinforcements."

Goodman looked at Tomislav. "Okay, how many reinforcements? When will they get here?"

Tomislav spoke into the microphone again and set it down. The reply was immediate. Tomislav's mouth dropped.

"What, what?" asked Goodman. Tomislav put the earpiece down, staring straight ahead.

"They said they sent a company," he said, monotone. "They'll be here in less than ten minutes."

"How many are in a German SS company?" asked Goodman.

Tomislav didn't even look up. "Between one hundred fifty and two hundred men."

"Oh, shit," said Goodman. The blood suddenly drained from his head.

"Yes," said Tomislav. "This is definitely shit."

"I'm going to get Amira in here," said Goodman as he started down the stairs, skipping steps as he went. "Get everyone ready!"

"To do what?" Tomislav yelled down the stairs. But Goodman did not respond. He ran through the building and out the door to the front gate. Rain pounded down on him.

He looked into the pitch-black downpour. *How the hell am I going to find Amira and her group?* He had no idea where she was, or where Zoran's main attack group was. *And even if I do, how will they know it's me and not shoot? Dammit!* He went back inside.

Tomislav found him and started to speak, but Goodman cut him off. "We gotta leave."

"Yes, of course. Now you want to leave," said Tomislav. "But first, you should see this." He led Goodman to where some militiamen were giggling over something excitedly. It was a stack of crates against the wall, partly covered by a heavy canvas. Tomislav told one of them to lift the canvas.

"Is that what I think it is?" asked Goodman. Stacks of green painted crates sat under the canvas, each one with the Nazi eagle and swastika stenciled across the front. A single giant word that needed no translation was stamped on every crate: "DYNAMIT."

"It is thirty-eight crates of dynamite," announced Tomislav.

"Wow," was all Goodman could say. *Oh, this is golden. What can we do with it?* Then he scowled. "Do we know how to blow it?"

Tomislav shrugged and shook his head.

"Oh, c'mon," said Goodman, irritated. "There has to be a way." He slung his weapon over his shoulder and put his hands on his hips.

Another of the men came running over, talking excitedly, too fast for Goodman to understand.

"He says there are other munitions in that truck." Tomislav pointed to the truck by the center wall that divided the loading area from the rest of the facility. They went over and looked. There were crates of rifle ammo, German potato masher grenades, flares, and linked machine gun ammunition.

Goodman said, "You think the grenades are enough to set off the dynamite?"

Tomislav shrugged again.

"Tell everyone to load up with as much as they carry. Then we get the grenades. Let's try to rig up some sort of wire or cable or something that will set off the grenades and blow the dynamite."

No one moved. They all just stared at him.

"Tomislav, tell them!"

Tomislav translated, and everyone sprang into action.

"Help me restack the crates and wedge a bunch of grenades between the stacks," said Goodman to Tomislav and the handful of men standing there. They moved the crates into two stacks, side-by-side next to the truck. The men brought several arm loads of grenades over. Others helped themselves to the newfound munitions, filling their packs and pockets with whatever else they could carry.

"Stick the grenades under the second crate, with the pull pins sticking out," directed Goodman. "Then run the end of the wire twice through all the rings." Tomislav directed another man to feed the wire through the grenade pull-rings once the crates were stacked on top of them. Goodman looked for the best place to run the wire.

Suddenly, there was a tremendous burst of gunfire not all that far away. The volume was enormous and sustained. Several explosions echoed and reverberated inside the large factory.

"Zoran's ambush," said Tomislav. "That's the SS counterattack."

"Right," acknowledged Goodman, barely thinking about it as his eyes darted around the loading area and his mind raced to conceive of something they could use to pull the wire that would pull all the rings out when the Germans were inside the building. A moment later, someone found some heavy-grade wire and brought it to the stack of crates. *What? There! Yes!*

Goodman climbed over the rear of the truck loaded with ammunition and pried open a box of grenades. "There!" he yelled. He waved over the man with the spool of wire. He grabbed the end and weaved it through the pull-rings of an entire row of grenades.

"What are you doing?" asked Tomislav.

"When the Germans show up, someone pulls the wire that is connected to these grenades which will pull the rings out...and boom!"

"That is a very bad idea," said Tomislav. "Who will do it?"

"Anybody. The wire is at least a hundred yards long!" exclaimed Goodman. "It's perfectly fine. Just...tell them to just run when they pull it. Tell them!"

"Yes, yes," replied Tomislav. He explained to the men what they should do. Their eyes widened, and then smiles spread across their faces. No one volunteered. *I didn't see that coming*, thought Goodman. He smiled and picked two of them. One of them began to argue with him, pointing at the grenades.

"What is he saying?" Goodman asked Tomislav.

"He says it won't work."

"Why…what the hell…get the extra guys out of here," said Goodman. "Tell them to wait by the wall until they see us." No one needed to be told twice, and soon Goodman was alone with Tomislav.

"Okay," said Goodman. "Let's wait a minute or two and then do it."

"No," said Tomislav. "We have to hurry and leave this place."

"Tomislav," said Goodman. "What's the problem?"

"These are not explosive grenades."

"What!"

"These are—"

"I heard you the first time. What are they then?"

"Incendiary grenades," said Tomislav.

"Incendiary grenades," he repeated. His face went numb. "Will this work?"

"It might—"

A sudden pause in the gunfire followed by a large metallic bang somewhere in the building caught them off guard. They both turned and listened for more noise from within the factory. A second later, they heard a loud squeaking and someone barking orders in German.

"Alright, time to go!"

Goodman wrapped the wire around his arms and jerked it hard. It came loose and a loud hissing sound emanated from the back of the truck. An orange glow filled the back of the truck and a shower of sparks danced on the concrete floor. *It's definitely lit.* "Run!"

They sprinted through the rain and to the half-wall they knew so well from earlier in the evening. Halfway across the street, Suleiman and the sharpshooter met them under the lamp.

"Hey!" yelled Goodman through the rain. "Look who made it!"

He grabbed Suleiman and pulled them toward the half-wall. Suleiman yelled something at Goodman, but Goodman ignored him.

Once they were all behind the wall, Goodman called out to Tomislav. "We're too close!"

"Yes, you're right!" said Tomislav.

"Follow me!" yelled Goodman. "Idi!"

No one needed any encouragement. Goodman led them back down the alleyways and across the main road again, following a narrow road up a slight incline. It circled around and crossed over a piece of high ground behind a row of shabby brick and stone houses. Frightened faces peered at them through doors and windows. Goodman looked back at the factory. They could see the roof from here.

"Stop!" yelled Goodman. Tomislav and the others slid to a halt and looked back as well. "We'll be able to see it from here. I think we're safe."

"You think?" asked Tomislav.

"Sure…" *I think so*, thought Goodman. Then he realized he had no idea how big the blast would be.

The group paused and caught their breath, not even noticing the rain. A moment later, the gunfire to the west of the factory subsided completely. Heavy machine guns that had been sending volleys of tracers into the sky suddenly stopped.

A number of large engines could be heard through the rain, which had let up slightly. Visibility was still limited to the silhouette of the factory that was now backlit by the lights on the far wall of the compound. The men rested with their backs against the wall of a house as the roof dribbled trickles of water just past their toes. The sounds of engines now brought the glow of headlights headed for the factory gate. They could hear the squealing of brakes and doors slamming shut. A moment later, drivers shifted gears, and engines roared. Goodman could envision them entering the loading area. *There was room for, what, eight, maybe ten trucks?* Goodman and his companions all breathed shallow, anxious breaths, waiting for what they hoped would be a satisfyingly catastrophic explosion. And they waited. And they waited a little more. They cast sideways glances at one another. Another minute passed. Nothing. Someone muttered something. Another man cursed. Yet another cursed and then spit into the rain-sloshed roadway. *It didn't work.* Goodman looked down. *Dammit, it didn't work!* He exhaled loudly and turned to Tomislav.

"Do you think…"

Tomislav shook his head.

"Well," said Goodman. "We should prob—"

He put his hand up to shield his eyes from the brilliant flash. The ground bounced beneath him, and the force of the blast sent roof tiles, rocks, and all kinds of now-lethal projectiles into the air. Raindrops turned into liquid bullets and pelted them, stinging their faces and hands. The scene before them lit up like the sun. A rainbow appeared around the factory, flames shot out through cracks in the upper portion of the brick and mortar, and the roof collapsed. Those tiles and bricks that had launched into the air now descended with the rainwater all around them. Each piece made a slight, stuttering whistle as it slapped through raindrops and impacted the road or a rooftop. Everyone took cover anywhere they could.

"Woah," said Goodman, awestruck.

"Fritzie is definitely shit now," said Tomislav.

Goodman listened as the last bits of brick pelted down around them. Another explosion flashed through the dark and rumbled like thunder in the valley. *Oh, my holy God*, he thought. He replayed the image of the blast in his mind. *Wow*. He shook his head.

"Maybe we should go," he called out to Tomislav. "You think Suleiman can get us to the rendezvous point with Amira?"

"We shall see," Tomislav replied.

# 42

## 0021 HOURS
## SEPTEMBER 28, 1943

GOODMAN AND TOMISLAV FOUND SULEIMAN, and the three of them quickly agreed upon a route to the rendezvous point. They ran through the outer neighborhoods and back into the countryside, to the farm where they were to meet up with Zoran and Amira. The rain had finally let up, and moonlight flooded the slopes above the valley. Goodman's nose, ears, fingers, and toes stung with the cold that rapidly sank in. What had started as a mild leg cramp was now in full force. Goodman massaged it as he walked, but it made little difference. Tomislav slipped, and Goodman caught him. Then he slipped and Tomislav lent a hand. They moved cautiously on the icy paths and edged their way through another small hamlet above the urban valley. Goodman looked over his shoulder and hoped that Amira and Zoran had completed their tasks and would join them soon.

A single, solitary shot rang out downhill to their south—the area west of what used to be the salt factory, which was now a thick column of dark smoke illuminated by smoldering fires. Then gunfire roared from the valley. Goodman and Tomislav looked at each other. *Shouldn't everyone be on their way here?*

"That's not good," said Goodman. "Is that Zoran?"

"Perhaps." Tomislav peered through the darkness toward the gunfire. "No, I think it is Amira."

Suleiman cleared his throat. "The rendezvous point is in that large field with the small hill in it." He pointed ahead uphill, to the right. Downhill to their left, the gunfire continued, punctuated by explosions and bursts of heavy machine-gun fire. An engine roared, and then a crashing sound echoed up from the valley road. Red and white tracers raced across the sky.

"We should go check that out," said Goodman. "They might need help."

Right then, they heard the roar of a man's voice. *That's Zoran!*

Goodman said, "We have to go."

"We cannot go into that," Tomislav protested. "That would be suicide."

"They need our help," said Goodman. "We won't go straight into that mess. I'm not stupid. We'll go wide to the right,"—he motioned with his arm—"so we stay outside the battle area. We'll stop before we see Germans or Amira's people."

"I think we should remain here until it is all over," said Tomislav.

"Fine, you stay here," said Goodman. He turned and called to the men to follow him. "Prati me!"

No one moved. They all looked at Suleiman, who kept his eyes down. Goodman fumed.

*What happens if Zoran gets killed or caught by the Germans? Or Amira?* He looked up and down the line of men huddled by the wall with him. *Do any of these guys know how to get us out of here? What happens to us—to me—if we get stuck here?* His mind raced with the possibilities. Every outcome was bad. His probability of getting out of Yugoslavia diminished quickly without the guiding hand of Zoran. *I need him. And Amira—*His mind shied away from the thought of harm befalling the fierce leader who broke down in his arms just a couple days ago.

"What are you going to say when they ask us where we were while they did all the fighting?"

Tomislav translated, and Suleiman said nothing.

"Nothing? Nište?" *I can't believe this*, he thought. *Amira and Zoran need our help. If we don't get out of this, I'm… stuck. And if something happens to Amira, to more of Musa's family, I'll be stuck knowing that I could have helped.* "After we just blew up that factory?"

Suleiman mumbled something to Tomislav.

"He says these are our instructions…" Tomislav let his voice trail off.

"Are you going to tell Zoran that you sat in that empty field while they slugged it out and died down there?" He pointed toward the hayfield. "I might be a foreigner, but I'm not going to do that." He looked at Tomislav. "Tell them." He did. *Suleiman doesn't know what to do here.*

Tracer fire fanned out across the sky, burning through the remaining cloud cover, followed by the stutter of heavy machine-gun fire. The sharpshooter from earlier stepped forward, holding his rifle like a pugil stick. He looked like a puppy that had just gotten dunked in a bucket of water. But he had a determined look on his face, like he had something to say.

"What you name?" Goodman asked him in Bosanski.

"Why are you talking to him?" Suleiman objected. "I am the—"

"Ušuti!" said Goodman. *Shut up.* He glared at Suleiman for a second or two and then turned back to the young sharpshooter.

"I am called Ademir, Effendi." Ademir bowed his head slightly when he spoke, then he pulled his shoulders back and stood like a statue.

"What you say we do, Ademir?" Goodman asked him. "We go or we stay here?"

All faces turned to Ademir. He lowered his eyes.

"It does not matter what I think, Effendi."

"No, you make think." Goodman pointed to Suleiman. "Him not leader. Me not leader. You leader. You say, we do."

"If I was the leader," Ademir pointed into the valley with his rifle muzzle. "If I was the leader, we should go there, Effendi." Another explosion lit up the early morning sky. "We help Zoran Pasha. We go to the guns."

*That's my man*, thought Goodman. He pointed downhill toward the raging battle and looked at Tomislav and Suleiman.

"We go to the guns."

# 43

TOMISLAV AND SULEIMAN RELENTED TO GOODMAN'S PLAN. From their current position, they would circle around to avoid walking into the firefight and set up an ambush on the main road to Tuzla. Once they were in position, Suleiman would attempt to contact Zoran or Amira so they could coordinate actions. Unless Zoran directed otherwise, Goodman decided they would protect Zoran's force from any more Waffen-SS or Ustaša reinforcements. The men stood, stiff and shivering from the cold. Goodman exhaled nervously. *They're ready.*

"Idemo," he said.

Goodman led them down the winding path from the rendezvous point, through small pastures and animal pens. Brilliant moonlight sparkled on every icy surface. The metal parts on Goodman's weapon became too frigid to handle, so he cradled it in his arms. The houses and their animal pens grew closer and closer together until narrow alleyways forced the men into a single file.

On the road below them, a heavy machine gun rattled away, sending tracers ricocheting in all directions. A loud explosion reverberated and sent a fireball into the air. Instinctively, Goodman and the men crouched down, taking shelter from the light. They exchanged concerned looks. *What was that? It wasn't artillery. An armored car? A tank? We should be okay as long as there aren't any tanks,* thought Goodman. He shook away the 'what ifs' that he could do nothing about. They continued down the slope. Families passed them headed uphill, away from the fighting. Men shepherded their children and wives away from the battle area, clutching bags and bearing worried looks. An infant cried out from under a blanket.

Goodman paused before they reached the last cluster of houses above the road. The sounds of battle had trickled off to a few shots that echoed in the crisp darkness. Goodman and Suleiman crept forward and found a row of small shops about thirty feet from a deep ditch that ran parallel to the road. They made their way back, and Goodman positioned the men just as he had seen Amira do in the forest before attacking the German convoy. Suleiman went off to find Amira or Zoran. They were somewhere a few hundred yards to the left, still engaged in a sporadic gunfight with someone. When he finished, Goodman assigned lookouts, again like Amira did, and the group sat down to rest.

In the stillness, exhaustion set in. Their clothing was soaked, and the cold sucked away their warmth. Men began falling asleep as they slumped against the walls of the shops. Even Goodman became drowsy once he settled into his place. He shook his head to wake up. *This is hypothermia,* he realized. He stood up to keep the blood moving and prodded the others to do likewise. They were reluctant, but most complied. Suleiman stumbled back into their midst and sat down opposite Goodman.

"You see Zoran Pasha?" Goodman asked Suleiman.

"Neh," he replied. "I was afraid of getting shot."

Goodman shook his head. "You no see them?" *C'mon, man.* Goodman stood tall to peer over the rooftops around them. *They can't be too far,* he thought. *Maybe he's got a point, though. I don't want to get shot by my own people either. They're tired and probably freaked out by the fighting. We need to protect Amira's flank. At least we'll get a few shots off at whoever comes from Tuzla before they reach her. That should be plenty of warning.* Satisfied, Goodman sat down again and folded his arms tight against his chest.

Occasionally, a burst of gunfire rattled through the streets. After half an hour, no more sound echoed along the Tuzla Road. *Maybe the Fritzies had enough?* But they had not seen any Germans retreating. *Maybe they don't have enough forces to send as reinforcements.* His hands still folded under his armpits, Goodman made his way to Tomislav and Suleiman.

"Is there any other way to Tuzla from here?" asked Goodman. "Could they go around us?"

Suleiman mumbled, and Tomislav translated. "He says the Tuzla Road is right here, and the river is only two rows of houses away from us. We would see them if they tried to get back to the city."

The men peered carefully over the wall. They saw nothing but darkness and the swirling of icy mist in the wind. Then Goodman looked at the ground. *What is that?*

It began as a flutter. Goodman thought it was the numbness of early onset frostbite in his feet. But it throbbed in a pattern. A vibration. A very slight tremor under the dirt. The vibration grew into a steady tremble. Men became agitated and murmured frantically to one another. The tremble grew into a rumble, and a metallic squeaking noise seemed to emanate from further west on the main road. An engine roared, and the metallic noise increase in pitch and speed. Goodman looked at Tomislav.

"Is that—?"

Tomislav crouched down. "Tank."

*No!* Goodman peered over the wall. Across the road and down fifty yards, there was a lone lamp post that cast a dim cone of light. But the tank, or whatever was coming, were still out of sight. Some commotion amongst the men on the right end of their ambush line drew Goodman's and Tomislav's attention. Tomislav ran in a low crouch over to them. After a brief moment's conversation, the whole group of men came rushing at Goodman, with Tomislav in the lead.

"What the hell are you doing?" snarled Goodman. "Get down!"

"The tanks!" said Tomislav.

"Yeah, there're tanks coming."

"What are you going to do?"

"Stop those tanks and whatever is with them."

"That is foolish," said Tomislav.

"Maybe, but we need to protect Amira and Zoran," said Goodman. "At least we can give them some warning." Goodman turned to the group that now gathered around them. "Two men at the top of those stairs," he directed toward the neighborhood behind them. "Four more down that way." He pointed down an alley which paralleled the road but was hidden from it. "And we need someone on that roof over there." He pointed to the top of a narrow, three-story house that dominated the neighborhood.

Tomislav selected the men and sent them on their way.

"Where's our marksman?" Goodman looked around. "Where's Ademir?"

"I am here, Effendi!"

"Good." Goodman took him by the arm and pointed uphill to a house with a flat roof. "Go up there."

"Yes, Effendi," said Ademir.

"When I shoot Germans here, you shoot Germans from there, yes?"

"Yes, Effendi!" Ademir took off for his assignment, and Goodman turned to the remainder of the squad.

"Where are you going?" Tomislav asked.

"I'm taking some guys to make trouble for the tanks," declared Goodman. "Those tanks can't get through. They'll tear up Amira and Zoran." Goodman counted the four men who remained.

"With four men?" called Tomislav.

"I want to hit 'em and get back here before they know what happened!" replied Goodman.

Tomislav shook his head. "How are you going to do that?"

"I want to go light and fast!" Goodman opened the flap of the rucksack nearest him. Small, green orbs reflected the ambient light around them. *Grenades from the factory*, he thought. *Good.* Goodman tapped the four men on the shoulder and motioned for them to follow.

"Prati me," Goodman said to the men. *Follow me.*

They followed. They rounded a small stone wall and took a hard right down a narrow stone staircase. At the last house before the road, Goodman found a small, protected space behind a low stone wall. The group moved in and set down their packs. Goodman peered over the wall and saw two tanks crawling forward side by side, headlights full-on. They were enormous. A searchlight swiveled from the tops of their turrets, scanning the neighborhoods and side streets. He ducked back down as the light flashed across the neighborhood. *I can't do anything about tanks*, he thought. *All I can to do is give warning to Zoran.* He reached into the nearest rucksack. *One grenade each, then we run.*

"Granate?" he offered as he pulled out the stick grenades.

Each man nodded in understanding and selected his grenade. They shifted down the fence a bit to give each other room to throw as Goodman peered over the wall and waited. The tanks continued to move at a snail's pace across their front, with only the ditch between them and Goodman's five-man assault team. As they passed under the nearest streetlamp, Goodman saw a mass of men close behind them using the tanks as shields. His gut clenched. *That looks like more than a hundred men.*

"*Infantrija!*" the man next to him whispered nervously. "Lots of infantry!"

Goodman nodded. *This changes things. If we throw a grenade and run, the tanks would probably ignore us and roll on. But infantry will fight back. That's what they do. They'll chase us. And there're only fourteen of us in total. Only four of us here.* He wished he had the rest of the squad. But he had surprise on his side. Plus, it was dark. And frigid. Not everything is against us, he figured.

One of the men smiled and dumped at least six more grenades out of his pack. Another pulled out two more from his belt and added those to the pile. The other men dumped their packs, and at least a dozen baseball-sized fragmentary grenades rolled out.

242

"Okay," said Goodman. "Four grenades each man." He put up four fingers.

Mischievous grins grew across the faces of the men around him as they eagerly reached for more grenades. A flash of mortality warmed him for a brief second. He was about to throw hand grenades at two tanks and a hundred German soldiers. *This is crazy*, he thought. He blinked icy mist away from his eyes and pictured himself crouching back down and letting the Germans pass. Waiting. *But for what? For something safer?*

*No. No, I can't run. Not now.* He clenched his jaw. *I'd never be able to live with myself, with that memory.* He thought of Amira. *I have to do this. For her. For Zoran. For Baba...*

He grabbed three more grenades and placed them carefully on the ledge for easy access. He shoved a fifth one into his belt. *My emergency reserve.*

"Gotov," said Goodman. *We're ready.* Two of the men nodded confidently. It made Goodman feel a lot better. Like it wasn't completely insane. Again, he suppressed the 'what ifs.'

The tanks rumbled directly across their front. At the rear of the infantry, two men walked fully upright, each with a wireless radio operator in tow. *Officers!* Goodman scowled. *They act like they're walking in a damn park. They have no idea what's coming.* He knew exactly where his grenades were going.

He crouched back down and exaggeratedly raised his arms and pulled lightly on the stick grenade's string to tell everyone to get ready. They all mimicked him, and everyone was shaking with excitement. Or maybe it was fear. Or the biting cold. Maybe all three. Goodman knew he felt all three, but there was a certain euphoria to seeing the tanks roll out across his front. Now the bulk of the infantry were directly to their front, outlined in the glow of the streetlight. Goodman nodded to the four faces beside him. He pulled the string on the handle hard. He felt the pop. *Fuse burning.*

# 44

"GRANATA!"

Goodman raised himself up and threw his first grenade in a high arc toward the SS infantry officers at the end of the column. The others quickly followed suit. He grabbed his second grenade and pulled the cord without waiting for the others. The next round of grenades was mid-air as the first five exploded in rapid succession. Goodman heard men on the road screaming above the rumbling of the tanks. *Good*, he thought. *Here comes more you sons of bitches.* The next grenades went off and ended the screaming, and the last volley followed a second later, exploding in the midst of the platoons as they scrambled for cover.

Goodman felt giddy, almost dizzy, like he was drunk. He snatched one of the round grenades, pulled the ring, and he threw, and then clumsily fished around on the ground for another. *Last one*, he thought to himself. He threw it high over the wall, and it bounced on the road. Several shots rang out in the dark, followed immediately by a blast.

*Now, we can leave. There's no way Zoran and Amira could miss all that.* He realized he had not taken a breath through the entire grenade attack. The cold burned his throat when he finally inhaled. He swallowed hard and waved to the others. *Let's go!*

Suddenly, the tanks' brakes squealed. The black-armored behemoths rocked back and forth as they came to a halt. The electric shock of getting caught red-handed struck Goodman. He quickly took cover behind the wall again and gripped his icy cold MP40. *They've gotta know we're close.* He expected to hear the turrets rotate, or the machineguns open up, but the only noise was the deep idling of diesel engines.

A shot rang out from behind them and a German cried out in pain. *Ademir's at work*, thought Goodman. *Good.* He peered over the wall as another shot rang out, and a German stumbled, fell, writhed for a second, and became still. His rifle skidded into the ditch.

All across the road in front of him, German soldiers were scattered across the pavement. Some laid still, facedown, and some laid on their backs, reaching up into the air or hoarsely calling out for someone. Others were crawling or scrambling for the ditch on the far side.

*Where are those fucking officers?* He peered over the wall again. He saw at least one of the radio operators was dead on the road, but saw neither of the officers. A soldier ran across the road and dived into the roadside ditch right in front of him. Goodman's eyes followed the man and saw that at least a dozen Germans were already in the ditch less than ten feet from them. He gestured to the man next to him to throw another grenade. With a smile on his face, the man casually lobbed the grenade over the wall. They nodded in shared satisfaction when the blast went off.

Goodman picked up his weapon and motioned for the group to follow him. As they rounded the front corner of the house, Goodman opened up on the Germans in the ditch. The men behind him fired their rifles into the pile of bodies and then slid into the ditch themselves. The ditch was full of sloppy mud up to the tops of their boots. One of the men started slamming a German in the head with his rifle butt. It struck Goodman as especially vicious, but ended quickly. The roar of the tanks' engines was too loud to talk over, so Goodman gestured for everyone to get up to the road. They all crawled up the ten-foot embankment on their bellies.

Another shot rang out from Ademir's rifle, and it set off a lot of yelling on the far side of the road. Goodman pointed to the other men's grenades and then mimed throwing them across the road. The grenades bounced and bobbled into the ditch on the far side where they detonated. Several Germans emerged from the far ditch under a streetlamp further down the road and sprinted to the west—back toward Tuzla. Goodman let off a short burst of fire at them. One soldier stumbled, but his comrade caught him under the arm and helped him limp away.

"Dammit!" exclaimed Goodman. His first reaction was frustration at not killing all the Germans, but, deeper, he was relieved at their retreat. He hadn't anticipated committing to such a close fight. *Okay, now to get out of here without those tanks seeing us*. He lowered himself down the embankment to conceal himself. *Why are they still here, anyway?*

Suddenly, something that sounded like a stick swishing through water startled him, and a house behind the tanks burst open in a brilliant flash. Something swooshed again, and an explosion impacted the tanks, setting the side of the turret on fire. Goodman and the others slid back into the ditch for cover.

"What was that?" Goodman yelled. Two more swooshes and two more explosions impacted somewhere above and sent a shower of sparks over them. The men next to Goodman cheered.

"Rakete, rakete!" They yelled.

*Rockets? Someone is firing rockets! I guess Amira was better prepared than I thought.*

A long stream of machine-gun fire ricocheted off the tank turrets, and another rocket swooshed over the top of the ditch and exploded out of sight. Twin blasts shattered windows as the tanks opened up with their main guns simultaneously. Goodman's head throbbed, and he and the others hugged the muddy ground at the bottom of the ditch.

One of the tank's engines roared as it reversed. Machine guns on the hull and turret sprayed bullets wildly across the neighborhood. The stationary tank fired its main gun again, exploding something far off on the hillside.

*We're stuck here!* thought Goodman. *I don't want to get hit by one of those rockets.* The tank's machine guns opened up as the turret rotated back and forth, spraying the neighborhoods on either side of the road, tracers flying wildly into the air and penetrating the houses and fences like they were made of paper. Splinters of brick and mortar showered down on Goodman and the others. Showers of sparks lit up the ditch like daylight. Goodman made his way eastward, toward Amira's position. A rocket swished overhead from that direction and slammed into the nearest tank with an ear-splitting crack. He dived to the bottom of the ditch again.

On the road above, the rear tank rotated on its treads, scraping the road in a wide circle. Another rocket crashed into the road. The lead tank fired again, shaking the walls of the houses and bouncing the men in the ditch. A nearby house exploded and sent brick and wooden beams tumbling into the ditch. Then, the lead tank began to pivot on its own tracks as the rear tank fired its gun repeatedly to cover it.

The tank had rotated halfway when a series of rockets impacted the hull and wheels with ear-splitting explosions. Not a single rocket missed its target. A fractured road wheel tumbled into the ditch next to Goodman. Scorching heat radiated from it, and Goodman scooted away. The tank continued to rotate, and another road wheel fell off with a loud *clank!* Goodman felt the ground vibrate with the stuttering movements of the tank above. He heard a loud metallic *pop,* and the tank's track fell off completely. Goodman lifted his head just enough to see that the tank was stuck where it sat.

The tank that was, a moment ago, practically indestructible had become a forty-ton immovable bunker with a turret. The turret rotated, and the main gun pounded the neighborhood above with several rounds of high explosives and a seemingly endless stream of machine-gun fire. Suddenly, it ceased firing. The retreating tank screeched to a halt. The two monsters remained still for a moment, engines growling at idle.

*What are they doing?* Suddenly, both tanks opened fire. The nearest row of houses collapsed as gunfire swept back and forth across the neighborhood. Goodman and the others quickly brushed off hot ashes and retreated to the deepest part of the ditch. The rear tank crept forward and continued firing until its bullets were flying directly over the heads of the group in the ditch. Bricks and stone flew sky high. *They're panicking! They're trapped, but so are we.* Goodman pounded his fist into the dirt. He could hear yet more German soldiers call out to one another as they ran past at a full sprint, headed back to Tuzla. Both tanks fired their main guns one more time.

The rear tank roared its engine and moved to the disabled tank. Now bumper-to-bumper, the hatches swung open, and four men scrambled out of the disabled tank and over the turret of the other, where they hunkered down. Goodman raised his weapon and fired at the now-exposed German tank crew. The others fired, too, but had to take cover again when the tank commander swung his heavy machine gun around and sprayed the ditch with gunfire. Goodman changed magazines.

The last man out of the disabled tank threw two grenades into the hatch before leaping to the rear tank. The rear tank gunned its engines and raced westward toward Tuzla as the lame tank burst open with blinding white flames. Brilliant sparks showered down in all directions. Inside the burning tank, machine gun ammunition cooked off and rattled around the interior for a moment. The retreating tank's engine faded, as did the flames emanating from the dead tank.

Goodman raised his head slowly above the curb. He rubbed his eyes and let them readjust to the low light of the streetlamps. *They're gone!* he thought. *The Germans are all gone.*

# 45

GOODMAN STOOD UP IN THE DITCH and scanned up and down the road. The sky was slowly graying, and things were becoming clearly visible now. The road looked to be a lot wider than it had appeared in the dark. Surprisingly wide. *Like a runway with neighborhoods on either side.* He chuckled to himself. And then he turned around.

The neighborhoods were thoroughly scorched. People slowly, cautiously emerged from their houses. Families and neighbors called for missing loved ones, crying out when they were found. Some people wandered into the road, gaping at the carnage and destruction.

Goodman climbed and stood at the top of the ditch, suddenly very, very exhausted. One of his men laid down on the road next to the corpse of a German soldier, pulled out a cigarette, flicked his lighter several times, and smoked.

Goodman scanned the German bodies for the officers he targeted with his grenades. He found them. One lay on the road, his legs cut off at the knees and a crimson gash across his chest. The other was face-down in the muddy ditch on the far side of the road, clutching the still-attached handset of the radio. The radio was still attached to the radio operator, who was also dead in the ditch. He examined the radios. Neither functioned as far as he could tell. He and his men started to gather weapons, ammunition, and grenades. One man traded boots with a dead German.

"Govno!" someone yelled out. "Jebi se, Fritizie!" *Fuck you, Fritzie!*

Two men of Goodman's squad were yelling out curses. Another joined in, cursing and swinging fists at someone. They had a live German.

"Jebi se, Fritzie!" A rifle rose up in the air and swung down like a baseball bat.

Goodman ran over and saw it was not just one, but three German soldiers. Each bore the Teutonic script "SS" emblazoned on their collars. One was bloodied, but the other two were in okay condition except for the beatings they now absorbed. *Amira wanted prisoners*, Goodman thought to himself. *Well, Zoran wanted them. I think she would have rather killed them and been done with it. But now we have prisoners.* He remembered the demise of the captured Ustaši. *I'm not killing prisoners*, he decided. *Zoran can do it if he wants.*

"*Haha! Jebi se, Fritzie!*" another of the men bellowed. The others broke out into a chant. "Fritzie, Fritzie, Fritzie!"

A pair of militia fighters dragged a fourth German soldier by his suspenders. The SS trooper tried to push back, but a third man ran up and gave him a full-force kick to the groin. He let out a howl and curled into the fetal position, yelling what must have been obscenities. Goodman halted the abuse to inspect the man's uniform and rolled him over. *An Officer!* The three dots and four bars of an SS Captain caught his eyes, as did the shine of an Iron Cross around his neck. *Good catch*, he thought. He looked up at the militiamen. "Offizier!" he called out. They cheered.

A moment later, Tomislav and Suleiman brought the remainder of their group down to the road. They all gazed silently at the wreckage of the tank and the mess of bodies that littered the road. One of Suleiman's men was being carried by two others. He seemed fine except for his ankle that was wrapped and treated as if it were made of glass. When his comrades sat him down, he groaned and gestured for a cigarette. Tomislav and Suleiman halted at the sight of the four prisoners lying on the road. Goodman smiled at them.

"Here," he said. "Take them."

Suleiman gladly took charge of the prisoners and organized a guard for them. Someone came up with a rope and tied the four Germans together by the wrists and necks and then gagged each of them. The guards followed up with a smack about the head to remind them of the new order of things. *As if they need reminding*, Goodman thought. Then he remembered young Fritzie from the convoy. *This will not go well for them.*

Goodman counted the militia fighters on the road. They were short a handful of men. "This isn't everyone, is it?" he asked. Suleiman looked to Tomislav to respond.

Tomislav motioned for Goodman to follow him. They walked up the hill toward the narrow stairway. A pile of corpses in German uniforms completely blocked the narrow passage at the bottom. There were more German bodies mixed with militia bodies inside the adjacent house. Goodman was astounded. *There's gotta be at least twenty bodies here.*

"When did this happen?"

"Some Germans took cover right on top of us when the tanks started shooting," Tomislav explained. He pointed to two bodies at the top of the stairs. "Malik and Fethullah handled themselves well, but there were too many."

Goodman and Tomislav started back down the hill to the road and saw a large group of people approaching from the west. Amira's voice rang out as singularly identifiable. As she passed the dead tank, she pointed at Goodman and Tomislav, her face narrowed with anger.

"Oh, no," they said in unison. They guardedly stepped onto the road.

"You are still alive," she said. To Goodman, it felt more like an accusation.

"Yes, I'm still here," said Goodman. "Doing well, thanks."

"What did you do in the factory?" she demanded. "You were not supposed to invade it and destroy it, you fool!" She continued speaking much too rapidly for Goodman to keep up.

"What?" said Goodman. "But we killed a lot of Fritzies and Ustaša."

"Ha!" she scoffed. "Nište!"

Amira held up a single, brass-colored bullet casing in his face and screamed words that were completely new to him. Her point was clear enough, though. The brass casing clinked on the pavement when she threw it at his feet. Amira stormed off toward Tuzla with her militia leaders in tow. *I get that she's pissed*, he thought. *But that's a bit over the top.*

Goodman turned to Tomislav. "What did she say?"

"She said that you were not supposed to attack the factory."

"Yeah, I got that part."

"And that she wanted to use the explosives in the factory to destroy the main gate at the Planina."

"The what?"

"The Planina fortress. It is the reason we are here."

"Oh, that would have been good to know before."

"And she said we are to go to Tuzla and meet Zoran at the eighth precinct schoolhouse. She said that Zoran will deal with us then."

Goodman watched her walk away. "But we have—" He paused. "What's the word for prisoners?"

"Zatvorenike."

Goodman cupped his hands around his mouth to yell. "Imamo zatvorenike!" *We have prisoners!* He pointed at the bound and blindfolded SS soldiers sitting with their backs together. "Oficiri!" She ignored him and continued walking toward the city. He turned to Tomislav. "What did we do wrong?"

"Everything, apparently," answered Tomislav. "I did tell you we should not go into the factory." He drew a smoke and lit up. "And I said we should stay at the rendezvous point."

"Yeah, yeah, okay," he said. *Maybe blowing up the factory and attacking the tanks with hand grenades wasn't the smartest thing to do, but both worked. It worked a whole lot better than I thought it*

*would. And how was I supposed to know about the dynamite?*
"What's it gonna take with her?"

"There is nothing you can do," said Tomislav. "You are everything she detests."

"What? How can that be? We just killed a tank! And I don't know how many Nazis. We protected her from their counterattack."

"You represent something she cannot control."

"So, there is nothing I can do?"

Tomislav shook his head, and Goodman threw his hands up. *What the hell?* He recalculated the pros and cons of his—their—actions over the last twelve hours. *This is a win, right?* he asked himself. He looked over the destruction and sprawled out bodies on the road. *Isn't this what she lives for?* Goodman remembered the moment with her in the woods. *I thought we had some connection.* He scratched his head and shouldered his weapon.

He and Tomislav joined the river of men, horses, and wagons moving westward on the Tuzla Road. Members of the Majevitsa militia intermingled with civilians as they went. Goodman's squad paraded their prisoners through the throngs of fighters, exposing them to jeers and assaults of all kinds. One of Zoran's nephews grabbed the rope lead from Suleiman and led the line of prisoners over the edge of the embankment, letting the first one fall into the muddy ditch. All four splashed and yelled out in protest. An older militiaman pulled them back upright and got them moving in the right direction again. Now they were soaked to the bone and shivering.

"You know," said Tomislav. "There isn't much different between us."

"Between who? What do you mean?" The comment instantly angered Goodman. *What point is he making now?*

"Their machine lost this time, but there will be other battles. The larger machine is still at work. This is all just the working of the gears."

"No way." Goodman scowled. "I don't buy that."

Tomislav shrugged again and lit up a cigarette. He offered one to Goodman. He refused.

# 46

## THE TUZLA ROAD, EAST OF TUZLA

GOODMAN'S EYES WERE GLUED TO THE BODIES that hung from the archway over the road. The rain from several hours ago had frozen the bodies into solid blocks of discolored ice that swung gently in the frigid breeze. From several yards away, they looked to Goodman like slabs of meat hanging in a butcher's freezer. But up close, despite the ashen pallor and icy veneer, their former humanity was unmistakable. Icicles pointed downward from the toes protruding through their socks. Each of the men and women hanging there had signs around their necks.

"What do those say?" asked Goodman.

"The signs state that these people are judged and condemned as traitors and spies." Tomislav pointed at several of the bodies. "Collaborators, too. And this one's a thief of the people's finances."

"What's that sign say?" Goodman pointed to the sign that hung over the top beam.

"By order of the National Liberation Army and Partisan Detachments of Yugoslavia."

"Who is that?" asked Goodman.

"Them." Tomislav pointed to several horse-mounted men in olive-green tunics and wool coats with red epaulets. They held rifles across their laps, and one smoked a long, curved pipe as he carefully eyed the west-bound crowds. Tomislav averted his eyes as they passed the mounted guards.

"Do not look at them," said Tomislav. "They will take an interest in you if you appear to take an interest in them."

Goodman's eyes went to the boots of the man in front of him. "They look like Russians," he muttered to Tomislav.

"Russians they are not," said Tomislav. "They *are* Communists, but they are the Titoists. General Tito's Partisan Army."

"Aren't they supposed to be in the mountains somewhere?" asked Goodman. "Did we know they would be here?"

"No," said Tomislav. "I am certain Zoran is extremely angered by this turn of events."

"What do they want?" asked Goodman. "I mean, why are they here?"

"Well," started Tomislav. "They want control of Yugoslavia. Everything they do is toward that end. So, logically, they are here because they want control of Bosnia. They come to Tuzla because it is the chief administrative city in this part of Bosnia."

"So, what do we do about it?" asked Goodman.

"I'm not sure there is anything we *can* do about it," replied Tomislav. "They are rumored to have over a hundred thousand soldiers. They are well-equipped by the Allies, and they are well organized."

"Wait," Goodman put a hand on Tomislav's shoulder. "We give them equipment?"

"The British do, yes."

"What in the he—"

Tomislav interrupted with a hand on Goodman's shoulder, and they looked up. On the road ahead, beyond the gallows, a wall of horse-mounted Partisans halted the mass of people headed toward the inner city. A green-clad woman with a megaphone directed all citizens to retrieve their identification papers and to keep quiet. Partisan foot soldiers suddenly moved in from all sides, some forming a perimeter, while other pushed the crowds into lines. Each line led to a table, and a soldier sat at each table with an arm outstretched for the next citizen's identity book. He would examine it and give a nod to the Partisan officer standing behind him to let the family pass into the city.

"Checkpoint," said Tomislav.

"What do we—"

"Shh!" Tomislav put a finger to his lips. Goodman put his head down, too.

Mothers shushed whining children as fathers fished into their pockets. For a brief moment, Goodman made eye contact with a pair of eyes surrounded by dark purple circles. The woman turned her face as she handed her booklet to her husband. She adjusted a blanket over her shoulder as she tried to maintain her hold on an infant attached to her breast. Suddenly embarrassed, Goodman averted his eyes. Everyone took a small step forward and waited.

Several people successfully passed through, but not everyone. An argument flared up between the woman's husband and a soldier holding their identification books. Another Partisan with red epaulets on his shoulders intervened with a commanding tone. He examined the man's papers and waved another pair of foot soldiers to remove the man from the line. The man protested but was quickly silenced by a club to the face then and dragged to a side street. His wife kept her mouth closed and silently followed. Goodman wanted to intervene, but thought better of it. *There's nothing I can do here.* The soldier at the table waved the next person forward, and the line in front of Goodman moved forward a step.

A knot grew in Goodman's stomach. *I don't have papers,* he thought. *What do we do?* He looked to Tomislav. "We need to get out of here!" he whispered.

Tomislav put a discrete finger to his lips. Goodman glanced around for a way out, and his panic grew. *They have us surrounded.* He took another step with the mass of people pushing from behind. A Partisan officer strode through the crowd with a clipboard. He looked at Goodman and Tomislav, and then at their weapons, and made two checkmarks with his pencil before walking past without speaking a word.

"Perhaps they think we are volunteers," Tomislav said quietly as he glanced around.

"Tomislav!" whispered Goodman. "We need to go back and try a different way into the city." He pulled on Tomislav's arm, but his friend resisted. "Dammit, Tomislav, we need to get—"

Tomislav reached into his interior coat pocket and produced a fist-sized roll of cash. He looked at Goodman and cocked his head slightly, then put half the wad into Goodman's palm.

"You throw left, I throw right, yes?"

*Yes!* thought Goodman. *That's perfect.* He smiled and nodded his head.

"Now..." said Tomislav.

The cash flew into the air and began landing on people's shoulders before they reacted en masse. Long, neat lines quickly melted into each other, and a melee erupted. The crowd surged forward, overwhelming the tables and the guard force, who pushed back against them with batons and rifle butts. Another echelon of soldiers approached with their weapons off their shoulders. The crowd panicked and ran in every direction.

"There!" Goodman pointed to an alleyway—now wide open—and they ran for it. Several handfuls of militia and civilians alike followed them through the narrow passage. Shots rang out behind them, and Goodman sprinted across the next intersection. They took a side alleyway, and Tomislav peered back around the corner.

"We are safe," he said. "Go!"

Goodman ducked around the next turn, and they climbed a steeply inclined stairway. "What a view!" he said when they reached the top.

The city lay spread out before them, red-roofed buildings and houses enshrouded in mist, with hundreds of wisps of white smoke curling upward. In the distance, a quintet of stone masonry towers jutted upward from a rocky hillside south of the city center. To Goodman, it looked like a medieval castle.

"What is that?" he asked.

"That is the Planina fortress," said Tomislav. "Zoran's final objective. It was once the residence of the old kings of Bosnia. This is the symbolic seat of power, though the government administrative buildings are somewhere in the city's government quarter. What we did last night was just to get us here."

"So, we're supposed to occupy the fortress?"

"There's more to it than that," said Tomislav. "It contains the Nazi Waffen-SS Regimental headquarters and a blended Ustaša and local pacification battalion. It is the base of Nazi power over the entire Tuzla district and beyond, including the Majevitsa."

"So, we attack that... thing." Goodman studied the building and suddenly felt the tiredness he had been pushing off. He let out a loud sigh. *That looks so much worse than it sounded the other night.* "Where do we go now?"

"We are to go there, I think," Tomislav pointed downhill to a red, two-story brick building set behind a stone wall only a few blocks away.

When they arrived outside the compound, Amira was standing next to the entry gate with her arms folded. Her face was locked in a scowl. She locked eyes with Goodman and glared. Goodman tried to look away but couldn't. *What's her problem?*

"You should not provoke her," cautioned Tomislav.

"I'm not trying to," said Goodman. "I don't think she understands what we accomplished back there at the salt factory and on the road."

"Oh, I think she does," said Tomislav.

"Don't get me wrong," Goodman continued. "I wish I had known about the plans for the explosives, but that's not my fault."

"I told you we should not go into the factory," Tomislav reminded him. "But I am also guilty in this."

"Yeah, yeah." Goodman lifted his hand and put two fingers to his lips. "I'll take that cigarette now."

Tomislav obliged him and lit another for himself. More Majevitsa men arrived and congregated around them. Goodman looked down at the place where one of his toes had worn through his boot.

"You should have taken a pair of boots."

"Yeah," replied Goodman. "Should have." He looked up again and saw a concerned look on Tomislav's face.

"What?" asked Goodman.

Tomislav gave Goodman a nudge and pointed with his eyes. Goodman looked up to see yet another group of Partisan uniforms headed toward them. But this group looked… spiffy. Each man was clean shaven, dressed in clean olive-colored wool trench coats with red epaulets, and they all wore pistols in brown leather holsters. Large saucer-shaped hats crowned their heads, and their boots were noticeably shiny. Partisan soldiers marched in front of these men, shoving people out of the way.

"Those men are political commissars," said Tomislav. "It is not good that they are here. Inevitable, but not good. I know what such people do."

"What is it they do?"

"This is the vanguard of the Communist movement," said Tomislav. "It means they intend to set up a government here. They come with ideology, with promises they have no intention of keeping, and a lot of money, all to prepare the people for the arrival of the official commissariat. The new order. They are not from around here, so there are no complications."

"What does that mean?"

"It means they can jail, kill, or torture anyone they need to without reservation. They'll kill you for speaking against them. They'll torture you for being suspected of doing so. If they do not like you, they will find a reason to suspect you. There will be informants everywhere." He took a drag on his cigarette. "Probably already here."

The column of soldiers marched through the gate and halted in front of the schoolhouse. Commissars climbed the steps and went inside, escorted by one of the Partisan officers, who shoved the local guards out of their way. The officer in the middle had shoulder boards with long red stripes and large, shiny stars on them. Amira's expression deepened as she watched them enter the building.

"Was that—"

Tomislav finished his thought for him. "A general, yes."

"I didn't know we had generals," said Goodman.

"We don't," Tomislav said with a scowl. "That is General Konstantin Kozar, probably Marshall Tito's most aggressive and competent commander. Quite famous, actually."

"No joke?" said Goodman.

"He is not to be trifled with."

A junior officer came out of the schoolhouse and motioned for one of the sergeants to approach. Milosz also exited and motioned to Amira. The four discussed something for a moment, and the officer pointed around the front of the building. The sergeant nodded his head and saluted crisply.

"Things will not go well today, I think," said Tomislav.

"You don't say?" said Goodman.

Milosz and the officer entered the building, but Amira remained at the front entry. She called out to the couriers, who had banded together a few yards away from the steps. She told them to enter and deliver their messages. The sergeant started to interrupt, but Amira simply took a step toward him and said something too quiet for anyone else to hear. The olive-uniformed sergeant backed off and told his men to stand down. As the guards backed away from the doors, the couriers entered the building in a rush. Amira remained standing, legs spread to shoulder width, arms crossed, staring straight ahead. Tomislav and Goodman approached her cautiously.

"Amira, what's going on?" Goodman asked. "What do Tito's people want?"

She clenched her jaw and narrowed her eyes without shifting them. "They want us to leave Tuzla. They want the Planina."

"What does Zoran say?"

She turned. "What do you think Zoran says?"

A guard moved closer to them and eyed Goodman suspiciously.

"Mmm… right," said Tomislav. His face darkened.

"What?" asked Goodman.

"I think it is time we get our friend out of here," Tomislav said quietly to Amira.

"Yes," said Amira.

"I want to help—" Goodman said, but Amira cut him off.

"Help?" she retorted. Her expression narrowed into a glare that was full of anger, and she exploded. "Govno!"

"Amira Effendim…" He used the honorific to mollify her.

She cut him off and pulled him to the side of the building where she attacked with a loud and animated exposition, most of which Goodman could not understand. Yet, he definitely understood what she meant. She fumed through her nose and stomped back up the steps to the schoolhouse.

"She called me a bunch of names at the end there, didn't she?"

"Yes, yes, she did."

"What *can* I do?" asked Goodman.

"Nište."

"Nothing? There's nothing I can do?"

"I think it is best that you remain outside of her attention. Perhaps Zoran will get you to the British liaison with Tito's forces. They will get you back to your airplanes." He drew in on his cigarette. "Think of it. Soon, you will return to destroying the Germans by the hundreds or thousands with your bombs. Here, war is by the ones and twos until the Germans counterattack, and then..." He whistled between his teeth and waved with his cigarette. "We will likely not prevail over the Communists or the Germans, and none of us will survive."

Goodman's gut clenched at the thought of Tomislav, Ademir, and the other men he'd fought beside being wiped out by the Germans or other enemies. And Amira...

"I won't let that happen," said Goodman, barely hearing himself. "I'm... I'm here, and we're making progress. I'll stay and help. We've made it this far, haven't we?"

"Don't be ridiculous," said Tomislav. "You belong elsewhere. As you once said, your place is ten thousands of feet up there." Tomislav pointed skyward. "Besides, you are *a foreigner*. You have no say in the events here. It is not your *sudbina*."

"So now I'm just the foreigner to you? That's bullshit. Nothing I've done counts? Just pretend for a moment that we do have some say in when and how we go. We have purpose here beyond our *sudbina*. We have to. Even me, the stupid foreigner." Hurt at the dismissal, Goodman turned away.

Suddenly, he spun back toward Tomislav. An idea was forming in his mind. "There is something we can do. Right now."

"I'm listening," said Tomislav.

"What if we took the Planina anyway?"

"Impossible," replied Tomislav.

"Why?"

"Oh, let me see," started Tomislav. "First, it's a fortress and cannot be attacked directly. Second, the Germans are currently in possession of it. And the Partisans are here with their army to take it *from* the Germans. And may I remind you yet again that we no longer have the explosives with which to—"

"Yeah, yeah, yeah, tell me something else," Goodman interrupted. "If I really screwed things up at the factory as badly as

Amira says I did, then Zoran doesn't have a plan for taking the Planina garrison, right?"

Tomislav opened his hands to concede the point. Goodman pointed at the schoolhouse.

"Everyone in there is politicking, and meanwhile, the Planina is still in German hands. By now, the Germans have radioed their chain of command, and there are reinforcements coming. Reinforcements that even the Communists can't beat, right?"

"Perhaps." Tomislav conceded again.

"So, the longer things take in there, the greater the chances of the German garrison getting reinforced and all of us getting our asses kicked. But if we take the Planina, it puts Zoran back where he wants to be. Right?"

Tomislav just blinked.

"Doesn't that make sense? At least a little bit?" Goodman looked for some indication of acknowledgment in Tomislav's face.

Tomislav cocked his head to one side. "Yes, but…"

"Okay, then." Goodman stood up. "Let's go see the garrison for ourselves. It can't hurt to take a look. Besides, it'll keep me out of Amira's hair, won't it?"

"It would," he said.

"Well then," said Goodman with an air of victory. "We can kill two birds with one stone. Let's go check it out."

# 47

## TUZLA EIGHTH ADMINISTRATIVE PRECINCT

GOODMAN AND TOMISLAV WEAVED THROUGH THE CROWDS of townspeople and armed fighters of all stripes. They were forced to stand aside as column after column of olive-uniformed Partisan units marched by, followed by several groups in civilian clothing marked with red armbands. The pair approached a market area and saw several crews set up their horse-drawn mountain guns. Goodman was astonished to see the arsenal being unloaded. Gun crews busily unloaded shells and wiped down gun tubes while their compatriots unchained the horses and led them away.

"So Kozar's forces have artillery."

"It appears so," replied Tomislav as he took a moment to count. "Quite a lot of it, presuming this is not everything in—" Then, out of the blue, a familiar voice called out.

Goodman and Tomislav turned to see Musa's head and shoulders above the crowd as he waved at them. Goodman waved back. Musa wrapped them both in a hug, nearly lifting Goodman and Tomislav off their feet. They all reeked of old perspiration, slivovitz, and cigarettes. A handful of teenage boys arrived right behind Musa.

"Zhiv si, Effendi!" Musa said with a broad smile. *You are still alive!*

"Yeah, Musa, I'm still here."

"It is very good that you are still alive! Do you see what Tito's people are doing? They're going to butcher Fritzie." He smiled and gestured broadly at the mass of artillery and equipment moving about the market area.

"Yeah, it's something, all right," said Goodman. *I don't think Zoran shares your enthusiasm. And I have no idea if this helps or hurts my chances of getting out of Yugoslavia.*

"You know, Effendi," Musa said to Goodman. "I liked what you did at the factory last night. And the way you attacked the German tanks on the road. That was...*nevjerovatno*!" He made a gesture of an explosion with his hands and fingers.

*I don't know that word*, thought Goodman. "Neh razumijem," he said. "It's something good, right?"

"It means incredible, unbelievable," said Tomislav. "He's praising you."

"Yes, very brave," Musa continued. "Many of us heard about what you did. Very courageous."

"That's enough flattery," said Tomislav. "Does he owe you money or something?" The three of them laughed.

"Hvala, Musa," Goodman thanked him.

"It was an honor to fight with you," said Musa. "It will be again."

"Well," said Goodman. "I don't know when that will happen."

"God knows what today will bring," said Musa. "It will be soon."

Goodman nodded. *Honestly,* he thought to himself, *I hope not.*

A line of Partisan trucks piled high with crates and teeming with soldiers slowed as it entered the square. Everyone got out of the way and watched the long procession pass by. When the last of the trucks departed the area, the crowds filled the streets again and resumed their previous flows.

"Zoran's plan was to take the Planina, yes?" asked Musa.

"That *was* the plan, yes," Tomislav said.

"So how will he do it?" said Musa. "It is much more difficult now with the Communists here, yes?" He flicked his cigarette away.

"I don't think the Planina is for the taking, right at the moment," said Tomislav. "I don't think we are up for a fight against both the Germans *and* the Communists."

Musa blew a lungful of smoke into the air and looked around. "Perhaps we should stick closer to Zoran," said Musa. Then he lowered his voice. "There are some things you should know."

"What kinds of things?" asked Tomislav.

"First, they are arresting and executing people."

"I think we saw some of their work on our way into town," said Goodman.

"Yes, but those are not important people," said Musa. "Thieves and collaborators. I'm talking about big people. Tito's people came in with several lists of names. Some lists had more than a hundred names. People they were looking for. Some they questioned, some they arrested. And some of the people..." He leaned in and whispered, "some they just executed right there in their *own homes.*"

"Like who?" asked Goodman.

Musa stood and looked around again. "I'm not supposed to share," he confided. "This is for Zoran's ears alone."

"You will not get an audience with Zoran any time soon," said Tomislav.

"I should really wait..."

"Yeah, Tomislav is right," said Goodman. "Zoran is busy with some general."

"With the communist general, I know," said Musa. "But I must insist. It is for him and him alone."

"Well, Musa," Goodman began. "We'll share what we know if you share what you've got."

Tomislav's look was priceless.

"What do you know about this?" asked Musa.

"Nope," Goodman replied. "You go first."

Musa smiled and flicked his cigarette. He motioned for them to follow him. Around the next corner, he drew them in close. "Mostly rich people," replied Musa. "Political people. Many were members of Zoran's family—from his Tuzla cousins."

"Okay," said Goodman. "That is bad."

"Yes, but that is not the worst part," said Musa. "Some were sellouts to the Germans. Some were the government people—the big officials who did not jump to Tito's side when the Partisans arrived. Some unions and the companies did jump to their side, you know, like the tradesmen and the city worker unions. But some did not, and they are being hunted. Many claimed they supported the Partisans, but they secretly are working against them."

"Zoran does not know this," said Tomislav. "How do you come by this information?"

"I also have a few cousins who live here in Tuzla." Musa nodded to the group behind him. "Here's one you may be interested in." Musa grabbed one teenaged boy with patchy facial hair and dark circles around his eyes.

"This is my cousin, Ismail."

Ismail took a cigarette out of his mouth and smiled a big, dirty-toothed smile. "Zdravo!" He and Tomislav shook hands, and Tomislav wrung his hand afterward. Goodman learned why a second later when it was his turn to have his hand crushed in Ismail's insanely firm grip.

"Ismail is a rope maker," explained Musa.

"That explains it," muttered Goodman, pretending his hand did not hurt.

"I was taking him to see Zoran," said Musa. "But he is busy with the big generals. And Amira Effendim is angry. No one in our family who lives here knows how Amira has become, and she would scare my cousins away, so I can't tell her. My other uncles are hiding all over the city waiting for Zoran's command to attack, so I cannot tell them. That leaves you."

Goodman and Tomislav looked at each other. "OK," said Goodman. He jumped to throw out the first question. "What you know Planina?"

Tomislav interrupted. "Forgive my friend here." Tomislav gave Goodman a hard look. "What we want to know is what Tito's people are doing in Tuzla, and what is happening around the fortress. Can you tell us these things?"

*No, that's not what we want to know*, thought Goodman. *Why is he distracting this kid?*

Ismail appeared surprised by Goodman's strongly accented Bosanski. "Where are you from, friend?" He blew cigarette smoke out of the corner of his mouth.

"Cousin, don't ask questions," Musa scolded.

"He's from Spain," said Tomislav. "Now, what can you tell us?"

"I'll do better. I'll show you." Ismail led them across the boulevard and toward the river.

He explained that thousands of refugees were leaving the city to flee from the Communists, who just arrived last night, while thousands of others were flooding into the city to seek protection from the Germans' inevitable reprisals against the vulnerable countryside. The banks were out of cash, or at least they were *telling* people they were out of cash. Everything was up for sale or trade and the black market, which had been strangled by the Germans, was now flourishing as prices had skyrocketed because the communists were buying or confiscating everything.

The group arrived at a wide avenue that had once been double-lined with trees, all of which were now cut off at the ground level, leaving a remarkable view of the main north-south thoroughfare that led directly to the Jala River, the bridge, and the Planina Fortress on its bluff on the south side of the river. Several layers of Partisan army roadblocks halted their progress. Partisan infantry had already built bunkers and machine-gun nests on the rooftops and from southward-facing windows. A battery of anti-aircraft guns had their barrels leveled at the enormous stone walls.

"Many Partisans," said Goodman.

"Yeah," said Musa.

"This is a huge waste," Tomislav stated. "Zoran's plans are scrapped."

Goodman scanned the fortress walls, the bridge, and the approach down the boulevard.

"What you say about Planina?" he asked Ismail. "What can we do?"

"Come," said Ismail. "I show you."

"I don't think it wise to trespass the Partisan lines," said Tomislav.

"No, I can take you *inside* the Planina," Ismail emphasized. "It's dangerous, though, filled with Nazis."

Goodman and Tomislav looked at each other and then at Ismail as he sucked on the last of his cigarette.

"What do you mean you can get us inside the Planina?" asked Tomislav.

"I mean *inside* the castle," Ismail repeated.

"How is this possible?" said Tomislav.

"I worked there until yesterday." Ismail's eyes refocused on Tomislav's. "There is a *tunnel* under the castle and under the river." He drew his hands apart to mime a tube or tunnel curling up at each end. The hair on Goodman's neck stood up.

"A tunnel?" said Goodman.

Ismail blew smoke from his mouth. "Tell me, friend, do you really come from Spain?"

Musa leaned into the conversation. "Just answer them, cousin, and stop asking questions. Tell them what they want to know. Tell them how you know and speak slowly so our friend can understand." He nodded at Goodman.

"He made ropes for the Germans," Tomislav began to translate.

Goodman interrupted him. "I think I can understand what he's saying."

266

"They are a mountain army unit, and they have lots of ropes. I repair the climbing ropes and make new ones for them when the old ones are worn out. But I didn't just work *for* the Fritzies. I worked *against* them, too." Ismail smiled as he paused for effect.

"Tell them," said Musa, who was smiling by this point. "Tell them what you told me."

"Tell us what?" asked Tomislav.

"I have killed three Fritzies, and they don't even know it was me!" He bowed and tipped his hat to the group.

Musa smiled. "Tell them the whole thing."

"There were three people who worked in the ropes shop," Ismail explained. "Me, a shitty Serb named Slobodan, and our stupid Fritzie boss, Sturmmann Frankfurter—or something like that. He was a stupid German." Ismail took a long drag on his cigarette before continuing. "One day, this set of ropes came in that should have been burned or used for hanging laundry. But the Fritzies told me to fix them. They needed a lot of fixing, which I did, but I left a big cut in one and cleverly covered it up. *Very cleverly*, mind you. They made us put tags on our ropes so they would know who fixed each rope. I put Slobodan's tag on the rope that I cut. It just so happened that the Fritzies used that rope for practice one day, and two of them fell off the cliff on the north face of the castle. They looked at the tag after they found the cut and executed poor, stupid Slobodan on the spot. They shot him right in the head and threw him over the wall." Ismail laughed out loud. "Then they beat up stupid Fritzie Frankfurter and made him guard the toilet for a week." He smiled again. "It rained every day but one when it snowed yesterday. His boots got frozen to the toilet floor. It was hilarious." He sucked again on his cigarette. "Stupid idiot Fritzies."

"What does this have to do with a tunnel?" Goodman asked.

"So, yeah," Ismail exhaled yet another puff. "There is this tunnel that King Stephen used to smuggle his whores and other stuff. It is still there, going under the city, under the river, and into the castle."

"Such a thing does not exist," said Tomislav.

"It does, I assure you."

"Then surely the Germans know about it," Tomislav insisted.

"Ha! No," Ismail laughed. "The Fritzies do not know anything about the tunnel. They're not all completely stupid, but they don't know everything."

"How do you know that?" Ismail looked at Tomislav as he dragged in his smoke.

"The tunnel entrance inside the Planina is in the…" He made a bowl shape with his hands. "…shit cave."

"The what?" asked Goodman.

"The shit cave. Under the officer's toilet. You know, where the shit goes. The shit pit—"

Musa interrupted him. "You mean the cistern, you idiot."

"Yeah!" said Ismail. "The cistern." He took a quick puff. "In the main hallway where all of their officers sleep. They make all their soldiers sleep and eat outside, and they have to shit out through the holes in the castle walls over the cliff. It is outside, and it makes their asses very cold. Meanwhile, the officers sleep and eat inside and have an indoor toilet." He took another drag and continued. "One time, a couple months ago, the pit under the officer's toilet got full and made the officer's quarters smell like shit. So, they made me and Slobodan clean it out. That was when I found the tunnel. Oh, that was nasty." His face crinkled at the memory. He cleared his throat and spit onto the street, then sucked in more cigarette smoke.

"Does anyone else know about this tunnel?" Tomislav asked.

"No," replied Ismail. He sounded far too confident.

"Are you sure no one else knows?" asked Goodman.

"We must know for certain," added Musa.

"There are probably some old-timers somewhere around town who might know," Ismail said. "But I guarantee you that no Fritzie knows about it, and that stupid pig Slobodan is no longer with us…" He smiled again, remembering. He took another drag. "I even tried to tell the army people about it, but they don't have time for little people like me. All the army people think they know everything. They don't know anything." He took another long drag on his cigarette.

"The army people?" asked Tomislav.

"Yeah, these assholes," exclaimed Ismail, gesturing to the mass of Tito's olive-clad partisans that bustled around them. "I tried to tell them about the tunnel this morning, and they told me to shut up. So, to hell with them and their mothers. Now I'm telling you."

"And do you know where the other entrance to this tunnel is?" asked Tomislav. "And how sure are you?"

"Apsolutno," said Ismail. *Absolutely.*

Musa looked expectantly at Goodman, who was looking at Tomislav. "I think we should check it out," said Goodman. Tomislav frowned.

"Are you certain this tunnel goes from the city to the castle?" Tomislav asked.

"Does a Serb farmer sleep with his goats?"

Everyone laughed except Goodman. Ismail saw this and made a thrusting motion with his hips timed with a braying goat noise. Goodman smiled when he finally got the joke. *That's disgusting,* he thought. Musa's eyes moved between Tomislav and Goodman, and then back again.

"Are you guys thinking of invading the Planina anyway?" asked Musa.

Tomislav delayed his response with a long draw on his cigarette. "General Kozar would hunt us down and kill us for even thinking of trying to take their prize." He glanced at Goodman. "And they would certainly not allow our friend here safe passage."

*No,* thought Goodman. *No, they wouldn't.*

"And I think the Fritzies already have it out for you lot," Ismail remarked. Everyone nodded in agreement.

"What will Zoran say?" asked Musa. "Will he be able to do what he wants here?"

"We think he's talking about that with the Communists right now," said Tomislav. "Back at the schoolhouse. I doubt General Kozar will grant him the pleasure."

A shadow fell over the group, and everyone took another long drag on their smokes. Goodman hoped that Ismail and Musa would drop it. *I don't want any rumors to spread—rumors about me or about the Planina. Plus, I don't know if we can trust this Ismail character, cousin or not.* Goodman saw Musa was still looking at him. And he squinted ever so slightly when Goodman made eye contact with him. Then a grin spread across Musa's face.

"But you are thinking about it… aren't you?"

Goodman tried his best to project the blankest look he'd ever given.

Musa's smile got even bigger. "That is a great idea."

# 48

## TUZLA EIGHTH PRECINCT GRAMMAR SCHOOL

ZORAN KNEW MILOSZ WAS ON THE OTHER SIDE OF THE DOOR. He let him knock twice and wait.

"Pasha," Milosz said through the door. He knocked again and let himself in. "Zoran Pasha, pardon the intrusion, but there is a messenger."

Zoran ignored his deputy. He was of no mind to deal with petty administration. He was also actively delaying responding to General Kozar's request for an audience with the relevant factions competing for breathing room in the Tuzla valley. That was the compounding problem. The root problem was more deeply concerning to Zoran. *How did I not know about the close proximity of the entire Third Partisan Corps? They were supposed to be over a hundred miles from here. But now they are practically crawling in my beard.* He scratched his chin. *I had no information about that.*

*No,* he corrected himself. *Not 'no' information. Wrong information. I have been deceived. But by whom?* He realized he was still scratching compulsively, and he stopped. More urgently, he had this new problem. Kozar. He had issued demands which needed a good counteroffer.

Zoran envisioned himself standing at the forefront of the factions, with the citizens of Tuzla city and the greater Tuzla valley behind them surrounded by the entire population of the Majevitsa, with himself postured between the factions and the Titoists, with the Nazis behind them. *In the face of General Kozar, I must show autonomy. No, something more. Self-determination. Still too small. Power. I must display power.* Zoran squared his shoulders. *I cannot display anything that could give the impression of acquiescing to the great*—he sneered at the word—*the* great *General Kosta Kozar, Marshal Tito's best general and the commander of ten thousand Partisan troops. The dog's ass whose battalions butchered the last of my strongest allies.* He had seen for himself the burnt-out villages and swinging corpses of the chieftains of the six great Rodovan families in western Bosnia. *I'll always remember that. But I am still here. By the will of Allah, I am of my own making. Aside from that*, he reasoned, *only Mikhail and the unions remain as near-competitors for control of Tuzla city. Controlling the Majevitsa means controlling the Tuzla valley, which means controlling Tuzla city.* Zoran's own cousin stood in his way.

*I cannot kill him, as I will need the industrial unions' loyalty if I am to control the city. How do I control him? How do I put in check the man who is the wall around my enemies? I will need him later if I am to rule from this place.*

"Yes, my friend and servant," said Zoran. "The communists left this place less than an hour ago. What do they want now?"

"It is a messenger from Mikhail." Milosz lowered his voice. "From Colonel Zbrogan."

"What is it?" Zoran grumbled. "What does that greedy car parts merchant want?"

*He must want to strike a bargain with Kozar,* thought Zoran. He despised the idea, but he knew it might be necessary in some fashion. The lesser resistance organizations and families were no match for the military and financial strength of the Titoists. They had the supposed backing of both Stalin *and* Churchill, which also meant that their benefactor—the American Premiere—also backed the Communists. Zoran shook his head at the situation. He must take the Planina. Only then could he put into place his design against the Germans, the Titoists, the Ustaša, and his cousin the Unionist. I will retore the old order—a civilized order, not the despots, not the royalty, and certainly not the fascists or communists. But Mikhail remained in the way. *Curse him. Curse all of them.*

"Zoran Pasha," Milosz persevered. "I do not know what his message is. He would not tell me."

*More games,* thought Zoran. *I am weary of this.* Zoran scratched his head under his hat. "Yes, bring him in," he ordered. "And Milosz?"

"Yes, Pasha?"

"When you bring him, remain with us." *Milosz will be the unknown factor in the room for this messenger. If the man is a peon, I will force him to speak to my deputy in front of me. If the messenger is someone of import to Mikhail, then he will be discomfited by the lack of privacy to which he is surely entitled. I can use either.*

"Yes, Pasha."

Zoran met Milosz and the messenger in the front room. Milosz closed both sets of doors and seated himself after the primaries had taken their seats. Zoran studied the man across the table. *This is Mikhail's chief accountant,* he thought. *His money man, Durnević. Of all his servants, why would he send this man?* Zoran had half expected Mikhail to send his son to deliver any message of importance. But this was unexpected. *What is his angle? Does he seek to buy me off? Buy me out, perhaps? What machinations has he started? I need that information from under the carpet as well as that which is the purpose of this meeting. Or has the purpose of this meeting changed, and I am yet to learn of its true nature? I will wait for him to make his mistake. Then I will attack.* Zoran held his tongue and waited to establish dominance before speaking, as the senior authority, to set the tone and direction of the conversation. Milosz stood by the door.

"Why does this man remain with us?" Durnević demanded. "This is a most sensitive discussion, and I am under strict instructions that what I have to say is for the ears of Zoran Mehmetović Dudovič, and him alone."

Zoran erupted, and his chair flew against the wall behind him. "I will take your head and send it to your master after I've pissed on it if you violate my prerogative again." He lifted the hilt of his sword to signify the seriousness of the charge. To pull it all the way without attacking would be a meaningless gesture. The half-drawn sword was a symbol, a fully drawn sword a weapon that must be used. The man raised his eyebrows and pushed back from the table. Milosz pushed him forward again and put a blade to his throat.

"You may choose to address my master once again." Milosz balled up the man's starched collar in his fist and shook it once before lowering the knife. "But only once."

The messenger cleared his throat. "A th-thousand pardons, effend—" Milosz crumpled the messenger's collar again. "A thousand pardons, Zoran P-Pasha." Milosz let go of the shirt material and let the man continue. "I am Nemanja Durnević, accountant and creditor of the Union of Skilled and Unskilled Workers of the Tuzla Canton. I am here to—"

"Why does my cousin and brother-in-arms send his accountant?" Zoran countered. "If I wanted a report of financial records, then I would expect such. I do not care for Mikhail's financials." *That's anything but true,* thought Zoran. *I'd give up half my force to know what is in this man's head about where Mikhail's money comes from and where it goes.* He continued. "Why are you here?"

Durnević watched out of the corner of his eye as Milosz returned to his post, and then his eyes returned to Zoran. Zoran could see his mind calculating, trying to determine what or how much he wanted to divulge in front of Milosz. *Good,* thought Zoran. *He's uncomfortable.* Zoran interlaced his fingers on his chest and blinked. Durnević cleared his throat again.

"Zoran Pasha,"—he dipped his head slightly—"Colonel Zbrogan wishes to assemble a conference of the people's resistance groups to discuss a way forward with—"

"Mikhail wants to assemble a conference?" Zoran slapped the table. "Who has put him in such a place to call an assembly of his countrymen? Under what authority?"

"I am unable to disclose that information." Durnević's eyes flicked over to Milosz and back again.

"Unable to disclose the information," Zoran repeated. "I think you know I would not like it when I heard it." *Which sounds to me like my cousin believes one of the current armies is going to remain in control of Tuzla for some time. It is either the Germans—or the*

*Ustaša on their behalf—or the Communists.* "On whose behalf are you speaking?"

"I am only here to deliver a message," said Durnević. "From my master."

"Very well." Zoran folded his arms. "Let's get on with it."

"Colonel Zbrogan has contacted General Kozar and arranged for a meeting to discuss power sharing in Tuzla—"

*So, he is working for the Communists.* "Power sharing?" said Zoran. "With the Communists? Nonsense. Continue."

"Y-yes, Pasha," said Durnević. "He requests your presence at a conference tonight to discuss this possibility."

"Perhaps I should be there." Zoran feigned a tone of thoughtfulness. "To lend my support to Colonel Zbrogan. What are the arrangements?" But he did not care. *This is just a smokescreen. Any stupid messenger could relay this information. Why is this man telling me these things?* He ignored everything Durnević said about the food and drinks and about the order of ceremony. He ignored everything but the man's eyes. *There's something else,* Zoran thought to himself.

Durnević explained the levels of bargaining from initial position to final offer, with something about a contingency cash offer to reduce ill will if unmet expectations soured the negotiation. The sum was exorbitant but irrelevant, as it wasn't Zoran's money. Durnević's eyes were holding back. *He's testing me,* thought Zoran. *He wants to set me up for something. Mikhail knows I would not miss a meeting of this magnitude, given what he probably suspects of my aims.* Durnević went silent again.

"Of course," said Zoran. "Please tell your master that I will be happy to attend at his request." *Screw him and his request,* thought Zoran. *I'll be there regardless of my cousin's invitation. But get to the point, man, get to the point! You don't want to say it in front of Milosz, but I'll force you.*

"Very well, Zoran Eff—Pasha," Durnević caught himself. "Colonel Zbrogan will be pleased you accepted. Now, I have—" Zoran gave a slight wave of his finger, and Milosz jumped up from his chair.

"Thank you for your efforts, Effendi," Milosz said quickly as he ushered Durnević to the door.

"But—"

Milosz cut him off. "It was a risky affair, getting to us from across the city under the current circumstances." He opened the door for Durnević, but Durnević halted awkwardly. Obviously conflicted about what to do, he turned back to Zoran.

"Many pardons, Zoran Pasha," said Durnević. "But there is another situation about which I have been directed to,"—he glanced at Milosz and went ahead anyway—"to make an offer that will be pleasing to you." He paused again. "For a certain party in your custody."

The American pilot. *He's found a buyer! And he wants to be the broker, just as he is wont to do. Now, though, I have leverage.* Zoran's mind awakened to the financial and political possibilities he had calculated over the previous weeks. *I had doubted Mikhail had retained any such contacts. If he had them when I asked weeks ago, he would have responded much sooner. He's made new arrangements. But with whom? His initial offer will tell me. Now, the initiative is mine.*

"You wish to pay for the costs of my forces' occupation of the eastern suburbs of Tuzla?" Zoran pushed back. *Work for it, you criminal.* Zoran's mouth turned up at the corners.

Durnević opened his mouth to speak, but closed it again. His eyes betrayed his calculations.

"Uhhh, no, Zoran Pasha, I am referring to… the foreign party under your control…"

"A *foreign* party?" Zoran raised his eyebrows and put this hand to his chest, fingers spread. "What do I have in common with foreigners? What is the nature of this *foreign* party you reference?" Zoran gave Milosz a look of disapproving shock. Milosz stifled his smirk.

Durnević was clearly confused. "Do you not have a foreign guest within your control?" The lilt at the end of the question showed his utter disorientation.

"Will you please speak plainly?" Zoran leaned in as he said this. "You have learned from your master the skills of obfuscation and redirection." Zoran smiled to himself. "What is this foreigner or foreigners about whom you dance without committing? Out with it, man!"

"Zoran Pasha, I was led to believe that you had a foreign pilot or crewmember, either British or American, in your custody," Durnević asserted himself. "Is that not the case?" A vein in his neck bulged to match the one on his forehead.

Zoran waited for a long moment to pass, much too long for Durnević from the look of it. "Yes, I have had a pilot of the Allies with me for quite some time," Zoran said at last. The accountant's shoulders visibly relaxed.

"Ahh, so then," Durnević breathed easier. "I am authorized to make an offer in exchange for the services of rendering him to his military."

"Yes?" Zoran waited. *How much will your master pay for an American pilot of officer rank?*

"I am authorized to offer you five hundred thousand." Durnević said. "Cash, not credit, not commodities. Two hundred thousand in the old Yugoslav Kuna, the remainder in Reichsmarks. Cash. Today." He reached into his leather travel pouch and handed a once-folded piece of paper to Milosz, who read it—eyebrows raised—and handed it across the table to Zoran.

Zoran read the paper to himself. *German Reichsmarks.* "What rate the Reichsmarks?" He asked.

"Thirty to one," said Durnević as he straightened his tunic. "I believe that offer to be much more than generous. Colonel Zbrogan is using the occasion to demonstrate the close kinship he feels—"

"Shut up," said Zoran. He put on a face of stoic consideration. But internally, he was anything but placid.

Ten thousand Reichsmarks. Zoran doubted there were a thousand Reichsmarks in circulation in the entire Tuzla valley. *But ten thousand?* He stared into space as he repeated it in his head. *Mikhail has thrown in with the Germans, at least for this deal.* It had been many months since the council treasury had seen even twenty thousand Kuna and mere hundreds of Reichsmarks. *I have less than four thousand Kuna now. Five hundred thousand. But then, the man who took the salt factory and killed so many of my enemies would be gone. The sooner I accept, the more assurance of the money. The longer I wait, the greater the likelihood of some unfortunate act befalling him. And more is lost than just another foreign pilot—the man who attacked tanks with a handful of men!* Zoran never would have asked any of his men to commit to such bravery. *The man who broke the code as only he, a foreign guest could, and built a bridge to be within my—my what? My family? Neh. But what is he? He is only a foreigner. And this is the deal I've been waiting for. Far better than I anticipated. But to lose him now, on the cusp of taking control of Tuzla!* He thought of his dead son, and then of Amira. *What man for my daughter, than he? Could he...* An image of Mirzad's face flashed through his mind's eye. *My son.* Zoran scowled. *These are un-serious fantasies, irrational fears of an old man...*

"Well, then, Zoran Pasha," Durnević said. "Consider it a transaction with a one-time premium. One of note, I should say." He clasped his hands behind his back and rocked on his heels.

"Yes, so it is," said Zoran quietly. *Can I swing this club both ways?* he thought. *Will I be able to keep this American and extend the grace period of the offer for a few days, a fortnight, even? But what if he dies? Then there is no money and possibly no victory.* "Please tell your master I will consider the offer and transmit my reply soon." He handed the contract back across the table.

"What?" said Durnević. There was surprise in his voice. He fumbled slightly with the paper.

"Did you misunderstand me?" Zoran stood and drew in a breath. "Am I speaking Italian?"

"Zoran Pasha," said Durnević. "This is not a deal to trifle with. This sum of money is more than fair, more than generous! It was against my advice to Colonel Zbrogan to offer you this amount, but he insisted. Out of a necessity to overcome the discord of the past few months between your two houses, he said. Obviously, he is the master, and I am the servant, so I am but to comply. But, Zoran Pasha, you insult my master by failing to accept this proposition. You shall not hear another like it!" Durnević squared off with Zoran and slapped the contract flat on the table. His face was red, and the vein in his neck bulged again. Durnević put his hands flat on the table and fumed. "Sign it and hand the foreigner over to us immediately!"

Zoran's sword was already out of its sheath before the metallic ring reached anyone's ears. It passed cleanly through Durnević's right wrist with a slight ping as the bones separated from each other. Durnević collapsed onto his right knee and let out a silent scream as he gripped the stump.

Durnević gnashed his teeth. "Help me!" he growled while gripping his wrist. It took a moment before the blood began to pool on the floor.

Zoran stood over him and inspected his sword for blood. It was clean. "That is for your insolence in my presence and to my face!"

"If your master knew what he is worth, you would offer me ten times that amount!" Zoran heard himself say the words and decided to stand by them. He slammed the sword into the sheath with a satisfying *clank*. "Too bad your days of keeping accounts are over. Perhaps you can dictate your sums to an apprentice with good handwriting." He took a deep breath and blew it out at Durnević. "Milosz," said Zoran. "Bind this salesman's arm and deliver him to his master." Zoran raised his chin and looked down upon Durnević. "Tell your master that next time he intends to insult me, he will not get a living accountant in return!"

# 49

## CENTRAL TUZLA COMMERCIAL DISTRICT

THE CROWDS WERE BAD. Really bad. It took the group over twenty minutes to walk four blocks. Goodman, Tomislav, and Musa exchanged confused looks when Ismail pointed to the building across the street. The sign read *Tuzlanske Vjesti*.

"The newspaper building?" asked Tomislav.

"Da."

"The tunnel comes here?" said Goodman.

"Da," Ismail replied. "In the basement." Goodman remembered *that* word. "But there is a wall."

"Then how do you know it comes out in the basement?" asked Musa.

"When I went into the tunnel, and I went to the end," Ismail explained. "I could hear the printing presses through the wall."

"How does he know what those sound like?" asked Goodman.

"My brother is a mechanic there, or at least he used to be. I used to assist him with work."

Goodman studied the building facade. "It looks closed," he said. The building was boarded up, with signs stenciled in German posted every few feet.

"Fritzie shut it down months ago."

"It doesn't look like it is guarded," said Musa.

"It is not," said Ismail. "We can get in through the back."

He started to cross the street, but Goodman caught his arm.

"Get rid of the kids," he said. They looked at the quartet of younger boys who followed Ismail.

"But they're my—"

"Get rid of them," said Goodman.

"Do it," said Musa.

Ismail's posse wailed in protest when he told them to leave, so he shoved them back down the sidewalk. The boys resisted until Musa stepped in, and then the boys retreated through the crowd and up a sidewalk, throwing curses as they stomped away.

"This way," said Ismail.

He led Goodman and the others across the road and down a side street. After a furtive glance around, he kicked at a sun-bleached picket in the fence until it gave way. They quickly slipped through the fence and strode briskly across the lot filled with crates of rotting newsprint spools and various broken machinery. A set of stairs terminated at a door in the rear wall.

Ismail looked around again and jammed a knife into the space between the jamb and the door. He twisted and pried until Musa took over, taking the knife and working it until the door snapped open. Musa smiled smugly as he held the door for all to pass through.

Once they were inside with the door closed, the group moved quietly down the long, dark hallway. The upper windows at the far end gave enough light to move along the tiled floor. Ismail led the group past offices and closets and through a large, cased opening with stairways leading down and up. He descended the stairs into the darkness. He found a light switch, and a single yellow bulb sizzled at the end of a bare copper wire in the middle of the ceiling. Along one wall was a trio of doors.

Ismail went to one and opened it. He muttered something and tried the next one before shaking his head. He went to the third door and opened wide. Goodman, Tomislav, and Musa dipped their heads to enter. It was a large closet, lined with shelves of old light fixtures, tools, drop cloths, and other miscellanea. Several old doors were stacked on the far wall.

Ismail pointed toward the doors. "It is there."

Goodman, Musa, and Tomislav all looked over and between the doors. "I don't see anything," said Goodman.

"All I see is junk," said Tomislav. "We should go." Goodman's heart sank.

"It is here, I swear it," said Ismail.

He started pulling doors away and throwing them on the floor. The men coughed and waved at the clouds of dust and cobwebs he'd disturbed. They wiped their eyes to see a smiling Ismail standing at the far wall and pointing at the brick wall. Goodman felt the rough texture of the wall and ran his fingers along a raised seam. It went upward and curved to the left, where it met another raised arc at a point right at the height of Goodman's head. He stood back to look at the whole wall. It was an arched doorway, bricked over, plastered over, painted, and forgotten. *It is here!* Goodman thought.

"Is this it?" asked Tomislav.

"Yes," said Ismail.

"So, you're not full of shit this time," said Musa.

"Not this time, cousin."

"Are you sure this is it?" said Goodman. "This has to be real."

"It is," said Ismail.

"Let's find out." Goodman scanned around the closet and found a three-foot length of lead pipe. He gripped it like a baseball bat and approached the wall. Tomislav stepped forward and put his arm out to stop Goodman.

"Perhaps we should—"

Goodman made contact with the wall, and the pipe bit into his hands as it bounced back. "Ow! Dammit!" He rubbed his hands and saw he had barely scratched the paint.

He shook it off and gripped the pipe a bit more firmly. His second swing got him no further. Musa, who was smiling excitedly, offered to take a turn. Goodman let him have it.

Nearly bent in half under the low ceiling, Musa took a swing. The pipe clanged loudly, and a large chunk of plaster fell to the floor. Musa stood back and examined the wall. Layers of paint gave way to the whitish plaster and brown-gray stone and mortar behind it.

"Stand back," he said. Everyone took a step back. He swung again, but this time the air hummed, and the pipe impacted with a deep clunk. Several inches of plaster fell and crumbled on the floor. He swung again. More white chunks fell and broke on the floor. And again.

A rock the size of a large watermelon rolled lazily out of its pocket and fell to the floor. Musa peered into the hole and poked at it with the pipe. It was loose. He swung again. The pipe hit with a resounding gong, and the wall ejected two more stones. Musa poked the wall with the pipe, and the pipe pushed all the way through. He knelt and put his face to the wall.

"Govno!" he cursed and lurched backward. Musa ran into Goodman as he exited the room, face covered, spitting and swearing.

"What the—" Goodman's words were cut short by the warm wind blowing into the closet from the hole in the wall. It smelled like sewage. He, too, covered his face and followed Musa into the larger room. "Oh, that's terrible!"

"What is that?" exclaimed Tomislav as he pushed his way out of the closet.

Ismail strolled out casually. "I told you where this tunnel goes." He lit a cigarette and took a long drag as he watched the others try to compose themselves. "So now do you believe me?" He blew smoke toward the ceiling.

Goodman nodded his head as he coughed and spit on the floor. He could still feel the wind blowing from the closet. He held his breath as he dashed back in and crammed a pile of rags into the hole before withdrawing and closing the door. *This is it*, thought Goodman. *This is the tunnel into the cistern. This is how we get into the fortress. This is how we get Zoran into power. Then, maybe I can get home.*

"What do we do now?" said Musa.

"I think we should leave this alone," said Tomislav. "The risks are too great."

"We'll tell Amira first," said Goodman. "Then we tell Zoran everything."

# 50

## NEAR THE EIGHTH PRECINCT GRAMMAR SCHOOL

GOODMAN WAS UPBEAT. And so was Musa. But Tomislav threw a wet towel over their enthusiasm: there was simply no way the entire Majevitsa militia could sneak into the German Army's strongest garrison in the entire Tuzla region and take it over. Unthinkable, he said, but he agreed to at least consult with Amira. *If we can convince her*, thought Goodman, *then we can convince Zoran.*

Back at the schoolhouse, the group attempted to walk up the stairs, but the Partisan guards stood fast, rifles ready. Tomislav spoke to a handful of the Majevitsa militia, who huddled together across the road.

"They say that Zoran is still in there," he said when he returned. "Amira and Milosz are with him, but now General Kozar is controlling the negotiations. And it's not going well."

"Then how do we get in that door?" Goodman asked. He scanned the face of the building for a way past the guards.

"We don't," said Tomislav. "We wait."

"No," said Goodman. "We don't wait. We're losing time, right?" He looked at Musa. Musa turned to his cousin. Ismail got the hint.

"Follow me," he said. "I know how to get in."

Goodman laughed. "Is there anywhere you don't know how to get into?"

Ismail just smiled and threw his cigarette on the street. He led Goodman and the others around the block, through a dilapidated neighboring building, and to a wing of the school where the windows were boarded up and the doors were nailed shut.

"This used to be my school." Ismail tried to pull away one of the boards, but it was nailed fast, and he gestured for Musa to apply himself. Musa pushed him aside and easily pried the boards away from the window. Once they entered, Ismail led them down a hall cluttered with broken furniture and stacks of boxes. They could hear loud voices echoing down the corridor. Zoran's voice was distinctive when he made his demands, as he was now doing. Then, a calmer voice spoke up with measured, baritone authority. The others in the room agreed with something the voice said, but the argument spiked again. Goodman peered around a corner at the backs of more than a dozen uniformed men. Zoran yelled something and the other voice replied in kind. The severity of the arguing drew other Partisan and local militiamen around a corner. Suddenly, the hall was empty.

Goodman and the others made use of this distraction to get closer. They found Amira, arms folded across her chest, leaning against the wall opposite the door to the negotiating room.

"Amira!" Goodman whispered down the hall. "Pssssst! Amira!"

Her eyes widened when she saw the four of them approaching. "What are you doing here? Get out of here!"

"You need to hear this," Goodman whispered urgently. "We have an idea about the Planina."

"No!" She glared at him. "Is this from you? No! You did enough yesterday at the factory. Get out of here before you spoil the negotiations."

"Come, let's go." Tomislav pulled at Goodman's arm. "This is not the place for us—"

"You'll like this idea," Musa added. "We have a way into the Planina. There's a tunnel—"

"What?" She pulled Goodman and Musa down that hall, away from the commotion surrounding the negotiation. "What is this tunnel?"

"Under the city, under the river, and into the castle," said Goodman. He gestured for Ismail to come forward, which he did somewhat hesitantly. "He has been in the tunnel."

Amira looked Ismail up and down. "Who is this guy?" she demanded. "How can this be? How do you know it exists? The Germans have been there for two years, and no one has discovered this?"

"Speak up, cousin!" Musa hit Ismail on the back of the head.

Ismail stammered. "Th-There is a—"

"She is Effendim!" Musa hit him again.

"Y-yes, apologies, Effendim! Many apologies, Effendim! There is a t-tunnel that leads into the fortress. Under the river."

Amira put her hands on her hips. "You have not yet told me anything I can believe. How do you know of this tunnel? Where is this tunnel?"

"The Tuzlanske Vjesti building."

"The newspaper?" Amira scowled.

"We were just there," said Goodman. "We found the entrance in the basement." Musa nodded in confirmation. She looked at Tomislav, who also nodded, if somewhat apologetically.

Amira put her hands on her hips and bit her lip as she thought. Ismail started to talk again, but Musa glared at him to shut him up.

"Amira Effendim," Goodman used the honorific. "What your father wants… is what I want. I want the Planina, too."

Amira grabbed Goodman's sleeve and pulled him farther down the hall. Musa moved to follow, but Tomislav held him back. She glared at him, or through him, it felt.

284

"Why?" She spoke in thickly accented English. It caught him off guard. "Why do you help us?"

For a brief moment, Goodman could not speak. *How do I answer that?* Strange, disjointed thoughts raced through his head. He recognized some of them–the feelings, the images. Others, however, he could not have articulated if he tried. Then his thoughts became focused, specific. He thought of Jasminka. Her tears and her toothy grin. And he thought of Baba. His eyes darted to Musa for a split second. He remembered the old photograph of Zoran's family. *They're all here,* he thought. *They've been taking care of me all along. Amira, your family…is…what do I say? What do I say to you?* The trees, the temperature, the smells, the feeling of her hair and hands, he remembered everything about that moment when he held her in his arms as she sobbed. He felt the feelings rush back into him.

"I am here!" Amira demanded. "Speak to me or you shall never again speak to my father!"

"Your father's family." He finally said it. "Your family is…you, Amira, are important to me."

Her gaze held fast. She pursed her lips as her eyes traced something around his eyes. Then her eyes dropped to the floor. *What is she thinking?* Goodman said to himself. *I said the wrong thing. That was dumb. What was I thinking? At least I didn't say love…* He held his breath until Amira finally looked up. Her brow furrowed.

"You should know better than to bring this kind of nonsense to me," she said sternly. Goodman "We are in a tight space here with General Kozar and the other commanders' representatives. I don't know what you are think—"

Milosz suddenly exited from the negotiating room. "What is this about?" he demanded. "Amira, what are they doing here?"

"We think we can get into the Planina," Goodman said flatly. "There is a tunnel from the city into the fortress."

"Seriously?" Milosz looked him in the eyes, then glanced at Amira, and then back at Goodman. "Really?"

"They *say* there is a way into the fortress," said Amira. "They *say* there is a tunnel under the river."

"A tunnel?" said Milosz. He thought for a moment. "Zoran Pasha is desperate. Come with me." He led them into a classroom some distance away from the curious eyes and ears around the negotiation room. He closed the door quietly.

"General Kozar says he intends to attack the Planina and the other German outposts the day after tomorrow, before dawn," said Milosz. "He wants two more brigades in place by then. Only God knows why—he already has more than enough forces to take the fortress and the remaining strong points in the city at least twice. But he is a general, and I am nothing, so there it is. Regardless, he intends to begin shelling the castle tomorrow morning to destroy the Germans' will to fight." Milosz pulled out his pipe and tapped the bowl against the wall as he spoke to Amira. "Is this something we can do soon?"

"We have no—"

A crowd of saucer-shaped hats suddenly spilled into the hallway and proceeded down the hall, conferring busily over note pads and wristwatches. Several local militia commanders also emerged with a mix of rankled and vexed expressions. After they exited, Milosz led Amira and the others into the room. Zoran sat at the table and looked much less like a Pasha and much more like a man who had been put through the ringer. He looked up and gave his daughter an exasperated look. Goodman was unsettled by it.

"We are alone again, Milosz," Zoran announced. "Our so-called friends have once again proven that there are no friends in this world." He exhaled loudly.

"We still have an audience with General Kozar," Milosz countered.

"Hardly, my friend. We only have his attention because we bring forces to Tuzla city. Or *the People's city*, he stated... how many times? Twenty, twenty-five?" Zoran's look was distant, forlorn even.

"What do you bring me, Milosz?"

"Zoran Pasha, we, "—he corrected himself—"Amira has a way to achieve your earlier plans..."

"You are talking about the Planina?" Zoran asked in a hushed voice. "Those plans are dead." He gestured for someone to close the door. Musa checked the hallway and closed the door.

286

"That may not be, Pasha." Milosz gave Amira the floor.

"Father, we know of a tunnel that extends from the city into the Planina."

Zoran pushed away from the table. "We will die if we try this." He crossed his arms. "But do tell me about this... this tunnel," said Zoran. Amira pointed to Ismail at the same time Musa shoved him forward.

"Father, we have evidence of a tunnel that this man brought to us..."

"Y-Yes... Effendi—"

"He is Pasha!" Ismail flinched at Musa's correction and bowed his head.

"Many apologies, P-Pasha, there is a... the o-officer's toilet in the main part of the castle. A tunnel extends from the newspaper building downtown and enters the Planina in the room underneath the toilet—"

"That is the sewer, my young man..." Zoran fumbled with some papers.

"Begging your pardon, Eff—Pasha—but this is not the sewer."

"You are certain?"

"Y-Yes, Pasha," Ismail replied. "I have knowledge of the tunnel, its entrances. We are the only ones who know. I have worked there for many months, and I know the layout of the entire castle."

Zoran looked him over briefly. "And where in the castle is this... toilet?"

"Eff—Pasha, the... ummm... the toilets in the officer's quarters are in the southwest corner of the Great Keep, inside the Great Keep, under the great room."

"So, the officer's quarters are under the great room?" Zoran leaned forward. "Where is the radio room from there?"

"There is a room upstairs from the great room that has many maps, and it is where the commander and the other officers spend most of their time. The radios are there as well. The way is simple, but there are lots of corridors. May I draw it?"

Milosz nodded and took out a pencil from his pocket and rolled it across the table to Ismail. Ismail began scrawling on a piece of newspaper. The drawing was childish, but effective. Goodman

287

hoped it was accurate as well. When Ismail put his pencil down, everyone leaned over the table and studied the schematic. Suddenly, the idea was tangible. Goodman's mind was racing with ideas.

"Is this complete?" said Zoran.

"Y-yes, P-Pasha," said Ismail, straightening up a bit. "Yes, Pasha. To my best—"

"Shut up," said Zoran. "Tell me about the rooms."

Goodman watched Zoran's eyes dart across the sketch as Ismail described the general layout, including the radio room, the wall defenses, and the armory, but he admitted he had never seen some of the places in the castle they were inquiring about. After a minute of questioning, Amira and Milosz went quiet. "In addition to the munition area of the weapons room, there is a large munitions bunker in the central area, here." He pointed.

Zoran sat down again and leaned back. He exhaled through his nose. "What do we think of this?"

"The Germans have the fortress. They still have heavy weapons, and there are many rooms," Milosz countered. "And a garrison of at least, what, one hundred fifty Germans? That is too many."

Ismail timidly raised his hand. "Ummm... Effendi, not anymore," he said meekly.

"What do you mean?"

"There used to be more than two hundred Fritzies living here." He cleared his throat. "They also used to have sixteen tanks. Most of them left a month ago to chase the Partisans in the mountains. They have not yet returned. And last night, they sent almost everyone else to fight in a different part of the city." Zoran, Amira, and Goodman all exchanged glances as Ismail continued. "They took the last two tanks with them. But they also have not yet returned. Then they kicked me out this morning. That was after the Partisan Army arrived."

"Those tanks won't be coming back." Zoran nodded at Goodman. "And you have seen the entrance to this... tunnel?"

"Yes, Pasha," said Goodman.

"Father... Pasha," said Amira. "We do not know this city, and the people here are not... our people."

"Yes, I know, my dearest daughter," said Zoran. "I know..."

288

Tomislav cleared his throat. "Pasha, this is an extreme risk…"

Zoran's hand stopped him. Amira started to say something, but Zoran raised his hand again. No one spoke for a moment.

"Milosz," Zoran finally said.

"Yes, Pasha?"

"Is this worthy?"

"This is the only other thing to do," he said.

"Other thing?"

"Yes, Pasha. There is always the option to do nothing. But there is risk either way."

"Risk?" Zoran boomed. "Of course, there is risk! There is risk in even having this conversation after the conversations I've been having all day with this damned General Konstantin Kozar!" His fist hit the table.

"Yes, Pasha," said Milosz as he lowered his head slightly.

Zoran swept his hand at the map. "Even if an attack is possible, we must consider the consequences beyond killing the Germans. This will only be interpreted by General Kozar—and Marshall Tito, for that matter—as a slap in the face, will it not?"

"Very likely," said Milosz.

"Not very likely." Zoran stood up. "Definitely!"

Milosz nodded silently. Then Zoran grunted as he adjusted his leather riding pants and pulled up on his belt. Goodman tried to think of something to say. *This can't be the end.*

"Then, father," said Amira. "We could do this, but should we not? There are too many—"

"Amira Effendim!" he bellowed. His use of the formal reference provoked a visceral reaction from Amira. She shrank from him, and Zoran looked at Goodman.

"Američko…" This was only the second time Zoran had called him this. "Američko, tell me how you would take the Planina from the Germans."

Goodman looked around at all the eyes looking at him and took a deep breath. *What do I say? Don't be stupid.*

"I would attack before dawn through the tunnel, at the end of the guard shift," he began. "If the Nazis do it like the American army, everyone is exhausted at the end of their shift, especially the early morning shift. Do we know the Germans' guard shifts?" He looked at Ismail, and Amira translated.

"They do two shifts," Ismail replied. "At six in the morning and again in the evening. They used to do four guard shifts, but now, with the small force remaining in the fortress, they only do two shifts."

"Twelve-hour shifts," said Goodman. "That's hard to do. They will be tired." Milosz nodded in agreement. "An hour before their sunrise guard shift will be best to attack."

"Two hours," said Milosz. "The Germans always awaken an hour before to prepare themselves."

"Okay," said Goodman. "Two hours. The guards who are on duty will be exhausted, and the next shift will not yet be awake. We attack at four." He leaned over and rotated Ismail's sketched map of the fortress toward him.

"We enter here?" He pointed at the place where Ismail had drawn the toilet for the officer's quarters. Ismail nodded. "We enter here and take the officer's quarters. That should not be too hard since they will all be asleep. And, frankly, they're officers. They're not fighters. Once we take them, we tie them up…" Amira clucked her tongue. Goodman looked up at her, then at Zoran. "We can sell them back to the Germans."

"Good, Američko," said Zoran. "Good thinking."

"We tie them up or whatever…then we move here…" His finger traced the lines of the corridors and stairs up to the great room and to the radio room. "Here, we take the map room and radio room."

"Radio room first." Milosz pointed with his pipe stem. "Get the radio so they cannot use it to call for reinforcements."

"Right." Goodman nodded. "So then, this is where it gets tricky, I think." He paused to think. *Where do we go? Which do we attack first?* "We take the ammo bunker, so we control how long this fight goes on."

"But the bunker is in the middle of the yard where all the positions on the walls and the towers can shoot down on you," said Amira. "Father, this plan will not work—"

"Let the Američko finish," said Zoran. "No attack is ever easy. Especially this one. Let him find the path." Amira clenched her jaw and fixed her eyes on the sketch. Goodman continued, still watching her.

"We will attack along the walls here and here,"—he pointed at one side of the sketch, then the other—"and take this tower and these two towers. Then, well, we won't need to take the ammo bunker at all…"

Ismail cleared his throat. "There is always a squad in the bunker." All eyes moved to Ismail and then to the square he had drawn in the center of the fortress courtyard. "They operate the mortars and feed ammunition to the towers and wall defenses. I have seen them practice their tactics."

"Then we *do* need to take the bunker." Goodman pointed back at the hand-drawn square. "We'll do that as quickly as possible." He stood back. "Officers' quarters, the radio room, the map room, the towers, and the ammo bunker. What else?" No one said anything. "I think that is as simple as we can make it."

"Even the simple things can be difficult," said Milosz.

"This plan does not account for the building within the fortress," said Amira. "There must be dozens of rooms and many corridors. It will take many men to accomplish this operation."

"All rooms are controlled by hallways, and it only takes one man to control a hallway," countered Zoran. "And we have surprise as our best tool. The fortress is manned by a skeleton crew, and the interior will have almost no one awake."

"Pasha, this is big," said Milosz, sweeping his hand across Ismail's drawing. "We will need at least two hundred men for this."

"I was thinking twice that number," said Amira. "This is not our ground. Our men are accustomed to fighting in the forest, with hills and streams to help us. This fortress has corridors and many rooms. That will mean many casualties. But too many men will be difficult to get into the newspaper building. Impossible, even. And we will only be able to employ small arms, as the ranges inside are very close. Father, I do not like leaving machine guns behind." She took a breath. "This is not our ground."

"My daughter," said Zoran. "Just last night we took the factory from the Ustaši and the Germans. We killed many enemies and destroyed two of their tanks. This is a good omen for us."

"We will still require many men for this operation," said Milosz.

"We cannot afford that many," said Zoran. "You get thirty."

"Thirty?" Milosz and Amira exclaimed. The minuscule number shocked Goodman. *There's no way...*

"Pasha, this—" Milosz spoke, but Amira cut him off.

"Father, this cannot be done with thirty men!"

Milosz tried to agree, but Zoran cut him off.

"Kozar's people are *watching* us!" Zoran slammed his fist into his hand. "They know our numbers here in Tuzla city. Kozar has directed that all non-Partisan leaders are to remain with him while our brigade remains outside the city. For our protection, he says. So, we must be separated. However, I am allowed a small force for my personal protection. A force of thirty armed men..." Zoran saw the disbelief in the faces around him. "We must make Kozar believe I am complying with the promises that I just made to his face not half an hour ago!" He paused. "Listen. All of you. We must lie to our enemies with our words and with *apparent inaction*. But our truth will be movement, but the lie must be stillness. The lie must be many times bigger to make the truth improbable. And we need not fight alone. I will talk to Colonel Zbrogan. He says he is also not of one mind with Kozar and his Partisan Army. Zbrogan will provide forces."

"The Tuzla unions, Pasha?" said Milosz. "Must we?"

"Father," said Amira. "Including the Unions will be a..."

"It will not be a problem because I say it will not be a problem!"

Everyone went silent. Milosz and Amira looked at the table. Zoran glanced at his watch.

*I haven't seen disagreement like this before*, thought Goodman. He felt a tightness in his chest. *Whoever these other people are, Zoran seems to be the only one to think it's a good idea.* Goodman did not like what was happening. "Who are the Unions?" he asked.

Tomislav whispered to him. "They are Zoran's—"

"They are allies!" Zoran cut him off. "They are allied with us against the Germans and Communists." His words shut down the group. He cleared his throat.

"Now, for tonight," Zoran continued. "I will be dining with the great General of the People, Kosta Kozar, and his staff in one hour.

Milosz, you will be with me, but I want your deputy to remain here for a...special task. General Kozar has seen fit to bestow us with some wireless radios so we may remain in communication with our forces and with him. And so he can spy on us by listening to our conversations. I want you to take possession of those radios immediately. You will have a radio here and a radio at our camp outside of the city. You will use these radios to talk about normal, routine things to make them believe we are sitting still. For contact with our attack force, we will use messengers until you capture the radio room."

"Father, I want my men fighting, not talking on the radio."

"I wish it," he said.

Amira clucked her tongue.

"Amira!" Zoran boomed. Everyone flinched.

"This is absolutely necessary," he said, in a gentler tone. "Amira, you are my only daughter. And tonight, you have a baby brother once again to care for—this mission. I want to know both of you survive this night. This is not negotiable." Zoran put his pipe in his mouth and chewed on the mouthpiece.

"Yes, Pasha," she said.

Zoran's look shifted to Milosz.

"Yes, Pasha," said Milosz. Goodman and Tomislav voiced their understanding as well.

Zoran's eyes moved across the group, but they fixed on Goodman.

"So, Američko," said Zoran. "You do great things, eh?"

"I'm just trying to help..." said Goodman.

"But you like the fighting, eh?" Zoran didn't give time to answer. "You like fighting on the ground, not just in the air? Perhaps you found something you enjoy about killing after your adventure at the factory? Or was it before?" Goodman could not answer this question. The memories of the bodies at the farm, watching Tomislav finish off the Ustaše fighters on the hillside, and other instances of the very close and very personal killing he saw rushed back to him. And the ones that he killed himself. *I can't deny that I've done it, and I would do it again in each situation. Maybe even more. But no,* he thought. *I don't like it. Not at all.*

Zoran resumed. "Does not matter. You've got some salt on your food now. But this is going to be something different. Are you ready?"

"Yes, Pasha."

"This will be more than shooting a bunch of pigs in the woods. You will be up close. This will be murder. Can you murder?"

The sound of the word made a knot in his stomach. "Yes, Pasha," said Goodman. He's not wrong.

"Was this your idea?" Zoran's eyes narrowed. "This attack through the tunnel?"

"I may have had something to do with it," Goodman replied.

"Well, I'll tell you something," said Zoran, bending at the waist to lean toward Goodman, leather creaking on leather as he did so. "That explosion at the factory was beautiful! The only people you pissed off were Amira and Milosz, because they wanted those explosives." Amira and Milosz looked at Zoran. "And the Germans, of course—the Germans and their Ustaša dogs. But I was very pleased that we were able to send so many of them to hell with one act of fire. Beautiful."

*Act of fire.* The words lingered in Goodman's ears. *That was quite the explosion.* He tried not to think about the destruction afterward.

"Listen, Američko…" He wagged a finger at Goodman. "You have my only daughter with you on this operation tonight, and you are going to cut the dragon in the gut. I want you to cut him to pieces. But be wise. And this goes for all of you: I want you to slay only who you must. We will need as many prisoners as possible to sell to General Kozar. That may be the only way to achieve the glory we seek *and* survive it afterward."

"And something else," Zoran added. "*Govno!*"—he slammed his fist on the table—"I wish I was going on this operation, but I must be at this damned dinner tonight. It is essential in living the big lie for Kozar. But I remind you—they are watching us." He pointed at everyone around the table. "They have spies everywhere. I have a spy assigned to me, and so do you, Milosz. He is waiting for you when you leave here. All of you be discrete, especially you, *moj strani sin*. They seek you."

Goodman's ears perked up when he heard the words. Amira's head jerked toward her father at the words, too. *Did Zoran just call me his foreign son?* thought Goodman. Zoran continued.

"…for you especially, that means keeping quiet. Kozar doesn't know about you. Not yet, at least. Pretending to rescue you will be a skin on his wall. I won't let that happen."

Goodman nodded that he understood. He was also very aware of the scowl on Amira's face.

Milosz tapped his watch. "Pasha, we must not be late. We must talk to Colonel Zbrogan about the attack, which I'm sure will not be difficult. But those of us on this mission tonight haven't much time to prepare."

"Yes, yes, Milosz," said Zoran. "You are correct. Amira, my daughter, please pick your men wisely. Only thirty." He took a deep breath and exhaled. "I'm going to go now. I will want updates as often as possible."

"Yes, Zoran," said Milosz. He followed Zoran out of the room after giving Amira and Goodman a look. When the large double doors slammed shut, Goodman, Amira, Musa, Tomislav, and Ismail stood in silence around the sketch.

"We must succeed," said Amira.

She was already looking at Goodman when he raised his eyes.

"This has to work," she spoke directly at him. "Or we will all die tomorrow, one way or another."

Goodman nodded ever so slightly. *Exactly what I was thinking.*

# 51

## CENTRAL TUZLA COMMERCIAL DISTRICT

GOODMAN AND ISMAIL LED AMIRA AND THE ASSAULT FORCE through the inner city, keeping mostly to the alleyways and side streets. The city at night was cold and empty. An occasional streetlamp illuminated an intersection here or a length of storefronts there. These, they avoided. Near the city center, Ismail halted abruptly at the end of an alley.

Across the street, the newspaper building was fully illuminated and swarming with Communist Partisan troops. A stream of uniformed men and women carried typewriters and boxes into the building and returned to get another armload of materials from a column of trucks that lined the street on both sides. Other Partisans stood guard at the street corners and held torches to illuminate the scene around them. Goodman's heart sank.

"Govno!" said Ismail.

"Who are these people?" said Goodman. He peered around the corner and turned back to Amira. "These guys weren't here before."

"What is this?" Amira was furious.

Musa and Tomislav crept to the corner of the building to get a look for themselves. Their faces fell when they saw what had transpired over the last six hours. Ismail let loose with a string of curses.

"This is done before it starts," said Amira. She looked behind them. "Where are the Unionists? We must warn them not to come."

"Too late," said Musa, looking up the street behind them. A large company of heavily armed men marched toward them.

"No, wait," said Goodman. "This isn't over. Ismail! You with me." He grabbed Ismail and looked at Amira, Musa, and Tomislav. "If this works, do what we do."

Goodman pulled Ismail out from the corner and led him diagonally across the intersection. Ismail went with him, but Goodman could feel the apprehension.

"Do what I do," Goodman whispered. "If anyone wants something, you do the talking."

"Why me?"

"Because I'm not from around here! Razumiješ?"

Ismail started to resist, but they were already at the line behind the nearest truck. They stood there for all of three seconds before a Partisan officer singled them out.

"Šta radiš ovdje?" he demanded.

Ismail froze. The officer repeated himself. Goodman faked a cough, hoping to prompt Ismail. He finally squeaked out a response.

"W-We are here to c-c-carry goods for the P-People's Army, effendi." He bowed his head.

"Do not call me effendi," said the officer. "I am a Captain of the People's Partisan Army."

"Y-Yes, sir." Ismail managed to speak. "We are—"

"Do not call me 'sir' either. Use Comrade Captain to address an officer of my rank."

"Yes, um, y-yes, Comrade Captain."

"We do not need your assistance," said the captain. "We have everything in order." He swung his head around. "Where is the Partisan Labor Supervisor? Where is my Labor Brigade?" he demanded of someone not immediately visible. No one answered.

Goodman prodded Ismail. "Tell him we're it!" he whispered.

"Sir…umm…Comrade Captain! We are your Labor Brigade, sir!" Ismail stood to attention with his hand raised in a crooked salute.

"The two of you? Where is your Labor Commander?"

"I don't know, Comrade Captain."

*This isn't going to work*, thought Goodman. *Ismail's not cutting it, and I don't dare try to talk to this guy.* He looked back at the alley and only saw Musa's and Tomislav's faces looking back at him. As quickly and discretely as possible, he waved at them to come over. At first, no one moved, and he waved again. Goodman's heart sank when still no one approached from the alley.

Then Amira stepped into the light.

Right after her, Musa, Tomislav, and the entire assault force— including the newly arrived Tuzla Unionists—marched across the intersection. The Partisan Captain's jaw dropped as he watched them extend the line leading to the rear of the truck all the way to the alley. Amira ordered the group to stay in line and then stomped her way to the front. She rendered a crisp salute at the Partisan Captain and stood to attention. *Nice touch*, thought Goodman.

The captain returned the salute. "Who are you?"

Ismail sprang to life. "Comrade Captain, she is the Labor Commander."

Goodman let out the breath he had been holding. *Good*, he thought. *Ismail's finally functioning.*

"Shut up."

"Ye-yes, Comrade Cap—" Ismail finally shut up.

"Yes, Comrade Captain," said Amira, glancing quickly at Goodman. "I am…the…Labor Commander." She stood to attention a little too crisply. But her theatrics worked.

The Partisan Captain looked at her from head to toe and then at the assault force standing behind her staring at him. "You are armed," he said. "I specifically requested laborers, not infantry. I cannot use infantry here. I would be brought up on charges of misappropriation of military resources." He sighed out loud and looked at his wristwatch. "How many of you are there?"

Amira sounded off. "One hundred twenty comrades, Comrade Captain."

"There are supposed to be three hundred laborers, and I get a hundred twenty infantrymen!" The captain shouted. "How am I supposed to support the Propaganda Battalion *and* the Headquarters Battalion if they refuse to give me sufficient manpower?"

The captain looked at his watch again and shook his head. "Very well, unload these trucks into this building. All excess inventory goes into the yard behind. Be sure to store the excess inventory off the ground and cover it with the tarpaulins in these last two trucks. Many of these trucks are loaded with printing paper for the People's Revolutionary Newspaper. It must not get wet. Do you understand?"

"Yes, Comrade Captain." Amira saluted again. The officer returned her salute and stormed off down the line of trucks into the darkness. Amira turned to Goodman. "What do you think you are doing?"

"Getting us into the newspaper building, that's what." Goodman took a few steps toward the rear of the truck. "Just carry your box."

Goodman stepped to the rear of the truck and shouldered a heavy wooden crate. He followed the laborer in front of him up the front steps and through the door. Inside, he followed directions to drop the crate in one of the offices and then went back to the main corridor. He caught Ismail by the collar and pushed him toward the rear of the building—to the door leading to the basement stairs. After he made sure that Amira and the others were behind them—and the Partisans directing traffic were not—he pushed Ismail through the doors. Ismail, Goodman, and Amira descended the stairs while Musa remained in the hall. He redirected each of the assault force members after them.

"Get the hammers," said Amira. "We must get—"

Just then, a very loud whirring noise obliterated their conversation. On top of that, a rhythmic mechanical sound dominated the whirring noise. They all looked upward to see a vent shaft from the above room that carried the sounds from upstairs.

"That," Ismail yelled over the sound and pointed at the ceiling. "That is the printing room upstairs!" They heard the *clink-clickety-clunk, clink-clickety-clunk* of the presses one floor above. "It is exactly how I heard it through the wall."

Ismail opened the closet, and the warm, humid stench rolled out and gagged them.

"Well... I believe you." She held her arm over her mouth. "Hammers, get up here!"

Musa and another barrel-chested militiaman heaved large sledgehammers that looked as though they had seen their share of plaster and stone. Musa stepped into the closet, cursed the stench, and took a swing. The dull thud made a four-foot crack in the plaster right below the hole they'd made earlier. His second swing caused a huge part of the wall to collapse into the tunnel. Another, more powerful wave of the warm stench overcame him, and he stumbled backward out of the closet, his hand over his mouth, eyes squeezed shut. The smell reached Goodman and the rest of them, and they retreated from it, gaging and cursing. *My God, that's terrible*, he thought. *I hope it clears out.*

"This is our path," said Amira, ripping a rag from a shelf and tying it around her head to cover her mouth and nose. "Again!" She coughed. "Hit the wall again."

Musa waved for the other hammer-wielding militiaman to go ahead. He stepped inside the closet and let out a curse. He hit the wall, and a large piece of stone collapsed with a heavy crumbling sound. Then, rather than take another swing, he vomited and stumbled out. Amira motioned for the Musa to finish the job. He grunted loudly as he heaved his hammer against the brick. Two more swings and the entire bricked-over portion of the doorway crumbled into the foul darkness. Musa poked and chipped at the remainder to widen the entrance. He cursed and came back out of the closet, wiping his eyes and spitting on the floor.

"*Duhove* took a shit in there," he muttered.

*Can't say I would have thought of it that way*, thought Goodman. *But that is exactly what it smells like.* He glanced at Tomislav, who had withdrawn to the far end of the room.

Amira came forward to inspect the hole. She blinked to clear her eyes, then muttered a curse as she lifted her lantern and entered the closet. Curiously, the lantern glowed extra brightly when the flame met the warm wind. *That's methane gas!* thought Goodman. *I hope there isn't enough to explode.* Amira whispered for Ismail. He entered the closet and peered into the hole next to her.

"Does this look like the way to you?" Amira asked Ismail, trying not to inhale too deeply. Ismail coughed and held his arm over his mouth.

"Yes," he said, blinking as he inspected the walls inside. "This is it. I was here before." They both exited the closet to face the group. "The fortress is there." He pointed into the darkness.

"Okay—" Amira stifled a cough. "We go now."

300

# 52

## BASEMENT OF THE TUZLANSKE VJESTI NEWSPAPER OFFICES

A MAN IN A BLACK WORKER'S UNIFORM SHOVED HIS WAY THROUGH THE CROWD to the closet entrance.

"You are joking with me!" he exclaimed as he covered his mouth and nose with his sleeve.

"Mirzad!" Amira barked at him. "Your men will enter the tunnel after we have—"

"I insist that you call me 'Director' in front of my people," Mirzad responded.

"Fine," she said. "Director Mirzad, wait your turn to enter the tunnel!" She turned away from him before he had a chance to respond. A quick nod to Musa, and he shoved Ismail into the tunnel. Amira entered after him. "*Idi!*" she ordered. Ismail obeyed and marched ahead, holding a lantern in front of him.

"Who was that guy?" Goodman whispered to Tomislav as they crossed the threshold into the closet.

"He is Colonel Zbrogan's oldest son and deputy commander." Tomislav ducked into the tunnel and stifled another cough. "He is leading the Tuzla Unionists in the attack tonight."

"Sounds like he's going to be a problem."

Tomislav shrugged and handed Goodman a lantern. He turned it up and followed Amira, who prodded Ismail to proceed faster into the tunnel. Musa had dropped his sledgehammer and retrieved his MG42 from one of his crew. The remainder of the Majevitsa men filed in after him, one after the other, cursing, coughing, and spitting. Someone gagged, and then someone vomited. The burst of bile splattered on the floor behind him, which triggered another man to vomit, then another. Goodman tried to increase his speed, but could go no faster than Amira, who stumbled and gagged as she went. Then Tomislav heaved behind Goodman. Finally, Goodman could no longer hold it back. *Oh, God, no...* He braced himself on the wall and heaved.

It burned his nostrils and throat. He cleared his throat and spit numerous times, but each breath of the foul methane air combining with the smell of bile only made things worse. The tunnel behind him was an erratic symphony of coughing, spitting, and multi-layered Slavic cursing. Amira turned and glared. Goodman sensed her frustration, but there was nothing to do but go forward. *Keep going!* Even if there was a sudden change of plans, there were a hundred and some-odd men in the tunnel behind them, all headed in the same direction and increasingly desperate to get to the end. Even if the end of the tunnel was in the heart of a Nazi-occupied fortress.

Except for the low ceiling, the going was easy. The tunnel was more or less straight and angled downward about fifteen degrees. He ran his hands along the walls, which were carved flat, or maybe plastered or cemented, and were dry as old bones despite the humid air. Amira's pace abruptly slowed, and she turned to Goodman.

"Stairs," she whispered. Goodman turned and whispered the warning to Tomislav. There was no handrail, so he braced himself on the walls. The humidity increased sharply. At the bottom, the floor continued downward at a distinctly sharper angle. The floor and walls here were slick. Rivulets of water reflected the lamp lights along the walls.

*Splash. Splish-splash, splish-splash, splish-splash.* Ismail halted.

"Keep going," Amira said to him.

"There is water," said Ismail.

"So? How much further?" she said. "Does it go deeper?"

"Yes, it goes much deeper," Ismail said. "We are under the river."

Goodman watched Amira's lantern hover motionless for a moment. *She's deciding what to do*, Goodman thought. *What is there to do? Do we go back?* He looked at the ceiling. *We're under the river...*

"Idi!" Amira ordered.

*Slosh, slosh.* Ismail protested.

"Idi!"

Goodman took his first steps and felt the water lap over his boots. Three more paces, and the frigid water soaked into his socks. Within two more paces, he felt the *squish-squish* of waterlogged boots. Each step went deeper and deeper into the water. *At this rate, the water will be up to the ceiling in about fifty yards.* In his descriptions, Ismail had said nothing of the tunnel's length, nor the downward angle. Nor the water. The going got more difficult as the water deepened. The water passed his knees, and Ismail kept moving, prodded along by Amira.

"This is only *a little* water?" Amira growled at Ismail.

"Izvinite, but more water has come in…"

"No kidding," said Goodman.

When the water soaked the bottom of his shirt, Goodman was forced to hold the lantern high enough to bump the ceiling with his knuckles. A few yards more, and the water soaked him up to the armpits. Then, Ismail's lantern went out. Amira cursed when her own lantern extinguished a minute later. She halted.

"Can you see ahead?" Amira asked.

"No… I can't see anything," Ismail cried out. He was panicking.

Amira grabbed Goodman's arm and lowered his lantern. She lowered it so water ripples licked at the oil flame, casting a shimmering light down the tunnel. She stood on her toes to see as far down the tunnel as she could above the water line. Goodman squinted to see how far the shimmering went before the water met the ceiling.

"I can see the tunnel rising," he said to her.

"How far?" She squinted.

"About ten more yards." He pointed. She exhaled in relief.

"You! Go!" she directed Ismail. He was huddled against the wall, shaking his head.

"Idi!" she yelled.

He hugged the wall tighter and shook his head. Musa approached and tapped his cousin on the shoulder. Ismail did not respond. He gave Ismail a shove, but Ismail put his head down and shook his head.

"He doesn't know how to swim," said Musa.

Amira slapped him across the face. Ismail whimpered and sank into the water up to his chin. She went to hit him again but stopped herself.

"Perhaps this is not possible," she said.

Musa put his hand on his cousin's shoulder to try to roust some yet-to-be-discovered bravery, but to no avail. *Oh, c'mon, man!* thought Goodman. *Get moving. We can't stop.* He looked ahead at the darkness and behind at the string of lanterns and dimly lit faces. *We're here*, he thought. *We can't stop.*

"I'll go," said Goodman. He pushed past Ismail, tilting his lantern to hold it out of the water. He stepped forward cautiously, feeling with his feet along the floor five feet under the water's surface. The space between the surface and the ceiling narrowed, and Goodman felt the closeness. He hoped that the water did not trap him under the ceiling. The water reached his neck as he bumped his head on the ceiling, which caused the fuel oil to spill and set a small patch of the water's surface alight. The flame bounced along with the ripples of Goodman's passing. As the lantern's frame scraped the ceiling, the flame in the lantern sputtered. Then his head bounced against rock. *Ow!*

Goodman cocked his head to one side to keep his mouth out of the water and stepped forward. He sputtered bubbles out of the putrid water with each breath as his feet shuffled forward. He cupped his hands around the base of the lantern to keep the water from splashing into the basin around the wick.

Goodman estimated he had advanced about ten yards, yet he was still chin-deep in the water. *A few more yards, and I'll know either way,* he thought. *Don't let this be the end. Don't let this stop us.* He took an extra-long, slow-motion stride. The vent cap on the lantern scraped the ceiling and chipped the glass globe. He took another long stride. And another. And another.

The water level was below his collar now. He took several longer strides, and the water was down to his chest, though the ceiling was a few inches lower here and forced him to crouch even more. *But the water is going down.* He exhaled. *Good.* Anything felt possible now.

"Hey!" he called back to Amira. "It's okay! The tunnel goes up from here. And there's light ahead! Follow the light!"

He heard several muffled voices sloshing and splashing. Goodman held up the lantern.

"Keep coming!" he said.

Amira came up first, more or less swimming. She was completely drenched, and her hair was matted to her head. Goodman grabbed Amira's hand and pulled her toward the soft glow ahead. She gripped him tightly. Despite the frigid water, her hand warmed in his. It was the second time they had touched and the feelings from when he held her in the forest came rushing back to him. He pulled her close to him and only let go when she could touch the floor again. It was still too dark, so he could not see the look on her face. He wished he could have.

Musa arrived next, dragging his cousin behind. The rest of the Majevitsa men, and the Tuzla Unionists behind them, slowly slogged their way forward toward the faint greenish glow. The remainder of the tunnel was wide, wet, and sloped upward gradually until a set of three steps elevated the path to a landing that took a gradual leftward turn. Goodman and Amira turned the corner together and saw the vague greenish glow was better defined. And then the stench of human waste hit them.

"Damn!" said Goodman, squinting against the foulness.

Amira fished for her watch somewhere inside her coat. She rubbed the face of it, trying to read the time in the dim lantern light. She let out a gasp.

"What?" asked Goodman.

"It is almost four!" She held the watch up for him to see.

"Let's move," said Goodman.

Amira ran ahead of him. He picked up his own pace, as did Musa, Ismail, and each of the men behind them as they gained their footing. The glow took on the shape of an arched casement. Amira reached the open casement and abruptly stopped, teetering on the ledge. Goodman saw why when he ran up behind her. They had reached the cistern.

*Oh, my Lord...*

Months of human waste sat in six small mountains, illuminated by slivers of light penetrating through cracks in the ceiling above. A small sea of liquid surrounded each of the mounds. Goodman and Amira pulled their collars up over their mouths and noses and scanned the space, looking for another door. Goodman could make out a square opening above the opposite corner, but something was covering it. There was a ladder immediately below it.

"Musa!" Amira whispered. "Get your stupid cousin up here!"

He shoved Ismail forward.

"How do you get that door open?" she asked him.

"It is just a wooden door. There is no lock," he replied. "There is probably a brick or something holding it down."

"How do you get across?" asked Musa. He, Amira, and Goodman looked at Ismail. Tomislav appeared, and terror crossed his face when he saw the pit.

"You walk," said Ismail.

"You mean in the…"

"In the shit?" he said. "Yes."

Ismail promptly stepped past Amira and down into the muck. His steps made a *shlick-shloop-shlick-shloop* sound as he crossed the pit. Goodman felt woozy. He did not know if it was from the noxious fumes or the realization—however predictable it was—that he was now going to wade through several feet of excrement. Ismail reached the ladder. He climbed and could not open the door at the top.

"Too heavy," he whispered.

"Musa!" Amira whispered. "Musa, get up there and open that door!"

"God help us," Musa muttered as he stepped off the ledge and into the muck.

"See if you can lift it," Amira directed him. "And be quiet. We are in the Planina!"

Musa nodded and quietly climbed the ladder. He reached for the wooden plank and suddenly stopped.

"What?" said Amira.

"I hear some—" Musa froze.

A door creaked open above the ceiling. They all heard crisp, hard-sole boots cross the stone floor and saw the light stream down when a plank slid away from one of the toilet holes. Then the hole darkened.

"Oh, no," Goodman muttered to himself.

The German officer grunted loudly and then let the previous night's dinner descend with a sickening plop. He wiped himself, grunted again, let the paper fall, and then light shone down into the pit again before the officer slid the plank back across the hole. The German's hard-soled boots clanked across the stone above. Musa waited for the door to clank shut and the footsteps to fade before he reached for the plank above his head again. He slowly lifted it and pushed it aside before poking his head up, then looked back at Amira and Goodman.

"Dobro je!" he whispered. *It's good.*

"Thank God," Goodman whispered.

Amira jumped down into the mess and high-stepped to the far corner, where she followed Musa up the ladder and into the officer's latrine. Goodman searched back and forth for a path of lesser filth, but ultimately decided to just deal with it. He stepped down and could barely contain his disgust. He gagged as he reached for the ladder. *I wish I could puke again.*

# 53

### 0430 HOURS, SEPTEMBER 29, 1943
### PLANINA FORTRESS OFFICER'S LATRINE

THEY WERE LATE. Amira was stressed, near frantic. And Goodman could see it plain as day.

"I'm going to get a look around," said Ismail when he finished scraping fecal matter from his pants and boots.

"No, cousin, wait!" whispered Musa.

"Don't worry," replied Ismail. "I know this place very well. I'll be back."

He silently closed the door behind him. While he was gone, Musa pulled Amira and another Majevitsa militiaman from the chamber. Others climbed out and all set to scraping their boots.

A minute later, Ismail returned, smiling. "The way is clear. They are all asleep."

"Good," Amira replied. "You do something like that again, and I'll slit your throat." Ismail froze.

In less than two minutes, the room was packed with men, all trying to wipe excrement from their boots and hands. Dozens more were awaiting their turn to cross the Worst Place in the World. Goodman turned his attention to Amira.

"The plan is still good?" he asked.

"Yes, we take this hallway first," she whispered. "We take as officers as prisoners as possible and then kill the rest."

"Okay," Goodman replied. "You take the first door, I'll take the second?" She agreed, and he moved next to Musa at the door.

She nodded and then tapped Musa on the shoulder. "You open the door when I say."

He nodded in reply. Amira scanned the room behind her to account for her men. More were climbing the ladder, but the room was already too full. The under-the-breath cursing ceased when everyone heard another door open in the corridor outside. Goodman's and Musa's eyes widened as the hard-soled boots came closer to the latrine door. They each had a death-grip on their knives, eyes on the door. Musa had his other hand on the handle, ready to yank it open. To Goodman's relief, the footsteps passed the latrine door and continued until they heard a knocking sound.

"Oberleutnant Shultz!" came the voice from the hall. A moment later, an unseen door unlatched and creaked open.

A very sleepy voice groaned something incoherently. More German commands followed, with the man named Schultz relenting to whatever the directive was. The first man departed the way he had come, and his footsteps faded. Schultz's door closed. Goodman looked at Tomislav.

"He's coming out in a moment," Tomislav whispered. They turned their attention back to the crack in the door.

# DEEP IN THE PLACE OF THE DEAD

A moment later, Oberleutnant Schultz came out and closed his door behind him. He was muttering under his breath as he walked down the hall. Goodman watched through the crack in the door as he passed the latrine and reached for the door at the end of the corridor. But he paused and turned around. Goodman moved away from the crack in the door as Schultz approached the latrine. He glanced at Amira. From the look on her face, he could tell that she already knew what was about to happen. And so did he.

Her eyes were afire as she motioned for everyone to stand away from the door. That was difficult with more than twenty men in a space that was intended for six and more climbing up the ladder. The footsteps in the hall came closer, and everyone braced for the encounter. Knives up. The young Oberleutnant Schultz's all-black SS uniform filled the doorway as he opened the door.

Musa reached out and grabbed a very terrified Nazi officer by the collar. Amira pistol whipped him across the face, and others quickly grabbed him and smothered him on the floor. He fought for all of two seconds before he had the air knocked out of him. They bound and gagged him and rifled through his pockets. Musa threatened to punch him. Oberleutnant Schultz shook his head in his attempt to communicate that he would not resist. Musa clocked him anyway, and his head hit the floor. They left him there.

Amira crept out and signaled for the others to follow. She silently directed her men to cover each of the ten doors. Each room housed two or three officers according to the information from Ismail. When each door had at least three men poised outside, Amira counted down with raised fingers and then eased a door open, as did Goodman. Amira's opened with a loud squeak, and she stormed inside. All the others charged into their assigned rooms. Goodman threw his door open wide.

The two SS officers in Goodman's room were asleep in their clothing. Beside their cots, their personal effects and weapons were neatly hung. One man never woke up before Goodman whacked him on the head with the butt of his submachine gun. The man in bed on the other side of the room opened his mouth to yell, but Musa's giant hand smothered him. A small, muffled sound came out, and Musa leaned in with all his weight. The man fought back briefly as the other militiaman swung his weapon and knocked all the air out of him. He wheezed and folded into a fetal position. And that was how they tied and gagged him. After tying his hands and legs, Goodman shoved a rag in to the unconscious man's mouth and wrapped his head with another piece of cloth.

Similar experiences played out in the other rooms. There was one German who managed to let out a cry for help before his attackers reduced him to a whimpering pile on the floor. One other SS officer pulled a pistol from under his pillow, and his attackers nearly beat him to death with it.

Amira used a German officer's uniform to wipe off her boots before exiting. All the officers were bound and gagged and then consolidated into one room, each getting at least one more solid punch to the ribs or about the head. Some protested. Others rolled limply to the floor and remained motionless. Goodman was surprised more by the sense of satisfaction he felt than the brutality of their treatment of the officers. *This is my war now.*

The militia ransacked each of the rooms. The overall take was six more MP40 submachine guns with ammunition, several pistols, also with ammunition, and several pairs of binoculars, goggles, and other premium military grade accoutrements. Most of the personal effects were quickly claimed and pocketed. More than a couple of Iron Crosses and Knights Crosses ended up in a militiaman's pocket for later story telling.

Amira quietly consolidated her men back into the corridor after having assigned two of them to watch the officers, with instruction to slit the throat of whoever made a sound. She was interrupted when other sounds emanated from the latrine. Apparently, the Tuzla Unionists had also arrived.

# 54

UNIONIST DIRECTOR MIRZAD WAS THE FIRST OF THE BRIGADE TO EMERGE from the lower chamber. The next Tuzla Unionist fighter to emerge must have slipped or fallen off the ladder, because excrement covered him from head to toe. He let loose a string of curses before Mirzad shushed him.

"Was that tunnel your idea?" he said to Amira as he scraped his boots on the floor.

"There was no other way," said Amira.

"What is he doing here?" Mirzad pointed at Goodman.

"He is one of us," she said.

*Did she just say that?* Goodman was shocked to hear the words. For an instant, he questioned if he understood correctly. *One of us.* He smiled.

Mirzad grumbled, but Amira ignored him and gave him an update.

"There are fourteen prisoners in the back room. This man,"—she pulled Ismail by the sleeve—"is our guide. He will lead you to your point of attack. When we have the radio room, you may attack the towers and whatever else you want. Remember, we will share the armory and split the profits from the prisoners, yes? You still agree to the terms, yes?"

"Yes, of course," said Mirzad. Amira shot Goodman a quick glance. *What was that? Does she think they'll go back on the deal?*

"Now, let's get on with this," said Mirzad.

Dozens of armed men streamed from the latrine and stood shoulder to shoulder, jostling one another in the corridor. Goodman checked his weapon while Amira issued final instructions to her men. It was loaded, and he had ten more magazines. His pistol was good, too, and he put it back in his coat pocket. He raised his MP40 and flicked the safety off. *I'm good to go.*

Ismail slowly opened the door at the end of the corridor and peered around the corner. He stepped forward and started up the stairs. Goodman, Amira, Musa and his machine gun team, and the rest of the Majevitsa militia followed. Ismail reached the landing and whispered to Goodman and Amira that this was the Great Hall where the Germans assembled before shift change. Amira glanced worriedly at her watch.

*Almost time for the next shift to show up*, thought Goodman. *If Ismail's information is correct.*

They faced a large, cased opening to the left into a gallery with several doors on each of the walls, and a large, metal-banded door at the far end. A set of stairs continued upward to the right. Here, Amira directed Musa's machine gun team to take a position aiming across this main room.

"The radio room is upstairs," Ismail whispered to Amira. He pointed up the curved staircase, and she nodded. Goodman saw her glance at her watch again. 4:58. They were running dangerously late. Amira had a very concerned look.

Goodman pointed to himself and raised four fingers after pointing to the men behind her, then up the stairs. Amira nodded vigorously in agreement. Goodman waved to Tomislav and started up the stairs to secure the staircase and prepare to assault the radio room.

Goodman approached the door at the top of the stairs. This was supposed to be the radio room, according to Ismail. But he'd also admitted that he had never been allowed up here. There was a sign in German on the wall: FUNKRAUM. He waved to Tomislav to read it.

He whispered, "This is it."

*Okay, good.* Goodman nodded and leaned forward to listen through the door. Someone yawned loudly, but he heard nothing else. Amira silently joined them at the top of the stairs.

"All is good, yes?" she whispered.

He nodded in the affirmative. She signaled for her assault team, and all four of the men readied themselves to force the door. Goodman crouched and prepared to aid in the attack on the room.

A sudden burst of machine-gun fire from downstairs hammered their eardrums. The suddenness made Goodman jump.

"Idi!" Amira screamed. Men tripped over each other, trying to get out of her way as she leapt down the stairs three and four steps at a time. Goodman yelled for the four men to knock the door down, but the door swung open on its own. Goodman's eyes met a young German's.

A young SS enlisted man, who stood at all of five feet, four inches tall and weighed in at no more than a hundred forty pounds, stood aghast as the door swung open. His feet left the floor when the first man hit him, and his pistol, barely drawn, flew into the air. He grunted loudly as they trampled him. Goodman opened fire.

Their submachine guns spewed rounds into the room, ricocheting in all directions. Sparks flew, wooden furniture splintered, and bodies twisted and fell as Goodman and his men emptied their magazines. They quickly stepped aside as the next handful of men leapt past them and unleashed a second wave of gunfire into the room. Goodman stepped in and let loose his submachine gun at two Germans who appeared from behind a desk. Mere seconds into the fight, eight SS officers and enlisted men, plus three black-clad Ustaša officers, lay dead on the floor. Goodman quickly peered under the row of tables and fired his weapon at a wounded radio operator as he frantically fumbled to get his pistol from its holster. Goodman walked around the table and stood over him. He put a second round through the top of the man's head and scanned the room quickly, but his eyes returned to the radio operator at his feet. *I just did that*, he thought. *Woah.*

"What did you say?" asked Tomislav as he entered the room.

"Nothing."

Map boards, gridded tracking boards, and charts of all kinds hung on the walls, and other documents fluttered to the floor, some burning or smoking. A small wooden desk fell over under the weight of the dead German officer lying on top of it. Smoke began to fill the room.

"Nothing," said Goodman. He changed magazines. "Where are Amira's radio men?"

"I do not know."

"See if you can get the radios working!"

Tomislav went straightaway to the large radio sets. The noise from downstairs sounded chaotic.

"Prati me!" Goodman yelled to Amira's fighters as he sprinted down the stairs. They stomped down the steps after him and joined the melee in the gallery.

Goodman positioned himself next to Amira as she emptied her magazine into a cluster of camouflage-clad SS troopers charging at them. Goodman dropped three more of them before the others scattered. Musa's machine gun team spewed hundreds of rounds into the room, and Nazis crumpled to the floor. Goodman tried to avoid fellow militiamen as they fired away at the Germans, but the fight was already out of control.

"We need to push them back!" he yelled above the noise.

Goodman tapped Amira on the shoulder and pointed at Mirzad, who had just appeared at the cased opening from the corridor with his men right behind him. Goodman waved to get his attention and made a wide sweeping gesture toward the fight in the Great Room. *Attack, dammit! Attack!*

The Tuzla Union fighters threw themselves en masse at the Germans. A hundred-odd armed men shot at each other point-blank and wrestled or stabbed each other in hand-to-hand combat using pistols, knives, bayonets, and bare hands. Goodman's MP40 jammed, and he slid around a corner to clear it. A hand reached for his face, and he quickly swung his weapon at it. The hands came again, and he clubbed the attacker across the face and over the head. He balled his hand into a fist, but a pistol cracked from behind him, and the SS trooper fell backward. Amira stepped to Goodman's side, pistol raised. She fired again and again until another SS trooper went down, then she changed magazines. Goodman reloaded and aimed. The twisting and swirling tides of the fight temporarily confused his aim. There was no clear shot, so he held his fire.

One of Musa's machine gunners began firing wildly into the swarm of men. *What is he doing?* Goodman put up an arm to stop him, but it did no good. *He's going to hit our own guys!* The man kept firing until Musa knocked him sideways.

Several groups of Germans retreated away from the carnage in the gallery. Mirzad's Unionists swarmed down the corridors after them. Musa and a handful of Majevitsa men sifted through the wounded and dead. Three men dragged a gravely wounded comrade away from the mess, and a medic set to work on him. Others hopped or limped to the corridor. The Majevitsa radio operators appeared.

"Get up to the radio room, immediately!" Amira yelled, pointing up the stairs. They ran.

Goodman was looking through the dead for ammunition or grenades when the door at the far side of the Great Room swung wide, and several astonished faces in SS camouflage appeared. One of Amira's men yelled something primal, and the room burst into gunfire again. Goodman went to his knee and unloaded his entire magazine in one long burst. Dropping his magazine, he raced to the door and inserted the next one. He got to the door and pulled it shut, involuntarily stepping back when he saw dozens of Germans sprinting across the courtyard at him. He turned to Amira with a look of terror.

"They're coming!"

# 55

## THE GREAT ROOM, PLANINA FORTRESS

GOODMAN STUMBLED AND FELL BACKWARD OVER A BODY in the doorway as bullets thumped at the door. He kicked in vain at the door to close it. Musa lowered his shoulder and rammed it shut. Musa lowered the bar and backed away from the drumbeats of bullets impacting the far side of the heavy door.

"How long,"—Goodman gasped for breath—"until they break it down?"

"Bullets will not open this door," said Musa.

Gunfire echoed from multiple corridors as the Tuzla Unionists pressed their attacks against the remaining pockets of Germans. Goodman knelt and replaced his empty magazines with unused ones from a German's ammo pouch. Amira surveyed the carnage in the gallery and looked back at the door. Bullets continued to thump on the far side.

"Now what?" said Musa. He coughed and waved away clouds of acrid gun smoke.

"We should check the radios." Goodman turned to Amira. "Your father's going to want to know."

He and Amira climbed the stairs to the radio room. Two of the radiomen came bounding down together and passed them in a rush. Ismail was with them.

"We need to replace some cable!" one of radiomen yelled.

"And I know where they keep it!" Ismail called back as they disappeared down a hallway.

A trio of pistol shots rang out from the radio room. Amira and Goodman looked at each other and dashed up the steps, weapons ready. They burst into the room together. The room was filled with smoke. Goodman could see no one.

"Tomislav!" Goodman yelled. "You alright?" No answer. *Oh, no!* he thought. "Tomislav!"

Amira kicked a chair out of her way and made for a corner of the room. A small fire drew Goodman's eyes to a space behind a desk. He ran around it and saw Tomislav reaching into a metal box, trying to retrieve pieces of burning paper from within. Tomislav cursed out loud when a piece burned his fingers. He glanced at Goodman and Amira before reaching in to pull more papers out. Goodman pulled him back.

"What are you doing?"

"Trying to stop the fire!" Tomislav pocketed his pistol and got up to his knees. He pointed to the body of a nearby German officer and the Majevitsa radioman lying next to him, face down, blood streaming from a bullet hole in his neck. Amira rolled him over. It was Mustafa.

*Not Mustafa*, thought Goodman. The boy who led him to safety from the ambush after he first left Baba's village. The boy who grew up too quickly. And now, the boy who died too soon. Goodman exhaled loudly, emotionally deflated by the sight. He and Amira helped Tomislav to his feet.

"What happened?" asked Goodman.

"This guy,"—Tomislav pointed at the SS officer with blackened fingers—"This *sturmbannfuhrer* was trying to destroy their codebook, and our man here tried to stop him." He pointed at Mustafa's body. "But he got shot."

"Why didn't you stop him?" Amira demanded.

"I tried!" said Tomislav. "I got here as fast as I could." He held his pistol up. "I tried to save the codebook, but…" He gestured to the charred pages and fragments scattered around the floor. "It's gone."

"It does not matter," said Amira. "What of the radios?"

"They are in working order, we think," said Tomislav. He pointed up a circular metal stair that disappeared into the ceiling. "The antennas are good, but the power supply was cut. The others went to get a new cable—"

A thunderous explosion shook the castle.

"What was that!" Goodman exclaimed.

"The door!" Amira sprinted toward the stairwell. "Get the radios working as quickly as you can!"

Another explosion followed. Then another in quick succession.

"You got this?" Goodman asked Tomislav. Ismail and the other radio operator entered the room, dragging a spool of cable between them.

"I am no radio expert," said Tomislav. "But they are."

Musa yelled from below. Goodman and Amira sprinted down the stairs to see Musa taking aim at the door as another loud explosion impacted outside. The door rattled against its hinges. Goodman instinctively took cover against the wall.

"What are they doing?"

"They're trying to open the door—what do you think?" Amira yelled at him.

Another blast sent sparks into the room. The heavy wooden bar across the door dislodged and tilted when the metal clasp that held it clanked to the floor. Another blast knocked the door inward a few inches, wrenching the ancient iron hinges. A cloud of gray smoke and a sliver of light shone through the crack above the door.

"Isn't there a way to stop them?" Goodman yelled over the blasts. Amira crouched to her knee and took aim with her weapon from behind a stone column. Musa readied his machine gun. Goodman looked at the men around the room, waiting for the onslaught. *There has got to be another way.*

One rifleman stood out like a candle in the smoke. Ademir. Ademir the Sharpshooter from the salt factory. The boy who could hit a gunner on a rooftop in the dark. In the rain. Under fire. Three times.

"Hey! Ademir!"

Ademir looked around for who called him. Goodman caught his eye and waved him over.

"Yes, Effendi!"

"I'm no effendi!" Goodman replied. "Follow me!"

Ademir followed him up the stairs. They ran through the radio room where Tomislav, Ismail, and the others were trying to splice an electrical cable. He reached the circular stair and began to climb, with Ademir right behind. Cables jammed the passage way, and it took some effort to climb without tripping or getting entangled. The roof hatch was open, and Goodman emerged on top and dropped below the knee-high-wall that surrounded the rooftop. The sky was a solid gray.

Like fingers in a stone glove, four stone towers jutted upward, with a fifth tower—by far the tallest—only about fifty yards away. He could see rifle barrels poking through some of the vertical black slits of each of the towers, but, thankfully, there were no such spaces on the near side of the main tower.

Goodman crept to the low wall and peered over it. Four stories below, he saw the large dirt mound of a bunker with a sandbagged doorway and trench built into an L-shape. Four German soldiers stood in front of it. One of them aimed a long tube at the base of the wall below him. The soldiers around him turned their faces and *wham! wham!* The rocket blasted twice: once while leaving the German's shoulder launcher, and a split second later when the high-explosive warhead detonated on that giant, oaken door leading to the gallery. The stone structure vibrated under him.

"Ademir! Get up here!" yelled Goodman. Ademir climbed through the roof hatch and crawled up next to Goodman.

"You see Fritzies?" Goodman pointed. "Down there!"

Ademir peered over the wall. His eyes quickly scanned the surroundings, then lowered to focus on the bunker below.

"Yes, Effendi." He nodded and pulled his rifle to him.

Goodman watched as Ademir seated his rifle into his shoulder and leaned in toward the rear sight. When Goodman took aim, Ademir calmly reached over and laid a hand on Goodman's arm. Goodman understood what he meant: *stay down, don't move, I've got this*.

Ademir put his cheek onto his weapon's shoulder stock, exhaled, and waited. Anxiously, Goodman looked up. Movement in a firing port in the far tower's wall caught his eye, and he saw a glimmer of flesh. Young Ademir exhaled long and slow and waited. The double blast of the anti-tank rocket rocked the courtyard again, and Ademir gently squeezed his trigger. The rifle jumped into his shoulder.

Goodman cautiously peered over the wall again and saw no more movement in the slit on the tower. Ademir cocked and aimed at the same place. He waited. He blinked to refocus, squinted again, and waited. The courtyard echoed loudly with another blast, and Ademir's rifle jumped again. Goodman watched a German helmet fall out a window.

"Do you see those guys down there?" He pointed out the SS trooper with the long-barreled anti-tank weapon, and Ademir nodded. "With the..."—Goodman didn't know the word for what it was—"the... the *bomba...*" The bomb.

"Effendi, do you mean the *panzerfaust*?"

"Yeah," said Goodman. "That guy. Kill him!"

"Yes, Effendi," said Ademir. He lowered his muzzle and let another bullet fly without waiting for a rocket blast. Goodman peered over the top of the wall and saw a dead German with the long tube lying next to him. Ademir fired again, and a German fell into the pit surrounding the bunker in the courtyard. Another shot, and another German stumbled and fell to his knees, then rolled onto his back. Ademir quickly drew back and rotated his bolt open as the other Germans in the courtyard ran for cover.

"Do you have enough ammunition?" Goodman asked.

"Yes, Effendi." Ademir lugged a heavy canvas satchel toward the wall. "I have bullets, Effendi." He proceeded to load them into his chamber.

"Right," said Goodman.

Ademir pulled up to the wall again. He cocked the bolt to chamber a new round, squinted through the sights, and fired. Goodman watched a rifle fall from the top of the farthest tower. Ademir cocked, aimed, fired, then wiped his brow with his sleeve and glanced at Goodman. A smile beamed across his face. The smile disappeared as he cocked his rifle, aimed, and fired again. Goodman lowered himself into the hole in the roof. He looked back at Ademir one more time.

*Glad he's on our side.* Goodman quickly scanned the surrounding towers, walls, and the walkways between before he put his head down and descended the stairs. *Now, how do we take those towers? And that bunker?*

# 56

## EIGHTH PRECINCT GRAMMAR SCHOOL

MILOSZ HESITATED before he apprehensively touched Zoran on the shoulder.

"Pasha," whispered Milosz. "Zoran Pasha…"

"Hmmm?" Zoran blinked his eyes open.

"Zoran Pasha," said Milosz. "The attack is on. We've received a report of fighting *inside* the Planina."

Zoran sat upright, fully awake. "Is it Amira? And the American?"

He looked to the radio operators, seated at the table on the opposite wall. Under the dim light of an oil lamp, they huddled around a humming radio set. They tweaked the dials, their ears strained for a hint of a transmission from Amira's assault force. The air was warm and thick with the scent of the oil smoke.

"No, Pasha," said Milosz. "The report came by courier from Colonel Zbrogan."

"Nothing from Amira?"

The radio operators shook their heads. "No, Pasha," said Milosz.

"My daughter…" Zoran exhaled loudly through his nose and shook his head. This was the decision he knew would be difficult: when to commit the rest of his forces to guarantee the attack is successful. *Do I go or do I wait?* He adjusted his bandoleers and then stood up, making further adjustments to his ensemble to give himself time to think. *To wait is to further the deception against Kozar*, he thought. *But to assault the Planina could hasten the victory. Or merely tip my hand if my daughter does not control the gates. I cannot fight the Germans and the Communists at the same time.* He massaged a tightness in his chest. *My little flower…*

"Milosz…"

"Yes, Pasha?"

"Let's get to the bridge." Zoran stood. "And send a runner to deliver this decision to Colonel Zbrogan."

"He may not want it," Milosz warned him.

"He does not need to want it," said Zoran. *I cannot leave my daughter to die when I can attack and save her.* Zoran thought of his beloved son. And then he thought of that strange American. *I need to save them all*, he thought.

"What about General Kozar's people watching the schoolhouse?"

Zoran felt the hilt of his sword, and it gave him courage. "To hell with Kozar."

"Yes, Pasha."

Minutes later, Zoran's four-hundred-strong force—less the thirty under Amira's command—departed the warehouse district and snaked through the alleys and back streets of Tuzla toward the stone bridge over the River Jala. The bridge that linked south Tuzla to the Planina Fortress. The link between himself and his daughter. *And this foreign-born son of mine.* Between his now and his future, as well as the link between the once great past and the future restoration of his people to greatness. *How could mere stone be so pivotal in my family's history?*

This hour would produce one of only two possible outcomes. Victory would restore the pride of his people and elevate him to power. Anything other than complete victory would be an abominable failure and spell his destruction and the condemnation of his people. Words of failure raced through his mind. *Debasement. Dishonor. Shame.* He flinched and shook the thought away. *That cannot be. It must not be! God would never want that.* He ran faster.

"Milosz," said Zoran. Despite the cold, he was already sweaty and breathless from exertion. And anxiety. "Time is against us. We must hurry!"

"Yes, Pasha!"

*God willing.*

# 57

## PLANINA FORTRESS RADIO ROOM

GOODMAN FOUND ISMAIL AND THE RADIO OPERATORS scratching their heads over the radio sets. They twisted dials and listened for anything close to an audible signal through the headphones. One of them spoke loudly into a microphone and waited. Sporadic gunfire echoed from elsewhere in the fortress.

"Does the radio work?" asked Goodman as he descended the stairs.

"Neh." Ismail shook his head. "Ništa."

"Can you make radio work?" said Goodman. He only saw the two of them in the room. "Wait! Gde Tomislav?" *Where is Tomislav?*

"He went to the commander's office," said Ismail.

"Where is that?"

Ismail pointed toward the main stairs leading down to the great room. "Down the stairs and up the next set of stairs when you turn left around the corner." Goodman replayed the directions in his head as he dashed down the stairs where two of Amira's men were firing their rifles through the crack in the door, and two others were loading theirs.

The commander's office was the only door at the end of a long corridor. Goodman heard papers shuffling, drawers sliding open then slamming shut, and Tomislav's voice cursing.

Goodman stepped silently into the room. A huge desk with a conference table in front of it dominated the room. Maps and notebooks covered the table, which was backed up by a large Nazi flag with its Swastika centered in the white circle on its blood-red field, and the Waffen-SS standard with the iron eagle perched above. Chairs still lined the bare stone walls. Behind the desk, Tomislav was hunched down in front of a bookshelf.

"Tomislav?" Goodman said.

Tomislav spun around with his Walther pistol aimed directly at Goodman.

"Whoa, woah, woah!" Goodman yelled. He held his hands out in front of him, shielding his face. Tomislav quickly lowered his pistol.

"What are you doing here?" said Goodman.

"I—I'm looking for information that may be of use to us," Tomislav replied. He attempted to close a cupboard as he stood, but a broken latch bounced the door open again. A *safe*.

"What are you working on down there?" asked Goodman.

Tomislav looked agitated as Goodman approached and glanced down at the open cupboard door. Goodman rounded the table, and Tomislav pointed into the cupboard.

"I found a safe," he admitted. "I thought it important."

"Yeah," Goodman knelt to inspect the dial on the safe. "Did you find the combination?"

"N—No," he said. "We should go."

"Yeah, right." Goodman watched Tomislav close a satchel and loop the strap over his shoulder. "What you got there?"

"I had nothing to hold ammunition," replied Tomislav. He picked up an MP40 and chambered a round. "Now I do."

"I thought you didn't do gunfights," said Goodman.

"This seems to be a prudent time."

"Yeah…right." *He's acting odd. What was he doing in here? What's really in the bag?*

Tomislav exited the room and ran down the stairs. Goodman followed. Musa and about a dozen Majevitsa men met them in the Great Room. They looked utterly exhausted. Several sat down with their backs to the walls and wiped their faces on their sleeves, which were covered in grime and streaked with sweat.

"What happened?" asked Goodman.

"What?" said Musa, extra loudly.

"What happened?" Goodman yelled back. *He must be deaf from the gunfire.*

"There's a lot of fucking rooms…too many rooms!" Musa cried out, breathless, exhausted. "The unionist fighters needed help with the last of the Germans in the castle." Colonel Zbrogan's people streamed into the great room and collapsed against the opposite wall.

Goodman looked at the men firing through the door to the courtyard. "What's going on with them?"

Musa wiped sweat from his face and yelled back. "The Germans are very tough. The Tuzla Unions tried to attack from one of the other doors against the towers, but the Germans are fighting from the towers. And from the bunker. It blocks the door."

"Where is Amira?" Goodman yelled. Musa shrugged his shoulders. A loud burst of gunfire echoed from one of the corridors. Then Amira's voice shrieked out over the noise. Several explosions reverberated through the stone structure.

"We need to get to that bunker!" yelled Goodman. "I'm going!"

Musa just waved him on and struggled to lift himself to his feet.

Goodman crossed the great room and entered the corridor producing the most noise. There he found Amira with most of her fighters jammed against the walls, avoiding the gunfire from the door to the courtyard. Goodman elbowed his way through the crowd to her.

"Where have you been?" she demanded.

"I've been busy!" he retorted.

She ignored his response and started issuing commands to the Majevitsa fighters and the Unionists alike, and Tomislav translated for him.

"We have cleared out the Germans from every corner of the main structure. Zbrogan's people took the first tower," he said. "But they are stuck with no way to move across the walls to take the second tower. The other towers are still under German control."

"So is the bunker!" said Goodman.

One of Amira's men ran to them with a heavy satchel. He let it fall from his shoulders with a loud *clunk,* and several long-handled German *Stielhandgrenaten* potato masher grenades rolled out. The bag was full of them. Amira picked up two and crammed them into her belt, then picked up two more. The others did the same as she unscrewed the cap at the base and unraveled the pull-string. She looked at Goodman.

"Well, *Američko*, are you going to be useful? Or should I put you in a safe place?"

Goodman could not tell if she was teasing him, or if she was really irritated. Regardless, he picked up two of the grenades and unscrewed their caps. He met her eyes and glared at her. She smirked back at him. He decided on some choice words for her when this was done.

"Get the rest of the men!" she barked at the nearest militiaman. Less than a minute later, the surviving Majevitsa warriors appeared. Only sixteen of them.

"Did you get through to my father on the radio?" she asked her radio man.

"No, Amira Effendim, we did not."

"It does not matter," she said. "Soon we'll have control of the Planina and—"

"And your father and mine will walk across the River Jala and through the open gates into their Planina!" It was 'Director' Mirzad. "And we will control Tuzla!"

"The Planina will be my father's seat!" she retorted.

Goodman sensed a growing argument. "Right now," he interrupted. "We have to take the towers, right? Right?"

His words were ignored. Both Mirzad and Amira were strangling each other with their eyes. Goodman nodded to Musa, and they both stepped forward.

Goodman gave Mirzad a hard shove against the wall and jammed his pistol into the man's neck. Mirzad's eyes narrowed and shone darkly. Musa stepped in right behind Goodman and stared into Mirzad's face. Goodman released his grip on Mirzad's collar, but Musa remained postured over Mirzad, who was at least a foot shorter than Musa.

*Good*, thought Goodman. *That little bastard*. He turned to Amira. "We only have a little time."

"Yes, you are right." She pushed her hair out of her face. "We go from here to the first tower and then to the ammunition supply bunker."

"Yes, of course." Mirzad agreed.

"And you will attack the remaining towers at the north, east, and south walls."

"Yes, Effendim." Mirzad looked each of them in the face and then looked at his watch.

"Two minutes?" said Amira. She glanced at her watch and put it back in her pocket.

"Yes, Effendim." Mirzad turned and ran back the way he came.

Amira looked at Goodman in the eyes and nodded ever so slightly. *Thank you for backing me up*. At least that was what Goodman took from it.

"Tower number five is the key to the Planina defenses," she said. "However, the passage to the tower is blocked by debris, and the Germans are covering it with machine-gun fire. We cannot take it yet! Musa, you will attack through this door along the west wall and take tower number three. From there, you will assist the Unionists with gunfire against the other towers."

"Yes, Amira Effendim." He straightened up confidently and dipped his head.

"You and I will take the bunker?" said Goodman.

326

"Yes, you and I will lead the attack against the ammunition bunker," she replied. She turned back to Musa. "Once you have taken tower three, do not stop shooting. I will bring you ammunition from the bunker. When the other towers are properly suppressed, we will attack through the tunnel and take tower five. Musa, take your men, and God be praised."

Musa bowed again before directing his fighters to assume positions and prepare to attack. Amira turned to Goodman.

"Američko, you are to come with me." He bowed.

"What is this?" she said. "You are bowing to me now?"

"I am learning, Amira Effendim…"

"Good. See that you don't die." But their eyes stayed with each other for just a slight moment. She looked away before muttering, "My father would kill me."

*Wait, what?* Goodman thought it wise not to acknowledge the remark. But he felt a wave of something come over him. In his gut, he wanted to say something, but he held his mouth shut. She turned away and took on her usual harshness.

"Prati me!" she called out as the fighters—Majevitsa and Unionist alike—changed magazines, chambered rounds, and shouldered their packs again. "Is the way clear?" she asked the men at the door.

"To the bunker, yes, Effendim," one replied. "Most of the Fritzies have abandoned the bunker and fled to the towers."

She peered through the crack. Goodman looked over her shoulder. Three Germans were sheltering from Ademir's precision fire under an overhang, and at least two more were visible in the entrance to the ammunition bunker. One took a frantic shot upwards at Ademir and quickly took cover again. Amira glanced at her watch.

"We wait for Mirzad's attacks," she said. "Then, when the Germans are firing up at them, we attack." Everyone nodded, and Amira put her watch away. She stood at the door, watching.

A cry let loose from somewhere above the courtyard, and machine guns filled the air with white hot lead. The noise reached an immediate, ear-piercing crescendo. Amira lowered herself into a cat-like crouch with her MP40 tucked into her shoulder. The weapon vibrated in her hands, and spent casings leapt into the air.

"Idi!" she screamed.

Goodman and Musa yanked on the door, and it fell loose from the crumbling stone around the hinges. It landed with a resounding clap on the floor.

"Prati me!" she screamed again. She was first through the door and emptied her magazine into the mouth of the bunker. A German soldier fell backward into the sandbag wall. Goodman stepped out and fired his own weapon. The SS troopers under the overhang crumpled to the ground. The last one ran for his life and died before his head hit the rocky ground.

Goodman, Amira, and the others charged the bunker. Sandbags split open, and sand sprayed into the air as rounds tore into them. A German rose to fire but fell into the opening. Two men running next to Goodman went down with loud grunts. Goodman dropped to the ground and sprayed the remainder of his magazine at the camouflage-clad Germans as they desperately tried to withdraw from the frontal assault. A handful of them chose to attack instead. Goodman fumbled his fresh magazine, and it skidded away from him. He reached into his pouch for another, but the Nazis were already running toward him. Goodman pulled his dagger as the first trooper leapt over him, firing and scattering hot brass cartridges. Goodman's blade caught the second Nazi in the leg. The man fell and clutched his thigh, his pant leg red with blood. His eyes met Goodman's, and he reached for his pistol.

Goodman jumped on top of the man and rammed his knife into his torso over and over again. The German clawed at Goodman's face. Pressing down with his hand into the man's neck, Goodman jammed the blade in one last time. The Nazi's hands and arms went limp. Goodman fell over into the red dirt, heaving deep breaths. A spray of dirt brought him back to the moment. He saw giant Musa lead his men into tower three. *Good*, thought Goodman. *Plan's working*. He rolled over, reached for his next magazine, inserted it, chambered a round, and looked for Amira.

She stood at the bunker's entrance, crouched behind the collapsed sandbag walls, exchanging fire with the Germans holed up in the trench around the bunker. Others were protecting her from gunfire from the towers and positions on the walls. Goodman crawled across the open courtyard and joined her.

"The Germans are fighting hard!" she yelled as she changed magazines.

"No kidding!" Goodman let loose with a burst around the corner. Another burst answered it from within the bunker. "They have all the ammo!" He fired again, and the unseen Nazi returned with several shots of his own. Then the firing paused.

Goodman peered around the corner. *His weapon is jammed!* Goodman thought. He looked at Amira. She thought so, too. He pointed to her and himself and counted down with his fingers: *three, two, one...*

Goodman aimed around the corner and let loose a stream of bullets, which thumped into the other side of the sandbags. Then, together, he and Amira leapt over the sandbags and rounded the first corner. One German soldier was there, on his knees, struggling with the charging handle of his weapon. Amira shot him in the face, and the man fell backward.

Still together, they rounded the last corner and charged down the steps into the bunker, weapons blazing. Their twin muzzle blasts split the darkness like lightning. The interior of the bunker was enormous and packed with shelf upon shelf of ammunition crates, shells, explosive rounds, and numerous other containers. Goodman glimpsed the bloody and terrified faces of the last two German holdouts and the two *Stielhandgrenaten* sticks dropping from their already dead hands to the floor. One bounced, then the other.

*No!*

The electric shock of terror swept across his skin. Blood surged into his ears, and every muscle contracted. Goodman stumbled backward and rammed into Amira, who was already scrambling away. He shoved her up the stairs and into the daylight. He heard a scream. They stumbled, and Amira slipped and caught herself. They clawed to get away. Goodman tripped again.

The ground lifted him into the hot air, and, before his sight left him, he saw the fortress walls and the fiery yellow and gray clouds rush at him. But everything was upside down, spinning. He heard nothing but a loud hiss.

✷✷✷

# 58

## GRAND BALLROOM, ROYAL STAR HOTEL, CENTRAL TUZLA COMMERCIAL DISTRICT

GENERAL KONSTANTIN KOZAR STORMED OUT OF HIS ROOM. That explosion was far too large to be anything unimportant. *Why did no one report an engagement to me?*

"What the hell was that?" he demanded as he buttoned his tunic. The medals on his chest jingled and his boots squeaked on the floor. His aide-de-camp fell off his cot in the hallway and scrambled to his feet.

Kozar kicked the door open to the command center before the sleepy-eyed guard could reach the doorknob. The night watch officer put down his radio handset and stood at attention, clipboard in hand. Nearby, eight young female radio operators scribbled in their logbooks, trying to piece together what the various units were telling them. Other young officers hounded them for more information.

"Wake the hell up, you lazy bastards!" Kozar demanded. "What was the source of that explosion?"

"Comrade General, we are trying to verify the origin of the blast," said the watch officer. "Also, Comrade General, we have confirmed reports of gunfire at the primary German garrison in the Planina Fortress, south of Tuzla City. And we have a report of thievery inside the newspaper offices."

"Theft? What? Who gives a damn about that? Tell me where that blast came from!" said General Kozar, scanning the wall-sized map of northeastern Bosnia while he buttoned his tunic. His eyes traced the lines of the various German Army and SS units to their locations in and around Tuzla. He ignored the Ustaša unit symbols. He considered them to be nothing but brutish, semi-useful idiots of the Germans. *Untrained animals.* His mind quickened with calculations of time and distance to make sense of the fragmented information before him. "Are the Germans staging an escape?"

"We do not yet know, Comrade Gen—"

"The entire Tuzla valley woke up twenty seconds ago, and my staff has no idea what is going on? Dammit!" He slapped the map board, sending notes and pushpins clattering to the floor.

"No...I mean...Comrade General...we are trying to confirm, Comrade General. There are conflicting reports..."

Kozar moved to the map of the Tuzla valley tacked on a wall where a large gilded-frame mirror once hung. He read the unit and operational symbols scrawled in various places in and around the city. He refocused on the Planina.

"What are you doing?" he muttered to himself. "General Dietrich's corps is still in the Konju Range. Now, which of your garrison commanders is panicking?" His eyes bounced between the five positions still held by the Germans or the Ustaša.

"What was that, Comrade General?" The watch officer and the operations officer stood to attention.

"Shut up!"

"Yes, Comrade General." The men backed away. The watch officer thumbed through a wad of notes the communications chief handed him and pointed to a location south of Tuzla. "The explosion is reported to have come from the Planina Fortress, south of the city—the German SS regional command and headquarters garrison for the Fifth Mountain SS Division. General Johann Dietrich, commanding."

"I know who the commander is, dammit! Tell me something I can act on!"

Kozar scratched at the scruff on his chin. *Someone is trying to break out of my encirclement,* he thought. *Johan, are you trying to flee?* Gestapo headquarters, an SS anti-partisan battalion... and the Nazis' primary arms and munitions depot for the region. *The SS has the remnants of a strike battalion, but they are hardly fit for anything other than local security. The Ustaše battalions are battalions in name only, able to deploy only a few scores of soldiers at most. Undisciplined soldiers, at that.*

Several other officers filled the command center and harassed the radio operators for some bit of new information to share with the general. The staff operations director, his tunic un-buttoned, assaulted the radio operators with his own questions. Each of them shouted to be heard over the others as the poor radio operators shouted into their radio microphones.

"Comrade Colonel!" called out an operations officer, a major. "The Planina is not attempting a breakout!"

"So, which garrison is attempting a breakout?" replied the operations director. Kozar turned to listen.

"None, Comrade Colonel," said the major, thumbing through the notes being shoved into his hands.

"None?" Kozar interrupted.

"None of our units are reporting being engaged," the watch officer told him.

Kozar turned from the operations director to the watch officer. "Then who is shooting?"

The senior watch officer turned back to his stack of notes and desperately hoped for someone else to speak up and take the commander's attention away from him. The operations director shook his head. Kozar's vice commander folded his arms and stared at the map. Kozar narrowed his eyes. He thought about the faces around the table at the dinner last evening. Faces of the resistance militias. *That mountain hillbilly—what was his name? Dudovic. The one who called himself a pasha or some other Ottoman nonsense. He seemed to be the most resistant to the agreement. But he could not hope to outmatch my forces. Or would he?*

"Where are our brothers from the Majevitsa?" Kozar asked, his head cocked to one side, awaiting the answer.

"Are they not in the east precinct?" said his senior watch officer.

"Do not answer my question with another damned question!" Kozar's face reddened. "Find me the answer!"

"As of the top of the hour," said one operations officer. "They were all in the East Precinct school and the warehouses on the edge of the city."

"I said now!" Kozar clenched his jaw. "Not almost an hour ago."

The watch officers turned to their radio operators and repeated the questions, which then were repeated to other radio operators across Tuzla Sector. Kozar pretended to study the map board as his operations officers and watch officers looked over the shoulders of the radio operators, reading their notebooks as they scribbled. One of the radio operators tugged on the senior watch officer's sleeve. He motioned for her to stand.

"Comrade General!" called out one radio operator. "They are no longer in their designated holding areas!"

"What!"

Another young lieutenant raised her arm. "Comrade General! An armed force…" She pressed a finger to the ear-piece on her headset. "A large, armed force…is moving…into the central districts of Tuzla." She closed her eyes to listen closer. "…from the east."

"Who is that?" demanded the watch officer. "What unit is that?"

She removed her earpiece and looked up at him. "No identity, Comrade Colonel."

"How large?" said Kozar.

"Battalion or larger, Comrade Gen—"

"Govno!" Kozar pounded on the map, sending more pins and notes to the floor. "They were supposed to be under surveillance!" He turned back to the map. *Where are you going? If you are gone, I'll make you suffer. The Planina. He wanted the Planina, at least our sources said as much. Do I respond and deploy my forces? Or do I simply sift through the detritus when you are spent?* He spun on his heels. "Stop them! Stop them immediately! Close down the central district! Do not allow them the reach the Jala bridge!"

"The bridge, sir?"

"Yes, they are going to the Planina!" Kozar snatched his greatcoat from the hook outside his door and stormed down the main stairwell, barking orders to whomever was within earshot. "Get my driver!"

His aide-de-camp and driver chased him down the steps with armfuls of map cases, hats, coats, and pistol belts. A column of officers followed in their wake, donning their hats, belts, and overcoats as they went.

# 59

## PLANINA FORTRESS COURTYARD

GOODMAN FELT SOMEONE HEAVE HIM UP BY HIS COLLAR and then drop him. A face he did not recognize looked down on him, then, just as abruptly, the face disappeared. He laid his head back down on the hard stone. Muffled sounds filtered through the mass of dirt in his ears. He lifted his head and opened his eyes again. Thick, dull clouds fogged over his brain, and confused thoughts made no sense of what he saw. Bodies, rocks, jagged beams of roughhewn wood, mangled weapons, broken crates, a twisted set of metal shelves. He shook his head. *What happened?* His left hand did not work quite right. *What the hell—?*

Bursts of gunfire cut through the fog and brought him back to the horrible now. He blinked and wiped his face repeatedly. Propping himself up, he scanned his surroundings. Machine guns ripped the air and sprayed tracers in all directions. Men ran along the walls, fighting and shoving one another. Someone fell from the wall across from him, while others climbed the stone staircases. A large, jagged shadow loomed over him. He looked up and scowled. *There should be a tower there.* Tower Five was not there, at least not all of it. Several tons of gray stone and mortar lay strewn across the courtyard in front of him. Bodies of men sprawled in all directions, intertwined with the beams and brick. Lots of the bodies wore German uniforms, and a few men were clad in the skins and thick linens of mountain folk. Then, his eyes snagged on a feminine shape.

*Amira!*

Goodman half dragged himself, half crawled over to her. Unsteady arms dropped him short, and he pulled himself to her. She lay on her back, her hair covering her face, her limbs twisted and covered in debris. He pushed the largest of the boards away, then brushed hair and dirt away from her face before lifting her eyelids, one by one. Glassy dullness was all he saw. *No pupillary response.* He thought he felt a pulse in her wrists, but his own shaking made him unsure. He felt no breaks or separations in her arms, legs, or neck. His hands came up dirty, but no blood. There were lots of cuts and abrasions, but no penetrations of her torso, no bones protruding. He lifted her head to feel for lacerations, and his hands came back sticky and dark red.

He tore a strip of cloth from her tunic and wadded it up. Blood poured from the unseen wound when he tried to apply the makeshift bandage.

*Oh, God, no!*

Goodman pressed the bloody rag to the back of her head. Blood pooled on the stone beneath her. *Dammit, Amira!* He cut her vest into strips with his knife and bound them to her head.

*Don't you die! Don't you dare die!*

He hunched over her to apply more pressure to her wound. A blast showered them with dirt and gravel, and he threw himself over her to shield her. He felt the heavy clods and rocks pelt his back. A loud cheer drew his attention, prompting him to raise his head.

Musa exited Tower Two, leading a long line of Germans, humbled and harassed, with their hands over their heads. A mix of Majevitsa men and Unionist fighters herded the Germans to a corner of the courtyard and shoved them to the ground. Goodman sat up and looked down at Amira. *I'm sorry, Amira,* he thought. *I don't know what else to do for you.* He realized he was clenching her hands, but he could not let go. The pressure behind his eyes compounded the throbbing already drumming through his head. He did not know what he was waiting for. He tore himself free, let out a sob, and wiped his eyes.

Goodman searched for a weapon and found a functioning MP40 that was still loaded. He limped over toward Musa, but Musa busily ran from man to man, urging them to keep up their fire.

"What are we doing?" Goodman yelled above the gunfire.

"That's the last tower!" He pointed at Tower Four. "But we're running out of ammunition! Mirzad's people are almost out as well!" The lower floors of the tower belched black smoke, which proceeded to billow up the exterior walls. A stream of blood ran from Musa's shoulder down to his wrist. Goodman tore Musa's sleeve and wrapped it several times around the wound. With exhausted eyes, Musa casually glanced at what Goodman was doing.

"Where's Amira?" he asked. Goodman looked at him and shook his head. Not a word was spoken. Musa's arms went slack, and his mouth dropped. He fell against the stone wall, dazed.

Another loud cheer went up from all around them, and the gunfire ceased. Goodman and Musa looked up at the last German stronghold in Tower Four. A white flag protruded from the uppermost level. Gray and camouflage-clad men crowded against the parapet on the rooftop. More pieces of white material appeared from the firing ports.

"Now they want to surrender!" said Musa. "The tower's still on fire!"

*Let them burn.* Goodman's head was full of angry, vicious thoughts. He mostly just wanted them to die. Everyone. The Nazis, the Ustaši, the Chetniks, the Partisans. All of them. *Just die.*

"What do you want to do?" Musa asked him. With Amira gone, now dead, that left Goodman to figure things out until Zoran linked up with them.

"We need…" Goodman forced words but struggled with the thoughts. "We need to put them, the Germans…all of them…into a place to keep them until Zoran comes…"

On Tower Four, the uppermost door burst open and German soldiers streamed out onto the short catwalk to the outer wall and down the stairs. The bunker in the northwest corner also sprouted several white flags, and men walked out, arms raised, into the guns of the Tuzla Union militia. Columns of oily black smoke from Tower Four and the ruins of Tower Five soared into an otherwise royal blue sky. The gray crater that was once the ammunition bunker still smoldered.

Goodman suddenly felt sick and took a knee, then fell to his hands. Bile filled his mouth and spit. He gulped down cool air and listened to his breathing. He looked up at the sky. Musa was still there, bloodied, holding his machinegun like a toy. The boundary between cold shade and warm morning sun sliced the western wall of the Planina Fortress in half. Goodman stood up, and then he, too, was split between the shade and the light. He squinted into the sun, looking for Amira, half hoping he would see her walking toward him. But she did not.

She was still exactly where he last saw her.

# 60

## THE RIVER MARKET, SOUTH CENTRAL TUZLA

ZORAN AND MIKHAIL'S COMBINED FORCE ARRIVED AT THE BRIDGE just ahead of the trucks carrying the bulk of General Kozar's reinforcements. Zoran smiled grimly at the Partisan guard force commander as he pushed past him, just ahead of the chaos of several hundred men surging into an already crowded plaza. Fighters from both sides pushed and shoved their way into positions along the riverbank and nearby buildings. Just as Zoran directed, his men wedged against each other—and the Partisan soldiers already there—to claim rooftops and balconies facing the river. A punch here and a jab with a rifle butt there grew into numerous fistfights, but no one had seen fit to kill a fellow countryman. Not yet, at least.

"Zoran Mehmetović Dudović!" General Kozar pushed his way through his ranks. "What is this thing that you are doing?" He marched past a large stone fountain in the middle of the boulevard.

Zoran met his stare and straightened up. "General Kozar, you are an outsider here. This is a Bosnian matter!"

Kozar looked around at the men staring at him, giving each a good look, cementing himself in each man's mind. He used his flanks of aides and wireless radio operators as a phalanx. Dozens of fighters of all stripes turned to watch the encounter. More than a few switched their safeties off.

"Colonel Zbrogan!" Kozar put his hands on his hips. "I am even more surprised to see you are a part of this ridiculous enterprise." He set his jaw. "Walk with me, both of you," he said. "The air here is full of passions." Kozar led them to a stone parapet at the edge of the riverbank, where he withdrew a cigarette from a shiny silver case. Zbrogan accepted a cigarette when Kozar offered. Zoran refused, and Kozar slid the case back into his pocket.

"What is this, Zoran?" Kozar began. "Colonel Zbrogan? I know what you are doing."

Several loud explosions echoed from the fortress as streaks of tracers arced high into the sky and burned out. The three men paused to look over the river at the gray rock walls and towers. Black columns of smoke drifted upward into the sky.

"This is disappointing, Zoran, very disappointing. Not ten hours ago, I believed we were of one mind on how we approach this problem of the German Army in the Tuzla Valley. I have the forces, the artillery, the resources of People's Liberation Army, and the legitimacy of the People's Congress. You have a few hundred volunteers, mostly farmers and tradesmen, I think, yes?"

Neither Mikhail nor Zoran said anything.

"Did you know there are more than 180,000 members in the People's Liberation Army? Yes, I personally believe there are many more than that, but that is the official count. We don't want to appear too strong, as it may threaten our alliance with the Allies. Speaking of our western Allies, you have one, don't you? An American, I believe, yes?" Kozar cocked his head to one side.

This concerned Zoran. *How does he know about the American? How much do you know, you godless pig?* Zoran said nothing in reply.

"Well, in any case, I have made inquiries into your American, this pilot that you found somewhere, so it is good of you to keep him safe. After all, it will look very good when Marshall Tito engages next with the Allies for more support. They will see how good we are with their lost pilots, no?"

"You are not Bosnian, General Kozar," said Zoran. "This is Bosnia. You may have anywhere else in Yugoslavia. Leave our homeland for us. Bosnia is for the Bosnians."

Kozar pulled his cigarette from his lips. "Zoran, you are such a dreamer. You know this can never be. The people's revolution must be allowed to flourish. The old ways of living, governing, and thinking are dead. Or, in your case, they are dying." Kozar put his foot on a rock and gestured toward the fortress. Gunfire echoed as he spoke.

"Do you hear that? Colonel Zbrogan! I know *you* are of sound mind. That is the sound of your people, your family, dying. I give you some credit for infiltrating the fortress. I do not know how you got in there, but you did, and now your people are paying for your arrogance."

Kozar inhaled cigarette smoke and slowly exhaled, letting the smoke curl around his head and swirl away in the wind before resuming. "In the greater picture, your backward ways will not exist in less than a generation. We must modernize. We must unite behind the Party and the people... the people. The people, Zoran, and the Party are one. This…" He gestured back toward the forces arrayed across the tops of buildings, on balconies, in storefronts, and along the riverbank. "This war will end, and Marshall Josef Tito will be in control of all of Yugoslavia. Perhaps more, who knows? We will be in command of the economy, the military, the engines of industry, and Yugoslavia is strategically located at the crossroads of Europe, Asia, and the Mediterranean. This is the beginning of the rise of the People's Republic of Yugoslavia. Get on board, Zoran, or get shoved off."

Zoran ground his teeth. *You miserable son of a bitch.* It was all he could think.

Kozar took another drag on his cigarette. The sound of gunfire abated, and all three men glanced across the river. A thick column of oily black smoke rose from one of the towers. Zoran pointed a thick finger at the surrounding hills.

"So, if you are in charge, then where are these people who follow you that you speak of?" Zoran took the offensive. "They do not live here. Do you have them in your shirt pocket, eh?"

"Zoran…" Kozar flicked his cigarette over the wall. "Shut up. You do not appear willing to reason, so you will be given the heel of my boot. Give us the fortress and give us the American pilot. And we may return to you your lives and lands. For now, at least." He turned to Mikhail. "Colonel Zbrogan, I extend the same offer to you and your people. Your people are at least modern and educated, building the engines of industry for the coming age. Do not go down with these…these mountain people."

Kozar put his hands on his hips. "I give the two of you ten minutes to decide your fate." He gave one last hard look at the two of them before walking back to his staff, who had gathered by the fountain.

Zoran looked at the castle walls and thought of his daughter as he made his way back to the bridgehead with Mikhail. They climbed over the low rail and stood at the line where the bricks of the market plaza met the stones of the bridge. Zoran examined the massive doors at the other end of the bridge, only fifty yards away. *Have you won the day, my daughter? The shooting has stopped,* he thought. *What has become of you? What has become of my future?* He rubbed his left shoulder, suddenly realizing that the throbbing ache had become a stabbing pain in his chest. Zoran exhaled loudly and put his hands on his hips, then bent over at the waist.

# 61

## PLANINA FORTRESS, SOUTH OF TUZLA RIVER MARKET

GOODMAN HEARD MIRZAD BEFORE HE SAW HIM. He was magnanimous. Goodman glanced at Musa, and they both watched Mirzad descend the stairs from the north wall.

"This is a great day!" he cried out. "We have the Planina! The greatest battlement between the Sava and Sarajevo! Be proud, men, be proud!"

He raised a fist into the air and cheered for his men, a few of whom responded, albeit with much more somber tones. He strode up to Musa and Goodman with his arms outstretched. They did not reflect Mirzad's celebratory mood, and his smile disappeared when he got close.

"What?" he said. He looked around as the men from both militias herded the prisoners into the bunker-turned-crater and consolidated captured equipment into large piles. "This is a great day! What is wrong with you?"

Musa and Goodman turned to the rows of dead and wounded fighters from both groups lining the walls. The wounded sat or laid together, but the dead were separated according to the Muslims from the Majevitsa and the Christians from Tuzla. Three men carried Amira's body on a blanket and set it down near them. Mirzad peered over their shoulders.

"Is that…?"

"Yes," said Musa.

"Oh…God be with her…" Mirzad crossed himself. "I shall pray for her soul, though she is not a Christian…" He shook his head and marched off. Goodman and Musa turned back to Amira's body and knelt beside her. Musa whispered a prayer under his breath. An older Majevitsa man approached and removed his hat to await their attention.

"What do you have for us?" said Musa.

"A thousand pardons, Effendi, but Zoran Pasha awaits on the other side of the river."

Musa and Goodman looked at each other. A new wave of exhaustion weighed them down.

"Open the doors!" Goodman ordered.

Men from the Majevitsa and Tuzla swarmed over the mass of debris the Germans had piled up to block the massive doors that formed the main entrance to the Planina's courtyard. Unionists and Majevitsa men alike cleared the debris in minutes, and lined up to pull the huge chains that controlled them. The chains clanked as they drew taut, and men's heels slipped and scraped at the earthen floor of the courtyard. The doors creaked at first, but jammed less than six inches apart. One of the older militiamen approached Musa and Goodman.

"The doors are stuck, Effendi," he said. "The Germans destroyed the gears, and the doors must be lifted. It will take some effort before we can get them open."

Musa shook his head. "Where is the Timović boy?" he said.

The older man turned and cupped his hands around his mouth. "Dusan! Dusan! Come here, boy!"

A short, dirty-faced teenaged boy who looked like he weighed in at all of ninety pounds ran up to Musa. His rifle was almost as tall as he was.

"Here I am, Effendi!"

"Go tell Zoran Pasha the Planina is ours," Musa told him. "Hurry!"

"Yes, Effendi!" He turned to go, but abruptly stopped and stared at Amira's body. "Is that Amira Effendim?" The look of shock on the boy's face was unmistakable. "She is dead?"

Goodman felt a sour knot in his stomach. *This is going to be a major problem*, he thought. *What will Zoran do if—when—he finds out? That won't go well for whatever that mess looks like outside the walls. Do we tell him? Can we not tell him? Is that even possible? How could I keep this information from a father—her father?* He knew how vital Amira is—was—to Zoran. *She's his everything.* He shoved the next five minutes through his mind repeatedly, and every outcome of either choice was disastrous. Only a few minutes separated every sad ending from the other. *Zoran will find out soon enough. There will be time for that*, Goodman decided. *But not now.* But the boy was already tearing up.

"I no think Zoran know her death." Goodman's pidgin Bosanski suddenly felt insufficient again. "This big problem for Zoran." Musa gave him a puzzled look.

"Say nothing to Zoran!" said Goodman.

"He is right," said Musa. "Say nothing!"

The boy wiped his tears. "Y—Yes, Effendi…" He sniffled.

Musa dismissed the boy to find Zoran. The boy weaved his way through the rows of men at the gate and disappeared in the narrow space between the ancient oak and iron doors.

Goodman turned back to Amira's body. He stroked hair from her face and arranged her arms back to her sides. Her skin felt cold. Dead cold. *This is going to kill Zoran.*

"Don't do that!" Musa reached down and pushed his hands away from her. "It is not good for a Christian to touch one of our dead! We have our ways of caring for our dead."

"Why does that matter now?"

"It matters." Musa covered her with the blanket.

*What am I doing?* he thought. *I know this.* "Alright." He pulled a corner of the blanket over her shoulder, but pulled it back. He looked closer. *Goosebumps*, he thought. *She has goosebumps!*

Goodman stood up. "She's alive!"

# 62

## THE BRIDGE OVER THE JALA RIVER BETWEEN THE PLANINA AND THE TUZLA RIVER MARKET

ONE OF THE MAJEVITSA MEN APPROACHED MILOSZ and pointed to a boy running toward them across the bridge. Milosz turned and his face lit up.

"Zoran Pasha," he said quietly. "A messenger from the Planina…"

Zoran looked toward the fountain where General Kozar and his staff were paying very little attention to him or anything happening on the bridge. Zoran snapped his fingers at Colonel Zbrogan. Together, they walked toward the boy who was waving his arms.

"We have the Planina!" he cried out. "We have the Planina!"

"They did it!" Milosz exclaimed. "What now?"

Zoran looked at the Partisan generals by the fountain and turned back to Zbrogan and Milosz. He drew his pistol. "We are going *now*!"

Zoran ignored the pain in his chest and took off at a run toward the giant gate. Milosz hurriedly corralled handfuls of their men to get moving. He waved to others, and they, too, ran southward across the rampart to the bridge. Still others saw the motion and ran to catch up. A great tide of men and weapons began to flow across the stone bridge over the Jala River.

Some of Kozar's officers yelled for their men to rush the bridge, while others ordered them to halt. Partisans collided with one another, but quickly, hundreds of fighters of all groups rushed for the Planina. Then Kozar's officers started to get control of their people again, and only the Majevitsa and Tuzla Unionists continued to flow southward. They didn't notice the ranks of uniformed Partisans forming behind them at the north end of the bridge.

"But Zoran Pasha!" yelled the boy. "Zoran Pasha! Uncle, wait, there is more!" The boy kept getting shoved out of the way.

"Never mind, boy!" Milosz yelled at him. "We will all soon be in the Planina, and you can tell us then!"

At the north end of the bridge, where the bricks met the stones, three ranks of Communist Partisans each formed, their weapons raised, awaiting a signal to fire at the backs of the militia fighters dashing across the bridge. Hundreds more Partisans moved into position behind those ranks, obstructing the remainder of the militia fighters from joining their comrades already crossing the bridge. Numerous fights broke out. The fights soon merged into a very large brawl, with yelling and cursing. A single gunshot rang out, and everyone turned to see what it was.

"Zoran!" yelled Milosz.

# 63

ONLY TEN YARDS FROM THE PLANINA GATE, Zoran slowly turned to again face General Kozar. He watched Kozar holster his pistol and push through the crowd of Majevitsa men. Zoran puffed his chest out and squared his shoulders as he faced Kozar.

"Pasha!" Milosz exclaimed. "Look out!"

Zoran looked at Milosz, and Milosz's eyes told him to look to his right. He turned slightly, drew his pistol, and saw Mikhail's pistol aimed squarely at his face. Their pistols almost touched muzzles. Men of both armies gaped in bewildered horror at what their leaders were doing to each other.

"Zoran," said Mikhail. "This cannot continue."

"You piece of shit Serb," replied Zoran. "Mikhail, you are a coward. You sheep of the communists! Son of a whore!" His pounding heart screamed at the betrayal. His hands quivered with rage.

"Zoran, please," said Mikhail. "You are foolish to think we will survive this if you continue."

"You traitor!" Zoran shot back. "You wretched cur! You betray your people! You betray me!"

"No, Zoran," said Mikhail. "It is you. Your arrogance, your greedy lust for power! You go too far. You have brought us face to face with our destruction. It must end now before everything that remains is taken from us."

The two patriarchs stood there, glaring at each other, only a twitch away from destroying their families. Zoran's mind raced, fears dueling with determination. *Do I kill this man? My cousin?* He gripped his pistol. His aches grew more intense. *Zoran,* he thought to himself. *You might have been a fool.* He blinked when a bead of sweat dripped into his eye.

General Kozar's men held their position on the north end of the bridge, and hundreds more now lined the northern riverbank. The rooftops and balconies were now a collective mile-long fortress, with every eye and weapon focused on the three men at the center of the bridge. For a moment, the only thing anyone heard was water rushing over the rocks in the river below.

Kozar stood again with his hands on his hips. His holster was still unbuttoned.

"Did you think you could get away with this?" He raised his hand and swept the breadth of the fortress with it.

Zoran kept his eyes burning into Mikhail with pistol and sword ready. "I was doing you a favor, Kosta!" he yelled. "There were too many Germans!"

The general smirked. "Ah, yes, Zoran. You are most generous. A true man of the people, selfless in every way!" He waited for a response.

Zoran said nothing.

"Very, well," Kozar continued. "I'll take command of the fortress. The Party will be very grateful. We will commemorate this day for years to come."

"He's giving you a way out," said Mikhail. "Take it! Take it so we can end this."

Zoran watched a bead of sweat roll down Mikhail's face and disappear into his beard. Zoran was finding it difficult to breathe. The stabbing pain in his chest intensified. It clouded his thoughts.

"Well?" asked General Kozar. "What say you?"

Mikhail said nothing, and Zoran's arm began to tremble. Their eyes remained locked.

"Zoran!" yelled Kozar. "I will have the Planina regardless of what you do here. You can give me the fortress and live through this moment. Or you can die here, and I will take the fortress anyway."

Zoran and Mikhail remained frozen, locked in a silent struggle. The men surrounding them were unsure of what to do, whose eyes to avoid and, most troublesome, who to aim their weapons at. Kozar turned around. The ranks of Kozar's men parted to make way and closed in behind him. The lieutenants reminded their men to keep a watchful eye to their front.

Seeing his moment, the determined messenger boy ran to Zoran and quickly tugged on his sleeve before Milosz could stop him. Zoran broke eye contact with Mikhail and turned to listen to the boy.

"Amidža!" Young Dusan whispered urgently to his uncle. "Pasha, a thousand hundred thousand pardons—"

"Slow down young man," said Zoran. "Tell Pasha what you have."

"I'm sorry, Amidža, but…Effendim is dead."

Zoran's face went blank. He weakly patted the boy on the head and stood back up. Zoran's face was ashen when he turned sorry eyes to Milosz.

"Pasha, please ignore—"

Zoran lowered his pistol, and his other hand dropped from the hilt of his sword. His eyes shifted to some far-off place.

"Zoran…?" Mikhail lowered his own pistol. "What is it, Zoran?" He looked to Milosz, and they each reached for him as he fell.

Zoran winced and clenched his left armpit. His revolver clattered on the stone, and his legs faltered, sending him to the ground. Milosz and Mikhail knelt beside him and tried to keep everyone else back when they surged forward to what was happening to their pasha.

# 64

GOODMAN AND MUSA JOINED MIRZAD AT THE GATE, where they helped the men heave the large doors back onto the ancient gears. The posts fell into place, and the doors opened. Men of both militias walked through and suddenly paused at the situation on the stone bridge before them. Goodman, Musa, and Mirzad pushed through the crowd and trotted across the bridge to where the commanders were gathered.

Milosz stood and put his hand up. "Is Amira really…"

"Amira is here!" Goodman told him. "Amira is alive."

Relief covered Milosz's face. Then he moved so Goodman could see Zoran writhing on the ground with wild, unseeing eyes.

"What the—? What happened?" Goodman dropped to Zoran's side, where he quickly assessed what was happening. *No, no no no! Not this, of all things!* He looked at those around him. "He's having a heart attack!"

No one understood what Goodman said.

"Pomoch!" Goodman yelled as he loosened Zoran's bandoleers, belts, tunic, and boots. *His heart!* "Don't you people understand? His heart!" Goodman thumped his chest with his hand.

Milosz and Musa knelt to assist. Zoran squirmed and clawed at his chest. His breath was halted and he gasped several times, sending spittle into the air. He grabbed Goodman by the collar and pulled him down close. Zoran moved his lips, but only raspy whistles came out.

"She's okay, Zoran Pasha!" Goodman tried to tell him. "Amira is okay! Amira is alive!"

Zoran let go of Goodman and began to tremble all over. His back arched, and Goodman heard the air rush out of him. *I can't let his heart stop!* He reared back to begin thumping Zoran's chest, but Milosz caught his hand. Milosz shook his head when Goodman turned. They both watched Zoran's chest rise and fall one last time.

A shadow fell over them, and Goodman turned to see General Kozar. He peered over Goodman's shoulder. Goodman ignored him and turned back to Zoran, who had completely stopped moving. He leaned over Zoran to loosen more clothing but concluded there was nothing to be done. Zoran's pulse was undetectable, and his breathing was so weak, Goodman could not hear it anymore. A moment later, the last of Zoran's air left him, and Goodman sat back on his heels. Goodman closed Zoran's sheepskin vest and buttoned the middle button. *What now?* he asked himself.

"Dobro," said General Kozar. *Very well*. He turned and walked away. "Get me the American!"

Several hands grabbed at Goodman and pulled him away from Milosz and Musa. Goodman resisted for a moment, but his strength left him. He lost sight of Zoran's body after that moment of struggle.

"Make ready!" General Kozar's voice boomed again. A thousand Partisan weapons aimed at the men on the bridge. A thousand hearts pounded. A thousand trigger fingers tensed. The water babbled over the rocks below, but no one heard it. The primal decision to fight or to flee boiled through the minds of the militia.

Goodman strained against the men who held him back. He thought about his knife. *Only a few inches away...but then where would I go? I wouldn't survive getting off the bridge.*

The roar of a truck engine broke the stillness. A large, canvas-covered truck careened around a storefront, jumped the curb, lurched into the air, and bounced on the pavement. Men jumped to get out of its way, and thousands of eyes shifted to see who would dare interrupt this dreadful moment. The truck skidded to a stop behind the fountain, and several men leapt to the pavement. These men's uniforms were different from all the others.

*British Army?* thought Goodman. *What are they doing here?*

# PART 3: FULL THROTTLE

*"No greater love than this, to lay down one's life for one's friends."*
—John 15:13

# 65

THE SMOKEY MORNING SUNLIGHT TURNED GENERAL KOZAR'S FACE
A BLAZING ORANGE.

"You are not supposed to be here!" the General yelled at the
nearest British officer. "You are to return to my command post
immediately! This does not concern you or your mission here!"

Kozar directed one of his senior staff officers to intercept the
approaching group, but the newcomers pushed their way through
with impunity.

"General Kozar, sir!" said one of the British officers. "Would you
please give me the courtesy of a word? In private, please?" He
gestured to the side.

Kozar was obviously of no mind to comply, but something about
this man gave Kozar a reason to pause. *This was real power.* This
intrigued Goodman. *Who is he and what is he doing here? Is this the
escape network? So the British really are here with the Communists.
I wouldn't have believed it if I did not see it.* General Kozar stood as
it the elevated rim around the fountain was his pulpit. He refused to
step down, but he did permit himself to bend at the knee to listen to
the man. The Englishman spoke and gestured hurriedly.

Kozar's staff and several hundred others watched this discussion for what seemed an eternity. The other newly arrived British officers picked their way through the tense crowd. Some spoke decent Bosanski—good enough to get Partisans and militiamen alike to lower their weapons as they passed.

Goodman's heart surged. *This has to be the escape network we were briefed about. Or are they something else?*

The British officers placed themselves between the mass of militia on the bridge and the ranks of men awaiting Kozar's order to fire. General Kozar stood high again and bellowed.

"Stand down!" His voice echoed off the nearby buildings.

The mood along the riverbed changed dramatically. The many ranks of Partisan fighters complied and slowly, but gradually, all lowered their weapons. Machine gunners and riflemen alike on rooftops up and down the river plaza commenced to smoking. Zbrogan waved to his men to lower their weapons as Milosz ordered the men of the Majevitsa to lower their weapons as well. Many did so begrudgingly. General Kozar stepped down from the fountain and his conversation with the British officer continued. Goodman rose after he shrugged off the last of the hands that held him.

"You're English," he said to the nearest English officer. On his epaulets, he wore the royal crown and two diamonds of a colonel. The colonel did a wide-eyed double take and looked Goodman up and down.

"And you're an American," said the British colonel. "What the devil are you doing here? And why are you dressed like that?"

But before Goodman could respond, the colonel called to another British officer. "Major Birdington!"

"Sir?" came the reply.

"I found an American!"

"You don't say!" The one called Birdington approached, and both men gaped at Goodman like he was a wayward carnival freak suddenly returned to the fold. "We would very much like a word with you."

"What's going on?" Goodman said with a nod toward Kozar.

"Well," said the colonel. "Perhaps *you* could tell us. It seems that you and your friends here were about the go to war with the most powerful fighting force in Yugoslavia. Apart from the Nazis, of course."

"What section are you in?" asked the Major.

"I have no idea what you're talking about."

"I'm asking because the general will want to know."

"My name is Captain Michael Goodman," he answered. "I was—am—a pilot in the 513th Squadron, 376th Heavy Bombardment Group, 18th Air Force." Birdington looked at him blankly. "I went down after the Ploesti raid."

"No, chap, we don't want your cover story," said Birdington. "What *section* are you in? You must be with—what do you Americans call it—Operations Group Tennessee, no?"

"I have no idea what you're talking about." Goodman shook his head. He looked around to see who else was listening, then stepped in closer to the Brit. "What is going on here?" he asked. "Do you work with these guys?" He pointed to the communist Partisans swarming the bridge and riverside plaza. The other officer stepped closer and drew Birdington's attention.

"Sir," said Birdington. "Our American friend doesn't seem to be playing our song."

"Is that so?" said the colonel.

"No, sir, he—"

Suddenly, a woman's cry made everyone turn.

"Papa!"

Amira knelt by her father's body in the center of the bridge. Goodman pushed his way through to her. She looked up and Goodman saw a face as impassive as the stone that made up the bridge. Yet, he saw a single vertical streak of skin tone through the grime on her face. The tear finally dropped from her chin.

Her realization of her father's death seemed to signal to the Majevitsa that it was accepted—or expected—to acknowledge the death of their leader, their chieftain. Hundreds of men fell to their knees and mourned out loud. Hundreds more paused and hushed. Even the communist Partisans went silent as they streamed past the group on the bridge and into the Planina. Amira stayed as she was. Unmoved. Unmoving. Twin dark spots grew on her lapel as the first tears dropped. Goodman knelt beside her as the British officers cast shadows over them.

"Come with us, Captain," said Birdington. "You've got some explaining to do."

"I'm not going anywhere," said Goodman. "Not with you, and not yet."

Birdington continued. "I don't think you understand—"

"No, Major." Goodman stood and sternly opposed him. "You don't understand what I've got to do."

Amira cried out. Milosz, Musa, young Dusan, and Goodman stayed near her as men slowly stood and brushed themselves off. More than one coat or shirt was torn out of grief. Eyes reddened. Some men held their heads and wept. *How does one focus the anger for a death as random and yet so central as this one without a killer?* thought Goodman. *No one shot him. But the effect is the same.* Zoran Mehmetović Dudovic, Pasha of the Majevitsa, is dead.

The river made a gurgling noise as it flowed westward over the rocks, its peaks and troughs sparkling in the smoky sunlight. Men filed past and bowed their heads to Amira and to her father's body as they passed. Goodman stayed next to Amira until Musa and Milosz coaxed her to stand and retreat with the men who lifted her father's body.

# 66

THE BRITISH ARMY COLONEL STEPPED INTO THE CROWD of men surrounding Zoran's body. His hands on his hips, the officer nodded to himself as he inspected the body.

"Well, that makes things a tad easier." He turned and walked back toward the north end of the bridge with the major right next to him. Milosz looked at Goodman. Goodman was aghast at the man's callousness. He looked back and briskly strode up to the Englishmen.

"You bastard," he growled as he shoved the Colonel on the shoulder, causing him to stumble. Both the Colonel and the Major spun on their heels with expressions of shock on their faces.

"You just struck a superior officer!" exclaimed the Major.

"I doubt that you pompous English shit," Goodman stood poised to do more than just shove. "Do you know who that was?" He pointed at Zoran's body.

"I certainly do," said the Major. "And he was a significant thorn in the side of the Allied effort in an already distressed campaign."

"A thorn in the side?" asked Goodman. "You do realize who it was that took this castle, right? It wasn't your communist friends. Which I can't believe you're working with them. Do you know they're conducting mass executions of their countrymen?"

"I hardly think such extreme allegations are relevant," said the Major. "You really don't know who you are talking to, do you?" He turned to his colonel. "*Colonel* Blackbyrne, would you like me to draft a report of this unseemly incident for General Maclean?"

The Colonel feigned a pensive look for a moment. "No, Major Birdington," he said. "This man has obviously been working too closely with his assigned assets, and he has become emotionally entangled to them." He looked down his nose at Goodman. "Now, the matter of working at odds with the directed Allied efforts is a different story altogether. We shall confront this issue more directly once we have informed the respective chains of command. For now, we must restore order to this misadventure." Blackbyrne turned on his heel and strode toward the fountain, where General Kozar still stood with his staff officers.

"Very well, sir," said Major Birdington.

He trotted a short way to catch up to his colonel. Goodman watched them walk away. Tomislav came up and put a hand on Goodman's shoulder.

"Where the hell have you been?" said Goodman, suddenly irritated at his friend and his absences.

"I heard Amira was dead and Zoran was, well, doing something Zoran would do," replied Tomislav. "But neither seems to be true."

"Yeah," said Goodman. He drew in a long breath and exhaled slowly. "Welcome to the victory party."

Together, they watched the militia lift and carry Zoran's body northward across the bridge and across the plaza. A long procession of men carried the rest of their fallen out of the Planina Fortress. Everyone gave Amira a wide berth as she walked slowly behind her father's body. The back of her coat was dark with blood.

"Is that the British Army?" said Tomislav.

"Yeah," he said.

"And you do not go to them?"

The idea struck Goodman hard. He already despised them and had not even thought about it. For weeks, he had undeniably felt excitement about the idea of seeing Allied soldiers again, and he *did* feel a burst of excitement when he saw the familiar uniforms a few moments ago. But to go to them now? Or, rather, to put it the way he *felt* right now, to leave the militia with whom he had lived and fought hard over the past weeks had not occurred to him. *What am I doing?* he thought. *I should be over there talking to them. I should be discussing with them how they're going to get me out of here, back to Benghazi. Back to flying.*

"I'll get to it," he finally said. But he was suspicious of British motives. "I need to know what will happen here first." *Whatever happens*, he thought, *the British can't be allowed to screw over Zoran's people.*

"I've heard rumors of the British liaison with the communist forces," he said. "But I've never actually seen or met one before. I think I prefer ignorance to this."

"Me, too," said Goodman. He scanned the sea of gray and olive green-clad Partisan fighters on the bridge and swarming the plaza. Then he saw the British officers chumming up to General Kozar. They were at ease talking with the General and his staff, even smiling. Goodman looked at Tomislav and shook his head. "Well, shit."

"Yes. This is shit," said Tomislav.

"You have a cigarette?"

"Yes," said Tomislav. "Fresh from the pockets of a dead SS major." They both lit up and took a long, long drag.

Milosz called the militia commanders by name to lead the procession ahead of Zoran's body. The men carrying bodies of the fallen from the assault would follow. Last would be the able-bodied men with as many weapons and as much ammunition as possible. Milosz returned to the discussion with General Kozar. Many of the militia wept quietly as they carried their dead sons, brothers, or cousins on blankets or improvised stretchers over the cobblestone street. A group of Partisans herded a line of German prisoners over the bridge and into a neighborhood. Musa stepped away from Milosz and pulled Ahmet with him.

"What's going on there?" asked Goodman. They looked at the group surrounding Kozar and the British Colonel Blackbyrne with his minion Birdington patiently standing by. Milosz stood outside the circle.

"The Titoists and the foreigners are deciding what to do with us," said Musa.

"What does that mean?" asked Goodman.

"Milosz believes they want to make us a part of their army," said Musa. "He is going to try to argue against it, but..."

"But what?" asked Goodman.

"Zoran was our protector," said Musa. "He made deals with the other commanders that assured our solidarity with the other militias. Now he is dead, and the other commanders do not want to oppose Tito's Army."

"If they can't kill us openly," said Ahmet. "Then they want us to be their cannon fodder. Their slaves."

The four of them watched as Milosz engaged vociferously with General Kozar and the British colonel. Colonel Zbrogan stood nearby, not saying anything. *The traitor*, thought Goodman. The discussion was heated, and Milosz was all alone in it.

"Hell, if I stand by and watch that happen," said Goodman. Tomislav, Musa, and Ahmet followed him to the fountain. Goodman paused outside the circle for a moment, then he dived right in and confronted Colonel Blackbyrne and General Kozar.

"You cannot force these men to work for the communists—"

Colonel Blackbyrne cut him off. "Just who do you think you are?" Blackbyrne turned to his staff. "Get this man out of here."

Major Birdington and another officer started to move on Goodman, but Musa stepped between them and shook his head. Alarmed, Birdington and the other officer halted. Witnessing the interaction, General Kozar stepped back and folded his arms, clearly entertained by what was happening within the ranks of his Allied advisors. He whispered something to his aide.

"I've been fighting alongside these men," said Goodman. "And I've seen firsthand what they are up against."

"This is rather interesting," said Colonel Blackbyrne. "And just what is it, in your estimation, that they are up against?"

"Colonel," Goodman began. "They spend most of their time defending themselves against your communist friends here, *and* the Ustaši, *and* the Chetniks, *and* whoever else that comes along trying to rob them, kill them, and burn their villages, kidnap their families, or whatever else has been done to them. Then, with whatever time is left over, they are effective at fighting the Nazis. They would win the fight with the Nazis if this crowd would leave them alone." He put a finger toward General Kozar.

"I will not allow this sort of allegation to be voiced without evidence," stated General Kozar. "I assure you that this affront will interfere in the efficiency of our relationship. This American agent has been the source of much trouble in the internal relations of our people's resistance movement."

"And I assure you, general," said Blackbyrne. "That this is not the sentiment of this mission, nor of the British government and nor will it be. And I promise you that our American friend here will be firmly dealt with once his chain of command arrives."

"I should hope so," said Kozar. "This amateur attack on the Planina Fortress has upset the entire timetable for liberation operations in this region."

"Colonel, it's really very simple," Goodman stepped in. "These *amateurs* got here first. We had to fight our way here, by the way, and then we conducted a very successful assault, and this loser is sore about it."

A vein emerged on General Kozar's forehead. He opened his mouth to say something, but a large canvas-covered army truck roared into the plaza. The brakes squealed and a half dozen or so

360

men emerged from the rear of the truck. Goodman immediately recognized the American uniforms. They approached the gathering at the fountain.

"Sorry we're late, Leonard," said an American colonel. "One of the security battalions had the whole west side cordoned off and wouldn't let us through."

"The fog and friction of war at its finest," replied Colonel Blackbyrne. "And you've arrived just in time, Colonel. We were being lectured by one of your men as to the nature of the war here in Yugoslavia."

"One of my men?" said the American colonel. "I doubt anyone here would be that presumptuous."

"Well," said Colonel Blackbyrne. "Is this not one of your men, Colonel Anderson?" He gestured at Goodman.

"Who? Him?" said Colonel Anderson. "No, I've never seen him before. How do you know he's mine?"

"He claims to be a downed aviator," said Major Birdington. "We thought for sure he was reciting his cover story, if not a tad overzealously."

"Yes, he claims to have been fighting with this country militia for quite some time," said Colonel Blackbyrne. "This may be the man we've been receiving reports about for the last few weeks."

"Really?" Anderson said as he looked Goodman up and down.

"I'm right here, gentlemen," said Goodman. "I could answer these questions for you."

"Yes," Anderson replied. "So you are, but there is a bit of a crisis right now, so you wait in my vehicle and we'll talk soon. Charlie, would you see that he gets there safely?"

A young American Army captain stepped forward. "Yes, sir." He said. He looked at Goodman. "Come with me."

"Okay," Goodman agreed. "But the problem—"

"Not now!" said the captain in a hushed but gruff tone. "Just follow me, if you know what's good for you."

Goodman took the hint and followed. He looked back at Milosz, Tomislav, and Musa. They watched as he walked away. This was not the way Goodman wanted to leave them.

"What's your name?"

"Huh?" Goodman turned around again. "Captain Michael Goodman, Army Air Corps."

"Charlie Whitman." They shook hands.

"It's good to finally see Americans," said Goodman. It *did* feel good, after all. "I just met the British five minutes ago, and I've already had enough of them."

They climbed into the back of the canvas covered truck. The back was littered with half-eaten ration boxes and sacks of potatoes, with several loose potatoes scattered on the truck bed. Goodman noticed that none of them were rotten. He accepted a cigarette and the light when Whitman offered.

"So," said Captain Whitman when they were seated. "What the hell are you doing in Tuzla? We thought you were way east of here."

"I was," said Goodman. "How did you know to look for me? Did anyone else from my crew make it?"

"I have no idea," said Whitman. "We've been told that some American has been running around with his own mountain hillbilly army, blowing things up. You've really caused a problem for us with the Brits, and for the Brits with Tito's people."

"I'm not sure that killing Germans or Ustaši around here is a bad thing," Goodman retorted. "Who has a problem with that?"

"It's not so much the what as it is the who is doing it," said Whitman. "How did you get here, anyway?"

"Well, first," started Goodman. "I was shot down back in early August and crashed in the mountains northeast of here. These...hillbillies as you call them found me and took care of me. And when I got healthy enough to move, they moved me. But, well, things led to other things, and we ended up here."

"Assaulting the strongest German garrison in all of northeastern Bosnia?" asked Whitman.

"Well," said Goodman. "I'm not in charge of anything. These people took care of me and, since I couldn't get out, I've been trying to help them."

"If you had come under the real Partisan control, we would have had you out of here weeks ago."

"Yeah, that sounds nice, but the communists didn't find me." Goodman pointed at the procession leading away from the bridge.

362

"These people found me and they're the reason I'm still alive. There is no way they could have gotten me out because they were afraid of getting killed by this crowd you call friends. They don't trust the Communists, the Chetniks, the Ustaši and most of the other groups around here."

"That sounds about right," said Whitman.

"What's that supposed to mean?" asked Goodman, irritated at the dismissive tone.

"It means that Yugoslavia is FUBAR," said Whitman. "Here, Tito's people are the biggest resistance force and by far the best at fighting the Germans. The Brits want to back the winning horse, and they oversee Allied support in this region. So, the British are friends with Tito and we get to help them. Everyone else is on the outs with Tito's people, so they are on the outs with us. That's just how it works."

"So the British and American governments want the communists in control after the war?" Goodman was incredulous. "I find that hard to believe."

"It's the lesser of two evils," said Whitman. He kicked his legs up on the side of the truck and lit a cigarette.

"You know they kill people just for not siding with them, don't you?" asked Goodman, probing to see where Whitman's boundaries lie. "Their first people into a city are the political and propaganda officers, right?"

"Yeah, yeah," said Whitman. "We know about that."

"Well, do you know that they have lists of people they have been executing in Tuzla since at least two days ago? I saw the bodies yesterday."

"That we didn't know," said Whitman. "We heard rumors but didn't know for certain."

"What don't we know for certain?" asked another voice from the rear of the truck. Another American captain climbed over the tailgate and sat down, followed by a red-haired, red-mustachioed soldier wearing the chevrons and rockers of a Master Sergeant. The new captain whistled as he shuffled through ration boxes until he found one that fit his desires. He and the Master Sergeant noisily rummaged through and dropped it on the floor after picking out cans of peaches. They each set to work with a can opener before Goodman caught their attention.

"Who the hell is this?" said the whistling captain. They each lit a cigarette and let out of huge smoke puff into the middle of the back of the truck.

"Meet—what'd you say your name was?" said Whitman.

"Captain Mike Goodman," Goodman said flatly. He was less enthused about meeting his countrymen now that he saw where his loyalties diverged from theirs.

"Captain Goodman and I were discussing the politics in the former Kingdom of Yugoslavia," said Whitman. "Captain Goodman, meet Captain Brian Kidder and Master Sergeant Henry O'Keefe." They shook hands.

"Another officer," said Master Sergeant O'Keefe. "Just what Yugoslavia needs." Everyone laughed except Goodman.

"Yeah, but he's an aviator," said Whitman.

"Oh, good," said O'Keefe. "Then he'll be going home soon."

"Did the flight get approved?" asked Whitman.

"Should be Saturday," said O'Keefe. "If Bari Station gives the final clearance for a new location with Banja Luka currently under siege." He paused a beat. "So what was it we didn't know?"

"Our new friend here says that Tito's people came in with kill lists," said Whitman. "And they're doing it." Captain Kidder and Master Sergeant O'Keefe exchanged glances.

"Wouldn't be surprised," said O'Keefe. "You remember Banja Luka earlier this year?" The Americans went silent for a moment.

"A problem though," said Kidder. "We don't have an airfield for Saturday." He slurped loudly on the peach juice.

"Then you can go survey one," said Whitman.

"That would be a good job for you, there, Captain," O'Keefe agreed.

"I did the last three airfields," Kidder complained. "Why do I have to do it?"

"Because the good Master Sergeant and I have to be in the command post," said Whitman.

"But—" Captain Kidder began to protest.

Not interested in their conversation, Goodman lifted the canvas tailgate flap to look for Tomislav and the others. He could see Musa's head towering above everyone else near the fountain. It looked as if the negotiations were still going on. *What are they saying?* Goodman's heart felt a heaviness for Amira as he searched the procession. She was too short to see from here. He was suddenly deeply torn. He really wanted to go back to them. To her. But his desire to go home grew as well. Unable to determine which he wanted to do more, he scowled.

"So this is our big-time operator," said Kidder, drawing him back in. "The fabled American officer, of whom we have heard so much lately. So, what the hell have you been doing to create such a stir? Trying to be the next Sergeant York?"

"No, not me," said Goodman. *I just want to get out of here,* he thought to himself. "I wasn't doing anything in particular."

"Ha!" said Kidder. "A man who does nothing makes the Brit's *and* the Partisans' *and* the Waffen-SS most wanted lists." He gestured as if hanging pictures on a wall. "General Weichs, General Krempler, General Phelps, General Zeitzler and Army Aviation Captain—"

"Goodman," O'Keefe reminded him.

"Captain Goodman, yeah." Kidder continued to press him. "Seriously, what'd you do to piss off General Kozar and the Brits so much?"

"I just fought." Goodman nodded toward Whitman. "Like I was telling him, the people who found me after I got shot down helped me. I should be dead, but they took care of me. They are good people, and they're getting the short end of the stick in this stinking war. So, I helped out."

"No one is innocent here," said O'Keefe, blowing a cone of smoke out the rear of the truck. "Everyone is dirty. Dirty, dirty, dirty. Don't let anyone fool you. Watching this from an observer perspective, I can barely justify aligning ourselves with the Brits, for all they allow to go on. And no one is getting a real great deal out of this. Everyone is getting murdered here."

"After seeing it for myself," said Goodman. "Some are getting it more than others."

"True," said O'Keefe. He smothered his cigarette with his boot and lit up another. They all nodded.

"Regardless," said Whitman. "Kozar heard about you a little over a month ago and has been looking for you ever since. He's really been giving the British mission grief about you."

"And to us," said Kidder. O'Keefe and Whitman nodded in agreement.

Goodman scowled. "Why?"

"He thought for sure you were proof of a back door deal we had with the Chetnik resistance in Serbia," said Whitman. "Tito has always been jealous of the attention and support we've given to the other resistance groups. They have an agenda, and you and your mountain militia here don't fit into their plans. And they always want leverage over us to give them more money and more guns and stuff. So, for a time, the idea of you was useful to them. Blackbyrne has heard a lot about you—some of it's probably true and I'm sure most of it is not—so he's made it one of our tasks to find you and get you out. You are a legend in your own time, my friend. At least, that was what Kozar made you out to be."

"And it worked like a charm on the Brits," said Kidder, lighting his own cigarette.

"Ay, that it did," said O'Keefe, lighting his next cigarette. "I've never seen two colonels go at it over anything like Blackbyrne and Anderson did the other day." Kidder whistled through his teeth.

"Over me?" said Goodman.

"Colonel Blackbyrne wants your head on a platter," said O'Keefe.

"Hell with them," Goodman replied. "I'm an American. I don't work for the Brits."

"Remember what I said." Whitman spoke up. "The Brits are in charge here."

"Yeah," said Kidder. "And Colonel Blackbyrne is supposed to be friends with King George or something like that. You might be royally screwed." Kidder smirked at his own joke.

Goodman slumped against the sideboard. Then Tomislav and two other Majevitsa men appeared at the tailgate and Goodman's face lit up.

"Tomislav!"

O'Keefe and Kidder sat upright and reached for their pistols.

"He's one of the good guys," Goodman said. "Not a threat."

Tomislav carefully eyed the other Americans before he spoke. "General Kozar is allowing us to bury the dead outside the city and transport the wounded back to the Majevitsa. I thought you would want to see them off."

"Yeah," replied Goodman. "I definitely want to!" He jumped over the tailgate.

"Hey!" yelled Whitman.

"I'll be back!" Goodman yelled over his shoulder.

The clouds of smoke were thinning out, and the sun was shining brightly. Tomislav led him through the crowded plaza to the back of a large flatbed truck. There, more than two dozen bodies wrapped in blankets laid neatly side by side. Most were bloody, but one was not. From the size of the boots, Goodman knew it was Zoran. He approached to look at Zoran's face. It was relaxed, so unlike the contorted, pained look he had when the heart attack first killed him. He looked like he was sleeping.

Goodman looked up and saw Amira near the front of the truck. He thought about the first time he saw her, in the dark at the camp. And then he thought about the second time he saw her, the next morning, and how strikingly and dangerously beautiful she was, despite the scars. Or was his sympathy for her coloring his memory? It was hard to tell. Once, after that time in the woods when he shared about Jasminka, he had wondered what it would be like to feel her warmth. He knew it would not happen. *Either way, she's alone now,* he thought. *What is she going to do now?* He felt his energy drain away. The wind felt very cold again.

A commotion made him turn. Officers were shouting and men were moving again. General Kozar and his staff piled into the backs of trucks, engines roared, and rank upon rank of communist Partisans formed and marched back into the city. Medics ran back and forth to assist the many wounded. Milosz was nearby, calling out for his leaders to assemble their own men near the truck loaded with the dead. Tomislav put his hand on Goodman's arm.

"My friend," said Tomislav. "You should be happy to go with them." He glanced at the Americans watching from their truck.

"I know," said Goodman. "I thought I would be happy about going home. But…I don't feel good. About any of it." They both looked at Zoran's body.

"He is at rest now," said Tomislav.

Goodman nodded. Milosz called out to his commanders and men gathered.

Musa came up and put his ape-like arms around the both of them. "Some of us want to say something to you."

"To me?" said Goodman.

When Musa stepped back, a small group of old mountain men approached anxiously. Bloodied and covered in soot, one man stepped out from the rest. He was one of the men from the ambush against the tanks. He took Goodman's hand to shake it, and he gripped it. His hand was cold, gnarled, and thick with callouses. His knuckles were inflamed and arthritic. He trembled as he spoke.

"You came to us by falling out of the sky," he said in a high-pitched, scratchy voice. Goodman could barely understand what he was saying and had to concentrate. "And you were a stranger. You fought with us. You fought like a *lav*." Goodman did not know the word. The old man continued. "Now we know you. And you know us. Thank you, American, for all your courage. We hope that your family grows and there is much wine at your table." He smiled a toothless but sincere smile.

And then he kissed Goodman's hand. Goodman was surprised by this, but contained his reaction. The old man kissed it twice more. In turn, each of the men paid Goodman a compliment, took Goodman's hand, and kissed it. The most elderly of the bunch also held his hand as he spoke, trembling with age, and then kissed it six times, enough to make it feel a little bit awkward. But Goodman knew what this meant, and he would not dishonor the moment. He hugged this last old man, and the man hugged back, weakly, but surely. When he backed away, Goodman saw that all the eyes looking back at him were red and glassy. Goodman felt humbled, unworthy of this praise. These were hard, old men who killed untold numbers of their enemies. And now he had to leave them.

368

"Hvala vam svima." All Goodman could get out was to say thank you.

"Ma salama," they all said. *God be with you.* They all said an awkward goodbye, then turned to join their family units in the funeral procession.

"That never happens," said Musa.

"What?" said Goodman.

"Those men are better known for killing outsiders than speaking to them. They must like you."

Goodman thought about this for a moment. Finally, he asked, "what's a lav? I don't know that word."

"A lion."

# 67

THE TRUCK CARRYING THE BODIES OF THE DECEASED Majevitsa fighters belched blue-white smoke when the engine started up. Musa and Goodman shook hands and Musa departed for his position in the funeral procession. Tomislav stayed close. A whistle sounded from behind them.

"Hey, Goodman!" It was Captain Kidder. "Time to go!"

Goodman returned to the truck and climbed over the tailgate. Another American officer had joined the threesome in the back. He was about the extend his hand to greet Goodman when someone shouted. Partisans and militia alike pointed at the sky.

Thousands of faces looked up in terror. A small airplane slowly buzzed out of a cloud, probably three or four thousand feet above the ground. Goodman immediately identified it as a German Storch scout plane. Undoubtedly, it had already reported a large concentration of Partisan forces in central Tuzla to a German command somewhere. An attack was coming for sure.

Heavy machine guns opened up with a terrible roar that reverberating off the buildings and hills. Goodman's heart jumped when the more powerful anti-aircraft cannon opened fire. Each blast compounded the echoes of the other blasts. Tracers soared in long, swirling streams, but to no effect. The gunners fired anyway.

Officers and sergeants barked orders, but the noise drowned them out. Men ran in every direction. Trucks roared to life. Officers clambered into their trucks as they drove away. Drivers maneuvered through the surging throngs of fighters and into the narrow streets and alleys. People ran for the shelter of alleyways, basements, or any building they could get inside. Anything to get out of sight of that terrible little aircraft.

Within a few minutes, the trucks were well into the city, away from the openness of the riverside plaza. Several trucks convened at a large, tree-lined square and parked under the trees or tucked into alleyways. The driver of the American truck backed into an alley and turned off the engine. Everyone sat still and listened to the gunfire fade away. Slowly, people came out from their hiding places. No attack. *Why not?*

Master Sergeant O'Keefe was the first to climb out, followed by Kidder, Whitman, and then Goodman. With their eyes toward the sky, the other Americans led Goodman down the alley, through a bakery, and up a flight of stairs. Whitman unlocked a door and directed Goodman to a worn-out couch. The others went into separate rooms or to the table in what appeared to be a small eating area adjacent to the kitchenette. O'Keefe unpacked his rucksack as Whitman sat down at the table and opened his courier bag.

"So, who are you guys?" asked Goodman. Kidder walked out and glanced at O'Keefe, who looked back at him. They both turned to see what Captain Whitman would say.

"We are the American liaison mission to the Yugoslav resistance," said Whitman, not looking up from his notes. "Seconded to the British Special Operations Executive mission here for the same."

"I didn't know the Army had such a thing," said Goodman.

"Not exactly the Army," said Kidder.

"The Office of Strategic Services," said O'Keefe. "Or OSS, if you like."

"Never heard of you," said Goodman.

"Yes," said Whitman. "That is intentional."

"What do you do?" Goodman asked.

"A lot of things," said O'Keefe. "Suffice it to say that part of what we do is get you out of here and back home. But, otherwise, a lot of things we don't talk about."

"Classified?"

"Yup."

"Gotcha." Goodman stood to look out the window. "What do I do now?"

"You need to lay low," replied Whitman. "So Kozar has a chance to forget about you."

"There's a low probability of that happening," said O'Keefe. "But we just need to get you out of here with the least amount of difficulty possible."

"So you are the escape network?"

"Yes," answered Whitman.

Relief washed over Goodman. *I'm finally where I need to be.* "But what about the people I came here with?"

"What about them?"

"I need to see that they are taken care of."

"No, you don't," said Whitman. "That's not your job."

Goodman was about to protest, but the Master Sergeant spoke first. "They were getting along fine before you came," he said. "And they'll probably be glad to get you out of their hair."

"And until then," Whitman continued. "We have to accompany Kozar's forces as they assault the remaining German positions around the city."

"Speaking of that," said O'Keefe. "Who's going to relieve the colonel in the command post?"

"I'll take the first shift," said Whitman. "I have to be up for the midnight message traffic from Bari Station and Cairo Station. Kidder, you have the next shift with the Major."

"So, what? I just sit here?" said Goodman. "I'm not good with that."

"Doesn't matter," Whitman replied one last time. "Colonel's orders."

# 68

## 0720 HOURS, SEPTEMBER 30, 1943
## THE OSS APARTMENT ABOVE THE BAKERY, TUZLA MARKET DISTRICT

GOODMAN'S BREATH CAST A FOG in the middle of the window. Throngs of people moving in currents through the streets. The tides converged in the sprawling open market area. Footsteps climbed the staircase on the other side of the door. Captain Kidder and Goodman glanced at the door. Two knocks followed by three knocks and Kidder swung the door open and holstered his pistol. It was Master Sergeant O'Keefe.

"Colonel Anderson says he'll see you," he said.

"Me?" asked Kidder.

"No, sir," said O'Keefe. He pointed at Goodman. "Him."

Goodman glanced at them both.

"Well, get going," said Kidder as he sipped from his coffee cup.

Goodman buttoned his coat and shouldered his submachine gun.

"You won't need that," said Kidder.

"Right," said Goodman. He ignored the advice. "I'm ready."

"Follow me, sir."

Goodman followed him down the stairs and into the street. They jumped into the rush of armed fighters, civilian vendors, trucks and horse-drawn carts. Pigeons and chickens filled in the spaces between. A large, canvas-topped truck was parked at the front of the Royal Star Hotel. The hotel sign was dirt streaked and all of its lightbulbs were missing. O'Keefe rounded the back of the truck and climbed the tailgate. Goodman peered in after him.

The back of the truck was an ad hoc office and operations center. A map board hung on one side, opposite a large piece of plywood tacked with pieces of paper. A man sat at a small field desk in the front corner with his back to the opening. Captain Whitman was seated at a smaller improvised desk, busily scribbling notes in a small notepad. An olive-green radio transmitter was strapped to the bench next to him.

O'Keefe spoke to the man at the field desk. The man raised his head and turned to look at Goodman. "Tell him I'll be with him in a minute." O'Keefe returned to the tailgate.

"I heard," said Goodman. They both waited.

At length, the man closed his notebook. "I'm supposed to check in with the Intel shop upstairs," the colonel told Whitman. "Would you go in my place and please tell them for me that the Allied weather report for the next week is available?"

"Yes, Colonel."

Captain Whitman jumped down from the truck and waved to the Partisan guards, who eyed him with disdain as he entered the hotel lobby. A moment later, Colonel Anderson climbed down from the truck and straightened his jacket.

"Henry, I'll be a few minutes," he said to O'Keefe.

"Right, sir!" said the captain. "Do you want me to take the radio call at 1200 hours?"

"No, I got it," said Anderson. He climbed down the rear of the truck. "I'll see you before then." He turned to Goodman. "Let's walk, shall we?"

"Yes, sir."

Goodman followed the colonel around the side of the truck and walked down a side street, away from the hotel and busy main street. Two uniformed Partisans with pistols on their hips followed them around the corner.

"Sir—"

"Never mind them," said Colonel Anderson. "All members of the Allied liaison mission are followed. They are for our security, among other reasons."

They walked on for a while without speaking. Goodman had a hundred questions but waited for his superior to initiate. Their minders were never more than twenty yards away, but Colonel Anderson was able to keep them outside of listening range.

"So, you say you were shot down?" he said. "Is that how you got here?"

"Yes, sir," replied Goodman. "My mission was to hit the railhead at the oil storage facilities near Ploiesti, Romania. But the whole thing was FUBAR before we even got there. My ship got hit before we dropped ordnance. We made it out from the German fighter umbrella and got as far as the mountains north of here."

"You were lead pilot?"

"Yes, sir."

"Where is your crew?"

Goodman hesitated. Each of their faces flashed in his mind. "As far as I know, I'm the only one who made it," he finally said. "I was unconscious and rode my ship down to the ground. Never even bailed out. I should be dead like the rest of them."

"Well, then, your mission is not complete," said Colonel Anderson.

"I don't follow, sir," said Goodman.

"Tell me about your time with the hill country militia," Anderson re-directed. "Speak freely."

"Yes, sir."

Goodman described his life over the last three months as they walked through a series of side streets. The memories flooded back to him. He described his recovery, the unnamed village where he learned Bosanski, as well as local culture and politics of the war. The German patrol tearing apart the village looking for him. As if he wanted to pry the scab loose, Anderson probed him further about the village, the villagers, and their approximate location. Goodman described Baba, Jasminka, the Nurse, the young female spy who died. He did not want to think about Jasminka's tears. Why did he keep remembering Jasminka's dirty tears? He described how he met Zoran Pasha Mehmetović Dudovič and his Majevitsa militia. He recounted the first attack in the valley, the feud between the villages, the attack on the Salt Factory, everything that had happened since his arrival in Tuzla. The death of Zoran. Goodman talked about everything and everyone except for Amira, except to mention her as Zoran's daughter. He kept most of that part to himself.

Anderson asked almost no questions. When Goodman finished talking, they walked in silence for a while. Then, as they returned to the main boulevard, Colonel Anderson stopped.

"Thank you for your honesty," he said. "Your story aligns with our previous information. And it fills in numerous gaps in our information. Too bad you can't remember where that original village is located. We couldn't tell if the stories we got were of a new downed pilot or the legends of older ones. You have to understand that a downed Allied airman is a hot commodity around here. Everyone wants one. There is money and prestige involved on both sides of the equation."

"So I've heard," said Goodman.

Anderson continued. "Money is behind pretty much everything. At the lowest, the tactical level, money feeds mouths. It buys a bullet, a horse, a bit of information. At the strategic level, money feeds nations and armies. You and I are a part of the wartime economy. Each and every group fighting here, and everywhere really, is an entrepreneurial economic endeavor. High-risk, low probably of return, mind you, but a high, high pay-off if there is any to be had. A bad way of doing business, really, but some manage to make it work. The payoff is the destiny of their country, whatever that looks like. Money is the blood of ideologies."

"Never really thought of it that way," said Goodman. "What did you do before the war, colonel, if I may ask?"

"I'm a lawyer," he said. "I advised corporations in New York and Boston on overseas investments, mainly in Europe."

"I don't get it," said Goodman. "Now you do…whatever it is you do here. How does that happen?"

"I've been with OSS since the start," said Anderson, pulling out a cigarette and offering one to Goodman, who took it and the light from Anderson's match. "This is a no-frills outfit with some—shall I say—eccentric personalities and pretty wild expectations placed upon us at the highest levels of government. We operate based on capabilities, not so much by protocols. We recruit intelligent people.

Creative people. Brave people. As a corporate finance lawyer, I had to figure out how two or more parties, separated by distance and language, get what they wanted from a single transaction or from a net exchange across multiple transactions. This job is all about that. But, instead of financial profit, the end-product here is political power. The commodities in exchange are information, influence, and destruction...in that order, more or less."

Anderson paused to look at their minders, who abruptly turned to pretend to look at an empty storefront.

"I would have thought those would be reversed," said Goodman.

"You would be wrong." Anderson turned another corner which forced their Partisan shadow to hurry lest they dodge into a shop and exit the back door.

"Captain," said Colonel Anderson. "You seem to have a knack for this sort of thing. From what we understand about you and your situation, you gained the leaders' trust, somehow reinvented yourself from an aviator to a rather effective guerilla, and, well, you survived. That says a lot by itself." He stopped and looked at Goodman. "The Brits despise you because Tito and his people despise you. Tito's people despise you because you upset their plans. Now, I do not particularly hold dear any relationship to Tito and his forces, nor any other force here in Yugoslavia, for that matter. The cozy relationship between some of the British officers and the Communists makes me ill. But they *are* effective in counterbalancing the Nazis and their Croatian partners. They might even win, depending on what happens elsewhere in eastern Europe, especially the front. The British Prime Minister and our President have decided that communism is the lesser evil for Yugoslavia this year."

"I'm not sure where that leaves me," said Goodman. "I mean, what happens to me now? What happens to the militia?"

"Well," Colonel Anderson thought out loud. "I can't speak to the future of the militia, but I'm going to try to soften the blow with my own report to London. Colonel Blackbyrne has already composed his report, and it is very un-complimentary of your activities since you were shot down. Pretty scathing, actually. Nothing to be done about that, sorry."

"So, what am I supposed to do?" asked Goodman. He felt a little knot in his stomach.

"For now, we have a mission to sustain," he replied. "Your situation is out of my hands."

"I assume you'll be sending me home," said Goodman. "Since I'm not much use here."

"We'll get you out of here, but I would not expect much of a homecoming," said Colonel Anderson. "You may face court martial." Goodman halted mid-stride. "The picture of you that Colonel Blackbyrne's report painted to the British High Command is that you were aiding the enemy."

"Aiding the enemy!" Goodman exclaimed. "How can that be? Nothing could be further from the truth! I was almost killed by Nazis, the Ustaši, and by these sons of bitches, for that matter. It was only the hill country people that everyone keeps insulting that cared for me."

Down the street, their shadows sidestepped a few paces closer, no longer pretending to look at posters and signs in store windows. Colonel Anderson continued walking.

"That may be true," said Anderson. "However, technically, these hill country people have been working against the Allies," Anderson stated. "And I'll ignore your little outburst, as I know this is difficult."

"I apologize, sir," said Goodman. "But, we…er…they have been fighting the Nazis for a long time now. But they've also been fighting against the communists and the Ustaši. And the Chetniks. It only looks like they were fighting the Allies because the Communists have been attacking them."

"That will have to be part of your legal defense," Colonel Anderson said. "I'm being honest with you, Captain Goodman. Your long-term prospects are not great right now. Now, I do know a few good military attorneys. One works at Supreme Headquarters Allied Forces in England. I'll request London Station to connect you to him." He steered them around a corner and lowered his voice. "Right now, we have to focus on getting you safely tucked away with the others."

"Others?"

"We have eight other Allied airmen who have found their way into our care. You're not the first pilot to be stuck in this mess."

"Are they here?" said Goodman. "In Tuzla, I mean."

"Oh, no," replied Anderson. "We have a farm south of here. It's a little exposed, but we keep the activity there to a minimum. For now, Captain, let's keep our eye on the ball and get you to that farm. From there, we'll get you out. In your mind, try to set aside your future ordeal and the politics of what we're doing to win the war. You have one last mission to complete before then."

"What the hell, Colonel," muttered Goodman. "I was just trying to survive. I would be dead now if it wasn't for them."

Colonel Anderson looked him squarely in the eye.

"Yes, and you did a hell of a lot more than survive, Captain. You stepped way outside your element, beyond your training, and succeeded. Be damn proud of that. We see a lot of downed airmen through here, but none of them have ever done what you did."

The last part provided Goodman no comfort whatsoever. A wind blew down the street, raising dust and old newspapers in a swirl.

"When do I leave?" Goodman asked. "Should I just wait in the truck?"

"No, we don't exactly work like that," said Colonel Anderson. "Major Farish is another of our agents here. He has a contact with our escape network. They oversee our evasion mechanism and will get you to that farm and then out as quickly as possible. We already had a mission lined up for tonight to move some materials through our courier network. We'll exchange you for our usual courier since you're going to the same place."

"I'm not entirely sure what that means," said Goodman.

"It's not complicated," explained Anderson. "There is a bag of messages and some antibiotics that you'll carry with you as you move with our asset tonight. Whitman and Farish will prepare you as necessary." He looked up and saw the Royal Star Hotel at the end of the street. "Let's not go this way," he said. They turned around and almost ran into Tomislav. He was almost as surprised as they were to suddenly be face to face. Anderson's hand flew to his pistol.

"Tomislav!" Goodman exclaimed. "What're you doing here?" Colonel Anderson dropped his .45 back into its holster.

"I did not want to intrude," he stuttered slightly. "But Milosz said that the funeral will begin shortly. And then the Majevitsa brigade will depart with the wounded for the homeland. He wanted you to know…" His voice trailed off, hesitantly.

"Umm, thank you, Tomislav," Goodman said. "Tell him I'll be there soon."

"Captain, you are to remain with my people in the apartment. It is not safe for you in Tuzla."

Goodman's heart sank. "Yes, sir." He turned to Tomislav.

"Please tell—"

"I will," said Tomislav. Then he hesitated.

"What is it?" asked Goodman.

"Also, Amira wanted me to tell you she and a small detachment of her men will remain with you for as long as you are in Tuzla."

This news made his spirit leap. *She was staying.* He felt his pulse quicken ever so slightly. *But I'm leaving tonight!* He wanted very much to see her again. *How do I do this?* He did not even know what he meant by that. What did he expect?

Tomislav tipped his hat and turned around. Goodman and Colonel Anderson watched him walk away. He turned around once to tip a finger to his hat brim and quickly trotted away.

"Who is that?" asked the colonel.

"That man saved my life," said Goodman, still slightly high from the news. "More than once. If it wasn't for him, I wouldn't be here."

"Do you trust him?"

"I have to."

"No," said Anderson. "You don't."

"Could you walk away from someone who saved your life?"

"In war, I guess every man has to make that choice. Just make sure it's worth your life the next time. A life for a life, right?"

That phrase, specifically the Colonel's use of it, caught Goodman completely off-guard. He waited for the Colonel to say the one more thing he left unsaid. But he said nothing. They walked until they turned a final corner toward market and the bakery. *There's no way that's a coincidence*, thought Goodman. *He must have heard it from somewhere in his time in this country.*

"If all goes well tonight," Colonel Anderson said finally. "I won't see you again. Good luck to you."

They shook hands, and Colonel Anderson walked briskly to the hotel. One of the Partisan minders stayed with Goodman. Goodman sighed loudly and looked at the dark clouds blowing in from the north. He went upstairs to the room above the bakery. From the window, he watched his shadow hurry back toward the Royal Star Hotel.

# 69

## THE OSS APARTMENT, TUZLA MARKET DISTRICT

THE UPPER-STORY WINDOWS ON THE ROYAL STAR HOTEL reflected the last rays of sunlight piercing the otherwise gray western sky. It was already dark in the East and smoke from cooking fires all over the city mixed with the diesel exhaust of the Partisan supply convoys. Amira and her men had arrived on the street below. Goodman had discretely waved to her, and she had replied in kind, but was insistent on signaling for him to come down. The OSS men disallowed that rather adamantly.

"You ready, Goodman?" Major Farish called up from the bottom of the stairs.

"Yes, sir!" Goodman picked up his MP-40 from the table and checked for a round in the chamber. He cast one more look out the window.

On the street below, Amira, Milosz, Tomislav and Musa stood in front of the bakery together with another forty or so Majevitsa militiamen. A Partisan officer stood a few yards away with three of his soldiers, himself positioned between the groups. He shifted from one foot to the other, pausing only to pull his sleeve up to check his watch for the third time in a minute. Goodman turned toward the door.

Goodman descended the stairs and stepped outside. The warmth of the day had not yet left the stone walls and street, but the air had already cooled enough to show each exhalation. On the side street, Captain Whitman stood with Kidder and O'Keefe, all of whom were smoking, cradling their Thompson own submachine guns. They saw Major Farish with Goodman and extinguished their smokes. The Partisan officer approached Farish and spoke in an urgent tone. Farish shook his head and replied sternly.

"That is not what General Kozar directed last night, and not what Colonel Anderson agreed to."

"This is the new arrangement." The Partisan officer was indignant.

"Major Bogdanovič, there is no new arrangement," Farish's tone was measured but growing tense. "You were at the operations meeting last night as well as I. This is not the agreed arrangement of troops. You are to provide only yourself and your own personal security as assurance of mission completion. Not an entire infantry company."

"General Kozar is taking seriously the rumors of Ustaše units forming in the hills. It would be tragic if something happened to your mission this evening."

"Yeah, real tragic." Major Farish shook his head.

A large contingent of armed men and women, clothed in the olive wool uniforms and leather boots of the People's National Liberation Partisan Army, marched down the street toward them in three neat columns. The three Partisan soldiers loitering by the curb tossed their cigarettes over their shoulders and bolted to a stiff standing position and straightened their hats. The lieutenant commanding the arriving company halted his columns and barked his orders, all of which were followed with some precision.

The Majevitsa militiamen, for the most part, also stood up, albeit much more slowly. Most failed to bother to straighten any items of clothing or gear. They continued to smoke their cigarettes, pointing and smirking at the newly arrived company of Partisan infantry. A couple of louder-than-necessary scoffs attracted the ire of the company lieutenant, and he marched stiff legged over to the offending party, which then drew the attention of the entirety of the Majevitsa crew. Milosz intervened to assuage the lieutenant and prevent his men from beating him up and thus causing a riot. After a brief show of chastising the scoffers, he told the company lieutenant that discipline had been restored and that no offense was intended. The company lieutenant then stiffly marched over to Major Bogdanovich, saluted equally stiffly, and made his report. Bogdanovich dismissed him as his own staff lieutenant extracted a folded map from a leather shoulder case and handed it to him. He approached Major Farish as he unfolded it.

"Would you do us the pleasure of pointing out the location of your intended exchange point?"

"No, we're not going to do that," Farish responded. "I am adhering to the agreement of last night and we will conduct the mission accordingly. You are along for the ride, Comrade Major. Nothing more."

"General Kozar says otherwise." Bogdanovich puffed up just a little. "So, Major, shall we depart?"

"Yeah, looks like it." Farish stepped on his cigarette. "Goodman, it looks like your militia won't be necessary tonight after all."

"Yes, we will not require these...backward country criminals to conduct our operation," Bogdanovič added.

Farish ignored him and spoke to Goodman and the other OSS men. "Looks like the deal has changed," he said. "Colonel Anderson will have to deal with this later. We need to move if we're going to make link up."

*So now I have to just leave*, thought Goodman. *Like, right now.* Amira was already looking at him when he raised his eyes to hers. She wanted to say something, he could tell, but not with this crowd around them.

"Wait, sir, you mean we have to take that whole crew?" Kidder was incredulous.

"Yeah, sir, Major," said O'Keefe. "This is mission abort criteria."

Farish reflected for a moment. "No, you're right," he said. "This can't work."

"Why not?" asked Goodman.

"Captain, this,"—he gestured to the columns of partisans—"is not about a successful operation, this is about control," said Major Farish. "If it was about success, there would be a total of maybe eight or ten people dedicated to this mission."

"And only Americans," O'Keefe added.

Major Farish nodded. "In this sort of work, Captain, smaller is better. General Kozar, or his operations director, or his intelligence director, or all of them, are trying to exert control over what we do, when we do it, and how we do it."

"What next then?" asked Goodman.

"We wait," said Farish.

"So, I just sit here and wait?"

"His flight out is tomorrow night, sir," O'Keefe reminded the major. "It might be the last one out for the winter."

"What do you propose, Master Sergeant?" said Major Farish. "Bring over a hundred-fifty people to an asset linkup? At night? In unsecure territory?"

*If my choice is to get out now or wait six months*, thought Goodman, *I choose now.* Goodman had a flash of an idea. Raw and unfiltered, but it might help. *And Amira can help.*

"Major?" said Goodman. "I have an idea."

"Captain, I appreciate the tenacity," said Farish. "But you're untrained for this kind of technical work—"

"We need ideas, sir, beggin' your pardon." O'Keefe spoke up. "What's on your mind, Captain?"

"We can trick them, sir," Goodman began. "We all leave, but then some of us go to the real location for this linkup, and the rest of us lead these other guys on a wild goose chase. If we need, the militia can help." Amira perked up at the mention.

"That's a good idea," said Whitman. "Sir, that will do it. If you want to lead the primary mission, I'll run these jerks into the ground miles away from the linkup site."

"Bogdanovič already knows it's my gig," said Major Farish. "I'll have to lead the deception. In fact, if *any* of the officers are missing, then the Partisans will know something's up. O'Keefe, looks like you've got this one."

"Not a problem, sir." O'Keefe looked at Goodman. "I think a Master Sergeant can manage one little contact linkup. Captain, we'll need some of your militia after all."

"Amira Effendim?" She was already looking him in the eye. "Will you help us?"

"Whatever you require," she said. Her tone was business, but her eyes spoke something else.

# 70

FROM THE APARTMENT WINDOW, Colonel Anderson, Captain Goodman, and Master Sergeant O'Keefe watched Major Farish lead the other OSS officers, the Partisan Major Bogdanovič, and the entire company of Partisan infantry move out from the market square. Under a shop awning across the street, Amira and her men pretended to be napping. O'Keefe looked at his watch.

"We'll give 'em a few minutes to get out of our hair," he said.

"My surveillance man is still with us," said the Colonel, noting the man in the long overcoat leaning not-so-casually against a sign post half a block away. "I'll drag him to my new favorite restaurant across town."

"Which one, sir?" asked O'Keefe.

"No idea," said Anderson. "But I'm sure I'll find one."

O'Keefe snickered. "Good luck, sir."

"No, good luck to you all," he said. "Take care, Captain." He shook Goodman's hand and turned to O'Keefe.

Anderson descended the stairs and strolled across the street. The man in the overcoat hurriedly paralleled Anderson's traverse across the market square and out of sight. A few minutes later, Amira led Tomislav, Musa, and the rest of her men to the rear of the bakery, where Goodman and O'Keefe met them. O'Keefe led them straightaway into an adjoining alley.

"We're running late," he said. "We only have an hour of daylight and a couple of hours until contact time."

"I'm good," said Goodman. He looked at Amira. She was barely even breathing hard.

"Now, are your people good for this?" O'Keefe asked Goodman matter-of-factly. "I mean…we won't have any trouble, right?"

"No," said Goodman. "Their commander is very good. Besides, the militia is with me until I'm out of here. They made that promise and they intend to keep it. It's their honor."

"There will be no trouble from us," said Amira. In English.

O'Keefe glanced at Goodman and looked over Amira and the Majevitsa group.

"Good," said O'Keefe. "I don't like sprinting to a meeting site only to watch our contact drive away." Then he turned and spoke to the group in excellent Bosanski. "Once we cross the ridge north of the city, we're still two miles away from the linkup site. We'll keep off the roads as much as possible. Once we get into the woods, everybody is quiet!"

Amira nodded in agreement. She shot Goodman a glance. And a slight smirk. It made him feel good.

Tomislav put his hand on Goodman's shoulder. "You are going home tonight, yes?"

Goodman turned to see a big smile on Tomislav's face and two cigarettes in his fingers.

"No, thanks," said Goodman. Tomislav replaced one cigarette and lit the other.

"It is good that we got rid of the partisans," said Tomislav. "They could have been a big problem." Goodman nodded before Tomislav continued. "I will help you, my friend. After tonight, I may never see you again. Unless, of course, you get shot down over Yugoslavia again."

"You have been a good friend, Tomislav," said Goodman. "No offense, *moj drug*, but I have no intention of getting shot down any time soon."

"Yes, good, see that you don't." Tomislav's smile grew even bigger. Goodman couldn't help but smile himself.

O'Keefe unshouldered his Thompson submachine gun and waved a hand to everyone to follow him. The small force followed in a single file through the narrow alleyways between the shops of the commercial district, the manufacturing district, then into a neighborhood, and finally past small farms and pastures on the slopes of the north ridge. The last bit of pavement faded into stone, which then shifted to a dirt track that gained altitude rather quickly. Goodman's breathing became labored, but O'Keefe did not slow down but continued uphill into the woods as the last orange light faded from the sky.

At the summit of their third hilltop, O'Keefe halted the group and took a knee. The mostly clear sky and full moon allowed for good visibility, and Goodman could see an open field ahead of them, high with weeds and sprinkled with shining quartz slab headstones. A broken stone structure lay silently in the middle, glistening white in the moonlight. O'Keefe waved to Goodman and Amira to come forward and join him. They rose together and slowly approached the edge of the woods. O'Keefe held up his watch to read it by the moonlight.

"Ok, we made good time." He pointed toward the church in the field. "This is where we will run to if everything goes wrong, *razumijem*?"

Goodman and Amira both nodded.

"Good," said O'Keefe. "Follow me." He rose to his feet and quietly led the group around the edge of the field into the trees once again. A couple hundred yards in, O'Keefe halted behind a group of large, moonlit boulders. He quietly called for everyone to come to him. Goodman, Amira, Tomislav, and Musa all came in close.

When their noise finally ceased, he spoke quietly. "We're here."

# 71

## CONTACT LINKUP SITE NORTHWEST OF TUZLA

GOODMAN PEERED INTO THE DARKNESS, his vision fractured by the bright moonlight splintering through the trees. "What? Where?" he asked.

"See that road?" O'Keefe pointed to a dim ribbon of road lying about fifty yards beyond the boulders to their front. "It comes up from the west end of the Tuzla valley. That's where you meet your contact."

"*I* meet him?" asked Goodman. "I thought *you* were going to talk to him."

"The contact only knows about a single courier, not all of us," said O'Keefe. "Don't you speak the local tongue pretty well?"

Goodman felt his chest tighten. He didn't expect to have to do this on his own. "It's ok, but this is something else…"

"I'll go," Tomislav interrupted.

Goodman turned to look at him. *Thank you, Tomislav,* he thought.

"I'll go with him," Tomislav continued. "It will be better if the one who says the code words speaks fluent Bosanski, yes?"

"Ok, then," said O'Keefe. He handed Tomislav a pale blue handkerchief. "You make sure this is visible to the contact and ask him about *a mechanic in the town of Mošenik*. Be specific. Make sure you say it correctly."

"A mechanic in Mošenik," Tomislav repeated.

"Yes, if everything is good, he'll tell you he doesn't know the mechanic, but he can take you to Mosnik. Now you, Captain, you'll follow all directions from the contact. If the guy knows of something that would prevent this from happening tonight, he'll tell us—tell the two of you—another day and time." Farish's eyes shifted from Tomislav to Goodman, then back to Tomislav. "You good with this?"

"Yes. It is no problem." Tomislav put his hand on Goodman's shoulder.

"Yes," confirmed Goodman. He felt better with this arrangement.

"Good," said O'Keefe. He checked his watch and then squinted into the moonlit surroundings. "We'll set up a perimeter and wait. Captain, if things go bad, run back to these rocks and we'll make our way to the church together before we go back to town. We have about twenty minutes until the window for our contact opens."

Amira returned to the center of their position with Goodman and Tomislav. Master Sergeant O'Keefe opened his pack and pulled out a small radio set. He attached the antenna and tuned the receiver. He held the earpiece to his head and spoke quietly into the microphone. A slight crackling sound emanated from the earpiece, and he spoke again. Apparently frustrated, he shut off the radio and returned it to his pack.

"Something wrong?" asked Goodman.

"Signal's not strong here," said O'Keefe. "Just as well, though, then the Jerries can't DF us." He settled in against one of the rocks.

"What does DF mean?" Goodman asked quietly.

"It means direction finding," O'Keefe whispered back. "The Germans have special radio receivers mounted on trucks that can track a radio signal. It works like your radio beacon navigation system. They are pretty good at it, too. There are ways to broadcast that are safer than others, and this isn't a high priority right now. I can tell them when I get back tonight."

"What happens if they track the signal?" asked Goodman.

O'Keefe looked at him. "What do you think happens?"

*Artillery or Stukas.* "Right, sorry."

"No problem, Captain. Just be johnny-on-the-spot when the contact shows up."

"Will do."

"But if Jerry or the Ustaše hit us, then run back to the burned-out church and wait for two minutes for others to show up. Now, while you're there, in the southwest corner of the chapel inside the church is a wooden box under a broken door, lying on the ground. In the box are two loaded flare guns wrapped in an oilcloth. At the end of two minutes, whoever is still with us will be there. At that point, fire both flares, one after another, and then run. Run your ass off. We'll go all the way back to Tuzla by the quickest route. Don't wait for anyone after two minutes. The next people you see will be the SS or something worse coming for you. Got it?"

"Why fire the flares? Won't that tell the Germans where we are?"

"They'll already know where we are. We have to warn the main force in Tuzla," O'Keefe said. "Each of General Kozar's outposts has the same warning system. But we're a couple miles outside their perimeter. We'll have to give warning that we're coming, not just that the Jerries are attacking."

"Do you think that's a possibility?" asked Goodman. "That we'll have to run like that?"

"We have to plan for all contingencies but, no, we won't have to run." O'Keefe scratched his nose. "I wouldn't worry about that part too much. We've never been blown out of a linkup site. We haven't used this location before, so it's good and clean. And this part of the network was created just for this occasion. They'll get you to the farm with the other aviators. These guys we're meeting tonight are good." He paused. "And, if we don't get a chance to say it later, good luck to you, Captain."

"Thanks, Master Sergeant. You, too." They shook hands briefly.

They went quiet as Amira put Musa and his machine gun crew up in a small cluster of trees to cover the entire stretch of road to their front. O'Keefe checked his watch and showed it to Goodman. The window for the contact to arrive opened two minutes ago. The woods fell silent.

Eventually, Goodman's nervousness wore off and boredom set in. A cool wind whistled and made the trees sway and creak. An owl hooted somewhere in the valley in front of them. Another, much closer, returned the call. He looked up at the rare chance of seeing the owls and saw the stars twinkling above the trees. Polaris was right where it should be. The constant in a sea of chaotic change. The air fell still, and it felt to Goodman that the temperature climbed a couple of degrees. Somewhere out of sight, deep in the valley, a dog barked. The treetops told of a mild wind overhead. O'Keefe checked his watch again.

"Where is this guy?" he whispered to himself.

Goodman shifted his weight off his left hip. The pains of his old and new injuries aggravated him. Leaves crackled as others shifted to keep their blood moving and regain feeling in their legs or arms.

Amira silently crept between Goodman and O'Keefe. "Kamion," she whispered. *A truck.*

The two men next to her strained to hear anything above the night sounds of the forest. Sure enough, the sound of a far-off vehicle sputtered through the trees. It strained up a steep grade, and the driver jammed the gear shift hard. The diesel-powered pistons increased in tempo as the truck got up to speed. The sound downshifted in pitch, then increased again. Everyone's ears followed the sound of the truck as it traversed several switchbacks on the road below the ridge, still well out of sight. Another switchback. Another gear shift. Accelerating. A dim, yellow glow of headlights far to the right preceded the sound's movement back from left to right. Goodman shifted his weight slightly and O'Keefe put his hand on his shoulder.

"Don't move, Captain," he whispered. "Not until the driver stops and puts out his signal."

"Right." Goodman settled back into place. "Sorry."

The vehicle continued agonizingly slowly on its way up the lower road, then slowed even more to make the last turn onto the stretch to the group's front. Goodman squinted as the headlights swept across the woods at the turn and then illuminated the road. The driver downshifted, and the truck crept into view. The headlights flashed, then flashed again, and then two more times.

"There's the signal," whispered O'Keefe.

Goodman watched the car coast by. Then the brake lights cast a dirty, orange glow through the trees. The vehicle crawled to a stop just past where Goodman and the others lay.

The engine cut off, and the driver got out but left the headlights on. The hood squeaked loudly as he lit a lantern and leaned into the engine compartment.

"There," said O'Keefe.

*Time to move*, thought Goodman. He tapped Tomislav on the shoulder and slowly climbed to their feet. They both leaned forward to take a step, but Amira grabbed Goodman's arm. It startled him.

At first, he thought it was her farewell. But it was much too strong and abrupt.

"What's wrong?" he whispered.

She held him fast, silent. Listening.

"Captain," said O'Keefe. "Get moving!"

Amira's grip on Goodman tightened.

"Something's wrong," Goodman whispered.

"What?" asked O'Keefe. "What's wrong?"

"I don't know…"

"The contact has his signal out," said O'Keefe with an edge to his voice. "You don't want to miss him. It's time to go…"

"*Neh…*" said Amira.

"What's the problem?" O'Keefe whispered angrily. "Go! Move! Now!"

"What's wrong with Amira?" Goodman whispered to Tomislav. "Do we go?" He pressed forward, but Tomislav held back.

"I don't know," whispered Tomislav. "Amira, do we go?"

Amira studied the darkness before she turned to Farish and Bogdanovich.

"No, this is wrong," she whispered. "Something is wrong."

"Bullshit," said O'Keefe. "Sir, you gotta go!" He gave Goodman a shove.

Stumbling in the dark, Goodman looked for Amira and Tomislav. *What do I do? Do I listen to O'Keefe or Amira?* It seemed there was trouble either way. *This is how I get home. What am I going to do, stay here?*

"Let's go!" Goodman said, pulling his arm from Amira's grip. Tomislav hesitated.

"We must leave here," Amira said as she backed away from the road. "We are in danger!"

"Move!" O'Keefe was incensed. "Get your ass up there, Captain!"

"Tomislav, we have to go!" said Goodman. "I have to go." He took a step toward the road.

Tomislav stumbled and followed Goodman through the trees down the slight embankment and onto the road, trying to watch what was going on in front as well as behind them. They both crept as quietly as possible. Goodman was conflicted. *Maybe it would be better to make some noise, so as not to startle a nervous and probably armed contact. Yes? No? What do I know about this sort of thing?* He took his first steps onto the road about ten yards behind the glowing taillights. The front of the car hid the driver. Tomislav strode tentatively toward the red glow of the taillights.

Goodman and Tomislav froze when they heard another set of engines and gearboxes grinding on the lower road. The driver poked his head out from behind the hood and saw the pair approaching. Tomislav pulled out the powder blue handkerchief in his pocket and held it out toward the driver. Another grinding of gears echoed faintly through the trees.

"*Izvnite, Effendi,*" began Tomislav.

"Yes, what is it you want?" The driver raised his lantern. Goodman was blinded by the light.

"My car is disabled...do you know the mechanic in Mošenik?" Goodman saw that Tomislav's other hand was in his coat pocket, where he kept his pistol. He tucked his own submachine gun's shoulder stock into his shoulder.

The driver raised his lantern higher and spoke loudly. "What? What did you say?"

Tomislav repeated, "I asked you if you would be so kind as to take us to the mechanic in Mošenik." The driver was distracted by the engine noises emanating from where he had just driven.

Tomislav stepped past the rear bumper and approached the driver, one hand still holding the handkerchief and the other still on his pistol.

"I'm willing to pay you in Kuna or Dinar for a ride for my friend...do you know the mechanic shop in Mošenik?" Tomislav ventured the pass phrase. The driver looked at the kerchief and lowered his lantern.

"No," he replied to Tomislav. "But I will take you to—" The driver froze and took a step toward Tomislav.

392

"*Vuko!*" he exclaimed. The driver suddenly reached inside the passenger window.

Tomislav drew his pistol. "Stop!" he yelled.

# 72

THE DRIVER DIVED INTO THE CAR ANYWAY. Goodman fumbled to get his submachine gun up, but not before Tomislav's pistol pierced the night air like a thunderclap. The lantern crashed to the road and spilled its oil, which ignited in a small pool of orange and yellow flame. The driver rolled out of the window with a pistol of his own, but dropped it as his body slumped to the ground. He clumsily reached for the pistol with a lame arm, but Tomislav sent another bullet into him, sending more echoes into the surrounding trees. The driver's body rolled over like a pile of laundry next to the flaming oil. Goodman stared at the body, still shaking.

"What the hell, Tomislav?" He reached out to grab his friend by the arm, when, even with deadened eardrums, Goodman heard the other engines roar to life. "Who the hell is that?" Goodman felt his heart pound. "Tomislav, wha—"

Heavy machinegun fire shattered the night air and blinding white tracers fanned out wide across the sky. Goodman and Tomislav flung themselves to the ground as a shell swished through the treetops overhead and impacted on a faraway hillside. Heavy machine guns thumped the air, and the sky lit up in a disorienting light show. A bright light flashed from the north, accompanied by a loud crack and a blinding fireball. The crackling of rifle and submachine-gun fire sounded pitifully small against the heart-quaking thumps of the heavy weapons. The trees behind Tomislav and Goodman suddenly became a commotion of men trampling and stumbling in the dark, dropping equipment, and shoving each other.

"Hey, Goodman!" O'Keefe yelled from the woods. "Get your ass back here!"

Tomislav and Goodman were sprinting back to the woods.

"We must leave here now!" Amira barked at the two of them, her weapon in one hand and heaving a belt of machine gun ammunition over her shoulder with the other. Several men were arguing over something when another very bright and loud explosion stopped all that. Everyone turned and sprinted into the woods.

Goodman saw Musa trying desperately, unsuccessfully, to free his MG42 from a vine in which it had become entangled. Goodman tried to pull Musa off the gun, but he was married to it and would not leave without it. Amira cut the vine with her knife and cursed at Musa for being foolish. Tomislav yelled for Goodman to run as he disappeared into the dark woods. A brilliant searchlight bathed the entire forest in blinding light, silhouetting men in their panic. Large caliber tracers splintered through the trees to sounds of the deafening blasts of the guns that launched them. Goodman looked back to see headlights racing toward the car. The searchlight swept back and forth through the trees, followed by streaks of tracer fire.

On the road, the car lurched several times as shells impacted and pierced it. The fuel tank ignited in a yellow splash of liquid fire as the headlights flickered out. A long string of tracers swept back and forth through the woods, thumping into trees and snapping branches overhead, severing tree limbs that fell with a crash. Amira yelled as she ran to lead her men out of the melee, trying to keep some semblance of control as they fled. One of her men returned fire with his submachine gun, illuminating himself and the trees around him. German tracer fire cut him down with a scream. Several men dived for cover. Goodman slid behind a tree, caught himself, and sprinted as fast as he could.

Goodman and Tomislav burst out of the woods into the moon-lit clearing where the church was. They sprinted through the cemetery headstones and entered the rubble of the burned-out church. He ran to the corner of the sanctuary and found the crate, just as O'Keefe had described. He flung the lid to the side and found the oily rags. As he shook the flare guns loose and cocked the hammer, he scanned for O'Keefe. *Where is he? Where is everyone else?*

"Fire the flares!" exclaimed Tomislav.

"We're supposed to wait for two minutes!" Goodman sputtered, out of breath. He

"Fire the flare!" Tomislav said again.

*Right*, thought Goodman. *This, I have to do for everyone else. Everyone has to know.*

He raised the first gun and squeezed his eyes shut. The flare went up in a shower of sparks and burst into a bright red blossom two hundred feet overhead that slowly drifted on the wind. It cast a red haze on the church and surrounding field and trees. Goodman picked up the second flare gun, cocked the hammer, and the second flare went up and exploded. Dual hazy pink shadows danced about everywhere.

A moment later, O'Keefe, Amira, Musa, and several handfuls of militia emerged from the wood line. Goodman waved to them from the rubble, and O'Keefe sprinted through the cemetery.

"What the hell did you shoot the driver for?" O'Keefe demanded when he entered the church.

"Your driver..." Tomislav sputtered. "Your man...was a spy."

"No way!" O'Keefe growled back. The men were almost nose to nose.

"Hey, stop!" Goodman intervened. "Right now, we have to get the hell outta here. We'll figure this out later. Master Sergeant, take point and get us back to Tuzla. Let Amira and her men fight this fight. They wanted to be here."

"Roger that, Captain." O'Keefe stood upright and straightened his ammo pouches. He stepped over a pile of stones and into the darkness just as Amira and the others arrived.

"Amira!" Goodman called out. "Set up a squad here to keep the Germans away from us!" He pointed to the wood line nearest the road. "Then get them back to Tuzla!"

Amira was already on it. She directed Musa and at least half her force to take positions in the rubble. Suddenly, from somewhere to the east and not all that far away, another burst of gunfire erupted. The volume of gunfire grew and tracer fire arced over the trees.

"That must be the Major Bogdanovič's Partisan company," said O'Keefe. "They must have bumped into someone else on their goose chase!"

Everyone paused to take in the sights and sounds of that battle until, over the top of that cacophony, Musa let off his first burst of machinegun fire at the Germans advancing on the church. The other militia opened up as well, and then the woods sparkled with the Germans' return fire.

"Go to the city!" Amira shouted to Goodman and O'Keefe. "We will be right behind you. Now go!" Before they could move, she turned and screamed at her men in the second position in the tree line to open fire, thereby covering Musa and his men as they withdrew from the church.

Goodman turned and yelled to O'Keefe. "Due south, right?"

"Yessir!" And Goodman took off at a sprint with O'Keefe and Tomislav close behind while the twin battles raged behind them.

Goodman thought he was making good time, but O'Keefe sprinted through the darkness as if it was the middle of the day. He dodged trees, rounded small ditches, and crossed streams without slowing his pace. At the crest of the last ridge, he paused to listen before resuming the descending journey into the Tuzla valley. He paused a second time and raised his hand to halt the column behind him. Goodman stopped and leaned against a tree, completely out of breath.

"What's going on?" said Goodman, completely out of breath.

"Vehicles, sir," O'Keefe replied. "Coming up out of Tuzla. I think it's Kozar's forces responding to the attack."

"Yeah," said Goodman. "I think you're right." He listened to the engines and gears as they raced up unseen mountain roads. "Let's stay off the roads so nobody thinks we're Nazis attacking Tuzla."

"Right, sir," O'Keefe replied. "Permission to proceed?"

A loud crash of footfalls on brush filtered through the forest behind them. *It must be Amira and her people.* "Wait," said Goodman.

"I hear 'em," said O'Keefe.

"Can you signal them?" asked Goodman.

"You got it, sir." O'Keefe withdrew a small flashlight and clicked it on and off rapidly. Amira's face shone in the light a moment later.

"Turn that light off!" she growled.

O'Keefe tucked it away. "You got everyone?" he asked.

"Yes, we are all here. Let's keep moving," she replied. "I think the Partisans are counterattacking."

"That's what we think," said Goodman. "Let's go."

The group made it to the Tuzla outskirts at about 0200 hours. O'Keefe led Goodman and Amira's militia to the market square across the street from the bakery.

"Hvala, Effendim," Goodman whispered.

"It was nothing," she replied. He thought he saw a smile.

O'Keefe tapped Goodman on the shoulder. "It's time for you to get out of sight," he said. "I don't know what Kozar is capable of after tonight."

"Right," said Goodman. But before he followed O'Keefe into the alley, Goodman looked back at Amira. She was busy checking her people, issuing hushed orders. O'Keefe unlocked and held the apartment door open for him. As his boots clomped heavily up the steps, Goodman realized he had not seen Tomislav. He knew Amira, Musa, Milosz, Ahmet, and several other familiars of the militia were there. But no Tomislav.

# 73

## 0700 HOURS, OCTOBER 1, 1943
## THE OSS APARTMENT

GOODMAN FELT GROGGY, but Colonel Anderson looked like he had been up all night. Anderson gulped his coffee and refilled it from the blackened pot sitting over the brilliant blue gas flame. The floor of the apartment was warm from the bakery below, but the apartment itself was not well-insulated and the steam from the coffee fogged over the kitchen window. The faces around him glowed blue on one side from the early morning light through the window and, on the other, orange from the oil lamp hanging above the table. Whitman, O'Keefe, Kidder, and Goodman sat like schoolboys in the principal's office. The cup clinked on the windowsill as Colonel Anderson put it down, steam still rising from it, and exhaled loudly.

"Gentlemen," he began. "Someone from the British mission will be here shortly to help us make sense of what happened last night. Depending on who it is, what I mean by 'help us' is to either make life difficult for us and assert that we are too incompetent to have a role in the war in Yugoslavia, or perhaps genuinely help us. I also expect someone from Kozar's staff to arrive later to give us more grief. We need to have our story straight. So..." He paused. "What the hell happened last night?" He looked at Goodman and Master Sergeant O'Keefe. "Well?"

Goodman spoke up first. "The driver was th—"

"It was that guy who was with Goodman!" Kidder blurted out. "The guy who wears the business suit. He shot our driver. That's what O'Keefe said."

Goodman glared at Kidder. "His name's Tomislav and he shot the driver because the driver pulled a pistol on us. There was nothing in the plan about the driver pointing a gun at us."

"It's a midnight meeting in the middle of the woods with a guy who has never seen you and doesn't know what you look like," said Whitman. "I'd have a gun on you, too."

"Yeah," Goodman retorted. "But would you pull it out in the middle of the conversation?"

"Stop it, guys!" Colonel Anderson raised his hands to silence the captains. "Let's take this piece by piece. Were you in the right place?"

Master Sergeant O'Keefe was indignant. "Yes, sir."

"Did the driver make it at the right time and right place?"

"Yessir."

"Who made contact with the driver?"

"Me," said Goodman. "And Tomislav. He was the one with the signal. I figured his native tongue wouldn't spook the contact."

"That might have been what did it," said Anderson. "The contact was expecting an American." Goodman felt a little ill at this point. Colonel Anderson resumed his questioning. "Did this guy Tomislav have the signals right?" Everyone looked at Goodman.

"Yes, sir," answered Goodman. "He had the blue handkerchief out like Master Sergeant O'Keefe said and, from what I could tell, he gave the pass phrase just about word-for-word."

"Did the driver give the right response?" All eyes moved back to Goodman.

"No," Goodman shook his head. "He was confused. He started to say something, but...he stopped. Then he yelled something before he pulled out the pistol."

"What did he yell?" asked Whitman.

Goodman recalled the man saying the word *vuko*. Like when the wolves came around Baba's village. "'Wolf'," Goodman answered. "He said 'wolf'."

"What was that supposed to mean?" asked Captain Kidder. "Like a wolf in the chicken coop?"

"Dunno," said Goodman. "Never heard it used like that before."

Anderson put his hands on his hips and looked out the window at the early morning gray. He exhaled and his breath blew in a cloud against the window and cursed under his breath.

Master Sergeant O'Keefe spoke up. "It's FUBAR for sure, but it doesn't do anything to explain how the whole damned German army *also* showed up at exactly the right place at exactly the right time."

"Not only that," Whitman added. "They were using a pincer movement to trap us. That means they had a plan. It might have been hasty, but they had one. We got out only because they failed to establish a complete ring around you *and* us. But how *in the hell* did they know to be there in the first place?" He looked at Goodman.

"I don't know," said Goodman. "We're surrounded by the Communist army, which is surrounded by the German army in a place full of people itching to kill each other." He gestured to the window. "How do we know Kozar's people didn't do something?"

"They wouldn't put the mission at risk," O'Keefe replied. "They have too much at stake. Besides, what would be gained by giving you or us up to the Jerries?"

"Don't forget they had a bit of a tough time last night putting that little fire out," said Whitman. "They still hold the ground, but they took casualties."

"Did we figure out who it was?" asked Kidder. "Was it *Wehrmacht* or SS?"

"The Germans?" said Colonel Anderson. "It was SS. Kozar's people say it was an SS motorized reconnaissance company in support of the SD. We've seen them do this sort of thing before, but not this far into the mountains. At least not so far this year."

"How do they know SD?" asked Kidder.

"They found an SD Major from their station in Tuzla. Unfortunately, he bled out before they could interrogate him," said the colonel.

Whitman nodded ruefully, swallowing the last of his coffee. O'Keefe shook his head and finished his coffee as well.

"What's the SD?" asked Goodman.

"The SD is the *Sicherheitsdienst*," Whitman replied. "The intelligence arm of Hitler's crazies in the SS."

Goodman had heard of the secret police branch of German intelligence from newsreels. "The *Gestapo*?" he asked.

"No," said O'Keefe. "The Gestapo run ops *inside* the Reich. The SD runs spies outside the Reich and in the combat zones. Among other things…"

"So the deal just went south," said Kidder. "A lot worse. We're compromised. I mean, how else would they know about our man on the road last night?"

"Don't jump to conclusions," said Colonel Anderson. "There are several possibilities."

"It may not be us," O'Keefe suggested. "It could be something further upstream along the chain. Can we ask the Banja Luka team to re-assess their network?"

"Already did that," said Whitman. "Aside from being royally pissed off about their best front-end agent getting killed, they said they're clean. All the assets involved were under direct Allied control. Getting our people out is their big game and their ship is watertight."

"Is everyone in sector up to date on radio ciphers?" asked Colonel Anderson.

"As of 0500 this morning, yes, sir," said O'Keefe. "Amazingly, everyone in Europe made their time hacks last night with the right designators. At least London station hasn't sent out any destruction notices."

"So, it's not our communications." Anderson nodded his head slightly.

Goodman shifted forward in his chair. "Last night, O'Keefe was worried about the Germans tracking the Partisans' radios," he offered.

"Not possible with that quick of a response time," Whitman said. "That force was already travelling to the site from two different directions. You can't just pick up and move a force of that size that quickly. The SS is good, but not magical. They knew ahead of time."

"This hurts my head." Captain Kidder shook his head as he lit up a cigarette. "How to find a disloyal son of a bitch in a pile of dirty and double-crossing sons of bitches?"

O'Keefe held out his hand to Kidder with two fingers extended. Kidder took a long drag and put the cigarette between O'Keefe's fingers and then lit up another cigarette for himself. Both men blew clouds of smoke up into the air. Goodman sensed no one wanted to state the obvious and so left each other with an awkward silence. Until Goodman smashed it.

"So is it someone here?" said Goodman. "Here in Tuzla?"

"Has to be," said O'Keefe.

"It's not us," said Whitman. "And it's not any of Kozar's staff. We didn't even share the time or exact location with Bogdanovich. That's why he was so hot last night."

Colonel Anderson looked at Goodman. "What about your people? When did they know about the mission?"

Goodman sat up. *He said 'my people.'* Goodman cleared his throat. "The only people who knew the mission before we put everyone together in the street last night were Amira and Tomislav.

And I don't think she had a chance to tell anyone anything other than to be ready for a mission."

"What *about* that guy…this Tomislav?" asked Colonel Anderson. Everyone looked at Goodman again. "Did he disappear at all between the time we set up the mission and our departure?"

"To be honest," Goodman confessed. "I don't remember. I don't think so." His eyes fell to the floor. The group heard deliberate footsteps on the stairs. Two sets of boots. Heavy.

"Ok," said Whitman. "This is probably Blackbyrne or his sidekick Birdington, with someone from the intelligence section. They are *not* our friends. The colonel and I will do the talking." Everyone nodded.

"Not so fast, Captain," said Colonel Anderson. "I asked someone else to come earlier this morning."

The other OSS men looked askance at the Colonel, but before anyone could ask, the pair of footsteps halted outside the door. Two knocks, then three more. Captain Kidder moved to the door.

# 74

CAPTAIN KIDDER OPENED THE DOOR to see Major Farish with a British officer. A smile spread across Kidder's face.

"Major Churchill, good morning!" he said. He opened the door wide.

"Thank you, Brian," said Major Churchill. "Say, one of your militia folks downstairs wants to speak to your pilot."

Goodman stood up. "They guy with the suit and hat?"

"That is him," said Churchill.

"Let him wait for now," said Colonel Anderson. Goodman sat back down.

Kidder closed and locked the door. He leaned against it with his arms crossed. "You can have my chair, sir."

"Thank you once again, Brian," replied Major Churchill.

The chair scraped the floor as Major Churchill sat down. He took his hat off and placed it on the table. O'Keefe offered him a cup of coffee from the stove, which he accepted and placed on the floor. From inside his overcoat, he extracted a small leather-encased flask. He unscrewed the lid and poured a generous amount of the liquid into his coffee. Goodman saw Kidder smirk at Whitman.

"So, what have we today, Colonel Anderson?" he said as he replaced the flask and lifted the coffee to his lips. He frowned at the drink but still swallowed a mouthful.

"Well, Randolph, we have a security leak," Anderson began with arms folded. "And we are not entirely certain who it is. But whoever it is had access to the specifics of the mission last night. Ahead of time."

"Whom have we thus far ruled out, Colonel?" Churchill asked, placing the coffee cup on the table next to his hat.

Colonel Anderson cleared his throat. "We've ruled out compromise of Allied European covert communications. The next portion of our escape network still appears secure…"

"Except for the loss of a front-end transporter," Churchill added. "From what I understand, he was a first-rate asset."

"That's correct, unfortunately," said Anderson. He continued. "We also ruled out nearly all of Kozar's staff—"

"Nearly?"

"Well, Major Bogdanovich and his surveillance teams are a constant nuisance, and they could have heard or seen something that could have given them more than we knew. Aside from that infantry company they threw at us at the last minute."

"Yes, that is a persistent problem," Churchill mused. "But, given Bogdanovich's zealous ideals and his ambitions, he would not put his own mission—keeping all of you under control, that is—at risk, now would he?"

"No, but if he or his crew shared what they knew with someone else on the staff, which they should have—again, if they heard something—and they reported it to someone who does not share

Tito's or Kozar's tolerance of our liaison mission then…" Anderson let the idea float on its own.

Churchill finished for him. "Then they could have reported to outside parties who then informed the SS."

"That would be a pickle," Anderson added. "But not entirely unforeseeable. Just really bad to have it happen now."

"Or at all, really," said O'Keefe. "There isn't a good time for this sort of corruption."

"Yes, quite," Churchill confirmed. He leaned down to take another sip from his enhanced coffee. "To whom does the good Communist Major report on the general staff?"

"He says he reports to the operations chief," said Whitman. "But we know he reports to the Intelligence Bureau."

"Yes, that's that same controller for my own chaperone," said Churchill. He paused for a moment. "But if the leak is from the top of the Intelligence Bureau staff, then we would be experiencing a lot more of these sorts of things, wouldn't we?" He took another sip of coffee as everyone nodded in agreement. "What about this troupe of mountain folk that came in with your downed airman?" He bowed slightly toward Goodman.

"Well…" Anderson took a breath. "That is the last possibility that we can ascertain right now. We're not sure if he had the opportunity or means to get a message out, but Captain Goodman's minder in the group—what's his name?"

"Tomislav," said Goodman.

"Yes, he was the one who shot our network transporter."

"Really?" Major Churchill raised his eyebrows and glanced at Goodman. "I hadn't heard that part yet."

"I did not include it in my report," said Colonel Anderson. "Blackbyrne wouldn't see me with all the activity last night. I had Captain Whitman make the report to Birdington. Who knows what *he* may have said to Blackbyrne…"

"Major Reginald Baxter Birdington is a royal shit," Churchill muttered as he took another sip of coffee. "I wouldn't trust him to carry the King's underwear back from the laundries." He looked at Master Sergeant O'Keefe. "Might you grant me one of those cigarettes?" He reached a hand toward O'Keefe, who was burning out the last of his smoke. O'Keefe pointed to Kidder, who turned his hand over to say "*really?*" Kidder reached into his breast pocket and extracted a crumpled cigarette packet. He withdrew the last two cigarettes and lit them both with a flick of a lighter, then handed one to Major Churchill. Whitman made a two-fingered motion to his lips.

"Sorry, I'm out," replied Kidder as he tossed the crumpled-up packet at him. Whitman shrugged and let the packet fall to the floor. Everyone watched Major Churchill take a puff, scowl, and blow the smoke into a cloud over his head.

"I miss my cigars. The last bunch unfortunately fell into enemy hands last month with the last resupply drop." Churchill shifted slightly to look at Goodman. "Say Captain, tell me a little about your exploits here in the terror that is the modern-day Land of the Southern Slavs." He took another puff and let the smoke waft from his nostrils. Colonel Anderson folded his arms.

"Well, sir," Goodman began, casting a quick glance to Colonel Anderson. "I'm not sure what you've already been told…"

"Let me stop you right there," Churchill interrupted. "First, let's dispense with the pleasantries. We're a tad more cordial in our confidential conversations. And let's pretend I've not heard anything about you. Which is more or less true since Colonel Blackbyrne plays his cards close to his chest. I believe that's what you Yanks would say." He looked to Anderson.

"That is a saying we have," Anderson said. "And yes, Colonel Blackbyrne is not very forthcoming with information."

"Yes, he's a learned pupil and sycophant of General Kozar, his mentor of late," Churchill said this last part with a wistful tone. "Information is indeed power. Now, good Captain, please pardon the interruption and share with me as if I have not heard a thing about your time here." Churchill offered Goodman his flask. Goodman looked to Colonel Anderson again, who granted him permission with a nod.

"Captain Goodman, you can share everything with Major Churchill. He is an ally."

"Yes, sir." Goodman took Major Churchill's flask and took a sip. *It's whiskey, not slivovitz*. He handed the flask back to Churchill. "I was flight lead as part of a raid on some German oil facilities in Romania in August."

"The Ploiesti raid?" asked Churchill.

"Yes, sir."

"Good God, man," exclaimed Churchill. "What an imperial cock up that was."

"Yeah, I think if I had to do it again, I'd have peeled off with the other squadrons when we figured out my wing commander turned at the wrong checkpoint. Instead of approaching from the west when nobody was awake, we approached from the east a half hour after the attacks had begun and every German gunner was wide awake. I stuck with my squadron leader and, well, here I am."

"Duty will test your moral fiber." Churchill took another drink. "Please continue."

"So I went down in the mountains northeast of here," Goodman went on. "I think I was the only one of my crew to survive. Anyway, this group of mountain folk, as you call them, took me in, hid me in a cellar, and took care of me for several weeks. All things considered, they took very good care of me, medically speaking. But when it came time for me to move, we were attacked and then…things got…messy."

"Messy, how?" asked Churchill.

"This war looks different when you're in the middle of it," said Goodman. "Lots of people get killed for things that don't seem to matter. I'm accustomed to a different way of fighting. This whole place is a mess."

"That's an understatement," Kidder piped in.

"This group that brought me to Tuzla seems to have no friends. They live in the mountains. They survive by making deals with other groups. Their leader, a guy called Zoran Pasha—"

"Pasha?" asked Churchill. "He's a Mohammedan. And a man who seems to have an inflated sense of destiny. Pashas are from the Ottoman traditions."

"I don't know about that," said Goodman. "But he definitely believed in some kind of destiny he was supposed to fulfill. In each battle, he seemed to think it was a sign or something of what was supposed to be his rise to power. He called his people his army, but

I'd call it more of a family or clan militia. There's only a couple hundred of them at the most."

"How many engagements were you involved in?" Churchill asked.

Goodman thought for a second. "Five, I think. Well, the last few days are kind of a blur for me."

"I'm sure," said Churchill. "Not the normal bit of warfare for an aviator specialized in strategic bombing campaigns, is it? What with being accustomed to your place in the formation at a specified altitude, with a specified heading and specified bombload with aerial checkpoints and other such details all dictated to you and everyone around you. Not exactly in line with your resume."

"No," Goodman admitted. "This is pretty far outside my training."

"What role did you play?"

"At first I thought I was along for the ride," said Goodman. "I mean, I didn't even know where I was until recently. But later, I kinda got forced into a sticky situation. Several, actually. I took command of a small attack and,"—he looked around the room—"I think I did alright, given the situation. I mean, we took this garrison at a factory east of the city and destroyed two German tanks and an infantry company before attacking the fortress on the river. Zoran's militia is definitely effective, though they are kind of messy about it."

"Tell me about this militia." Churchill interrupted. "What are they about?"

"Well, Zoran's dead." He instantly felt a pit in his stomach. "He died yesterday after the assault on the German garrison in the fortress. His daughter, Amira, is their leader now, along with a guy called Milosz, who was Zoran's deputy. There are other noncommissioned officer-types, but those are the main ones."

"A woman commander?" asked Churchill. "Interesting."

"Yes, she...I don't know what to say about her." He was conflicted about her and wanted to protect what she had, even if the Allies wouldn't help. He also didn't want to share anything that could be used against her. "She's got a heavy load to carry."

"Stepping into her father's shoes, is she?" Churchill probed. "It's perfectly reasonable to—"

"No...no, I wouldn't say that." He searched for the words. "She's...driven," Goodman finally said. "She's driven, for sure. She's been abused, assaulted, I think. She's the only survivor of her family now, which I understand was pretty large before the war. She's all business. She can be vicious. Anyway, she's their leader now, but their force is pretty beaten up after the attack on the fortress."

"What do you think her intentions are now?" asked Churchill. "What is her motivation?"

"Revenge," Goodman assessed. "That is her rule. She didn't always agree with him, but I think she sees herself as a continuation of her father's will."

"Will she side with Tito's people?"

"No," replied Goodman. "Absolutely not. Her father did not trust them and she's not going to trust them. She thinks she's on her own now with people depending on her, especially with her father dead."

"What is she capable of?"

"Anything that will get her to a place where she can kill those who she thinks have anything to do with...with the suffering of her people." It felt wrong to share more about what he suspected of Amira's assault.

"Sounds to me like there are plenty of those," Churchill assessed.

"Except for all of you, here in this room, to my knowledge she's never fully trusted anyone besides her father," said Goodman.

"Trusts us?"

"She's still here." Goodman nodded toward the window over the road. "She wouldn't stick around if she didn't. I don't know why else she would be here."

"Perhaps that's because of your reward, my young captain. She has a healthy bounty coming to her on account of you being delivered here." Churchill puffed on his cigarette. "What of this man...Tomislav, you say?"

"Tomislav is the reason Zoran and his daughter survived," said Goodman. "Something went very badly for the militia last April.

Supposedly, Tomislav was the one who warned them about the attack that killed Zoran and Amira's village. And their family."

"What did he do before the war?"

"He was an actor."

"An actor?" Churchill's eyes lit up.

"A stage actor. Like Shakespeare and that sort of thing."

"Interesting. Where is he from?"

*Why would he ask that question next?* "He said he's from someplace that starts with a 'z' like Zabeg or—"

"Zagreb?" said Churchill.

"Yeah, that's it."

Churchill and Colonel Anderson exchanged glances. Then Major Churchill ground out the stub of his cigarette on his boot and stood up. The others stood up as well.

"Thank you, Captain Goodman, for your appraisal," Churchill extended his hand and Goodman shook it. "I'll return to my hole and continue digging for now."

"Good to see you again, Randolph." Anderson tipped a finger to his brow.

Churchill returned the gesture. "Oh, and Colonel Anderson…"

"Yes?"

"I shouldn't be overly concerned with any surprise leaks or otherwise deviant behavior from Kozar or his inner circle."

"Oh?"

"Yes, he thinks he's got us in the bag, so to speak. However, we've a mouse of our own in his house. I'll set an ear to the wall about the nasty surprise the SS gave us last night."

Anderson cocked his head to one side. "Okay, then. Thanks for that."

"Of course." Major Churchill smiled and put on his field hat, tipped it to one side, and walked through the door Captain Kidder opened for him. "Good day, everyone." Churchill put a finger to his hat and exited the room. His footsteps faded down the stairs, and everyone turned back to Colonel Anderson.

"Sir, I had no idea you intended to share so much," said Whitman.

"Well, speaking to Randolph Churchill is not the same as speaking to the British mission here in the Balkans."

"Yes, sir, that's what I meant," said Whitman. "Especially given who Major Churchill is…" The abrupt silence caught Goodman's attention. He looked at Whitman and then at Colonel Anderson.

"Who *is* Major Churchill?" The collective hesitation let the words ricochet in his mind for a second. Then it hit him. "Is he related to *Winston* Churchill?"

"Son," said Colonel Anderson. "He's Winston Churchill's son. It's no accident he's here."

*Woah*. The son of the British Prime Minister, considered a hero by millions of people in England as well as the United States.

"What was it that Major Churchill said there at the end?" Whitman asked.

"Oh, that," said Anderson. "It means that the British are running an agent somewhere inside Kozar's staff. He'll insert an inquiry as to what the staff *really* knows about what happened last night. You'll do well to keep that under your hats, gentlemen." He looked at each man in the eyes. "That's a direct order."

"Yes, sir," said the Captains and Master Sergeant O'Keefe.

"So is that good for us?" asked Goodman, unsure of the politics at work. "And since I'm still here, is that good or bad for us?"

"Good, for both," Anderson replied. "We know full well that Colonel Blackbyrne omits or modifies information in his reporting to Cairo, and his word will win out over our reports through OSS channels. But we can still get things the correct command attention through Major Churchill. Now, that said, is it a two-edged sword? Absolutely. So I use it deliberately and sparingly. Again, gentlemen, we'll never talk out loud about that little detail again." Everyone nodded, including Goodman.

"What do you want me to do now, sir?" he asked. "What's the next move to get me out?" His mind was already racing with the possibility of escape. He imagined himself getting smuggled through the countryside under a pile of hay in the back of a truck, then sneaking onto a ship late at night and debarking in Alexandria or Spain.

"For now," said Colonel Anderson. "We tread water. Without a secure ground network, we have no way to get you to the Partisan-controlled areas where we can bring in a transport to get you out."

"So I'm stuck." Goodman's heart sank a few levels.

"For the time being," said Colonel Anderson as he turned from the window. "Gentlemen, I think it is best to keep Goodman here until we can sort out this business about the leak. I also want to monitor this militia group who brought him here. They're the unknowns right now."

"Sir," said Goodman. "I need to tell you that I don't think Amira is a spy, and neither are any of her people with us now. She hand-picked them for the mission the other night. They hate the Nazis. And the Communists. And the other groups around this part of the world seem to hate them, too. I've been with them for months and I've seen it. And, as for Tomislav,"—this part hurt to say—"he's been my friend. Zoran didn't like him very much, but he trusted him to take care of me. And he has come through for them in the past." Then he added, "and for me, too. He saved my life more than once. I'm here, thanks to him."

Anderson considered this for a moment. "Ok, I want to work the spy on Kozar's general staff angle," Anderson said, then assigned tasks to the group. "Whitman, that's you and me, in light of what Major Churchill said. Master Sergeant O'Keefe, I'd like you to write up a message to send to our people with Supreme Partisan Headquarters and see if they can give us options for exfiltrating *all* our airmen now that Plan A is lying dead on a road in the middle of the woods. Captain Kidder, you and Goodman keep things tight with our militia. Goodman, can you ask the new militia leader to help keep an eye on her people? Especially this Tomislav character if he's an outsider…"

"I don't think that's an issue, sir. They're like family."

"You think families don't hurt each other?" Kidder pointed out. "Have you ever been divorced?"

"Never married."

"Nothing says screw you like a knife in the back from the ones you love." Kidder shrugged.

Goodman glared at him.

"We'll make it happen, Colonel," said Whitman.

"Good. Get to work, but keep everyone close. That goes for all of us *and* for the militia down there right now." He pointed out the window. "Keep them away from Kozar's people. Their politics are gas and dry timber right now. Let's meet here again in four hours and see where we're at."

"Roger that, sir."

# 75

DESPITE THEIR BEST EFFORTS, no one turned up any new information all morning. The SS units in the hills had withdrawn to the north and west. Goodman and Master Sergeant O'Keefe found nothing that would exonerate or condemn Tomislav. Colonel Anderson slapped the table and stood up, sending his chair skidding backward. Even Major Farish jumped. Master Sergeant O'Keefe stepped back to avoid Kidder's coffee that splashed on the floor. It was clear to Goodman, and everyone else, that the last four hours had not gone well for the Colonel.

"Gentlemen, we need to confirm this!" he yelled. "This man Tomislav could be a major liability if he is working for the SD. Or even if he's working for someone else, like Kozar or directly for Tito's central espionage group, or the Ustaše, for that matter." He paused. "So, how do we confirm this?"

"Could we ask Kozar's intelligence shop?" Kidder asked as he wiped up the spilled coffee on the floor. "They might know. I mean, Whitman, you're on good terms with their counterintelligence chief, right?"

"Yeah, but they're really tight-lipped about agents they're running and their targets," said Whitman. "I don't think they'd give us what we're asking for. At least not without having to give up some gold."

"You pay them in gold?" Goodman asked.

"Sometimes," said Kidder.

"Not literally." Whitman scowled at Kidder, then turned to Goodman. "It's a term of art for useful information."

"*Really* useful information," O'Keefe added. "Something you can act on, even if it's only to trade for something better."

"Gotta give gold to get gold," Kidder mused.

The group continued to work the problem over in silence. Goodman was troubled by the idea that Tomislav, who twice saved his life, could possibly be working for the Germans.

"What if we get Kozar's people to arrest him?" Whitman offered.

"What? How?" asked Major Farish.

"I don't know, we make something up," Whitman said. "Something like, well, like he's a spy working for the Nazis?" O'Keefe and Kidder perked up at the idea.

"That could work," said Farish. "But if Kozar's people find a reason to detain him, they'll find a reason to execute him. There's no guarantee that they'll even interrogate him to see what he knows. They'll execute him just to make a point. And *that* is a guarantee."

"And we don't want to get burned," said the Colonel. "Not with Kozar, and not with the Brits, either, if something goes wrong with that plan."

"Why are we all cloak and dagger about this guy?" said Whitman. "We can just pull him off the street and interrogate him."

"We don't even know if it is him!" Goodman exclaimed. "What if we're wrong?"

"Or just shoot him," said Kidder between puffs on his cigarette.

"Did I just say something, or am I talking to myself?" Goodman stood up and kicked the table. The room went silent.

"Take it easy, Captain," said the Colonel.

"Sir, we're going about this as if we know." Goodman looked at the other officers. *These guys are just going to kill Tomislav because they think they know something.* "We don't know."

"He's right," said Master Sergeant O'Keefe. "We don't know. We suspect, and that's a big difference. Let's not be so quick to condemn someone." He looked at Goodman. "After all, according to the good captain here, this guy we're talking about did save his life. That's a good reason to look harder."

"Twice," said Goodman. "He saved my life twice."

413

"OK, so how to we find out?" asked the Colonel. "If we feed him to the Partisans, we'll never see him again."

As the OSS agents looked at each other blankly, Goodman's mind raced. *I need to know*, he thought. *I don't believe he would do this. But I must know. We have to force this to a conclusion. I need to force this.*

"What about me?" said Goodman.

"What about you, Captain?" said Major Farish.

"Well, sir," replied Goodman. "I have a price on my head, right? Just because I'm here with you all doesn't mean the German reward for me is voided. Does it?"

"What are you getting at, Captain?" asked Colonel Anderson.

"I mean, I can't believe I'm saying this, but…the way I see it, we can make him an offer he can't refuse."

"Like what?" asked Whitman.

"Like…put me out there and let them try to get me."

Master Sergeant O'Keefe's mouth dropped.

"That's crazy," Kidder laughed, then choked on cigarette smoke in his throat.

"You would do this?" Colonel Anderson rubbed the scruff on his chin. All eyes moved back to Goodman.

"Is there a better way?" Goodman continued. "If Tomislav is working for the Germans and his goal is to get me for the money or whatever, then he should try at the first and best opportunity. Let's give him that."

"Would he still do that?" asked Whitman.

Goodman suddenly had a flash of realization. *The nonsense Tomislav said days ago about the machines at war and all that. This is what makes him go. He'll do whatever he thinks he's supposed to do as long as he can do it.* Goodman continued. "Tomislav believes the Germans will win. He believes he's part of a machine that will eventually join Germany. Especially against the Communists."

"That makes sense," said Sergeant O'Keefe. "He might be right. But this, it's a *big* risk to you. To us."

"I understand," said Goodman. *Will he really get me to give me up to the Nazis, after everything we've done?* Goodman felt

414

nauseated at the thought. *Have I really been that big of a sucker?* Goodman's eyes fell.

"Why don't we just keep him here, under guard?" said Whitman. "We keep him here until we get an evacuation flight."

"That is an option," said Major Farish to Colonel Anderson.

"But then we're stuck not knowing," said O'Keefe. "And this guy may be a threat, if he is indeed actively communicating with the Germans. That's a big problem for the whole campaign in the Tuzla valley."

"Let's keep this a hypothetical for now," Anderson began. "But what if we did that? *How* would we do that?"

"First, we pick a place that we can control," said Whitman. "That's not going to be easy here."

"Right," said Major Farish. "Someplace not *completely* filled with people, but with just enough people doing their daily thing to make noise to hide in."

"We make an airtight box around Goodman, so nothing and nobody enters or exits the box without our knowledge." Whitman turned to Kidder and O'Keefe. "Some of us go plain clothes, some of us in uniform so we can go heavy if we have to." He patted his Thompson submachine gun lying next to him on the table.

"What about getting Amira and the rest of the militia to help?" asked Goodman.

"No! Absolutely not," Anderson replied. "We need them to be normal. The best way to do that is to keep them out of this."

"He can't go all alone," said Whitman. "There's no way anyone with the slightest of idea of what he's doing would buy that. That would tell *me* it was a trap."

"If I can't go alone," said Goodman. "Then I certainly can't go with one of you. He'd never attempt anything against one of you."

"So, what *is* your idea?" Anderson asked.

"I'll go with Amira," he said. "He wouldn't suspect a thing if it were just she and I."

"You trusted this guy Tomislav," Kidder challenged him. "That's what got us here. Wouldn't she and her clan want the money, too?"

"She's already getting *your* reward money," Goodman replied. "She's never really liked the burden I put on her people, but she trusts me, and I trust her more than anyone else here because she's stayed true to her father's wishes."

"You may trust her," said Anderson. "I do not."

"Where the trust ends," said Whitman. "Control must begin. How do we control her?"

"I'll do it," said Goodman. "I know how to get her moving. "

Colonel Anderson cleared his throat. "Okay, since this needs to happen sooner than later, we'll go with this idea of Captain Goodman's." He pointed at Major Farish. "Slim, this is your operation. Make it tight, make it work. This is a one-time thing. If we miss or tip our hand, then Tomislav *will* take to the hills. Which is also an okay outcome, but not as good as catching him or getting him out of our hair permanently. We would like to know what he knows, if at all possible."

"*If* he's doing what we suspect he's doing," O'Keefe added.

"Right," said Farish. "And if he's a no-show, then he's not our man."

"Or he *is* our man, and we didn't sweeten the deal enough." O'Keefe mused as he stood up to stretch.

"Well then, cover it with icing and put a fucking cherry on it," said Colonel Anderson. He looked at his watch. "Figure it out and get it done tonight. We all still have our day jobs. Kozar's brigades will assault the remaining German strong points around the city within the next twenty-four hours. The war hasn't stopped."

# 76

## OUTSIDE THE BAKERY, TUZLA CENTRAL MARKET DISTRICT

"DO YOU KNOW WHERE TOMISLAV IS RIGHT NOW?"

Goodman walked briskly up to Amira, maybe too briskly, but Goodman needed to know everything right now. Now was no time for holding back.

"What is happening?" she asked, glancing at the OSS agents heading off to their various destinations.

"I asked you where Tomislav went." His stomach boiled with tension.

"He'll be back in—"

"No," Goodman interrupted. "I mean do you know where he is right now?" She looked sideways at him and pulled back half a step.

"No, I don't," she answered sternly. He could see her walls going up. *This is what I was afraid of. I don't have time to sugar her up. I need to know if my friend wants to turn me over to the Nazis.*

"Is anyone with him?"

"No. Why are you asking me these questions?"

"Did he stay with you all of yesterday? Before the mission last night?"

"Yes. No. I don't remember every minute!" she retorted. "Does it matter?"

"Yes, it matters!"

"Why?" Her face tightened into a stern mask as she crossed her arms. "Why does it matter?"

"Amira," Goodman softened his tone. "Please, just listen. Something happened last night that wasn't supposed to happen. Someone gave us up to the Nazis. And, right now, we—"

"And you want to accuse us?" Amira bit her cheeks and looked at the sky. Her hands balled into fists. "We are surrounded by our enemies and you...of all the people...you think we would do this thing? Us? My father's people..." She clenched her jaw. "You are nothing to us."

"So why did you help me?" Goodman stepped toward her. She said nothing.

"Was it for the money?"

Her head turned slowly, revealing her eyes and their very special kind of anger, before she unleashed a litany of curses at him.

Goodman tried to interject, but she continued with more insults. He retreated a step or two to let the storm pass.

"Amira, I don't even know what all that means…"

"Do you know *govno*?"

"Yes…"

"Good. That is you."

"Amira…"

She put a hand up and turned her head.

"Amira!" She turned back and walked directly at him.

"For my father," she said. "It was the money. You are money, nothing more."

"But why do you help me now?"

"Because I am my father's daughter…"

*Yes, you are*, Goodman thought to himself.

"Perhaps it is time for us to leave you with your people." She looked away, biting her lip. "Would you do this, say these things, if my father was still alive? Or are we just stupid mountain people to you now? You think I am *gedzhovitsa now, do you?* You would not be here, alive with your blood still inside you, if we just left you where we found you. And now…this…" She threw her hands up and started to walk toward the market stall.

"Amira, pricheki. Molim." *Wait. Please.*

"What? What do you want?" She sounded weary.

"You are right. I would be dead or captured if your people did not help me. You saved me," said Goodman. "And you are your father's daughter. I mean no disrespect."

"Then why do you say these things about us? My people are my family, my only family now."

"I did not say anything about you or your people."

She scowled as he continued.

"I'm talking about someone who was not with you a year ago. I'm talking about Tomislav." She pursed her lips and breathed through her nose.

"When did you first meet him?"

Her eyes floated to the ground.

"It was last spring, wasn't it?" he said. "Right after your father decided to start attacking the Germans and the Ustaši, wasn't it?"

"Yes."

She looked away.

*I need her to tell me the truth. But I'm about to lose her.*

"You lost a lot of people then, didn't you? After that time?" She squeezed her eyes shut.

"I lost all of my family then." Her eyes were reddened when they re-opened.

"I know," said Goodman. "I'm very sorry." He took a breath. *I need to her to open up*, he thought. "My heart broke for you when I heard of that, and then when I told you that Jasminka is still al—"

"Yes, thank you for that," she said. "Now I know we will not all die here." Her face relaxed.

"When did you first meet Tomislav?"

"It was in the beginning of the thaw," her voice cracked. "We wanted to protect the farmers so they could plant." She wiped her eyes, leaving dirty streaks across her cheeks.

"Was it before or after the attack on your family?" Goodman probed. "It was before, wasn't it? They didn't attack the farms, they attacked the villages. They knew the militia was far away. How did they know?"

She nodded slightly and brushed a lock of hair from her face. A tear followed the line down along her nose.

"How did he come to be with your people?" Goodman lowered his voice. "Did you find him? Did you invite him to join you?"

"He found us," she admitted. "He came to find us. He came to us with weapons and money. And information."

"He told me *you* found *him*," said Goodman. "And he said that his family is in hiding in Zagreb." Amira looked up at Goodman, wide-eyed.

"No, you are mistaken…" She averted her eyes. "He said he wanted to avenge his family's murder by the Ustaši. He hated the Ustaši. You are wrong." It was her last holdout.

Goodman tilted his head slightly to re-center himself in her vision. "No, I'm not."

"I don't believe it…" Her shoulders sagged. "He warned us about the attack on my village, but he came too late…" She choked on the memory before continuing. "But there was always…something between him and the rest of us. We thought it was because he was from the city, that he was a from a wealthy family, and an actor…not a hard-working man. But he was always loyal. And he always working hard to help us." She steeled herself and squared off with Goodman. "What is your proof?"

"He's the only one who could have spoken to someone about the mission," he said. "He knew the location and time of the mission last night. And he is the only one who we cannot account for every minute before we departed. He could have shared the information before we went to meet the contact."

"You only say that he *could have* done this thing. You did not say that he did do it. For all you know, *I* could have done this. So, what is your proof?"

"I don't have any," Goodman admitted. "Not yet."

"Why do you bring me here?" Amira looked at the market gate. "And why do your new American friends follow us?"

"They aren't," he lied. "I wanted to talk to you with no one else around."

"You are a liar." Amira stopped and put her hands on her hips. "One of them is watching us right now."

Goodman followed Amira's eyes to see Captain Whitman three stalls back, dressed in a dirty black work coat, loose-fitting pants, and a broad-brimmed hat. He averted his look and pretended to inspect a cart full of apples. Goodman couldn't return Amira's glare. *Dammit.*

"Then we have nothing more to talk about," she said. Her eyes flicked over his shoulder and Goodman turned around to see what it was. *Tomislav.* He had an armload of bread, a wooden skewer full of blackened meat, and a large metal jug sloshing clear liquid down his sleeve. Goodman exhaled through his nose. Then he faked a smile at Tomislav.

"Here, let me help you with that." Goodman took the water jug.

"Thank you," said Tomislav. "No one is following me, are they?"

Goodman glanced behind him. "No one I can see."

"Good."

"Anything I should know about?" Goodman watched Tomislav's face carefully.

"Ummm...no," said Tomislav. "The food is a gift from the people of Tuzla!" He led them back to the market stall and dropped the food on the counter. "Hey, everyone!"

Several of the men awoke with a start, looking confused, stretching or rubbing their eyes. Several jumped up and shoved past one another toward the counter. Tomislav caught the silence between Goodman and Amira.

"Is anything wrong?" he asked, looking at them both. Amira cocked her head to one side, waiting to see what Goodman would say.

"No," Goodman broke. "Everything's ok." He brushed his hands on his pants. "Thanks, though. I need to get going...Amira and I...are going to look at horses."

She gave him a dirty look.

"Horses?" asked Tomislav. "Whatever for?"

"You all need horses to get back to the Majevitsa," said Goodman. "You want to come with us? We're going to spend a little of Amira's reward money. I hear I'm worth a few horses." He let that float in front of Tomislav for a moment. He smiled as genuinely as he could muster.

"No, thank you," said Tomislav. "I'm no expert in horses, and thus I trust Amira's judgment."

Amira reached into the bread box and tore a loaf in half. She then peeled a strip of charred meat from the stick. Goodman motioned subtly for Amira to go with him. To Goodman's relief, she did. They only walked a few paces when Amira challenged him.

"What are you doing?"

"I'm giving Tomislav a chance to prove his innocence." He turned around and looked at the stall where Amira's men were devouring the food. He felt his heart sink when he saw Tomislav had already disappeared.

"Amira..." He nodded toward the stall. "See?"

She turned and whipped her ponytail around again to make eye contact with Goodman once more.

"What do I see?" She glared at him. "I see that you are a liar, too."

# 77

## TUZLA CENTRAL MARKET DISTRICT

GOODMAN WRESTLED WITH HIMSELF for the entire twenty minutes it took to follow the route that Major Farish had specified to avoid unwanted surveillance. He finally reached a draw. He could not make sense of how things had unfolded except if Tomislav was indeed a spy. This angered Goodman immensely. *How the hell could Tomislav have played me for so long? It wasn't just me*, he thought. *He played everyone. For months. There's no way he could pull that off for so long. But then, how else could the mission last night have been so badly botched?* His mind still resisted the idea. But he knew otherwise. Now, he had to convince Amira that there was something to it. Something worth pursuing. But she would never go with it willingly. So Goodman went with the false pretense option.

Goodman and Amira rounded a corner and Major Farish, dressed in mechanic's overalls, gave Goodman a slight nod and turned his head. Amira appeared to not see him. The others would be nearby, and that made Goodman feel slightly less vulnerable. Everyone except Master Sergeant O'Keefe was now somewhere in the market. He remained behind to create an impression of busyness in the apartment to keep Kozar's intelligence agents complacent. It worked. None of the OSS men had their usual shadows.

Goodman could tell that Amira was on edge. She said almost nothing for the entire walk to the market plaza. He had finally persuaded her with Colonel Anderson's offer to make purchases for the militia with his own operational funds, so any new acquisitions would not count against the reward money. They were far outside their support area and needed supplies for the journey back to the Majevitsa.

# DEEP IN THE PLACE OF THE DEAD

Most of the horse stalls were empty, but one or two traders lingered with their animals. Goodman halted in front of a stall housing three shaggy and underfed mountain horses. He looked around and saw Captain Whitman huddled against a wall with a group of old men slurring their speech with their afternoon slivovitz. A bulge under his long coat slightly betrayed his Thompson submachine gun underneath. Whitman pretended not to see him as he passed the jug.

"Why do you bring me here to look at horses?" She lifted the head of one animal and looked at its eyes and mouth. She shook her head and looked at the next one briefly before shifting to another stall altogether. "We already have horses. These are worthless."

At that very moment, something caught Goodman's attention. He almost missed it. One of the stable hands moved just a little too quickly for an adult male who lived a life around animals. The horses shuffled nervously because of it.

"I know," answered Goodman. He looked her squarely in the eyes. "I need to show you something."

"What? What do you need to show me?"

"Give me a minute," said Goodman. He scanned the area for the stable hand again. Nothing.

The two of them stood in silence, both pretending to look over the next group of horses. Goodman's eyes darted to a group of young men who spilled out of a cafe and into the street. At the center of their group were two young women with long, black hair wearing dresses that exposed their abundant cleavage. The group's carefree noise attracted smirks and sneers of nearby market goers. Old women huddled and whispered jealously. An older man emerged from the cafe scolding them and whipped at them with a rod. They cursed and mocked the old man and laughed their way toward the main boulevard. That was when Goodman saw the first set of eyes. Dark eyes.

The man stood in the window of the storefront, partly obscured by the activity reflected on the windowpane. Goodman quickly averted his own eyes and focused on the horse in front of him. He focused on his peripheral vision. *Is that what I think it is?* He glanced up quickly. The man remained where he was in the window.

*It is. He's watching me. It's not Tomislav, but he's watching me.* Goodman's pulse quickened and his hands suddenly started shaking. Goodman made eye contact with Whitman and cocked his head toward the store window. Whitman slowly turned to the bench facing the wall of drinkers to see through the window at the sharp angle. Whitman turned back and slowly reached inside his coat.

Several market goers strolled casually between stalls and storefronts. Another man, this one in a padded, dark blue coat, turned abruptly into an alleyway. Goodman was not the only one to observe this. Captain Kidder's freckled face peered out from the cab of a truck parked near the alley entrance. He tilted the side-view mirror to observe the man and gave a quick nod to Goodman. Goodman turned his head back to the horse. *This is it*, he thought. *Tomislav is near.* He deliberately slowed his breathing and fidgeted with the feedbag that hung from the gate.

"*Šta vidiš?*" Amira caught his eyes. "What do you see?"

"*Ništa...*" He concentrated on looking at the horse. "I don't see anything."

"You are lying to me again." Her ponytail swept her shoulder as her eyes swept the passageways between horse stalls.

"Someone is watching us," he replied under his breath.

"There are at least three men watching us," she replied. "Besides your American friends. The man you looked at in the store is the first, and his stable boy friend who just went away from the horse market. He is in the vegetable tables." She examined the horse's bridle.

*Amazing*, he thought. "I only see two."

"The stable boy, the man in the café window," she said flatly. "The third man is above the *ribnjak.*"

"The what?"

"The fish-man," she said. "The one who sells fishes. *Ribnjak.*"

Goodman turned and faked a wide-mouthed yawn. He pretended to rub his eyes and quickly scanned the far side of the market area. There, among the several carts and dealers hawking their products, was a striped awning over a large cart filled with meticulously organized shiny fish bodies. The fishmonger and his wife stood indifferently behind their cart. Goodman looked up and saw a long row of windows above the awning, then turned back before he looked obvious.

"There's a bunch of windows over there," he said.

"The one above the man who sells fishes was the first one I saw," she said as her fingers traced the ridges and valleys over the horse's bony frame. "He has not moved since we arrived here."

Amira walked away from the horse stalls into the midst of several slipshod pens full of skinny goats. They bleated incessantly and crowded each other against the far side of their pens as she approached. A fat herdsman seated behind a table all but ignored them as they approached. He incautiously flicked his cigarette into an empty stall before pulling himself upright and lumbering behind the partition between stalls. Amira halted at the end of the narrow passage in front of a small kiosk to look at the announcements posted there. Her eyes darted left and right.

Goodman eased his way through the pens to join Amira. He pretended to look across the animal pens and caught glimpses of the man's silhouette through the curtain that drifted in and out of the upper window. A gust of wind kicked up dust and hay into the air and people all around the market shielded their eyes. Goodman swatted at the dust in his face and blinked several times to clear his eyes. He looked up at the window again.

"He's gone," said Goodman. "The man in the window."

"Where?" Amira searched the row of windows.

"No idea," said Goodman. He glanced at the truck where Kidder sat. But now, Kidder was gone, too. *Did he see something? Did he move to follow the man in the window?* Goodman repositioned himself to see Whitman. He, too, was no longer sitting near the drunks.

"Where is everyone…" Goodman's observation was cut short by the looming figure of the fat herdsman with his club raised over his head.

*No!*

Goodman yanked Amira by her arm as the herdsman's club clanged loudly on the top rail of the fence. Right where Amira had been standing. Goodman lunged at the herdsman and landed a fist squarely in the man's face. Blood squirted across the herdsman's scraggly beard.

The herdsman's next swing went wild, and dust cascaded over them as the club dislodged a pole holding up the awning. Dust fell into Goodman's face and he choked. He tried to wipe his face, but the fat herdsman fell upon him and Goodman lost his breath with the impact. The herdsman reared back with his club but froze in mid-swing. His eyes widened and his mouth opened in a silent scream. The club fell from his hands, and he fell, face down, next to Goodman. Amira stood over him, bloodied knife in hand. A wave of relief washed over the adrenaline that still pulsed through Goodman's body. He used the fence rails to get up and saw Whitman running down the narrow passageway between pens. His Thompson was out.

"Get down!" he yelled.

Goodman and Amira fell into one of the goat pens just as the man in the blue coat emerged from behind a door with a revolver in his hand. Goodman and Amira struggled to raise their weapons as the goats stampeded over them to flee from this new intruder. The man in the blue coat saw them on the floor and aimed. Then his pistol fell from his hands.

Blood spewed out of this neck and washed downward across his chest. He tried to clutch at the gash in his neck, but his hands never made it and fell to the floor. His body squirmed violently before settling into smaller spasms. Kidder emerged from behind the door and wiped the blood from his dagger on the body before replacing it in his boot scabbard. He reached forward and helped Amira and Goodman up as Whitman arrived, with Major Farish right behind him. The goats ran amok as they tried to evade the sudden crowd of humans in their tiny space.

"Did you see him?" Farish asked.

"Who, Tomislav?" said Goodman. "No, just these guys."

"He's got to be here!" Whitman exclaimed.

"Maybe he's not here,"

"Lack of evidence of guilt is not evidence of innocence," said Whitman.

"What are you, a lawyer?"

"As a matter of—"

Whitman was about to respond when everyone alerted to a pair of shadows against a wispy curtain along one of the outer stalls. As Goodman and Amira crept toward the curtain, Whitman stepped over the low fence and sent the goats into another frenzy. One caprine leapt over the fence and charged into the curtain. The curtain fell and clouds of dust swirled in the sunlight. The two men on the other side sprinted for cover. Goodman gave chase, with Amira and the others right behind. *Tomislav! he thought.*

Goodman ran to the end of the passageway and turned into the open market area. His eyes bulged when an iron fist nailed him right in the chest. He blew his breath into his attacker's face and stumbled backward, out of breath. The attacker drew a black pistol from inside his coat and took aim. Goodman kicked wildly and the pistol bounced on the pavement. The man turned and sprinted into the crowded market before Goodman could catch his breath. In his wake, he left a crowd of fallen women and spilled contents of shopping bags rolling across the street.

Amira leapt over Goodman and dodged the fallen vegetables and herbs spread across the ground, but was blocked by the large rear ends of a dozen old women trying to recover their groceries. Goodman got up and ran through the crowd, almost knocking over another old woman already yelling curses at the inconvenience. She cursed at Goodman, too, as he ran by. The attacker disappeared into an alleyway on the far side of the market. Goodman slowed before rounding the corner himself. Amira caught up to him and they peered around the corner.

Clotheslines hung low over the stone floor. Numerous doorways and passageways branched left and right, providing space for more doors. And lots of places to hide. A door creaked open and slammed shut. Goodman ran toward it, but paused before he went farther. Too many doors. Too many corners. *This could be a trap*, he thought. He listened for anything that might help avoid that probability.

He heard voices. Men's voices. Ahead on the right. And the running footsteps of Whitman, Kidder, and Farish closing in from behind.

Goodman raised his hand, index finger extended as they slowed to a halt, breathing heavy. Goodman stepped quietly to the threshold and squeezed the doorknob. The voices got louder. Yelling. Arguing. The door was unlocked. He turned and gave a nod to the others. Farish and Whitman lifted their Thompson submachine guns from and aimed directly at the door. Goodman heard footsteps ascending stairs on the other side of the door and men's voices suddenly hushed. He turned the knob and opened the door. Goodman's eyes climbed the stairs to see the back of his assailant and there, one stair step above the man between them stood Tomislav. They each saw surprise and anger on the other's face.

"Tomislav!" Goodman raised his MP40.

Tomislav cursed and kicked the man in front of him squarely in the chest, sending him flying down the stairs. He slammed the door shut at the upper landing as the other man hit the bottom stair. Goodman fired into the man's chest and stepped over him. Goodman took three steps at a time as he climbed toward the door at the top landing. He reached for the doorknob and bullets burst through the door, sending splinters into the stairwell. Goodman flattened himself on the steps. Another three rounds penetrated the door and thumped into the ceiling over the stairwell. Goodman raised his MP40 but hesitated before squeezing the trigger. *Dammit Tomislav!* He fired a burst through the door. When no gunfire came back at him, he lowered his shoulder and fractured the inner door jamb. The door swung open.

The anteroom was small and sparsely furnished. To the left was a tiny, darkened bedroom and to the right was a small kitchen with a smaller pantry lined with shelves of foodstuffs. Directly ahead were two windows on the far wall, wide open, curtains blowing. Tomislav was nowhere to be seen. Goodman ran to the windows and looked down.

Below the window, Goodman saw a hole ripped in the striped awning revealing the fishmonger and his wife cursing over their now-disheveled market stall, their silvery fish scattered across the pavement. Tomislav sprinted across the market square, his coattails flying, a wake of people in disarray behind him. Goodman aimed his submachine gun but hesitated again, this time as fleeing bystanders obscured a clear shot. Tomislav quickly rounded a corner and disappeared.

"Dammit!" Goodman lowered his weapon. Amira sprinted across the square below.

"Hey!" he yelled after her. "He's gone!"

She ignored him and ran at full speed, her pistol drawn, her submachine gun bouncing on her hip. She dodged a car and rounded the corner where Tomislav had been just a moment before. The marketplace slowly recovered, and people went cautiously about their business. They looked over their shoulders at Goodman in the window and spoke to one another in hushed tones. The fishmonger and his wife salvaged what they could of their catch, each muttering to the other.

"Tomislav, why?" Goodman said to himself. "After all that we've been through…why?"

Captain Whitman put his hand on Goodman's shoulder. "At least we know now."

"No, I've been a blazing idiot," said Goodman. "I already knew. I just didn't want to admit it." Goodman let out a long exhale as a wave of remorse washed over him. "Now I have to kill my friend."

# 78

1822 HOURS
THE OSS APARTMENT

SOMEONE KNOCKED TWICE AT THE DOOR, then three more times. Colonel Anderson entered when Whitman slid the bolt and opened the door.

"Thanks, Charlie," he said as he dropped his map case and hat on the table. Whitman closed the door and locked it again.

"What's the word, sir?" Kidder awoke from his nap on the sofa and sat up.

"Well, our British counterparts are now in the same position as we are," Anderson replied. "They can't move around either."

"They're under house arrest, too?" said O'Keefe. He poured the colonel a cup of coffee.

"Thanks," Anderson replied. It was too hot to sip, so he put it down. "Well, Blackbyrne is calling it an operational pause."

"Really?" Whitman was surprised. "I thought for sure Blackbyrne had squeezed us out."

"He did," said Anderson. "But it backfired on him. He and I have both been declared *PNG* in the hotel. Colonel Razik kicked us out of our office space and now we're all out on the street. We are slightly better off than the Brits because we have this apartment. Blackbyrne and his people are homeless and looking for a place to hang their hats."

Kidder and Whitman snickered.

"PNG?" asked Goodman.

"*Persona non grata,*" replied Kidder. "It's Latin for 'screw you get out of my house' or something to that effect."

Whitman emptied his cup and poured himself a fresh one. "Sir, what about the incident earlier today with that Tomislav guy?"

"Kozar's people are not at all pleased with our *independent* operation, as they call it. They deny the existence of a Nazi informant network and assert that the entire action was fabricated."

"They think we made it up?" asked Kidder.

"No, that's what Blackbyrne told them," replied Anderson. "That we mishandled our asset and now we're cleaning up our own mess. Also incompetently."

"You mean me, sir?" asked Goodman.

"No, only partly you," said Anderson. "Your arrival and the whole thing with this Tomislav character fits the narrative of what the Partisans and—by extension—the British mission have been building over the past year or so to get us removed from this theater of operations. I think we know better, which is why I wanted you off the streets for the remainder of the day. Out of sight, out of mind, so to speak." He took a sip of coffee. "What I didn't expect was that all of us would be put into that same box."

Master Sergeant O'Keefe stood up to look out the window at the market square. "Any idea what they're up to that they don't want us around to see?"

"It might be that they want to clean house themselves," said Whitman. "Maybe find Tomislav and interrogate him?"

Goodman shook his head. *I should have shot him when I had the chance.* It was all Goodman could think about. He could have shot him through the door. And if he had, then there would be no questions left. *Dammit, Tomislav.* "What about Amira and her people?" Goodman asked. "What do they want to do with them?"

From the apartment window, Goodman watched Amira pace back and forth across the stall opening across the street. She hadn't spoken to him since she returned from her pursuit of Tomislav across the central part of the city. She had since deployed most of her men around the commercial district in hopes of spotting him again, but the Communists harassed them constantly and made it all but impossible. Goodman wanted to be down there, looking for him, hunting him.

"Don't know," said Anderson.

"But none of this fully explains why Kozar's people kicked us out," said Whitman.

"It might just be some new paranoia that came in over the radio," replied Anderson. "Tito kicks his liaison team out of his cave every time he runs out of coffee. The Communists conjure up a conspiracy to explain everything. It could be as simple and as dumb as that." He took a sip of coffee. "It doesn't change the fundamentals of the situation. The Third Partisan Corps has yet to take the remaining four garrisons around the city. They need to consolidate their positions in and around the city if they want to hold it against a German counterattack. They may not want us to see them struggling to crack that nut. Whenever that happens."

"They've been cycling tons of supplies through their supply dump down here," O'Keefe remarked from the large window. "It's been nonstop since you all left for your op."

"It might be some time yet before they have enough built up for an effective defense of this place after taking the garrisons," said Whitman as he scraped the last beans out of a can and set it down with a *clink* on top of the wood stove.

Anderson scratched his head and yawned loudly. "I just realized I haven't slept since yesterday morning," he said. "I'm going to take a nap. Wake me if anything happens." He tore off a hunk of bread from the large loaf on the counter and munched on it as he entered the bedroom. He partly closed the door but stopped to say one more thing. "And by anything, I mean anything *important*. General Kozar is important. An armistice between the Nazis and the Allies is important. Blackbyrne and his problems are *not* important."

"Roger that, sir!" Captain Kidder called back, suppressing a snicker. He stood up as the door clicked shut and announced, "I'm taking a nap, too."

"You mean *another* nap, sir?" O'Keefe snipped at him.

"Yeah," Kidder shot back. "Another nap." He kicked off his boots as he entered the other bedroom and closed the door. O'Keefe slumped down on the couch where Kidder had sat, crossed his outstretched legs, and pulled his hat over his eyes. Whitman, who had been scrutinizing map sheets, crossed his arms on the table and laid his head down. Goodman stood up and stretched. He had been sitting for too long on that lumpy, broken down couch. Besides, he'd already taken a satisfying nap a couple of hours ago. He rubbed his nose to expel the mildew smell.

A series of rumbles shook the room and rattled the glass in the large front window. Captain Kidder yelled "dammit!" from behind his door.

"Is it incoming or outgoing?" Anderson poked his head out.

Goodman and O'Keefe looked out the large front window. The group reached the conclusion it was it was outgoing fire rather than incoming, but short range like mortars rather than artillery.

"They're setting up a battery of howitzers," O'Keefe announced from the window. The others approached to see for themselves.

They watched the horse-drawn gun carriages make a wide circle on the market square. In a complex display of choreography, Partisan soldiers scrambled to deploy eight large cannons and

432

unpack artillery rounds from the wagons and covered trucks that circled the market square. When the cannoneers, loaders, and ammunition handlers ceased their frenzied activity, the battery was prepared to fire. But they did not fire. The commander paced back and forth, looking at his watch. After a few minutes, a horse-mounted messenger galloped into the square and handed a folded sheet of paper from his courier bag to the battery commander. He, in turn, handed the paper to his junior officer, who read it, saluted, and ran to his previous position behind the guns.

"Hey, guys," said Whitman. "Those guns are aimed right over the apartment here. They're gonna fire!"

The gun crews loaded shells and powder into the guns, locked the breaches, and braced for the next command. Their team leaders covered their ears as the cannoneers pulled their lanyards tight, looking to the section chiefs who, in turn, looked to the battery chief, who raised a small red rag. The section chiefs raised their hands. The commander looked at his watch. Goodman could see a slight nod between the commander and the battery chief.

"You don't want to be standing there, Captain," said O'Keefe. Goodman backed away from the window.

When the battery chief dropped his arm, the eight cannoneers yanked their lanyards. The howitzers erupted in unison, filling the square with an ear-splitting blast that sent shock waves reverberating off the buildings and down the streets and alleys. The large window facing the square shattered and thousands of pieces of glass cascaded through the apartment and across the tile floor. Goodman threw his arms up in front of his face as tiny shards pelted him and the others. Echoes of the blasts faded outside as the battery and section chiefs shouted commands to reload.

"Son of a bitch!" O'Keefe shouted as he brushed pieces of glass off his shirt and pants. More commands echoed in the market square. "They're gonna fire again!"

A second blast wave hit the apartment, knocking jagged pieces of glass loose from the frame which then shattered on the floor. Another round of commands echoed from the square and a third volley of cannon fire filled the square. A fourth, and then a fifth set of blasts reverberated throughout the city. Elsewhere in the city, other gun batteries fired and sent more echoes off the buildings and through the streets. Then all fell silent except for the commands from the gun chiefs. Clouds of acrid-smelling smoke rolled in through the now-windowless frame. Several moments of thumping from the distant impact explosions and rolling thunder shook the walls. The staccato of heavy machine guns and the thumping of mortar fire rolled down from the hills in a continuous drumbeat.

Goodman followed Kidder on his hands and knees toward the window and peered over the sill along with O'Keefe. The crews appeared to be done firing and were busy swabbing their massive gun barrels and preparing more shells. The commander conferred with his battery chief, apparently in violent agreement about something.

"Here comes our messenger," Kidder announced. Whitman and O'Keefe stood up in the now-empty window frame as a young Partisan soldier sprinted through the square and waved frantically at the OSS men. He yelled something Goodman did not catch.

"They're attacking the garrisons!" said Whitman. "General Kozar invites us to join him in the command post."

"Alright men," said Anderson. "Gear up!"

The OSS men ran to throw on their combat kit and ready their weapons.

"Goodman, get the door for our boy?" said the Colonel.

A second later, there was a knock on the door and Goodman opened it. A boy of not more than fifteen entered and tried to catch his breath. His Partisan uniform was several sizes too big.

"Here," said Master Sergeant O'Keefe. He handed the young Partisan a large portion of bread and a cut of meat. The boy ate it hungrily and gladly took the coffee Whitman offered him.

"Ask him what he knows," Said Colonel Anderson as he slung his submachine gun over his shoulder. Whitman spoke briefly, and the boy replied rapidly through mouthfuls of food and gulps of coffee. Goodman caught only brief phrases and individual words.

"They're attacking the strong points around the city," said Whitman. "One brigade is attacking each location. Supply trains are closing on the city now. This is the big push."

"So he *is* trying to get it done before the Germans counterattack," Colonel Anderson said, snapping his tactical belt closed. "He must be in a hurry." Whitman translated for the boy.

"Neh, comrade." The young Partisan shook his head. He went on talking.

Whitman offered more bread, which the boy took and wolfed it down. "He says their intel indicates there's only a handful of small SS reconnaissance detachments north and west of here, nothing with any serious combat power. And there is a blocking position fifteen miles outside the city, at the western end of the Tuzla valley. Kozar says that more than a thousand Partisans will be able to hold off a German attack for days."

"Whose intelligence is this?" asked Anderson. Whitman asked the boy.

"Kozar's," he said. "And Tito's. The Fifth Mountain SS Division and their tanks are all still engaged in anti-guerrilla sweep-and-clear operations along the Sava River. They think it will take them at least a week to disengage and reorganize for the movement here." He paused for the boy to add something. Whitman translated again. "And he says the Germans will probably need a major resupply before they head this way. At least that's what the official assessment from headquarters says."

"That's why Kozar kicked us all out of the hotel," O'Keefe concluded. "He didn't want us to spoil the surprise."

Whitman loaded his weapon and flicked the safety catch, then he shook his head. "They don't trust anyone."

"Would you?" said O'Keefe.

"Good point."

"Everyone ready?" Colonel Anderson called out.

"Roger, sir," said Whitman and O'Keefe in unison.

"Yes, sir!" said Goodman. He picked up his own submachine gun and threw his ammo pouch strap over his shoulder.

"Stand down, Goodman," said Colonel Anderson. Everyone looked up as he continued. "We have our assignments, and Kozar's commanders know to expect us. You're different. You are suspect in their eyes, which makes it unsafe for you. You need to stay here and keep out of sight."

"Unsafe? Really, sir?" said Goodman. "I just about got cut to shreds a minute ago and Tomislav is still out there with who knows how many people working for him! How am I supposed to be safe?" Anderson focused his stare on Goodman, but said nothing.

"Listen, Captain," O'Keefe stepped in. "It's not just this guy Tomislav we're worried about. It's not above Kozar's people here to engineer an accident for you. They've done it to their own, and we can't afford to let it happen to you. You really pissed them off. We're gonna get you outta here, but until then, you need to lay low." Goodman knew they were right. He put his submachine gun down on the table with a clunk.

"Okay," he said. "I'll stay here." He took off his coat and leaned on the back of a chair. "Sorry, sir."

"Don't do that again," said Anderson, opening the door. "I respect the energy, but keep it contained until you need it."

Goodman nodded in compliance.

Anderson spoke to the group. "I'm headed to the hotel and then probably to the north strongpoint, if that's still Kozar's primary objective. We'll meet up back here when the last strongpoint falls or twenty-four hours from now, whichever comes first."

The group agreed. Colonel Anderson exited the room and descended the stairs. The sounds of distant battles echoed into the room.

"Will do, sir," said O'Keefe. "Oh, hey, Captain Goodman?"

"Yes, sergeant."

"Something you should know," said O'Keefe. "When one of us comes back, we'll use our knock and then our challenge and password. You hear the knock—*only* the correct knock—then you issue the challenge, which is the word 'paper' and one of us will reply with 'tiger'. If you get the wrong knock or the wrong reply or no reply, come out shootin' like Machinegun Kelly. If someone tries to open the door *without* knocking, come out shootin' like Machinegun Kelly. Finally, anyone who ain't us tries to come through that door under any circumstances, come out..."

"I know," said Goodman. "Shootin' like Machinegun Kelly."

"Until then, keep the door locked and the table against the door."

"There's a problem," said Goodman. "I need ammo." He held up his magazines, only one had a handful of rounds left.

"There's a whole case of ammo for that thing in the bedroom," Whitman pointed to the back room.

"Whitman! Get your ass down here!" It was Colonel Anderson calling up from the street.

Captain Whitman picked up his helmet and made for the door. "We gotta get goin'!"

He and the others turned and ran down the stairs and caught up to Colonel Anderson, who was already up the street, headed for Kozar's headquarters. The others went in other directions, toward the sounds of the guns echoing from different parts of the city.

Goodman closed and locked the door before sliding the kitchen table against it. He found the case of ammunition and repeated 'paper' and 'tiger' to himself while he reloaded the magazines for his weapon. It occurred to him that he had not been left alone for weeks. He spent the remainder of that evening listening to the sounds of the battles around the city and trying to remain vigilant for anything threatening. His thoughts turned to Tomislav, Amira, and the others who were so important to him and his survival. He looked out the open window to see if she was still there. The Majevitsa militia and their leader were indeed still there, still sitting around the stall across the street. A few of them watched the activity in the market square, but the artillery soldiers prevented them from approaching the guns or anything else in the square itself.

At one point, he made eye contact with Amira, but she turned away after a moment. She remained facing the square, arms folded, deliberately not looking toward the apartment. Musa the Giant, however, stood and waved up at Goodman with a smile. He motioned for Goodman to come down and eat something, but Goodman yelled back that he was not allowed to leave. Musa grabbed a loaf of bread but was blocked from crossing the street by a pair of Partisan guards. He backed off and shrugged his shoulders at Goodman. Then he pointed at Goodman and made a motion of throwing the bread loaf over his head toward the window. Goodman nodded and held his hands like a running back. A moment later, the bread came sailing in through the window and bounced on the floor. Goodman picked it up and waved to Musa.

"*Hvala!*" Goodman called down to him. A handful of the militiamen clapped their hands in a round of applause, mocking the Partisan guards as they scolded them.

"*Molim, moj drug!*" Musa gave a slight bow and flourished with his hand. Goodman watched them and considered the moment. What's going to happen to them? How are they going to protect their families, their farms? The doubts mounted in his brain. He waved once more to Musa and the others before retreating from the window.

He pried opened a ration can and used his fingers to spoon the cold beans into his mouth as he devoured almost the entire loaf of bread. *Not bad*, he thought. When he finished, he wiped his hands on his pants and let out a loud belch as he reclined on the couch. The springs poked him through the flat cushions, but he was too tired to care. He ignored the mildew smell. He closed his eyes while he listened to the sounds of battle in the surrounding hills.

But his thoughts again turned to Amira and her family, now entirely made up of the surviving Majevitsa militia. He hoped they were going to be ok. They have to return to their mountains, he thought, but how will they be able to resist the communists? Will she give up power to the communists? He doubted so. That won't go well. So who do they fight first? The Germans, the Communists, or one of the other groups? The power gap between the groups was enormous, almost as incomparable as the batteries of artillery at General Kozar's disposal to the bolt-action rifles carried by many of the Majevitsa militia. Again, he thought of Amira. She never had a chance to have a normal, safe life. Is there any hope for something better after this? What will her life be like *after* the war? Will there even be an "after"…? Will Jasminka one day become another Amira? Goodman could not stop the thought that, through his actions, his mere presence even, he had contributed to undermining what remained of Jasminka's childhood. But what is childhood in wartime? Does that even exist? He let troubled thoughts swim through his mind as watched the shadows climb the walls. His eyes closed. Then he slept.

⁂

# 79

## SOMETIME AFTER MIDNIGHT, OCTOBER 2, 1943

GOODMAN FLEW OFF THE COUCH IN TERROR when the artillery rocked the market square again. Sprawled on the floor, Goodman covered his head with his hands. The series of blasts thundered throughout the city. He breathed easier once he heard the section leaders barking commands again without follow-on blasts. His breathing slowed, and he shuffled himself back onto the couch. It was still dark outside, but sleep would not return anytime soon. Strange dancing beams of hazy, yellowish light and opposing shadows made him blink his eyes wide. It took a second to realize that either the Germans defending the strong points around the city or the attacking Partisans were launching parachute illumination flares into the night sky. The blinding little suns oscillated back and forth as they descended. Intermittent machine-gun fire sent stuttered echoes through the streets. Distant mortars and artillery occasionally thundered as new salvos of flares were deployed into the sky. He sank into the couch and blinked his eyes to clear them. Then he heard a noise from the stairs. Another step. Then shuffles.

*Good*, he thought. *They're back.* He yawned loudly. He rubbed his eyes and got up to move the table away from the door. Goodman rubbed his eyes as he approached the table in front of the door.

He was about to move the table, when remembered to wait for the knock and password. *Paper, tiger, paper, tiger*, he thought to himself. He listened for a knock, a voice, something from the other side of the door. Nothing. *Am I just hearing things? I know I heard something on the stairs a moment ago.* A scrape like a foot drag on a riser. Now he was wide awake and very alert. *Maybe not…*

The doorknob squeaked and then stopped. It squeaked again. *Dammit! It's not them*, he thought. *Tomislav!* Just as he went to the couch, the dancing shadows faded into complete darkness. He ran his hands over the cushions, searching for his weapon, but his hands could not find it. The door pushed against the frame with a slight *clunk*. A moment later, there was a slight scraping sound emanating from the lock. Scrape, scrape, click, clink. *Somebody's trying to pick the lock!* He moved frantically for anything to use as a weapon. A bottle, food tin, anything.

The lock clicked, and the door bumped the table with a soft thud. The door pushed against the table with a slight scraping sound. A dark shape entered the room and paused silently while a second shape slipped through the door. In the semi-darkness, Goodman sensed that they did not see him yet. *Where is my damn weapon? It was just here!* One hand found his ammo pouch as the other hand found his weapon's canvas shoulder strap and pulled it toward him.

His empty bean can rang out sharp and loud as it bounced on the floor. The two shapes flew at him at once. One missed, the other hit him squarely in the stomach. His weapon flew out of his hands as he hit the floor. His head throbbed and his vision filled with twinkling stars. The man on top of him punched and his head bounced off the floor. He had a sudden sensation of nausea and almost passed out while the one hit him yet again.

Goodman clawed for the dim outline of the attacker's head. He found an ear and pulled *hard*. The attacker screamed and threw a punch that glanced off the side of Goodman's head, smashing the attacker's knuckles on the hard tile floor. He yelled out again as Goodman rose up and punched at the man's face. Warm blood spurted down Goodman's arm and into his face. The attacker fell over backward, and the second attacker took a swing at Goodman, but missed. Goodman kicked with both his legs, one finding its mark. The second attacker wheezed loudly and fell to the floor. Goodman scrambled to his feet. His head swam and his legs were unsteady. A third figure was suddenly running at him from the door, feet pounding hard on the floor.

Goodman grabbed a chair and swung wildly at the third man, missing at first. On his second swing, a chair leg made contact with the man's head and broke off, bouncing off a wall somewhere in the dark. Goodman heard the third man groan as he slumped to the floor. Holding up the chair with both hands, Goodman prepared to swing downward as hard as he could, but one of the first two men hit him with something hard. Goodman, the chair, and his attacker all fell against the wall and over the arm of the couch. With a vigorous kick, Goodman knocked the man's knees out from under him. Goodman stood and quickly slammed the chair down. The chair smashed on the attacker's head and the tile beside it. Only the frame of the back of the chair remained in Goodman's control. The rest of the chair fell to pieces.

One of the other attackers charged at Goodman with his arm outstretched. Goodman deflected the first thrust with the chair frame, and the second thrust as well, but lost sight of the attacker's third swing and felt the intense burn of a knife blade slice through his coat and into his forearm.

Goodman reeled. His next swing missed.

The attacker thrust again with the knife, penetrating clothing and nothing else. He pushed back but found nothing but air. The dark shape retreated to the door and disappeared.

Goodman quickly scanned the darkness for the next attacker. *Were there three or is there a fourth guy?* A brief hope that the other attackers, however many there were, had given up and exited the apartment gave Goodman a moment of elation, but the whisper of clothing rushing at him cut short the celebration. Goodman dodged this fresh attack, but they collided and slid to the floor. Goodman fought back frantically as he realized this new attacker had him pinned down. The man yelled something in Bosanski and another man stomped up the stairs and entered the room. A hand stifled his breathing. He jerked his head left and right, but to no effect. Panic at the loss of air surged adrenaline into him, and he thrashed his arms and legs, but they, too, were suddenly held fast. He felt a rope, a cord, something tighten around his ankles and arms. One last burst of energy helped him to shove the attacker at his feet against the wall. *Okay, next bastard…*

441

Goodman felt the blow to his head, and then the strength in his body left him. After one last flicker, the dancing lights on the walls around him faded away completely.

# 80

EXCEPT FOR TINY RAYS OF YELLOW LIGHT stabbing down on his face from the ceiling, the darkness that surrounded him was complete. *Where is this?* he thought. *I'm not in the apartment.* He tried to move, but he was stuck. His head felt heavy with dull throbbing waves that washed back and forth repeatedly. The could-have-been doctor in him imagined the consequences of so many blows to the head. He tugged at his bindings.

A deep voice filtered down from the room above. That same someone walked around the floor above and blocked the light for a moment. More talking. This time in German. *German!* But it sounded like it was only half a conversation. And the speaker's tone was stilted. More like talking on a phone. Another bit of stilted German ended with a loud click.

Other voices reached him. These voices spoke Bosanski. Then the same voice speaking German switched to Bosanski. More Bosanski in reply. Something about trucks in the morning. The Bosanski speakers were upset, upset about waiting, or wasting time, or something like that. Then he heard the word *Američko*. He strained to hear more of what was said. *They're talking about me.* Footsteps scuffled on the floor above, a door opened, and the footsteps clinked on metal stairs. The sounds descended toward him.

He tried to move, but his hands were tied together as well as his arms. He moved his legs and felt the tug on his arms, bound together by an unseen rope.

Keys jingled. A door behind clicked open. Someone stepped over him and knelt by his head.

"You are going to be moved soon." It was Tomislav.

"Jebi se," Goodman said back to him through the gag.

Tomislav laughed out loud. "Yes, you have learned to curse in our language! Good for you." Tomislav turned Goodman's head to look into his eyes. "It won't do you much good since its mostly German spoken where you'll be going." Tomislav cocked his head to one side. "I don't think I like the way you're looking at me. After all I've done for you…"

The slap stung, but Goodman raised his head in defiance.

"Oh? You have strength left in you." Tomislav made a fist and swung downward.

The double impact of the head punch and the bounce off the floor made Goodman dizzy. He laid his head down. Deliberate breathing allowed him to pretend the pain was less than it really was.

"Don't expend all your energy fighting me," said Tomislav. "You'll need to keep your wits about you when the SD get their claws into you." A chair scraped the stone floor. "For now, you should rest."

Goodman tried to say something pithy at Tomislav, but the gag made it unintelligible.

"So you decided to be a Nazi?" Goodman said. "You like their money better?"

"No, you idiot." Tomislav crossed his legs. Three clicks to get the flame to ignite the cigarette. "You should know better than to think I'd chase the money. Did you not listen before? I have always been a part of the German war machine. Always."

"Doe that include last spring?" Goodman played his hand. "Was that why you came to the Majevitsa in the first place? You came to kill Zoran."

"No, well, yes, but also no." A long exhalation filled the small room with sour-smelling smoke. "These are good cigarettes. Not the Serbian goat shit I've had to suck on for these last several months." He took another long drag and exhaled. "No, I did not come to kill Zoran. At least not immediately. I came to stir them up so they would oppose any who they met. We needed Tito's army to divert resources to fight these other, smaller clans. Zoran's militia was the last of the non-aligned groups in this region that constituted any real threat. By that I mean that we, ah, the Germans, would have to divert measurable resources to defeat. He was the hardest to get to while he hid in his precious mountains. He had to be drawn out. Once I learned of his aspirations, I made his goals into my goals. After losing his family, he attacked anyone and everyone he could find. I succeeded, then he succeeded, and then I succeeded again. Now he's dead, his militia is nullified, and I have you."

"You're a real jackass, aren't you? I mean, it takes effort to be this big of a—"

"Come now, Captain Goodman, such discourse is unbecoming of an American officer, no?" Tomislav uncrossed his legs and leaned in close to Goodman's face. "You ought to behave yourself for the remainder of your time in our custody, however long or short it might be. The SS interrogators will break you. That is for certain. Especially now that you know something about your own intelligence services' operations here. Seriously, you should think about cooperating. It will be better for you."

"To hell with that."

"We'll see."

*I can't let him win. Not on any level.* "But you haven't destroyed the militia," said Goodman. "Amira's in charge now."

"Ha!" Tomislav choked on the cigarette smoke. "She's nothing. My mission is almost complete."

"Almost?"

"Well, despite my earlier remarks, I do possess somewhat of a profit motive. By tonight, I will have delivered you to my German contacts, and they will pay most handsomely. Soon, I'll be able to return to my family in the posh Gornji Grad district of Zagreb, where I'll treat my wife and children whom I have not seen since last Winter to a long vacation in the mountains north of Ljubljana, perhaps I'll buy a chalet while I am there to extend my vacation, and support more of the theater which I enjoy so much. Perhaps I'll even do a little acting. Yes, that part was true." He took another drag and blew it in Goodman's face. The chair creaked. "And then I must visit my mistress from Kožarska Street and take her to the coast for a time. If she's still alive, that is. That will be nice." He sighed out loud. "I hope she is." Another pause. "Then, when I am bored again, I'll return to work. I suspect my contacts will focus my talents on undermining Marshall Tito's command group. That should be a challenge. And much, much more lucrative."

Goodman rolled over to look at Tomislav. "So you're just a gun for hire," he said. "All that noise and you're just doing it for the money."

"No, Michael, I am doing it because the Germans will win and I will be an important man in maintaining control in my corner of the Third Reich." Tomislav stood up and stretched. He cracked his knuckles. "It does not hurt to fill my accounts. Especially when the Germans cannot conceive of why someone like me would do this for free. Out of the goodness of his heart, so to speak. Apologies for not allowing you say *auf wiedersehen* to your Majevitsa comrades, but it cannot be helped. I think they liked you, after all the trouble you caused them. Even Amira, I suspect, has a special place in her heart for you."

"So tonight you put me in a truck and take me to wherever your master tells you?"

"No!" said Tomislav. "First, I have no master. I am my own. Second, I don't have to take you anywhere. The Germans will be here very soon."

"Who will be here?" said Goodman. "Your handler? I thought you didn't have a boss."

"Well, yes, I'm sure my German contact will be here, too. But I'm talking about the German Army, you stupid American shit. At least twenty thousands of Wehrmacht forces led by the Waffen-SS are marching or flying here as we speak. I believe the SS has an excellent commander in charge of the operation. This should be an interesting next forty-eight hours."

"Bullshit," Goodman charged. "You're making this up. You don't know anything."

"Yes," said Tomislav. "Defiant. And stupid." He rolled the cigarette smoke out his mouth and into his nostrils. "Everyone on General Kozar's staff, including his British intelligence lapdogs, believes the Germans are regrouping outside Banja Luka. They were, but that was several days ago. Now they are less than a day away and no one here knows anything about it."

"There's a thousand Partisans blocking the valley," said Goodman. "It'll take days to get here."

"Oh, you know about that, do you?" Tomislav sounded surprised, but only mildly. "That position was destroyed in less than one hour. One single bombing raid took care of that entire force. The survivors were all shot."

*Dammit.*

Tomislav looked at his watch and waved his hand back and forth. "Just a few more hours before the Stukas arrive. And then, well, you know." Tomislav's voice sounded like he was smiling as he uttered the word. "Boom." He chuckled.

*He's playing me,* thought Goodman. "There's no way everyone can be wrong," said Goodman. "You can't move twenty thousand Germans without everyone knowing." *Amira and Anderson's people need to be warned!*

"Oh, yes, they can. I know this. And soon you will know this." He took one last puff and watched it curl across the beams of light. "I am done with you." Tomislav flicked the glowing cigarette butt in Goodman's face and closed the door behind him. Keys jingled. His footsteps climbed the stairs, then slowed and stopped at the room above. Another door squeaked and clanked shut. Hushed voices again.

*I need to get out of here!*

Goodman strained against his bindings. Leather straps. There was no getting them loose. He felt around on the floor for something to cut them. Nothing. He wiggled over to the chair and pulled it down on himself. He felt the legs, rungs and crossbars for a sharp edge. The best was one leg that was slightly splintered, so he went to work on it. He tired quickly and paused. He tried again, but only managed for a few minutes before he tired out again and laid his head down on the damp floor. Distant rumbles of artillery vibrated through the stones. A large truck or tank thundered by somewhere on the street level. Goodman imagined a squad of SS troopers packing him into a box and driving for days to an interrogation center. And then the hell really started. The worst things Goodman could think of rolled through his head, one after the other. Then they repeated. And got worse.

# 81

GOODMAN SHIVERED AT THE COLD WIND that descended upon him through the floorboards above him. Or maybe it was the heavy clank of the exterior door slamming shut that woke him. Several German voices discussed something urgent, not bothering to speak in low tones. The upper door creaked open and heavy footsteps descended toward the lower door. Goodman looked around the dim space and saw nothing he could use to defend himself. He wiggled himself to aim his feet toward the door as the keys jingled again. *Dammit. What am I going to do? I can't go like this.* He pulled his wrists as far apart as he could. The straps still had no give in them whatsoever. *This isn't going to go well. God, please help me. Please, don't let this happen.*

The door swung wide, and several dark shapes reached for him. Goodman kicked his feet at the men entering the room. Something long and heavy hit him on the thigh and another something jabbed him hard in the ribs. The knife point of pain made him wheeze. He pulled his arms and legs in tight to protect himself. Several more blows landed on him, merely adding to the general aching he already felt. The next boot landed on his ribs.

"Okay, okay!" he yelled out. "Okay, stop! Please, stop!"

"Halt!" someone commanded. The beating ceased instantly. He heard the familiar clinking of his dog tags.

"You are Captain Goodman, Michael Amancio. Yes?" The voice had zero accent. The guy could have been from Iowa. "Identification number 95677443. Yes?"

*Name, rank, and service number are all I'm obligated to give,* thought Goodman. *And they already have it.* "Yeah." It was all he said.

"Mit ihn auf die straße!"

The several pairs of hands lifted him up. A hood was thrust over his head and tied at the neck. They carried him up the stairs. He felt the cold wind blow up his shirt and pant legs. A machine gun stuttered and echoed through the streets from somewhere not all that far away. More gunfire popped farther away. He heard Tomislav mutter something.

"Tomislav, you said they weren't taking me anywhere!" One of the men punched him in the throat. Goodman coughed and gasped for air.

"Šuti!" said Tomislav. "You are under their control now. You should obey them. Goodbye, Captain Goodman."

Goodman heard the metallic clank of a large truck tailgate and felt himself lifted higher. Then, he dropped and landed first on his shoulder. Hard. On the street. Tomislav argued with someone. The Germans sounded frantic. A pistol shot. Then all hell broke loose.

Automatic weapons and rifles unloosed a cacophony of gunfire that deafened Goodman. Hot brass casings landed on him. Then something, or someone, heavy landed on him. He felt the body wobble slightly with each bullet impact. He tried to push the body off him, but it would not budge. The gunfire continued, and he felt a warm liquid cover his neck and soak into his shirt. Someone yelled something in English and then more commands called out, but in Bosanski. A German voice yelled something and then his next word was cut short. The man coughed, spit, choked, and went silent. Two more pistol shots and lots of heavy footsteps approached. Goodman finally pushed the body off of him and someone untied and removed his hood. He blinked and wiped his face with his sleeve. In the early morning light, he could see it was Captain Whitman. Amira and Colonel Anderson stood behind him.

"Thank God," said Anderson. "You alright?

Amira interrupted. "You are good, yes?" Her concern for him sounded real. Almost a panic.

"Yes, sir," said Goodman. He looked at them both. "Da, Effendim. I'm good."

Amira and Whitman set to releasing the straps that bound him and helped him stand up. Bodies littered the alleyway around the truck. Goodman looked around at them. No uniforms. *These guys are all spies.*

"Tomislav is here," he said. "Somewhere." He turned and spoke to Amira. "Tomislav was here. There." He pointed inside the building next to the truck. The door was closed. Mostly. Amira raised her weapon and prepared to enter. Anderson and Whitman saw this and quietly waved their men over. Goodman lifted a machine pistol from one of the dead German agents. He checked the magazine and the chamber before he rotated the folding shoulder stock out to wedge it firmly in the crook of his shoulder.

"There's at least one room on this floor with a short hallway and one room down the stairs to the left." Amira nodded her head without taking her eyes off the crack in the door. He looked at her again. "I first."

Her eyes flashed at him. Her killer eyes. "Da." She moved aside slightly.

Whitman put his hand to the door.

"Wait." Goodman lifted a fragmentation grenade from Amira's belt. She watched him pull the pin. He nodded to Whitman, who eased the door open a few inches. It creaked loudly. Pistol shots thumped into the thick wooden door. Goodman let the spoon go free and tossed the grenade into the opening. Whitman pushed the door closed, and the grenade exploded. The door creaked open and Goodman, Amira, Whitman sprinted into the darkness, spraying their automatic fire as they went. Sparks flew everywhere. Goodman and Amira entered the upper room and saw a desk with a phone and several files spread out, unattended. No sign of Tomislav or anyone else. Colonel Anderson, Captain Whitman, and a handful of Amira's militiamen entered the room.

"Tomislav!" Goodman yelled as he sprinted down the stairs three at a time. He kicked the door open and quickly swept the room with his submachine gun. *No Tomislav.* "That son of a bitch." He turned to climb the stairs again when he felt a cool wind descend the stairwell. *Where is that wind going?* he thought. He peered into the darkness again and moved to the far wall.

There it was.

He had missed it before. He looked into the opposite corner and saw a second wall, not hidden, just set back from the wall he had presumed was the *only* wall. Behind it was a long, narrow hallway. Completely dark. Completely silent.

"Amira!" She was already behind him.

"You. Me. There."

She handed him a fresh magazine and they changed magazines together. Whitman descended the stairs to join them. Goodman stepped around the corner and led them into the dark. In less than twenty yards, they were engulfed by the pitch black. *Tomislav, where did you go?* He felt his way along a conduit that was bolted to the wall. The narrow tunnel curved slightly, and he saw a light ahead. He ran.

He tripped over something soft, heavy, irregular. It was a body. There was no way to see who it was, but to Goodman, it felt to be too short for it to be Tomislav. But he wanted it to be him. Amira caught up with Whitman right behind her.

"You got a light?" Goodman asked.

Whitman flicked his lighter. The body was not Tomislav's, but another man Goodman did not recognize. He had been stabbed multiple times. Goodman fished through the man's inner pockets and found a German identification book. A distant flicker caught his eye, and he looked up. A door slammed shut farther down the tunnel. It sprang open slightly and revealed a sliver of light.

"Tomislav!" Goodman sprinted toward the light. He peered through the door into a small landing at the bottom of a narrow stairway. Goodman pulled himself hand over hand up the handrails to ascend the steep, narrow steps. His arms and legs screamed with exhaustion. He burst into the backroom of a garment shop. Shelves piled high with bolts of cloth covered the walls and several foot-powered sewing machines lined the center aisleway. A row of electric lightbulbs hovered over the sewing machines. A door swung open and Tomislav aimed his pistol and fired three shots. Bolts of patterned cloth absorbed the bullets. Goodman aimed to return fire, but Tomislav disappeared. As Goodman knelt and pushed the door open, the wood over his head splintered with gunfire. Goodman fired several rounds in reply. Another door slammed shut. He and Amira stepped carefully into the adjoining room. The front of the store was a row of three large windows with a starburst pattern of thick tape across each one. Tomislav ran across the front and Goodman shattered the middle and leftmost windows with his automatic gunfire. He missed. Amira ran to the door, and he followed.

They opened the door to see an empty city street. A car door squeaked open, and they saw Tomislav get into close the door. The engine failed to turn over as Goodman sprinted. Tomislav tried again, and the engine roared to life. He found the gear, and the car skidded into the open street. Goodman let loose with his weapon and the car lurched into a parked car across the street. The weapon jammed and Goodman cocked it again as he stepped incautiously toward the car. He raised his weapon and emptied the magazine. Windows shattered and holes thumped into the body panels. The trunk lid sprang open and fell shut again. More rounds thumped into the steel body and warped the reflections of streetlights with the gray light of early morning. Without another magazine, Goodman tossed the MP40 aside and drew the pistol from his pocket. He checked the chamber and aimed at the driver's side window.

The door swung open, and a leg dropped out. Pistol raised, Goodman approached the car from the rear. An arm flopped out but rested on the leg. The arm bent at the elbow to reach for something but lacked strength and fell again, palm up. Goodman stepped to the door and put his pistol against Tomislav's temple.

"Whatever you're doing," said Goodman. "You need to stop." From what he saw, Goodman knew he no longer needed his pistol.

A steady stream of blood pooled on the street from both the leg and the arm that extended from the driver's seat. Tomislav's coat and shirt were wet crimson, and the entire windshield and dashboard were splattered with red. A wound on the side of Tomislav's head oozed dark, almost black blood. His head rolled toward Goodman, and his eyes searched back and forth as if he could not see. Tomislav licked his lips and tried to speak.

"Are you done?" he sputtered.

Goodman remembered his earlier conversation with Colonel Anderson. "No," he said. "No, I'm not."

"Good...good man," said Tomislav, straining for breath. He chuckled awkwardly and choked on it before spitting out a mouthful of blood. He motioned weakly for Goodman to approach with his wounded hand.

"What?" Goodman held his ground.

Tomislav gasped and sputtered. He licked his lips several times. He muttered something incoherently. Goodman leaned in slightly.

"It does not...does...does not matter." Tomislav drooled blood down his shirt. "I cannot see anymore. Are you there, you stupid American? You're dead." He coughed and spit up frothy pink. "All of you! Dead."

Something sprang out of Tomislav's hand and clattered to the street. A grenade spoon! Goodman dived away from the car as the grenade went off. His shoulder took most of the impact with the wall, but he blacked out for a split second. He opened his eyes again long enough to see Amira and Whitman running toward him. The skin on his face felt heavy, like it was detached from the underlying sinew and about to slide off his head like a mask. He closed his eyes and blew a loud exhalation. And it felt better.

# 82

## THE OSS APARTMENT

SOMEONE SLAPPED GOODMAN IN THE FACE. And again. And again until Goodman wrinkled his face and groaned out loud. "Cap'n, you there? Captain! Wake up!"

His head felt dull and thick. He blinked his eyes open and tried to focus and the faces hovering over him. He watched concerned looks morph into relief.

"Yeah," Goodman mumbled. "I'm here…"

"Ok, good. Let's get those bandages tightened up," O'Keefe directed.

Goodman felt someone tugging on his arm. Someone else gently lifted his head and pressed a cloth to it. He blinked again and saw Amira's face draped by her hair. She smiled sadly at him and looked up. Master Sergeant O'Keefe's face entered his view with Colonel Anderson, the OSS captains, and several of the Majevitsa militia crammed into the small apartment behind them. He was back on the same couch where he had been laying over twenty-four hours ago when he lost the fight with Tomislav and his men.

"How is he?" Anderson asked.

"He'll be ok, I think." O'Keefe sat back on his knees. "He's banged up, though."

Goodman tried to sit up, but O'Keefe gently pressed him back down. "Don't rush things, Cap'n. You've had a bad go of it." Goodman laid his head back down and exhaled.

"What happened?" Colonel Anderson stood over him, holding his Thompson on his hip.

"These guys," Goodman waved a limp arm at the blood on the floor next to the destroyed kitchen table and chairs. "They picked the lock and got the drop on me."

"Looks like you gave 'em a good fight, sir," said O'Keefe. "How many were there?"

"I don't know," said Goodman. "But…he said…"

"Who said what?" asked Anderson. Goodman pointed at Tomislav's leg protruding from the driver's seat.

"It was Tomislav…"

"We know, son," said Colonel Anderson. "They kidnapped you. But Amira and her people followed and led us to you."

"No, there's…" A coughing spasm cut him off. *They need to know.* Goodman fought through the cloud in his head. *They need to know about the attack!* He clumsily propped himself up on the couch.

"Take it easy—"

"No… there's more…" He cleared his throat again. Everyone turned back to Goodman. "Tomislav…" He breathed deeply to clear his head more. "He said…he said that the Germans were coming…"

"We know—" Anderson began, but Goodman cut him off.

"No!" Goodman sat fully upright and the pain exploded inside his head. "He said they're *already* coming! He said there's more than twenty thousand Germans coming right now!"

Colonel Anderson's face went gray. "And you trust what he said?"

"Those were his last words," replied Goodman. "I don't know how it would be in his interest to lie at that moment." He cleared his throat again. "He said we're as good as dead."

"Well, shit," Anderson muttered. "Whit, go back to the radio room and get a message to—what is that?"

A commotion from the square outside attracted everyone's attention back to the window. Amira pointed upward and cried out. "*Avion!*"

Everyone rushed to the window as the scout plane's whining engine echoed through the streets. Elsewhere in the city, anti-aircraft cannon and machine guns opened fire, filling the sky with white tracer fire and obscuring the high-pitched sound of the single-engine craft.

"Sounds like a Storch," Goodman observed, steadying himself on his feet.

"It is," said Whitman, searching the sky. "There! There he is!" He pointed at a tiny, t-shaped dark spot fading in and out of the clouds. Tracers from several gun emplacements soared after the tiny aircraft, sweeping back and forth. The scout plane raced his engine to climb into a cloud, chased by tracers as he disappeared. He reappeared a moment later, and the gunfire was louder than before, with tracer streams converging around him from all over the city. Suddenly, several streams shifted far to the west. Goodman's eyes followed them to their new targets. A trail of seven more aircraft emerged from behind a cloud. These had heavier, sinister sounding engines.

"Stukas!" Goodman yelled out.

"Oh, no," said Kidder, backing away from the window. Everyone else tore their eyes away and backed into the interior of the apartment.

"You don't want to be anywhere near the windows when those things dive," O'Keefe replied. They had only a second to wait for O'Keefe's prediction to be borne out. The Stukas' engines screamed as they began their dive sequence. Goodman watched the aircraft peel off with precision, one by one, into their dive. He followed Whitman and Amira into the kitchen, where they hunkered down behind the cabinets. The sound became unbearably loud as the Stukas' wingtip 'trumpets' and emitted their ear-piercing screeches that reverberated and amplified in the tight urban spaces. Tears streaked from Amira's eyes as she shielded her ears from the horrible sound. Goodman stuck his fingers in his ears and made himself as small as possible for what came next.

Next came the whistles of high explosive bombs loosed from the mounts in the wings. As the bombs' whistles grew in intensity, the Stukas' engines roared as they pulled up and away to avoid the imminent explosions and anti-aircraft fire.

The first bombs impacted some distance away, and the explosions cracked the air and rumbled through the streets. Shockwaves kicked up dust into the apartment. A second pair of explosions were further away, but still rumbled and shook the tiles on which everyone lay. Goodman's teeth rattled. Glass plates made a tinny sound as they shattered on the streets below. The anti-aircraft gunfire slowed to a trickle as the drone of the Stukas faded into the clouds. Rays of light filtered through the clouds of dust drifting through the large open window frame. Slowly, everyone in the apartment lifted their heads.

Goodman looked over the windowsill into a market square filled with swirling dust. The façade of a nearby building cracked loudly and slid into a pile of rubble in the street. Clouds of dust rolled across the market square as the last several bombs impacted elsewhere across the city.

"Son of a bitch!" Sergeant O'Keefe said out loud from his place near the couch. Everyone dusted themselves off and walked out of wherever they sought shelter.

"What do we do now, sir?" asked Kidder as he clapped the dust off his coat.

"We need to confirm if this is indeed a main force attack or just a raid," Anderson began his assessment. "I don't know long Kozar's forces will be able to withstand coordinated air and ground attacks. Assuming this is just the beginning of the preparation bombardment of a main force assault…" He looked at Goodman. "We need to get our airmen out of here ASAP. Charlie?"

Captain Kidder raised his head. "Yessir?"

"Get a message to Bari Station about a new pickup mission. Scratch the airdrop for tonight. I want it now."

"In the daylight?" said Kidder.

"Kozar will never agree to an air mission right now," said Whitman. "They're going to want to know about the gunfire this morning."

"I think they've got bigger fish to fry than worrying about us," O'Keefe observed.

"Hold on a second," said Colonel Anderson. "Charlie, finish your thought."

Whitman continued. "I think we should make everyone disappear. Goodman stays out of sight until we can get him out of town. Same with the militia." He nodded to Amira. "We dispose of the bodies and clean up the mess like they were never here. If we pretend nothing happened, and we stay on our pattern, then the German counterattack might keep whoever directed this kidnapping off balance long enough for us to get at least one step ahead of them." Colonel Anderson gave a nod of consideration.

"What does one step ahead look like?" asked Kidder.

Whitman responded. "We need to get our airmen out. All of 'em. Especially if there is a general counterattack coming." All eyes went to Colonel Anderson.

"You're right," Anderson agreed. "Whitman, that's your ball. Get it rolling."

"Yes, sir…"

The sounds of boots running up the stairs drew everyone's eyes to the door. It flew open, and Major Farish slid into the room. He caught himself on the table.

"Pack up everyone!" he yelled. "We're getting reports of massive, armored columns converging on Tuzla!" The mess of blood on the floor caught his attention. "What the hell happened here?"

"Slow down, slow down," said Colonel Anderson. "Armored columns from where?"

"From the west and northwest," Farish replied, out of breath, still looking at the corpses. "With motorized infantry from the southeast.

"That would be just about everywhere," Kidder remarked.

"And that eliminates access to all our airfields," Whitman added. "And kills the idea of getting out people out."

"How far out are these columns?" asked Colonel Anderson.

"According to Kozar's scouts, the lead elements are in the foothills around the Tuzla valley," Farish replied.

"Well, damn. That's only a few away hours at the most." O'Keefe looked at his watch.

"The reporting is inconsistent," Farish went on. "There is a report of SS reconnaissance vehicles at the Rimsky Canal Bridge. With artillery falling all over the high ground to the north."

Whitman's mouth dropped. "That's only minutes away from the church!"

"The church?" asked Goodman.

"It's where we have the other airmen stashed," said Colonel Anderson. "We need to get them and you out of there." He looked at the surge of activity in the market square. Convoys of trucks, heavy with ammunition and other supplies, roared by on the street below. Long lines of infantry units double-timed their way through the district. Civilians scurried the narrow alleyways to avoid the crush of military equipment. Three large trucks loaded with artillery, explosives casings, and powder charges pulled into the market square. Dozens of men clambered aboard to download and assemble and stack their shells under a store awning.

"Gentlemen," Anderson announced. "Getting our airmen out of the Tuzla valley is our number one and only task right now. Do we have any airfields that are not likely to have fresh Panzer tracks across them by lunchtime?"

Whitman and O'Keefe unfolded a large map of the region across the table. After a brief scan across the center of the map sheet, they shook their heads. Then O'Keefe pointed at a spot and looked at Whitman, who returned a sideways glance.

"No, it's too close to the Partisan defensive lines," said Whitman. "Besides, it's a grass strip and it's been raining. No good."

"What about this one?" said Kidder, putting his finger on a dashed line with a small airplane symbol on it.

"Too short," said Whitman. "C-47s need at least two thousand feet to take off."

Goodman's eyes followed the long stretches of road leading out of the city. He followed the one major road to the east. Simin Han. *That's the name of the town where the salt factory is, or was. There's that long stretch. That's more than two thousand feet.*

"Sir, if I may," said Goodman.

"What do you got, Captain?"

"Well, sir, there's one possibility east of here," said, spinning the map around to show the Colonel and Major Farish. "The Tuzla Road." Goodman leaned over the table to see the map. "It is a highway, and it should do nicely as a landing strip.

"It won't work," said Kidder.

"Why won't it work?" Goodman asked.

"It's a highway," said Kidder. "That's not an airstrip."

"That's why it will work," Goodman replied. "It's long, straight, and flat."

"Headquarters doesn't have a survey on file," Kidder added. "They'd never authorize a landing on an unseen stretch of road."

"It's not unseen," said Goodman. "I walked it a couple of days ago. I can draw you a picture right now."

"How fast can you do a survey?" Anderson asked, point-blank to Whitman. "How fast?"

"Well, sir," Whitman said. "If everything is perfect on the ground, about three hours. Or I can do a map survey, but HQ doesn't like those."

"You have twenty minutes to do a map survey," Anderson directed. "HQ will have to take it. We'll mark it when we get there." He looked at O'Keefe. "Master Sergeant, gin up a message to transmit the survey, and shift tonight's drop to a daylight pickup for as soon as they can get a mission together."

"Wilco, sir," said O'Keefe. "Use the usual authenticator?"

"No," said Anderson. "Use the emergency code. And don't bother to encrypt it."

"Send in the clear?"

"No time to waste," replied Anderson. Whitman and O'Keefe looked at each other as they sat down to their tasks. Kidder whistled between his teeth.

"Kid, get us a truck," said the Colonel. "Whatever it takes."

Captain Kidder nodded and grabbed his weapon and ammo pouches on his way out the door. Amira stepped up to the table to see the map.

"What of my people?" she said. "What do you need or want from us?" Her eyes flitted from Goodman to Anderson.

"Amira…" Said Goodman. He switched to Bosanski. "*You need to get out of town. Get your people back to the Majevitsa.*"

"I decide what my people must do," she said. She glared at him.

"General Kozar won't authorize any forces to protect the landing zone," Whitman stated. "We need security at the landing strip. Can she and her people be our protection?" Anderson looked right at Amira.

"Sir," Goodman interjected. "With all due respect, the militia needs to get out of town ASAP. If the Germans are coming with this large of a force, then a hundred militia won't make a difference." He looked at Amira. She looked straight back at him.

"Yes," she said. "We will provide men and weapons for this mission."

"Amira," said Goodman. "You need to get out of town as quickly as possible."

Amira looked him in the eyes. "My father wanted to get you out of Yugoslavia. I *am* my father's daughter, as you said. We will protect you and your airplane so you may return to your people." Amira turned back to Colonel Anderson. "I have enough men to assist."

"Perfect," said Colonel Anderson. "Goodman, you're a multi-engine-rated pilot. Assist Whitman with his survey. Make sure we don't break a C-47 transport when they land."

"Yes, sir." Whitman nodded to Goodman.

"Good," said Anderson. "Ok, everyone. Keep to your routine. And that means I have to attend a tactical update with the general staff that starts in…" He turned to Major Farish.

"Fifteen minutes."

"That's you and me?" asked Anderson. Farish nodded.

"Sir, we need trucks, too, sir," said Whitman. "The one we have is too small."

"I can get you trucks," said Amira.

"You sure?" asked Colonel Anderson. "Two large trucks?"

"Two large trucks? No problem."

# 83

## TUZLA CENTRAL MARKET DISTRICT

CLOUDS OF WHITE SMOKE BELCHED FROM THE EXHAUST PIPES as Major Farish and Captain Kidder ran up to the tailgate. Under the canvas cover sat Goodman and more than two dozen of the Majevitsa militiamen. Musa wore his habitual grin as he wielded his MG42 machine gun over the tailgate. Master Sergeant O'Keefe squatted next to the team's radio transmitter with a mess of cables and antenna parts at his feet. Amira sat behind him on the bench. She was stone faced. Waiting.

"Is Whitman up front?" Farish asked. Goodman nodded.

"Good," Farish replied. "Tell him where we're going."

"Hey, good luck to you!" Kidder raised his hand to shake.

"Thanks!" Goodman reached down from the truck. "And to you, too!"

Kidder turned to say one last thing. "When you get to Italy, have a bottle of a nice cabernet or something for me!"

Major Farish chuckled. "That's French."

Goodman snickered and gave Kidder a thumbs up, then helped Major Farish climb over the side. The second truck started up with a cloud of smoke, full of the militia. Whitman held up the map for Goodman to see. He scanned the contour lines and web of road networks for the familiar arrangement of hills on the north side of a major road, the built-up area around the salt factory, and the long east-west straightaway of the Tuzla Road. He put a finger on it.

"That's it?" said Whitman.

"Yes," said Goodman. He pointed at the place where he estimated that he and the others attacked the German tanks and infantry company just days ago. "That's it. Did we hear back from your people?"

The truck lurched as the driver put the truck in gear and accelerated out of the alley.

"We got the message out," Farish yelled over the sound of the engines. "And we got an acknowledgement."

"So, we're good to go, sir?" asked Goodman.

"They only acknowledged receipt of the message. They didn't say if they would send a plane to a new landing zone."

"So, we're not good?"

"We'll see," said Farish. "We communicated the urgent nature of this pickup, so if anything does come, it'll be a Dakota."

Half of Goodman's flight school class went to cargo planes, the other randomly selected half went to bombers. He considered the Dakota, a twin-engine cargo plane with a hundred-foot wingspan. Unarmed. Not all that maneuverable. Dubiously called the Gooney Bird. He ran calculations in his head from his memory of how wide the Tuzla Road was. *Ought to make it*, he thought. *We'll see how this goes.*

The lead truck turned a corner and immediately skidded to a halt. Partisan soldiers, militia, and civilians packed the road. The driver leaned on the horn to no effect.

"Oh, c'mon," Whitman said out loud. "Idi! Pozurite!" *Let's go! Hurry!*

The driver put the truck into gear again and edged forward into the crowd. Several Partisans and civilians immediately showered him with expletives. Whitman urged the driver to go until a young Partisan officer raised his hand in front of the bumper and approached. The young officer climbed up to Whitman's side window and barked orders in Bosanski when he was taken aback by the pistol Whitman held just below the window. Whitman slowly shook his head. Then people in the street began yelling and running, colliding and falling, abandoning carts and children in the street. A finger pointed to the sky. Goodman, Whitman, and the officer looked up. More Stukas!

A column of Stuka dive bombers rolled over their wingtips into their attack dive. The screams were overwhelming. Each plane pulled out of its dive, obscured by the tall buildings. Explosion after explosion after explosion rocked the city. Towers of gray and black debris and orange flame climbed into the sky. People trampled each other to get under shelter or into the side streets or the alleys between buildings.

Another plane roared overhead, just above rooftop level, and let loose with a long burst of machine-gun fire. The black cross of the Luftwaffe was clearly visible on the wings and vertical section of the tail. Broken glass cascaded from building edifices to the streets below. Another plane screamed by just barely above the tallest buildings. A fraction of a second later, two small, black projectiles zipped overhead and crossed the gap between buildings. Before Goodman's brain could process the bombs falling, explosions shook the buildings next to them. A large building on the next block collapsed in a giant cloud of gray dust. People screamed. Two more fighter-bombers roared over, loosing four more bombs each that impacted near the river. Pillars of smoke and dirt jumped into the air over the skyline. Their thunder echoed for quite a long time. Goodman and the others in the trucks rose from their hiding places. The boulevard was suddenly devoid of people.

"Go!" Goodman yelled. "Go, go, go!"

Engines coughed and belched large clouds of smoke. The trucks lurched violently into gear and everyone in the rear of Goodman's truck fell over as the truck careened down the street. In succession, the trucks and passengers swayed left and right as drivers avoided other vehicles and carts abandoned by those who had fled the attack. The lead truck skidded around a corner and smashed through a wooden cart. Wood panels flew into the air as crates of produce disintegrated. Egg yolks splattered across the windshield. Chickens squawked and shed feathers everywhere. The second truck finished off what was left.

Partisan infantry units had recovered from the attack and filled the streets again as the lead truck rounded another turn. The driver punched the horn but was ignored. He hit it again and again. He looked haplessly at Whitman and Goodman as he downshifted.

"Crap!" Whitman yelled. Amira also cursed.

But she braced herself as she stood up, raising her submachine gun. She yelled at the driver to go and sprayed bullets into the air. Goodman joined her, firing his own weapon. Surprised by the gunfire, men and horses scrambled to get back into the alleyways as the truck roared past. Once clear of the worst congestion, Amira looked back and smiled at Goodman. She reloaded, as did he. The driver made a hard-left turn at the river road and bounced over the curb. Everyone hunkered down and gripped something to keep from flying out of the truck bed.

Goodman and Amira both looked across the river. The Planina Fortress was there with the stone bridge that would never leave their memories. Goodman shot her a quick glance. Her ponytail trailed in the wind as she watched the bridge disappear behind them. A thousand thoughts about her clouded his mind.

Here, the road had three large, fresh craters in it, which the drivers easily by-passed at speed. An overturned truck was still smoking as soldiers attempted to right it with levers and horses. Heavy machine guns opened up on unseen aircraft somewhere overhead. Amira, Goodman, and Farish scanned the sky for the gunner's target. It was right behind them.

Two large, twin-engine Ju-88 fighter bombers came in low over the riverbed. Their nose-mounted machine guns peppered the

Partisan rooftop positions along the riverbanks. Dirt clouds, slivers of concrete, and chucks of broken road flew into the air as the gunners tracked in on the two trucks. The driver swerved left and right to avoid hitting people and livestock and smashed a signpost. The planes roared past so closely that Goodman saw a nose gunner grinning at him as the empty brass casings showered down around them. Goodman, Amira, and Major Farish each emptied a full magazine at it. But the pilot peeled upward, undeterred. The tail gunner opened up on the river road, but their gunfire was scattered and ineffective. The aircraft rejoined the others in their formation at altitude and headed northwest.

Entering the eastern suburbs, the driver deftly steered the truck through the narrow streets between shops and neighborhoods. Here, the streets were empty except for soldiers preparing defensive positions between buildings and on the rooftops. Miles behind them, another flight of Stuka dive-bombers flew high overhead toward the city and made their terrible assault on the downtown area. Farish shook his head as they watched enormous jets of dirt and yellow-orange fireballs rise above the buildings, folding into plumes of oily black smoke. Huge columns of smoke drifted lazily over the remainder of the valley, mixing with the gray cloud cover. That worried Goodman.

"How low is the cloud ceiling supposed to be?" he asked Farish over the sound of the wind and the engine noise.

"I don't know," he yelled back. "Bari Station usually transmits the weather forecast with the air operation's instructions! But they didn't send any instructions because they never transmitted an air ops plan!"

"What does that mean?"

"It could mean nothing!" They braced as the truck hit a bump. "Or it could mean that the transport wasn't approved, and nobody is coming for you!" The truck swerved again. "It's probably fine. We just need to get there. First, though, we need to pick up the other airmen."

Goodman had forgotten about the other airmen the OSS had been protecting. He looked at the sky with skepticism. The dark clouds were on the leading edge of a front coming in. Airplanes don't fly if they can't see. And, with the mountains between them and the Adriatic, Goodman worried about whether the air operations director would allow such a risky mission, however necessary it may be.

The driver downshifted and steered the truck onto a dirt road headed south toward a small hamlet. Black and gray explosions erupted on a low ridge about a mile away, sending rumbles across the landscape and drawing everyone to stand up to see what was happening.

"That's artillery!" Farish pointed at the ridge. Goodman nodded.

On an opposing ridge directly to the north, a Partisan mortar unit lobbed shells against the likely places where German artillery observers were positioned. The shells swished overhead.

"Get off the road!" Goodman yelled, pointing out a formation of aircraft sweeping in from the west. The driver slowed and pulled into a thicket of bare trees. A flight of three fighter-bombers struck hard at the Partisan defenses on that same ridgeline that was pummeled a moment earlier by artillery. 250-pound bombs detonated in quick succession, and the entire flight banked hard and swooped in low over the positions again. The staccato of the heavy machine guns echoed off the hills. The planes made another pass and then reformed overhead.

"How long do we have, sir?" Whitman called to Major Farish.

Major Farish looked at his watch. "Less than an hour," he replied. "If they come at all. I gave them a pretty narrow window. Though I'm wishing now I hadn't."

"We might not have much more time than that," said Whitman. "Unless the Partisans can hold out against the Waffen-SS."

"We'll see." Farish looked at the sky.

"Pazi!" Amira pointed to the ridge, still smoking from a dozen large fires. "Vojni tenki!"

German Panzers were descending the near side of the hills to the south less than half a mile away. One of the lead tanks fired its main gun and a house burst apart. Partisan infantry streamed out of a nearby barn just seconds before it, too, was destroyed by tank fire. Almost twenty armored beasts rolled down the slopes and into the harvested farm fields.

"Move!" Whitman yelled at the driver. He pointed at a church steeple that rose above the surrounding rooftops. "There! That's where we're going."

The driver nodded and gunned the engine. They skidded to a halt directly in front of the church doors. A priest dressed in black robes stepped out from the main doors. An American pilot emerged cautiously with a Russian submachine gun. Three others walked out with relief on their faces.

"The Jerries are comin'!" an airman yelled.

"That's why we're here," Whitman responded. "Get your stuff!"

"What stuff?" said another airman. "Let's get the hell outta here!"

The airmen ran to the truck. Two more exited the church with a man in a pilot's uniform between them, his arms draped over their shoulders. Musa helped lift him into the bed of the truck. He smiled as he helped each of the others into the back of the truck. An American Lieutenant Colonel helped a British officer navigate the curb with his improvised crutches and spoke to Captain Whitman.

"Thank God it's you guys," he called out. "The Germans are bombing the hell outta the commies!"

"No kidding," said Whitman. "Get everyone into the truck."

Ten more men in American and British flight uniforms spilled out of the church, followed by a priest and two young men carrying a young airman on a stretcher. He was in rough shape. Goodman leapt down to help lift the stretcher into the truck. He climbed back in and Musa closed the tailgate. The man's bandages were old and reeked of infection. Goodman lifted one set of wraps to inspect his wound and regretted it. He tightened the bandage. Good thing we're getting you home, he thought. The rear of the first truck was now a rolling hospital, and the second truck was overflowing with armed militia. Musa climbed aboard the rear truck and readied his machine gun on the cab rooftop. Amira stood next to him and looked at Goodman. She gave him a half-smile.

Major Farish climbed over the tailgate and joined Goodman, standing behind the cab. He rapped on the hood. "Let's go!"

# 84

THE DRIVERS DEFTLY MANEUVERED THEIR OVERWEIGHT TRUCKS through the narrow streets and bounced over the curb onto the main east-west highway. The Tuzla Road. Goodman almost did not recognize it without the hundreds of people surging into Tuzla from a few nights ago. It was vacant now. The gallows were still there. But new bodies swung from the old ropes. *I'm not going to miss that.* The intersection

"This is it!" Goodman yelled. "Turn here!"

The driver swerved around an abandoned sandbag bunker and accelerated down the boulevard. A mile or so later, the roadway widened and the hills to the north steepened. The stair-step effect of the houses looked familiar.

"We're here!" Goodman yelled. "This is the middle of the strip."

The truck's brakes squealed and ground to a halt.

Major Farish stood tall and looked around. "What is that?" He pointed down the road.

"That's a dead Panzer," said Goodman. *I forgot about that.*

"You didn't say anything about a tank in the middle of this landing strip!" said Whitman.

"A C-47 doesn't need that much room?"

"At least sixteen-hundred feet," Whitman said. "Bare minimum."

*That's close*, thought Goodman. "Ok," he said. "Might be a problem."

"You think?"

"Calm down," said Major Farish. "We're not dead in the water yet." He tapped the driver on the shoulder. "Let's go check it out."

He accelerated, then slowed and halted next to the tank. All the bodies had been removed from the roadway and the roadside ditches, as had the discarded weapons and other various other artefacts of the battle that occurred here. The rain had washed away all but the darkest scorch marks and small divots where the anti-tank rockets had blasted away the pavement. A rainbow reflected from the pool of diesel fuel mixed with the rainwater.

"How high does a C-47 sit on its landing gear?" Goodman asked.

"It's low," said Whitman. "Neighborhood of five or six feet."

The tank stood at least ten feet tall. The sky suddenly darkened, and Goodman looked up. He flinched as the first spit of rain stung his face. He saw the hazy wall of the downpour sweeping down on them from the East.

"Damn," said Whitman. "We don't need that."

A hard wind blew and chilled Goodman's neck. He looked to where it was blowing in from. Ninety degrees off from what it was just a minute ago.

"No," Goodman said out loud. Amira and Whitman turned. "No, no, no. The wind is all wrong." He looked up and down the wide boulevard. Trash blew down from the hillside neighborhoods and tumbled across the pavement.

"Yeah," said Whitman, looking into the sky. "This is serious weather."

"Is it too much wind?" Major Farish asked.

"Depends on the pilot," said Goodman. "I've landed in worse, but I had a nice regulation width and length airfield with ground support and emergency crews. And I wasn't trying to take off again right away. It would help to have a windsock."

"Well, let's do what we can to help," said Major Farish. "Ideas?"

Goodman looked at the diesel fuel pooled around the Panzer. He reached into his pocket and pulled out the SS lighter that Tomislav had given him. He waded up a piece of cloth and lit it. When it was fully aflame, he tossed it toward the broken treads. At first, the flaming rag just sat there, the flames dancing sharply in the wind. *Ignite, damn diesel fuel. Ignite!* Suddenly the fuel flashed blue and ignited and raced around the tank. The wind fed the flames and smoke blew southward and climbed into the sky.

In the back of the truck with the radio, Master Sergeant O'Keefe pressed his finger to his earpiece. "I got 'em!" He snapped his fingers in the air and everyone turned to listen.

"Roger, Pipeline, this is Coalminer. I copy one six minutes out…roger, standing by. We are on site at the landing zone. How copy, over?" He paused and squeezed the earpiece harder. "How do you copy, Over." He shook his head and looked up at Major Farish. "Well, I had 'em." He removed the earpiece. "Not sure if he heard me at the end or not. From what I could hear, the pilot says rough weather is coming in fast. They have a fighter escort assigned to them, but they have yet to make contact. He thinks they're lost in the weather. He wants to know about weather conditions and if the runway is secured."

"It's as secured as it's gonna get," said Major Farish.

"Roger that, sir." O'Keefe turned back to his radio. He put the earpiece to his head and tried again to contact the pilot.

"Ok, let's set up the marshalling area back there." Major Farish pointed down the road toward Tuzla.

Everyone climbed aboard and held on. The drivers eased their trucks a half-mile down the road and halted where the boulevard narrowed and curved. When the engines shut off, all they could hear was the wind and the occasional rumble of explosions far to the west. Amira jumped down and positioned her militia in the buildings and rooftops in a wide perimeter around them. Goodman attended to the injured airmen. He directed others to apply pressure to the stretcher-bound pilot. The infection was very gangrenous, Goodman observed. *He'll probably lose that leg.* Amira stood on the back of the truck and watched her men deploy to their positions. Musa stayed on the truck with his machine gun trained down the road. He watched the sky intently.

"Strange how quiet it is here," Whitman mused. He scanned the clouds with his binoculars.

"Let it stay that way," said Major Farish.

Goodman watched the Major check his watch for the fifth time in less than a minute. Then Goodman felt the cold, light tap on his shoulder. Again, this time on his back. Another on his back. Then two more. Spits of rain tinkled on metal. Goodman's heart sank.

"No…" he muttered.

"This might be the end of this show," said Major Farish. "Pipeline doesn't usually like landing in bad weather."

Everyone shifted back and forth on their feet to stay warm. *The cold won't help us take off*, thought Goodman. And the imminent ground assault by twenty thousand Germans. *If this doesn't go...hell if I'm going to go back to Tuzla with the bombing and the artillery. Do I stay with these OSS guys? Or do I go with Amira back to the Majevitsa?* Amira joined Goodman by the truck. She looked up at the sky and held her hand out, palm up. A forlorn look drew her face down. She knows, Goodman saw in her eyes. *She knows this is a bust.*

"Holy cow! They came!" Major Farish exclaimed, pointing upward. Goodman and the others looked skyward for the small, black silhouette somewhere amongst the clouds.

And there it was.

A single C-47 Dakota transport in dark green camouflage paint with a white star painted on its wing and another near its tail descended fast and swept over the northern ridgeline. The low droning of the engines was barely perceptible over the wind. Goodman looked at the smoke streaming from the tank. *Still a strong crosswind*, he thought. *I hope this pilot's good.*

He ran up to the rear of the truck and got O'Keefe's attention. "Tell the aircrew that the smoking tank is the leading edge of the runway. It is a two-four-zero heading. It will also indicate the cross winds!"

He nodded and pressed a finger to his earpiece. "Roger, Pipeline, this is Coalminer! I read you loud and clear!" O'Keefe gave a triumphant thumbs-up. "Roger...we are in position. The tank that is on fire is the leading edge of the runway, heading two-four-zero. There's a northerly crosswind as well. Over." He pressed the earpiece to his head. A moment later, he gave Goodman a thumbs-up. Goodman couldn't help but smile. *I'm going home*, he thought. *I'm finally getting out of here.*

"Pazi!" One of the militia cried out from a nearby rooftop. Heads turned. "Tanki!"

Tracers flew over their heads and stabbed at the transport plane on its approach. High explosive shells swished overhead and impacted in the hillside neighborhoods. The bright red streaks chased the plane as it banked hard and away from the highway.

470

Whitman cursed out loud as everyone dived for cover. Then the deadly red streams descended and tracers zipped right over their heads. Giant coal-colored Panzers rumbled from behind buildings on the south side of the Tuzla Road. Amira redeployed her men to the reinforce the southern roof top positions. The volume of gunfire surged.

"The infantry is assaulting from the right!" Whitman yelled out.

Goodman spotted several dark figures dashing between buildings. A whitish sparkle in a second-story window sent tracers into the rear of the truck next to him. Goodman raised his submachine gun and fired at the window. Musa swung his MG42 around and poured a stream of deadly fire into the alleys and buildings up and down the street. Bullets pinged off the truck's metal body panels and chipped the wood frame, but he kept firing at the infantry. The radio transmitter popped and fizzed as solid core machine gun rounds penetrated and shattered the sheet metal case. Master Sergeant O'Keefe fell backward and scrambled out of the truck.

"Radio's out!" he yelled. "Get down!"

Everyone else took his cue and jumped from the trucks to take cover on the ground. Most of the airmen were unarmed and took shelter behind the large truck wheels and engine blocks. One American pilot was cut down and fell to the pavement next to a Brit, each man dead where he lay. Everyone else laid flat on the ground, huddled behind the large tires. Bullets zipped over them, missing them by inches or throwing slivers of stone or dirt in their faces. Another man nearby screamed in pain before going silent.

"We can't hold this position!" yelled Major Farish. He looked around at the north side of the road. "We need to withdraw to the houses back there!" He pointed and Goodman looked. *That's too far back! We can't hold the highway from there.* He pivoted to look for the C-47.

The plane continued its long bank away from them. Out of sheer anger, Goodman raised himself to his knees and emptied the rest of his magazine at the German-occupied buildings before O'Keefe pulled him back to the ground. The other pilots and aircrewmen cursed and pounded their fists on the pavement in angry despair.

Amira looked at Goodman from behind a now-flat truck tire. Her eyes said everything. *What should I do?* they said. He had never seen her like this before. Frozen. Unable to act. *She needs to get out of here.*

"Amira!" yelled Goodman. "Amira! Run! You, your people, go from here!" *If she stays too long, she'll get caught. And I know what will happen to her. I can't let that happen.* "Amira! Go!"

"I cannot," she yelled back. She emptied her magazine and yelled to her men to keep up their fire.

Goodman started to crawl over to her when a tank blasted a nearby house into the air. It disintegrated and broken masonry and red roof tiles showered the ground. Machine gun rounds creeped closer and closer as the rocks and debris splintered around them. The truck sparked and smoked as machine gun rounds tore it up. The front quarter-panel clanged loudly on the pavement. Goodman hugged the ground behind it. Amira's eyes locked on his, swelling with tears. He felt the terrible rumble of the approaching tanks through the pavement. One of Amira's men got up and was immediately cut down. He writhed in pain and slowly expired. *God help us. Please God.*

# 85

THUNDEROUS ENGINES ROARED OVER THEIR HEADS as heavy cannon fire split the sky. Explosions thumped through the pavement and shook Goodman's insides as six P-40 Warhawks flew over at rooftop level. The red nosecones meant the 99th Fighter Squadron. He'd seen them before, peeling off from the bomber formations to destroy German and Italian supply trains. *Damn, they're low!* He thrilled at the sight of them, engines screaming, making their wide, inverted arcs for another run at the Germans.

In their second wave, two more fighters dropped their 250-pounders right into the midst of the Waffen-SS infantry positions. Twin blasts shattered walls and launched entire sections of masonry into the air that landed with a heavy, sickening crunch. The infantry immediately scattered into the alleys and doorways away from the road. Two more planes targeted the lead tanks with thumping cannon fire. One turret flipped over and slammed into the ground with a bright yellow flash. Sparks filled the air. The remaining tanks withdrew downhill from the highway and the gunfire nearly ceased.

Goodman looked at the sky and questioned if the Dakota pilot was still willing to risk the landing. Please land, he said out loud. *One in ten thousand pilots would even attempt to make this landing. He's gotta have stones.*

The C-47 lined up again for landing more than a mile away. Tracer fire swept across the plane's path but from behind them! Goodman turned and saw that three German vehicles now approached from the west. Tracer fire streamed from their machine guns mounted over their drivers' heads.

"Musa!" Goodman waved at him and pointed at the vehicles approaching. Musa rotated his machine gun and opened up on the Germans. The trucks swerved, and one crashed into a building. "Keep firing!" yelled Goodman. He emptied another magazine at the trucks.

Not a second too soon, two more Warhawks' heavy guns rattled overhead and dumped brass casings over the road as they made their attack run on those same vehicles. Two vehicles burst into flames and the remaining truck retreated into a side street.

As the C-47 Dakota touched down half a mile away, just past the dead Panzer, the Warhawks pulled away. The pilot taxied the transport plane over the pavement, skillfully swung the tail round and slowed to a stop only yards away from the trucks. The cargo master had already opened the troop door and waved for the passengers to climb on.

Several pilots sprinted to the aircraft. The militia helped carry the wounded airmen and hoisted them up the ladder. It was a painfully slow process, and the Warhawks did their best to turn the surrounding neighborhoods into a living hell for the attacking

Germans. Pass after pass, they dumped cannon fire into the German positions. On one pass, they were low enough for Goodman to see their faces, and he felt an instant connection. He instinctively waved to them.

"Goodman!" Whitman yelled above the noise of the aircraft engines. "Good luck to you!" They shook hands.

"You, too! Thank you! And, thank you as well, Sergeant!" He shook Master Sergeant O'Keefe's hand as well.

"Good luck, sir! Now get the hell outta here!" His smile was grim, but sincere. He shoved his weapon's butt stock into his shoulder and turned to face the direction of the German gunfire.

Goodman turned around to look for Amira. *Where are you?*

"You better get going, sir!" O'Keefe urged him toward the transport.

He started for the plane when he saw her. Her hair was blowing from under her cap, her weapon held firmly with the strap over her shoulder, her clothing and the side of her face a muddy black smear. Flecks of blood dotted her face.

"Amira!" He had to yell, but he had no idea what to say here, now. "Thank you!" He immediately felt dumb for uttering such a trite sentiment. Yet, he meant it. How do you thank someone who got you this far? Through everything? "I mean—"

She put a hand to his mouth. Then she reached for his hands and held them in an iron grip. Her eyes held him in her stare and they stood there, motionless. He looked for an emotion to display across her face. Or a word. Or something. Anything. There was nothing. Yet, she stood there, gripping his hands in the ice-cold drizzle.

"Go!" she yelled over the engine noise. "You go!"

"Cap'n! You gotta go!" O'Keefe yelled over the gunfire. "The pilot says the fighters are seeing more Jerry tanks crossing the river. You gotta get outta here!" He and Major Farish broke Amira's grip and shoved Goodman toward the plane.

He looked over his shoulder and saw her watching him climb the ladder. A burst of gunfire drew her attention, and she ran to join Musa and the others as they returned fire to protect the plane. Another burst of machine-gun fire sent them all to the pavement again. Goodman could see the flickering of muzzle flashes in the windows. Enemy machine guns tore into the surrounding buildings as Musa's own MG42 ripped into the attacking infantry. One of the distant tanks fired a shell that swished high overhead and impacted on the hillside behind them. *How do I leave them all here?*

Goodman climbed aboard and lowered his hand to Major Farish, who climbed up and made his way to the cockpit. Goodman helped the cargo master pull the troop door closed and strapped himself into a seat next to it. *Ok*, he thought. *Let's get out of here*. The plane did not move. The engines did not throttle up. Bullets pinged against the aluminum skin and daylight poked into the fuselage. One of the airmen screamed and fell into the center walkway. Blood spurted from his neck and Goodman released his harness and crouched over him to apply pressure. "Get moving!" Goodman yelled toward the cockpit. The plane surged with thousands of horsepower and bounced across the pavement. *Finally*. Goodman set to saving this man's blood.

Then the plane slowed to a stop. *What the hell?* Goodman and a handful of others craned their necks to see why the pilots aborted the takeoff.

"Goodman!" Major Farish yelled. "Goodman! Get your ass up here!"

Goodman directed another American pilot to put pressure on the bleeding man's wound and picked his way through the mess of injured airmen to the door separating the cargo area from the cockpit. He stepped aside as Major Farish and one of the British airmen pulled the co-pilot out of the cockpit and laid him down on the floor. Another stream of bullets pierced the aircraft's skin over his head and showered him with little flecks of aluminum and plastic. He ducked down next to the radio operator.

"Get in there and get us off the ground!" Farish pointed into the cockpit.

Goodman climbed over the co-pilot's bloody torso and slipped into his seat. The pilot handed him his headset, then flicked the intercom switch.

"I don't know who you are, but I hope you're multi-engine rated!"

"I am!" Goodman searched the instrument panel. They flinched as a bullet pinged against the metal window frame and a crack jumped across the windshield.

"My left arm's no good, so you need to take the wheel!"

Goodman looked and saw the blood covering the man's legs. "You okay?"

"Yeah..." His voice was strained.

"I got it," said Goodman. He flicked the fuel control switch to increase the fuel flow to both engines. Then he reached over to the propeller pitch control arms and shoved them three times to FULL HIGH PITCH. He released the brake and felt the plane ease forward slightly. *She's ready to fly. Like right now*.

"Good," the pilot said through his headset. "Now, let's get the bloody hell out of here, shall we?"

"Roger that," said Goodman. He pushed the pedal down and the plane straightened out.

Goodman made one last visual check out his windscreen and watched with horror as a stream of red tracers swept across the nose and stitched a path of holes right across the cockpit. Bits of metal, plastic, and glass sprinkled across his lap. The pilot slumped forward, and his head rolled to the side. Goodman saw glassy, lifeless eyes behind the goggles. *Danny, not again!* Another bullet pinged off the window frame. He caught the white muzzle flash in the corner of his eye. Dark shapes sprinted toward him from the row of houses on the north side of the road.

"No, you don't!" he yelled. He pushed the window slide open with the muzzle of his MP40 and sprayed bullets at the dark shapes until he ran out of ammo. "Dammit!" Goodman shoved hard on the throttles and the plane lurched forward. Another hole appeared in the aircraft's skin next to the window.

The Warhawks passed directly over the plane in another low-level gun run down both sides of the road. Tracers streaked in both directions as the Dakota picked up speed, jarring Goodman violently as the wheels bounced along the ground. A flash of light lit up the interior as a blast shook the plane. Goodman suddenly realized he was about to fly again for the first time since his crash. The sensation was familiar, yet felt ancient, like walking into his grandparents'

476

house after years' absence. Another bullet pinged off the fuselage as the plane picked up speed.

Goodman felt the tail lift off the ground. He held the plane steady, unsure of the minimum takeoff distance. Then he saw a black hulk in the middle of the road about five hundred yards ahead. *There's that stupid tank! Damn it!* He tried to push the throttles higher, but they were already metal-on-metal. The dead Panzer grew closer, faster and faster. The Dakota seemed to lumber down the pavement. *I have to clear that thing*! He stared at the smoking black hulk, now less than a quarter mile down the road. *I'm nowhere near takeoff speed. She'll stall if I pull up now, and then we're dead.* Goodman envisioned the landing gear shearing off and the Dakota spinning out of control and smashing into the stone buildings if he hit that tank.

*Do I abort?* He reached for the throttles. *I can't take off on the other heading, the wind will be the wrong direction. I'll have to taxi back and turn around again. The odds of surviving the round trip are zero.* The airspeed indicator read only sixty knots. *I need at least a hundred.*

*I need to bounce it. That's it*, he thought. *There's no other way. Bounce it right over the tank and then I'll have the airspeed to get up. The landing gear ought to take it. Right?*

He pulled back lightly on the yoke and the plane lifted a few feet off the ground, then bounced back down on the pavement. Only three-hundred-fifty yards to go. He lifted the wheels off the pavement again, and down she went and bounced again, much harder this time. Two-hundred-fifty yards to go.

"What're you doing up there?" someone yelled from the cargo compartment.

"Goodman, what are you doing?" It was Major Farish. "Can you fly this thing?"

"Sit the hell back down!" yelled Goodman. "I mean, Sir!"

Goodman let the plane accelerate for as long as he could. One-hundred-fifty yards. He pulled back again. *Please, please get up. Get up!* One hundred yards. He could clearly see the tank sitting in front of him. The ride smoothed out as the main landing gear left the ground. One more bounce. He saw the boulevard rise to meet him again. He pulled back on the wheel. *Please get up! Please...*

To Goodman, it felt like the plane hiccupped when the dead Panzer skipped under the aircraft. The plane rose and the airspeed dropped. One-two-zero knots. One-ten. One-zero-zero. Nine-zero. He felt the lift wash away, and the plane sank slightly. The indicator arm on the instrument panel squeezed the red line that meant stall airspeed for a standard load for a C-47 transport.

Goodman hated to do it, but he pushed the control yoke away from him and the nose of the plane dropped. The propeller blades chopped at the air. He pressed the pedal to steer into the slight crosswind and felt the airframe shudder. One last bounce and the Dakota caught the lift she needed. *Yes! Now, climb!* He pulled back on the yoke.

She stayed up but still did not climb. The houses on the northern hills were level with him. A column of smoke from the site of the salt factory streamed diagonally skyward, and the plane flew straight through it, getting a slight bump from the warm air of the still-smoldering fires. The air smoothed out, and the aircraft found lift. Goodman watched the altimeter ease slowly upwards.

The hillside neighborhoods slipped by the wingtips, then hilltops eased by in slow motion. He saw the houses, towns, roads, valleys, and forested hills that surrounded him for months fly by in mere minutes. *We should be out of range of anything the Germans have by now*, he thought. *One four-five knots. That's good.* He pulled back harder on the wheel and the low gray cloud cover enveloped the aircraft. Water droplets streaked across the windscreen. The turbulence suddenly increased again, but Goodman managed to keep climbing.

Once at six thousand feet above sea level and safely inside miles of opaque water vapor, Goodman leveled off and flew by instruments. He reached for the flight books and proceeded through the emergency systems checklist. Ordinarily, his co-pilot would be the one to call off the instruments, but he did it himself now. Again. This, too, felt oddly familiar. Coldly familiar. He switched the radio from INTERCOM to EXTERNAL, and it crackled immediately.

"—line, Pipeline, this is Red Dog Leader. Can you read me, over!"

*I guess I'm Pipeline*, thought Goodman. "Red Dog Leader, this is Pipeline."

"Good to hear from you, Pipeline. We thought maybe you dug yo'self a tunnel into one of them mountains, over."

"Negative, Red Dog Leader, I'm here, but I'm in bad shape. What were your instructions, over?"

"Pipeline, we gonna escort you all the way to Italy. Can you make it? Over."

"Roger. Can do," replied Goodman. He looked over his instruments. "I'm heading one-niner-zero, altitude five-niner-zero-zero, over."

"Roger all that. We'll pick you up on the other side of this storm system."

"Roger." Then he added, "Red Dog Leader..."

"Right here, Pipeline."

"Thank you. Over." A pause.

"Roger that, boss man. We goin' back to radio silence. Out." The transmission clicked off.

Goodman leaned over and pulled the map board from under the dead pilot's leg. His eyes traced the pencil-drawn lines across the regions of greens and blues and the many swirling brown contour lines. The pencil lines terminated at an airfield near a town called Bari, on the Italian coast of the Adriatic. *Never been to Italy*, Goodman thought to himself. He looked at the compass and corrected with a dip of his wing. Finally in a place of control and safety, he took a breath. *I finally know where I am.*

Goodman still had his weapon on his lap. He pushed it onto the floor and compared his stopwatch to the air chart. "Ten minutes to the coast and we're clear!" he yelled back to whoever might be listening.

Farish repeated to the airmen in the cargo compartment. Everyone cheered. His headphones crackled.

Goodman rubbed his chin and realized his hands were grimy with a swirled mixture of brown, red, and black filth. He wiped his hands on his pants and slumped in the harness with his hands on the yoke. He fidgeted.

Something was off. He felt ill again, and his head felt like there was a spike through it.

His hands began to shake. He clenched his fists, tried to hold his hands still, and then finally clutched the control wheel as strongly as he could. Squeezing his eyes shut, he choked back the rush of emotion that flooded out of him. He quietly wept angry, resentful, guilty, ridiculous, stupid tears. And then, the faces—and everything associated with them—came back to him.

Amira.

Zoran.

Jasminka.

Baba.

Tomislav. *You bastard.*

*Amira. I left you. I should have brought you with me. What becomes of you now?*

"You alright?" Major Farish yelled over the noise of the engines and the wind. He put a hand on Goodman's shoulder. "You okay?"

Goodman simply nodded and habitually gave the major a thumbs up without turning to look at him. He focused on scanning the amorphous grays and whites outside the aircraft.

The Dakota finally broke free of the cloud cover. The silver-blue sky over a sun-bleached Adriatic coastline with a blazing Adriatic horizon made him squint. He looked over the instrument panel. Then he scanned the horizon. He looked again at the instruments. *Everything is fine*, he thought. *This is good.* The brilliant, sparkling water and warm sun on his face made him feel better.

*Kind of like heaven,* he thought to himself.

Even better, the P-40s of the famous Red Tails were there, an echelon of three off each wingtip, just like they said they would be. Goodman waved at the flight lead, and he saw a gloved hand give a salute. Goodman returned the gesture before turning to look down the interior of the plane at the men also seeking to go home. They were all looking at him. Waiting for the good news.

"We're clear!" yelled Goodman.

Loud cheers. So many faces.

# 86

1745 HOURS, OCTOBER 3, 1943
1709TH FIELD HOSPITAL, BARI SOUTH AIRFIELD,
SOUTHERN ITALY

THE EXAMINING DOCTOR BARELY LOOKED UP from Goodman's medical chart.

"So, Captain," the examining doctor began. "You are not in the best shape, but you could have been much, much worse, given your circumstances over the past several weeks." He told Goodman that his injuries were healing satisfactorily, but that he was substantially malnourished and dehydrated, which he already knew.

"Yes, sir," Goodman agreed. "Did the lab work show anything I need to know?"

"Well, yes, actually," said the doctor. He described the initial blood lab report indicated low lipids and other things Goodman reasoned would improve with a more normal diet. Goodman also already knew what came next. "I strongly suspect you've got a mild concussion. Nothing to be overly concerned about, but you should have another thorough examination done at your next command. Avoid hitting your head and get lots of rest. And it won't kill you to get some good food in you."

The doctor prescribed painkillers, bedrest, and double rations for the next three weeks. "Above all, sleep and eat," he said. "Eat a lot of meat, potatoes, vegetables, you know, that sort of thing."

"That," said Goodman. "Is exactly what I'm looking forward to the most."

The doctor congratulated him on his successful return to Allied territory. They shook hands, and he offered to let Goodman use his office to put on his new uniform. Goodman thanked him and followed him behind a curtain. The room contained only a small wooden desk, a folding cot with a pile of wool blankets, a footlocker, and a full-length mirror.

"My God," he said out loud when he looked into the mirror. *I look terrible.* With the scraggy beard, sunken cheeks, numerous scrapes and cuts, and dark circles under his eyes, his face was hardly recognizable. *This is like looking at the ninety-year-old me.* Goodman dropped his hospital gown and was utterly dismayed to see himself.

He could see his ribs and the gaps between. His pelvic bones jutted outward, and his skin sagged slightly. Ugly purple and yellow bruises covered him. And there were discolored scars just above his knees where he recalled the instrument panel on the Jessica Joy cutting into his legs. Goodman felt himself shrink with a deep sense of loss. He tenderly felt the sensitive burn mark under his left arm. *I don't remember that,* he thought to himself. Next to it was the knife cut from one of Tomislav's men. *I do remember that.* Despite being issued the correct sizes, the new pants and shirt felt huge on him. After he finished dressing, he found the out-processing desk. Major Farish already had his discharge paperwork in his hand and four bottles of acetaminophen.

A warm wind hit Goodman as Farish held the door for him. Outside, a driver with a jeep greeted them and held the front seat forward so Goodman could get into the back. The driver stomped on the start button, and they kicked up dirt and rocks as he accelerated out of the hospital parking area. The sun and warm wind felt good. *Very* good.

"Let's get some food," Major Farish suggested.

"That's a great idea, sir," said Goodman. "Chow halls any good?" The idea of food was all-consuming. Even if it was Army food, it was better than the highly suspect foods he'd consumed over the past couple of months.

"I know a place better than any Army mess," said Farish. "First, though, let's check in so we don't come up on a report."

"Headquarters then, sir?" said the driver.

"Yeah, thanks, Tommy."

"Yes, sir!" Tommy slammed on the brakes to avoid a trio of Army ambulances. "But then we eat at the usual spot, right, sir?"

Major Farish smiled. "Sure, Tommy, my treat."

"Yes, sir!" Goodman could almost hear the grin on Tommy's face.

Tommy accelerated and performed a deft maneuver around a disabled 5-ton truck and skidded back onto the road. He wove between two flatbed trucks and took a small side road to a long, squat building at the end. After so many weeks of cold, damp weather, the dry heat, the dusty air, the brilliant blue sky, the crunchy grit in his teeth, it was all very visceral. It all felt good, but unreal. Inside, Goodman felt awkward. Like *he* was out of place, AWOL even. He felt guilty. *Why do I feel that?* He dismissed that idea. Was it the weeks of tension that were hard to let go? *Maybe I just need to rest. That must be it.*

The jeep spewed dirt and rocks into the air as the driver steered into a parking area. A sun-bleached American flag snapped in the wind atop a leaning flagpole. The driver slowed to a stop directly in front of the double doors.

"We'll be back in a minute," said Major Farish. Tommy merely nodded as he put the gear into neutral and jammed the parking brake with his foot.

The official-looking sign stenciled on the front of the building read:

D COMPANY, 2765TH AVIATION MAINTENANCE
ADMINISTRATIVE GROUP (PROVISIONAL),
15TH AIR FORCE
BARI AIRFIELD, ITALY

And below it was another sign, this one hand-painted:

FIXING THE WORLD, THREE COPIES AT A TIME

"What is the Aviation Maintenance Administration?" said Goodman. "And don't tell me it's classified."

"We thought it would help everyone want to stay as far away as possible," said Farish. "And, yes, it's classified." Then he smiled. "Welcome to OSS Bari Station."

"Thanks, sir," said Goodman. "The sign works, by the way." They both snickered as they approached the main doors.

Before Major Farish could reach the door handle, a U.S. Army colonel emerged with two Military Police sergeants on his flanks. Goodman eyed their "MP" brassards with a growing pit in his stomach. The colonel looked him up and down and looked at his clipboard.

"Captain Michael Goodman?" said the colonel.

"Sir—" Major Farish raised a hand to intercede but was brushed aside by one of the sergeants.

"Yes, sir," said Goodman. His chest tightened and his head swooned.

"Captain, you are under arrest."

# AUTHOR'S HISTORICAL NOTE

Many, many terrible things happened in Yugoslavia in 1943. The mission that propelled my hero on his journey, Operation Tidal Wave, really did happen on August 1, 1943, and was an attempt to cut off the Third Reich from its strategic petroleum supplies. The mission was an operational disaster with little strategic effect. Most of the hundreds of aircraft that flew that mission did not return to base at all or intact.

The German invasion two years prior unleashed a three-way civil war that ended not when the Germans were expelled, but when Josef Tito's Communist Partisan army destroyed or subjugated everyone else afterward. The British Special Operations Executive (SOE) really did conduct operations in Yugoslavia, attached to Tito's army headquarters and those of his divisions. The American mission there was run by the Office of Strategic Services (OSS), and there were indeed ugly politics between the Allied agencies. Those were not the only ugly politics, however.

The clash of native ethnicities and religions brought far, far worse consequences. The largely Catholic Croatians, the Muslim Bosnians (to whom Zoran and his clan belong), and the Orthodox Serbians played a brutal game for keeps. Those groups brought out the worst in each other, which gave rise to ethnic cleansing, concentration camps, mass murder, systematic raping and pillaging, and brutal subjugation of the survivors—all tangible results of overlapping remnants of empires. Tito kept that under control, more or less, until his death, when those exact same animosities clashed again throughout the 1990s.

My association with the region and its troubles began when America and her NATO allies intervened via peacemaking and peacekeeping missions that went under several names from 1993 onward (Operation Joint Guard, Joint Endeavor, etc.). Sadly, the nations of Europe's Balkan region still suffer inter-cultural angst and political instability to this day.

# ACKNOWLEDGEMENTS

My thanksgiving and praise first and last to Elohim Elyon, for everything.

To my Wife. Thank you for your love and patience, and for your tolerance when your patience ran out. Each time. I hope you are proud of my work. Thank you for being my wife. I love you.

Thank you to my daughters. I spent a lot of time away from you to write this story. I hope maybe one day you'll read this and be amazed, as I am amazed at how wonderful you are. I love you.

To my Mom & Dad. From childhood, you raised me right and let me explore my world and myself, and then I went off and did things. Now I did this. Thank you. I love you.

To my *other* Mom & Dad. Thank you for raising such an amazing daughter and blessing our marriage. This is good. I love you.

To my developmental editors: Sophie B. Thomas and Randall Surles. Your intelligence, your writers' hearts, and your wise editorial counsel were always exactly what I needed to hear. Even if it meant killing my 'darling' scenes (may they rest in pieces). And to my Line Editor, Laura Graves, thank you for always being right!

Thank you to my family, friends, and brothers-in-arms, and everyone who gave me meaningful feedback from the very first ideas and excerpts I sent out years ago to my readers who endeavored through the entire manuscript help shape the book I now send out into the world. Finally. And special thanks to R.Y., K.S., and R.H. in my writers group. Our interactions were very encouraging.

Thank you to my coffee shop friends, where you kept me caffeinated, encouraged, and allowed me to occupy seats for years.

Also, thank you to my platoon sergeant, MSG Andrew Zybas, for coaching me through that deployment to northeastern Bosnia back in 1997. You inspired me for the remainder of my career.

Unpaid, unsolicited plug: thank you also to Shawn Coyne for the Story Grid and its constituent ideas and methods. I can't tell you how much this helped me and will guide my thinking about the craft of writing forever. I hope you discover the penultimate meta story you seek.

May all your households know truth, wisdom, peace, joy, love, contentment, and prosperity.

# ABOUT THE AUTHOR

Matt Erlacher lives with his family in North Carolina. He is a retired U.S. Army Special Forces officer and combat veteran of multiple tours in three different combat zones. His first deployment was to northern Bosnia-Herzegovina in 1997, where he led his rifle platoon on numerous patrols in and around the Tuzla valley and the Majevitsa mountains.

While this story is not based on any single person, Matt's grandparents all served the greater good in the Second World War, and Matt's great uncle, 1st Lieutenant Richard Shoenthal, was a Liberando B-24 pilot. Check out his crew's page at the 376th Heavy Bombardment Group's website:
https://www.armyaircorps-376bg.com/shoenthal_richard_crew.html

Please consider helping combat veterans recover from their time in service to our great nation. Writing this book helped me. Many of us, our beloved dead and the troubled living, have never fully come home. We all left a piece of ourselves somewhere.

*Deep in the Place of the Dead* is Matt's first novel.

*De Oppresso Liber*

# THE LAST WORD

My inspiration for the title comes from the Bible:

*When I was deep in the place of the dead,*
*I called out for help.*
*And you listened to my cry.*
—Jonah 2:1

www.ingramcontent.com/pod-product-compliance
Lightning Source LLC
Chambersburg PA
CBHW061506020726
47502CB00006B/1958